# Healing Water

## The Search for Hunter Wipley

By T.A. Beretta

PublishAmerica
Baltimore

© 2008 by T.A. Beretta.
All rights reserved. No part of this book may be reproduced, stored in a retrieval system or transmitted in any form or by any means without the prior written permission of the publishers, except by a reviewer who may quote brief passages in a review to be printed in a newspaper, magazine or journal.

First printing

All characters in this book are fictitious, and any resemblance to real persons, living or dead, is coincidental.

PublishAmerica has allowed this work to remain exactly as the author intended, verbatim, without editorial input.

ISBN: 1-60610-634-1
PUBLISHED BY PUBLISHAMERICA, LLLP
www.publishamerica.com
Baltimore

Printed in the United States of America

*Dedicated to my mother, Kelly,
who taught me the book is better than the movie.*

# Chapter One
# James, the Document, and the Legend

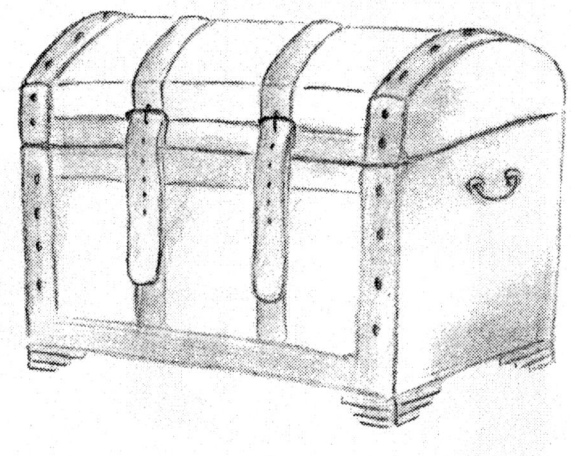

James Greene stood in his father's office filled with both curiosity and fear. The strange document he had just found hidden under the hardwood floor was still clutched tightly in his nervous hands.

"What is this?" James asked himself, as he quickly unlatched the leather-bound cover and opened the document. What was worrying him most right then was that at any second, Rex, the most violent man he had ever known could walk in that room and catch him. But, James decided almost immediately to allow necessity to overpower these worries; hoping this might be the one thing that would help solve his problems he rapidly flipped through the document until he came to its first page. There he began reading the typed words…

At the time I found researcher, Hunter Wipley's, memoirs they had no order and no formal index. Instead, there was this mess of handwritten pages scattered around on the bottom of a large trunk. Since then I have pieced together what I believe is the best representation of its contents, and added in this introduction on how I came to possess such a rare collection.

James stopped there, immediately realizing he didn't have time for introductions, he flipped a few pages ahead until he came to some older, handwritten page. He knew he was running out of time, but this discovery was so different than anything he had ever seen before that he just couldn't put it down. At least, not until he found out what the document was about. So, he quickly began reading again…

*June 15, 1951*

*The fountain of youth is not a new idea. In fact, the story of this special water, which is said to return and sustain youthfulness to all who drink it, has been around for over a thousand years. This romantic idea drove a countless number of explorers to travel to and search almost every corner of the globe hunting for this 'miracle water'. Still, and after all of their attempts ended in failure, the legend managed to live on and continued to be passed from one generation to the next. This so-called myth baffled both scientists and explorers for hundreds of years, but then in the early 1900's a secret break through occurred and changed important details of that legend forever.*
*This alternative story, which is still mostly unknown, claims that in 1909 there was a discovery of an island off the coast of Florida with absolutely pure water which had the ability to heal people of any disease or illness. This perfect water was said to have been the first produced by*

*the earth and was considered the source of all life. Not only did this powerful water heal, but it supposedly extended the life-span of humans, animals, and plants alike.*

*The scientific community agreed that a popular legend such as this would never change so drastically without real evidence to support and cause it to. Knowing this, I searched for and found that evidence and would like to provide it here in this document. I believe this rare information proves the new legend to be the accurate one, and finally solves the mystery of the fountain of youth.*

*Hunter M. Wipley*

James reluctantly stopped reading again and looked up from the strange document. He still had no idea what to make of his new discovery, but he believed it had to be important. *Why else would it be hidden*, he asked himself?

As intriguing as the document was and no matter how much he wanted to continue reading it, fear that his own physical well-being was in jeopardy caused him to act otherwise. He knew that the only way he could further investigate his new discovery was to escape back to his room with it; this being the only place left in his house where he still felt somewhat safe. With James' dying father in the hospital now, there was no one to stop his step-mother, Debra, or her violent friend, Rex, from taking over the home. James didn't even want to think what Rex might do if he caught him in the office again.

Throughout the past three months now things in James' life had gone from bad to worse. He had a bad feeling someone was to blame for his father's condition, and only a few days ago he had decided to try and prove it. He felt that if he could at least find out the truth it might somehow help both him and his father.

You could say James' desire for seeking out the truth was in a way born within him. The past three generations of Greene's (James' father, Joe, his grandfather, Jack, and his great grandfather, John) have all in fact been detectives; and good ones at that. Ever since James' great grandfather John began the family business, Greene Private Eye in 1930 and passed it on to his only son Jack, the Greene family name has been synonymous with quality detective work. That tradition continued as the business was then passed from Jack to his only son Joe, which it still remains to this day, seeing as James is still only fifteen years old and too young to take over yet.

Along with the family business, the skills needed to become a good detective were also passed down to the next generation; the only difference was this began at a very young age. This tradition posed a problem for James because he was in fact the first Greene boy who did not want to grow up and become a detective. The family business seemed boring to him, but of course he still learned it and pretended to be interested, so as not to let down his own father. Still, secretly he hoped to become a great pilot one day. He loved the idea of flying, but had yet to set foot on a plane due to his phobia of heights. To try and replace the actual experience of flying he watched movies and read books on aviation. He collected anything and everything he could get his hands on that pertained to flying planes.

Over the past fourteen years James had lived a mostly normal life (if you exclude the detective work he helped his father with). One of the only real tragedies before now was that his mother, Mary, had died over ten years ago due to cancer. Afterwards, James and his father, Joe, lived alone and James liked it that way. Joe Greene spent most of his time running the family business and teaching James, he never really had much time for anything else. The two of them were living as well as any father and son could without the love and help of a woman around.

Either way, that all quickly changed a year ago, after Joe Greene meet Debra Hawking and supposedly fell in love with her. A few months later the two were married and Debra immediately moved in with James and his father. Debra seemed nice to James at first and for a while he actually liked her, he even thought of her as his second mother. He had no way of knowing who she really was, but not long after Joe Greene was admitted to the hospital Debra's true nature was revealed. As James' father grew deathly ill, Debra began seeing other men and bringing them over to the house. She was acting violent towards James now and it got worse with each passing day. Eventually Debra began bringing over a rough man named, Rex, who she said he was just a friend, but James knew better. Soon thereafter, Rex began staying over more frequently and eventually he moved into the house. This man was very intimidating to James, to the point of being abusive. He was an alcoholic and James had a hint he was a hardened criminal. Needless to say James stayed locked up in his room most of the time now, hoping to stay out of harms way.

With his father left alone and dying in the hospital James had little options and felt he was running out of time. It had been over two months since he had last heard news of his dad's condition, and since then his step-mother and Rex had become more and more heartless-something just had to be done.

One of the first things he noticed, after deciding to fight back, was that lately Debra and Rex had been searching around the house looking for something. Of course he had no idea what that was, but he knew he needed to find it first. And as luck would have it his detective training was already paying off, in more ways than one.

During James' search around the house today, which began only a few minutes ago, is when he had actually first laid eyes on the mysterious document. Shortly after finishing the first handwritten page and looking up from it, is when he heard the sound he had been dreading most. It was the sound of the front door opening, and that meant Rex had come home early again. With this simple sound James' worst fear had become a reality, and now he needed to figure out something fast if he wanted to escape with the document and not end up in the hospital because of it.

As he debated his next move James' indecisiveness instantly turned to panic when he heard Rex's heavy foot-steps enter the kitchen. He knew now that he'd never make it out of the office without the abusive mad-man catching him. He had simply waited too long.

"Come on, James, think," he whispered to himself, as he hurried over into the office closet. There, he cautiously pulled off two of his father's old coats from their hangers; using one to cover up the document and the other as a decoy. He then moved swiftly out of the closet and over to the door. He felt his heart pound as he slowly peered out into the hallway. The feeling of relief rushed over him as he saw that no one was there. He tried to act as casually as possible as he walked down towards his room with a different coat under each arm and the document wrapped up inside of one. *It's only ten feet away,* he told himself as he turned the corner and suddenly looked up. Standing in front of him like an angry bear was Rex.

"What do you think your doing?" Rex growled, as he stood between James and his sanctuary.

James' heart pounded. "Uh, I was just, getting a—"

"You were just getting what?" Rex interrupted, as he stood towering over James; his dark, greasy hair and beard looking unwashed and frightening. "You were just snooping through my stuff again weren't you?" He hissed, his breath smelling strong like alcohol.

"No, I was getting a couple of my father's coats that's all," James said.

"Your father's coats huh," he said, as he inched closer to James. "How many times do I have to tell you to stay out of that room!" he shouted. "I guess the only way you're going to learn is if I go in there and burn everything else of your dad's, huh… Then you wouldn't have any reason to go in there now would ya?"

James hesitated and then courageously argued back. "No, you can't do that, that's all my dad's stuff and when he gets back from the hospital—" Rex suddenly grabbed James by the collar.

"You don't tell me what I can and can't do, you understand me? And like I told you before, your dad isn't coming back." The harsh words seemed to hurt James more than the rough hands that were grinding into his neck. He fought back the tears that were beginning to swell in his eyes, and that's when Rex finally let go and grinned.

"Who needs two coats anyway," he laughed as he ripped one out of James' hand. "This is your last warning punk," he said, poking James in the chest with each word. He then turned around and walked away.

James immediately dashed into his bedroom and locked the door behind him, he then unfolded the remaining coat on his bed, wiped his eyes clear and smiled. Knowing he had just outsmarted Rex was totally worth the sore neck he was going to have tomorrow; plus, James knew that in order to find out the truth about what was going on with his father he was going to have to continue taking chances like this.

"That was a close one, but it could have been worse," James told himself, as he took a good look at the leather-bound document for the second time.

He wiped some more dust off its cover and then turned it over on his bed; he wanted to find out everything he could about the strange document his father had hidden away. He had a lot of questions about what was going on around the house lately and thought maybe this would be the thing that provided some answers.

As he examined the pages, he again took note that some looked different than others. The first few pages in the front were typed and on much newer paper than the rest. He slowly turned back through until he got to the older, handwritten pages and stopped when he found an interesting title page that read:

## *The Island of Healing Water* by Hunter Wipley

*So, it's like a journal or something. But still why would it be hidden?*
Since he had been taught to think like a detective, James naturally treated the strange document as if it were a piece of evidence or some clue that might help him. The document was an interesting find to say the least, and he was going to make sure he figured out everything he could about it.

James turned back to where he had left off in the introduction and was about to began reading there again, when out of nowhere loud yelling came reverberating down the hallway. He immediately knew the screaming was coming from his step-mother, Debra. She had most likely arrived home drunk and was now fighting with Rex as usual. Even though this kind of thing had been occurring more and more often, James still found it to be very disturbing; just another thing to add to the long list of reasons why he hated being there. One of the great things about James though, was that despite all these depressing realities he still kept a positive outlook on life. He would just tell himself over and over again that things were going to get better, and that he was going to find a way to fix his broken world, even if he was only fifteen years old.

James sat nervously on the bed in his room and listened as the fighting between his step-mother and Rex escalated. He was biting his nails when he suddenly heard a scratching at his door. He quickly jumped up, hid the document under his bed, and hurried over to the door. He opened it just enough to let in his little black dog named Buddy. James felt bad that he had forgotten about the small pug faced dog he and his mother had saved from the pound so many years ago.
"You okay, Buddy?" James said as he bent down and hugged the little dog. Just then there was an explosion of glass and a few more screams from what sounded like the living room. Buddy jumped up on the bed and hid under a pillow as James sat down beside him and continued to listen. The screaming turned into what sounded like more violence and then, for some unknown reason it

ceased... After a few moments of complete silence James heard the front door suddenly slam shut. The house then once again returned to being unusually quiet. *Maybe too quiet.* The absence of noise made James even more anxious, realizing that if his step-mother had left Rex there alone he might try to take his anger out on him. So, as a precautionary measure James decided to barricade the door with the chair from his desk. After wedging the chair in-between the knob and the floor, he walked over and sat on top of his desk, he then turned and pulled open the window behind him all the way. He figured that if he needed to he could now jump out and escape from Rex. He had actually arranged this set-up several times before and it always made him feel a little more secure during these uncertain times. James knew that when living with an abusive alcoholic it was always a good idea to have an escape plan.

He looked out the window and scanned the dark front yard, trying to see what vehicles if any were left in the driveway. After a few seconds of staring, he gave up and decided now to just sit tight on top of the desk with Buddy and wait. He had to be sure both Debra and Rex were gone before returning back to the document he so desperately wanted to read.

As he sat staring at the door knob and listening for any signs of Rex in the house, he held Buddy in his lap and stayed poised to react. After several minutes of intense waiting, the air from outside quickly rushed in and seemed to demand his attention. James turned slightly on the desk as he felt the cool air again. He looked up at all the bright stars that were scattered out over the dark June sky, and for a moment he forgot all about his problems and instead remembered how great his home life used to be. He turned back to the door and reached into his pocket, he pulled out a small, black and white photo of his father. James smiled as he stared at the dark-haired, handsome man in the military uniform. He turned the picture over and there on the back was a note his father had written to his real mother.

*I'll always fight for you, Love your husband, Joe*

James still remembered the story his mother had told him about the day his father had given her the picture along with a dozen roses. It was the day before he was due to be shipped over seas to fight in the war. James' mother told him she knew then that they would always be together till the very end, and she was right. The sad thing was that the end came entirely too soon for her.

*HEALING WATER*

James couldn't remember everything because he was far too young (maybe five or six), but he remembered when his father told him that his mother couldn't come home anymore because she had gone to heaven forever. When the breast cancer finally took her life it changed James' and his father's forever. No matter how much it bothered him, James took comfort in knowing that they were beside her throughout the entire ordeal. And when he tried hard enough, like he was doing right then, he could still see her beautiful smile and hear her sweet, sweet voice.

James smiled at this memory as he turned the photo back over and took another look at his father. The similarities between him and James were undeniable. Everything about them was the same, from their dark, brown hair and eyes, to their slim physique; they even had an identical dimple on the right side of both their faces. The only difference between them at the moment was that in the picture his father had a short, military hair cut, while James' hair was kind of long right now and had to be pushed to the side since his step-mother wouldn't take him to get it cut.

He put the photo back safely in his pocket, and then got up and went over to his bed. It had been a while now since the front door was slammed shut and he had still not heard anything.

"I think they're both gone," he whispered, putting his ear up to the wall. Buddy jumped up on the bed and began to wag his tail.

"That's good news, huh?" James said, as he sat back with Buddy beside him and stared at the chair wedged under his door, deciding it best to leave it barricaded for the night. He also decided to turn off the lights in his room, to make it look like he had gone to sleep. He did this often since he was rarely ever sure Rex was actually gone. There had been many nights that James made the mistake of wandering out of his room only to find Rex stumbling around the house in a drunken, violent haze.

*I won't make that mistake again…* he thought, *I'll shut the lights off and get my flashlight, then I can start reading the document again.* He hated living like this, always having to constantly look over his shoulder in order to feel safe, but he didn't have a choice right now he had to be extra careful.

After a brief search through his desk drawer, he found the small flashlight and turned it on; he then walked over and flipped the overhead lights off. The room went instantly dark; the only light now was coming from the end of the flashlight which James was pointing across the room at his bed. He kneeled down beside the wooden frame, aimed the flashlight underneath and grabbed the document. He got back under the covers and situated himself, Buddy, and the strange pages. With the room dark and the flashlight on, it caused it to look like there was a small, glowing, blue tepee on top of James' bed.

"Okay, let's figure out what this thing really is," James whispered with enthusiasm, as he opened the strange document for the third time. The leather cover still felt oily and the pages had that familiar musty smell; which caused Buddy to start sniffing the air like a bird-dog. James turned to the very first page again and began reading the rest of the introduction…

In the year 1949 a new theory on the fountain of youth was spreading throughout the scientific community like wild fire. During this time an American researcher named, Hunter Wipley, took off on a very bizarre and dangerous trip aboard his sailboat during hurricane season. He left from South Grove Harbor in Florida, and the last reported sighting of his small vessel was taken two days later and fifty miles off shore in the Gulf of Mexico. It was never known what his reasons or motivations were for taking the trip, but after a couple weeks at sea with several storms and one hurricane, there were no more reported sightings given and no sign of the explorer's return, it appeared that Hunter Wipley had most certainly gone down with his ship and perished at sea. There was a lengthy search operation that went on for weeks and covered hundreds of miles, but nothing was ever recovered. Hunter Wipley would not be seen or heard from again until over five years later.

It was then on a warm day in June 1955, as the afternoon sun was beginning to set on the gulf in Florida, when out of no where there appeared a small, mangled sailboat floating into South Grove Harbor. When the rescue boats were sent out and the owner and name of the wrecked boat was identified over the radio almost the entire town heard that it was Wipley and began making their way down to the docks to see if it was true; no one could believe that Wipley was still alive. As they towed the wrecked boat up to the docks people gasped at how destroyed it was, they were amazed that it was even floating. After a short time an older man with light hair and matching beard appeared out of the rescue boat, everyone was amazed to see that it was indeed Hunter Wipley. He was flanked on both sides by emergency people helping him to the ambulance. By this point, the crowd around the dock had grown to several dozen people; everyone from children to reporters was watching. People were yelling questions from all directions: 'Where have you been Hunter?' and 'Are you okay Mr. Wipley?' Some of the people who were closest to him said that he actually looked healthy and that he even smiled and waved before entering the ambulance. After a couple days in the hospital and dozens of examinations from many different doctors it was deemed that Mr. Wipley was healthy, but that he was suffering from severe memory loss. He couldn't remember where he had been for the past five years or even his own name. It was a total mystery to everyone.

Shortly after leaving the hospital though, Mr. Wipley disappeared yet again. At first, everyone talked about and speculated where he had gone to this time. His boat was missing from the harbor again but no one knew anything else. It was one of the most bizarre tales in years, but was soon overshadowed by other more outrageous reports of the times. After several months people in South Grove stopped talking about Wipley, and eventually forgot about the story all together, but not everyone. A young boy named Manny Jones (who lived in South Grove Harbor, and was eight years old during the time that Wipley was found) had vowed that one day he would in fact solve the mystery of where Wipley had been during those five years. He said that he knew Wipley had found something amazing and that it was his destiny to find it too.

I met Manny after moving with my family to South Grove when I was ten; it was then that I first heard the story of the great explorer, Hunter Wipley. It was all Manny ever seemed to talk about, that and how he was going to solve the mystery and become famous for it. Manny always said that he knew Wipley had found something incredible during his five year absence, and that he was meant to find out what that was, he even seemed somewhat obsessed with the idea. Still, Manny and I became best friends and soon afterwards I began reading short books and articles on Wipley and I too became interested in the story. We ended up doing research together and trying to solve the mystery. We worked together on this project all through our teenage years, but eventually we grew up and the idea faded.

After high school ended I went off to college and Manny stayed in South Grove. We lost contact and it wasn't until eight years later, when I was sent back to Florida by the company I worked for (H.A.I. Historical Artifacts Incorporated), that I would see Manny again. I was contracted by this company to travel around the world to different auctions and buy antique merchandise. I had arrived in Bogstown, Florida a few days earlier then expected, and it was then that I ran into my old best friend.

Two hours later, we were standing together on a large dock in South Grove Harbor staring out at the vast ocean. It was then as we both shared stories about our current lives that Manny once again brought up the tale of Hunter Wipley. This time,

## HEALING WATER

Manny began telling me a different version of the story, one he had never told me before. He said when he was eight years old he was one of the many people on the dock that day watching as they brought Wipley and his tattered sail-boat in. He said that he was in front of all the adults, watching as they helped Wipley to the ambulance. Manny then whispered that it was then, as Mr. Wipley was walking by, that he looked down winked and discretely handed him a small note. I asked him what it said and he paused, and then handed me a small, folded piece of paper; he told me that I was the second person he had ever shown it to. I carefully unfolded it and inside was written the sentence, 'If you want to know the truth, find my document'. There was also a symbol at the bottom of the page that looked like a hieroglyphic; it was three wavy lines one on top of the other. Manny said he had never been sure what the note meant, but that the symbol at the bottom was an ancient universal marking that was used to indicate water sources. Manny said that when he went to talk with Wipley about the note he had already disappeared again, and no one knew anything about where he had gone to. Manny said that he had continued still after all these years to try and solve the mystery. I figured this note was what had been fueling Manny's desire to find out the truth for so long.

Manny then when on to tell me that eight years ago, after I had left for college, a young man named Ray came to South Grove Harbor looking for Mr. Wipley; claiming to be his long lost son. Manny said he met with the young man and told him the same story he had just told me about the note. He said this young man, Ray, then told him about a collection of documents he had which Wipley had apparently left for him before he disappeared again for the second time.

Among these documents was one that he said told the story of where Wipley had supposedly been during those five years. He said the document told of a mysterious island Wipley had discovered which had water on it that could heal anyone. Manny told me that the young man promised to meet up with him the next day and show him the document, but never did.

Now that I was grown up I didn't care much about the legend of Hunter Wipley any more. I don't think I even believed any of Manny's stories that day, but the very next day when I was at the auction in Bogstown, I was completely astonished to find out that all the stories were one hundred percent true.

James was about to turn to the next page when his flashlight suddenly became dim. He gave it a firm shake, attempting to restore power, but this only helped for a few brief seconds. Soon, the light returned to the dull, yellowish color it had been. He wanted to keep reading the document but that meant turning the light in his room back on, and he just didn't want to risk it. He knew he'd be nervous the entire time and he figured he'd continue reading more tomorrow.

"Oh well, it's probably getting late anyway," he told himself, as he checked his father's old watch under the dull light. "Wow, it's almost one in the morning… You getting tired yet Buddy?" he asked pointing the flashlight at his little dog who he found was already curled up and sound asleep. "Just like I thought, sleeping on the job again," he said with a grin.

James closed the document and slipped it under his spare pillow. He then began adjusting his blankets and that's when the flashlight finally went out. It was dark as night now in the room as James laid back and pulled Buddy away from edge and closer to his side. It felt good to stretch out and relax in peace and quiet for once, and it wasn't long before James slipped into a very deep sleep.

That night as James slept he dreamt that he and his father were out on an old sailing ship at sea. They were approaching land when all of a sudden their ship came under attack. Canon balls were flying through the air and blasting massive holes in the wooden side of their ship. James and his father scrambled behind a row of nearby barrels for cover. As James peered over the top, he saw the ambush was coming from a ship that looked similar to theirs, but had black flags and torn sails. James' father then handed him a telescope and as he looked through it he was appalled to see Rex walking along the deck of the attacking ship carrying a torch in his hand. He was laughing as he used the torch to casually ignite huge canons which were all aimed directly at James and his father's ship. The explosions continued to rock their vessel violently and before James knew it he and his father where force to abandoned ship. They both dove overboard into the cold, salty, ocean water and tried now to swim for land, but after a minute James' clothes were so waterlogged and heavy that it was becoming a serious struggle just to stay afloat. With every passing second, the fight to keep his head above the water became more and more difficult. As a wave lifted James up and tossed him about, he suddenly heard his father yelling for help. He looked over and there in the choppy ocean water he saw his dad's head appear and disappear above and below the water like a fishing bobber. There was no way of mistaking it, his father was drowning. James sprang into action, quickly paddling over and grabbing his father who was gasping for air, "I got you dad!" James shouted as he strained even harder now to keep both his and his father's head above the salty water. He continued to try and swim towards land with his father in tow, but eventually the extra weight just became too much, and they both started to slowly go under. With one final burst of energy, James fought to keep them afloat, and then, after his last breath of precious air the ocean rushed over them and everything went dark and cold. The last thing James heard as he and his father sank together was the sound of Rex laughing from above.

# Chapter Two
# History Repeating…

    James awoke the next morning in a light sweat; he was lying completely sideways on his bed with the sheets and covers on the floor. He sat up and wiped his forehead in relief as he realized it had all just been a dream. He looked over and noticed Buddy sitting on the floor staring up at him halfway under the sheet, with his ears perked up in an alarmed way. James figured he must have been mimicking his nightmare in real life, since Buddy and the bed looked the way they did.

    "Can you believe it Buddy," James said to the little dog as he removed the sheet from his furry head. "I can't even escape Rex in my dreams." He reached down and scratched Buddy behind the ear until suddenly he remembered the document. He flipped the spare pillow over, but it was not there. He began to fear he had dreamed it as well. In a brief panic he scattered the rest of his pillows out of the way and looked down in between the headboard and mattress. There, stuck a few inches from the floor, was the document. He reached down and pushed the pages until they fell and landed under the bed. James grinned as he stood up and stretched. As usual, he walked over and pulled back the curtains covering his window.

"Well, that's a good start," he said, after looking out and seeing the driveway empty. *Debra and Rex must have stayed out all night*, he thought, *I hope they stay out all day too.* But he knew this was unlikely considering they usually never stayed gone for long.

Over the next half-hour, James made his bed, took a shower, and got himself and Buddy something to eat. Afterwards, he went into the large, unorganized, living room hoping to find the phone. This room used to be neat and elegant, with twenty feet high ceilings, a marble fireplace and oversized leather furniture. But now it looked more like a scrap yard, since Rex had taken the furniture and left the room filled with trash and boxes of his junk scattered everywhere, which made it tough to find anything. James knew it was a long shot but still he walked over to the cordless phone base, where the phone should have been, and looked down. As expected it wasn't there; he did notice however that the red light on the answering machine was flashing, indicating there was a new message waiting to be heard. James sat down beside the small table, moved a sock out of the way and pressed the play button-

'You have one new message,' the electronic female voice announced. 'Saturday at four-thirty a.m.' "James, James are you there?" mumbled the female voice on the other end. James knew right away it was his step-mother. "Well, since you're not awake—just listen, we've got to go visit someone and, we'll be gone till tomorrow night, so don't leave or mess with anything... You hear me? And..." Suddenly James heard Rex in the background. "Just give me the phone... What she meant to say was you better hope I don't catch you snooping around the house again," Rex barked. "I'm getting tired of you nosing around you little punk..." The machine then beeped and James knew the message was over.

*Ugh, I hate that guy,* James thought, as he shook his head in anger. In a way, the message was good news though, he knew now that for the first time in three months he would actually have the house to himself for the day. It almost seemed too good to be true. As he sat and debated what it was he wanted to do with the unexpected freedom, he also wondered who it was Debra and Rex were going to visit. He felt this whole situation with the two of them seemed to keep getting stranger, and he needed desperately to figure out why.

After going over several options in his head, he couldn't think of anything else he wanted more than to see his father. He knew this was next to impossible, since he had no way of getting there and the hospital was over three hours away. So, instead he was going to try the next best thing: to call the hospital and attempt to find out how his father was doing. He hoped maybe this would put some of his worries to rest. He had wanted to make this call again for a while now; the last time he called the hospital he was told that some new policy prohibited anyone from giving out personal information concerning any patient over the phone. He knew this time he needed to come up with a brilliant plan before he made the call.

As he thought about it he continued his search for the phone. This took ten minutes and covered the entire first floor of the house, eventually leading him to the bathroom where he found the cordless receiver under a dirty, wet towel. *That's great,* James thought. He wanted to cuss Rex out for breaking all the other phones in the house, but instead channeled his anger into constructive thoughts as he searched the phonebook for the hospital's number.

"What was the name of that place?" James asked himself, as he ran his finger down the long list of hospitals. He didn't know the hospital's number since they had recently moved his father to a new specialized clinic. He did know, however, that it was somewhere in the town of Hartsfield, and that was just enough to spark his memory.

"Here we go," he said as he stood at the kitchen table and circled Community North Hospital. Filled with anticipation, he began dialing the numbers when he suddenly stopped. *Go back over the plan again,* he told himself, remembering what his father had taught him. If he didn't want this to turn out like last time then he needed to be convincing and get the hospital to break its policy. He figured that if he could just get someone to tell him his father was still alive that it would make all the difference in the world. It was like torture not knowing anything at all.

"No, I know he's still alive, he's got to be." James said, as his little dog Buddy wagged his tail at his feet. After going over his plan again in his head, he knew it was a risky one, but he figured if it worked it would be well worth it. He slowly picked up the phone again, and with his plan in mind he once again began dialing the numbers. He sat nervously at the table as the line began ringing…

"Hello, this is Community North Hospital how may I direct your call?" a woman on the other end said.

In a voice deeper than his usual one, James professionally said, "Yes, I needed to get some information on a patient of mine in your hospital."

"Okay, may I ask who is calling?" the woman asked. James hesitated for a brief second as he stared at the phonebook below him.

"Yes, this is, Dr. Duncan and I'm in a bit of a hurry," James announced, as he stare at the same name on the next page over. The women on the other end stayed silent for what seemed like hours; James could feel his heart pounding as he impatiently waited.

"Okay," she finally said, "I'll transfer you, one moment please," and then the line began to play elevator music. James sat with the phone tight to his ear as thought after thought raced through his mind of what to say next. Without warning the phone began ringing again...

"Yes, hello Dr. Duncan, how are you doing today sir?" a man asked.

"Fine, fine," James continued in his fake, deep voice.

"And what is it we can do for you today, sir?"

"Yes, I need some information on a patient of mine in your hospital, I'm uh," James paused, almost forgetting his next line. "Yes, I'm doing some follow-up work and don't have time to drive over there right now. The patient's name is Joe Greene." James explained as a light sweat broke out on his face. His nerves weren't made for lying, that much is true. The line went quiet for a couple seconds, which caused James to think the man on the other end had gotten wise to him and simply hung up.

"Hello," James said, desperately trying to conceal his nerves.

"Now Doctor Duncan you know I could get in trouble for giving you this information over the phone, I know you're two hours away but—"

James suddenly interrupted. "Yes, well, you know I had two nurses call off today and this would really help me out. They've done this for me before you know, and I wouldn't ask if it wasn't very important—"

"All right, all right," the young man said, "give me just a minute and I'll see if I can find his attending nurse." And just like that James was on the phone with his father's nurse.

"Hello this is Tammy, what can I do for you Dr. Duncan?" The young woman quickly asked.

"Well," James sternly said, "how is my patient, Joe Greene, doing?"

"Um, let me check here," she said, and James could hear her tapping several buttons. "Okay, here we go, yes, it looks like Mr. Greene was responding well to the treatment at first," she said and then paused.

"What do you mean at first?" James demanded.

"Well," she said, and he heard her hit a few more buttons, "after the first week of his new treatment Mr. Greene lost consciousness again, and then I'm afraid he slipped into a coma two days ago, he has been unresponsive ever since."

James' heart sank after hearing this, he almost hung the phone up but then he heard the young woman speak again.

"But there is something odd in the chart here," she said, "It looks as if Mr. Greene was trying desperately to communicate something before he went completely unconscious. It says here that he kept repeating something about pages that are hidden in his office; he said he needed the pages. We're not sure why he was saying this, but apparently it was something he thought was very important. We did in fact call and ask Mr. Green's wife about it yesterday, but she said she didn't know what he was talking about."

James froze, he wondered if it could be the same strange pages he had found yesterday. But what were the chances of that, and why would his father want the document so badly?

"That doesn't mean anything to you does it Doctor?" She asked, after a few moments of silence.

"No, not really," James said, still thinking about what he had just heard. "Does it say specifically what he was talking about?" James slowly asked, giving less effort in disguising his voice now that he was deep in thought.

"No, it doesn't say anything else about it here in the notes," she said. "But I might be able to speak with the nurse who was scheduled that night and find out if she heard Mr. Greene say anything else about it."

"Yes, that'd be great," James quickly said, as he continued to ponder this bizarre information. He couldn't believe his dad had gotten better but was now even worse than before. And out of all things to say, why would he mention those pages? None of it made any sense.

"Now who is this again?" The young nurse curiously asked, after Buddy started barking in the background.

"Doctor, Doc," James stammered as he tried to quiet Buddy. Suddenly it dawned on him why he was barking. *No it can't be*, James thought as the young nurse on the other end of the phone was getting upset.

## HEALING WATER

"Hello? Who is this?"

James immediately hung the phone up and threw it on the table. It was not even two seconds later that he heard the nerve racking roar of Rex's old, diesel engine as it pulled into the driveway. James hastily closed and covered up the phonebook, he and Buddy then ran from the kitchen to his bedroom down the hall. James heard the front door opening at the same time he closed his bedroom door. He slowly locked it, and then stood there with Buddy at his side and listened. *What is he doing here*, James thought, *it's not even noon yet... The message said they wouldn't be back until tonight*. He felt that nervous tingle go through his body again for what seemed like the hundredth time this month. It was the kind of feeling you get when you mix fear and hate together at the same time. *I've got to figure out what that document is*, he told himself, as he stood perfectly still at his door listening. He heard heavy footsteps enter the kitchen, and then stop. A few seconds later the steps got louder, they approached the hallway and stopped again. James held his breath as he waited. Finally, the footsteps continued on down passed his room and then disappeared. James knew it was Rex, but he had no idea what he was doing there.

James stood there for another minute; and as he did he couldn't help but feel some sort of weird bliss come over him. It was yet another strange blend of feelings brought on this time by thoughts of his father still being alive, but also being in a coma. Still, as he stood thinking about this, he told himself to look on the bright side, not everything had turned out bad. In fact, he had in his possession something that was apparently very important to his father, the document. Maybe his father thought the pages could help him somehow. Even though James had no idea why or how they could help, he was going to be sure to figure that out, this much he did know.

After a few minutes of waiting and hoping Rex was going to leave again, James finally accepted that his short lived freedom was over; he knew Rex was there to stay. After barricading his door again for protection, he grabbed the document from under his bed. This time he looked at the pages with a newfound respect.

As Buddy lay sleeping at his feet, James sat at his desk wide awake scanning over the pages with keen eyes, this time trying desperately to find some clue to why this thing might be so important to his father. He went right back to where he had left off last night and continued reading. As he finished that very next page he suddenly realized what the introduction was claiming the old document to be. The idea hit him hard and as the epiphany grew he flipped back and began to reread the last page again to be sure...

Now that I was grown up I didn't care much about the legend of Hunter Wipley any more. I don't think I even believed any of Manny's stories that day, but the very next day when I was at the auction in Bogstown, I was completely astonished to find out that all the stories were one hundred percent true.

It was there at the auction, as I walked around the displays showing off each collection, that I took special notice of a large, old trunk which was full of maps and papers. I stood staring at the collection for several minutes. What was really grabbing my attention were the initials H.W. signed on many of the documents. Even the crest on the outside of the wooden trunk read H.W. and I remember saying to myself, 'Could this be, Hunter Wipley's actual collection?' I tried to look down through the protective glass case and read some of the documents lying on top, but the handwriting was too small. I then found and read a very brief description on the other side of the case, and was absolutely amazed to see the name Hunter Wipley at the top. I then read the sellers name and found it to be one Ray Wipley, Hunter's long lost son, it was all true. I couldn't believe it, Manny had been telling the truth this whole time. The documents of Hunter Wipley really did exist, and for some reason his son was selling them.

I immediately called Manny and left him a message. I knew I had to buy this collection no matter what the cost. Lucky for us no one there had ever even heard of the researcher Hunter Wipley before, so I was able to purchase the entire collection for two thousand dollars. It all seemed too good to be true. It was an amazing discovery for me and I knew Manny would be absolutely beside himself. All of our youthful dreams were about to come true. We would finally know where Wipley had actually been and possibly where he was now. The idea of becoming famous was growing in my mind like it had in Manny's for so many years.

After the auction I immediately drove the four hours back to Manny's and as we got the trunk inside and opened it we found dozens upon dozens of documents and maps, some of which were not even in English. We began searching through the pages, trying desperately to find the document Manny had been looking for his entire life; the document that told where Wipley had been during his five year disappearance. We read page after page of stories Wipley had written throughout his lifetime. They documented everything from: places he had traveled, to people he had met, and things he had researched.

After several exciting hours the night turned to morning and the pages got fewer and fewer. It was beginning to look like we might finally be running out of luck. But then I picked up a flimsy, leather-bound document that was also handwritten. I started to read the messy writing and knew right away that I had found what Manny and I had been looking for; it was the answer to the mystery of where Mr.Wipley had been for all those years. We both took turns reading aloud the story, and after the first dozen pages it was apparent where Wipley claimed he had been. Wipley's son was right, according to the pages he had wrecked his sailboat on some small, unknown island somewhere in the Gulf of Mexico. But the incredible part of the story was that Wipley claimed that this island had water that could heal any man and cause him to live twice as long as he normally would. 'I have finally solved the mystery of the fountain of youth, it is a myth no longer,' Wipley wrote. Then to our amazement the document even gave rough directions to the island's location. After reading this Manny lost it. He immediately accepted it as fact and even began packing to go find the island. I believed it had to be the first document in existence claiming to know the location of real healing water. I knew it had to be investigated, because if proven to be true it would have to be one of the most valuable documents and greatest discovery of all time.

    James stopped there, the concept of the document was mind-boggling. He flipped a few pages forward and examined the old, handwritten section. He looked up and stared out his window in deep thought. His young mind was trying to wrap itself around what he had just read.

    "Could it really be," he asked himself, as all his thoughts began to connect, and questions erupted in his brain. For the first time the young James Greene actually wished he was a great detective like his grandfather had been. *Was there really an explorer named Hunter Wipley, could this old document really be the same one he wrote fifty years ago? Is there really such a thing as healing water?* James was a smart young man and usually knew what was real and what was make believe, but this time he wasn't so sure.

    He soon began to read the older, handwritten document and as he did the line between reality and fantasy slowly became blurred. He asked himself if the situation he was in was just causing him to be unusually gullible and desperate. But if the pages were not real then why would his father have mentioned them in the hospital, and why would he have hidden them? James looked back down at the flimsy, leather-bound document. Most of the pages did look old, and they were handwritten… But could this really be a long-lost document, and could an island like this really exist? The next thought to strike his young mind was a bold one. *Maybe this is why the pages are so important to my dad, because they are true and he knows they could save his life.*

James' heart pounded as the idea settled in. Had his father found and hidden away one of the most valuable sets of directions ever, and if so, where had he gotten them from, and why would he have hidden them under his dirty, office floor and not in a safe somewhere? The questions continued to pour out, but James knew the answers would be nearly impossible to find out right now.

"Come on James, how can this story be real?" he finally asked himself, feeling foolish for ever contemplating the idea. "Yeah right, magical, healing water, sure…"

The more James went back and forth with this dilemma the more frustrated he became. He couldn't decide if he believed the document was real or not. Finally, he stood up, opened his desk drawer and jammed the document inside. As much as he was wanted to continue reading it, he felt that the idea within the pages would only give him false hopes and then eventually let him down. He figured only a kid would believe in a story like this, and he stopped reading comic books years ago. After all, he should be looking for real ways to help his father right now, right?

For the next two hours, James lay in his room and tried to ignore the mysterious pages in his desk drawer. He turned on his small television in the corner of his room and tried watching some boring reality show, but his imagination was still flooded with visions of finding this healing water and saving his father… Eventually, he couldn't take it anymore and jumped up, walked over, and got the document out of his desk. He opened and flipped through the pages until he came to the last one he had read. He turned to the next page, and once again saw the title: The Island of Healing Water, by Hunter Wipley. The handwriting on the first fifty or so pages was somewhat difficult to read, just like the introduction had said; but James took his time and read through every page carefully. Even if it had been written in a different language he still would have figured it out; nothing was going to keep him from understanding this document.

As he continued reading, the story that unfolded before him seemed to be even more realistic then he had first imagined. With each passing page James believed more and more of the legend. He read on into the evening, and at around nine that night James finally finished Wipley's document. It was an amazing tale and James' imagination soared. Maybe it was the situation he was in or the fact that he was fifteen, but for whatever the reason he believed the story in the document was mostly true.

James asked himself, why couldn't he find this island too and take back some of its healing water to save his father? The concept seemed simple enough. And as the idea began to slowly take hold of him he flipped back through the old pages and read over the rough directions to the island again. Wipley had written that the island sat in the Gulf of Mexico; he even gave specified coordinates to the place: 25 degrees north latitude by 88 degrees west longitude. Everything seemed obvious enough to James, the only unexplainable part of the entire document was that the introduction section strangely cut off after the author and Manny found the document. There was simply nothing else written by the unknown author after that. James wondered why this was. *Maybe something happened to the author and Manny Jones,* James told himself. *Maybe they died trying to find the island and couldn't finish the story. Or maybe they did find the island and it was so great they never came back to finish it? But why would they leave the document with the directions behind?* He argued with himself.

Despite this inconsistency, the idea continued to evolve in James' young mind. But, as with any good detective, he still continued to question certain aspects of the story and feel torn about its validity. Besides, he told himself, even if something like this healing water did exist somewhere he had no idea how he would ever get there... He didn't even have his driver's license yet and very little money in his savings account.

As excited as James was with his new discovery and the ideas it generated, he knew he needed to get some sleep soon. Tomorrow was Monday and that meant he would get to escape the house and go back for his last week of school before summer break. He didn't even want to think about what it was going to be like around the house that summer without his dad around. He remembered last winter when his father was still healthy he had promised James that they would build a pool together that coming summer. This memory made him feel even more alone and soon James tried to replace it with a good one, but those were becoming harder to come by with every passing day. He knew he was going to need help if he hoped to find out anything else about the document. James had no way of knowing, but tomorrow was going to be a rollercoaster ride of ups and downs that would inevitably lead him to some answers, along with even more questions.

# Chapter Three
# Neil and Pop Kelly

    The next day, after James got out of school, he began walking home with his best friend, Neil Kelly. He and Neil had been best friends ever since first grade, and even though Neil was just as tall as James he was stocky and weighed about fifty pounds more. He had sandy blonde hair, which was always combed perfectly, and he wore Hawaiian party shirts all the time, even in winter. He was like an odd mix between a surfer and a professional wrestler. Once James asked him why he never wore normal shirts and Neil told him that he was preparing for life on the beach, after of course he became rich and bought a house on one. Two friends could not have been more different, but the strange partnership for some reason always made for a good team; James, the brains and Neil, the muscle perhaps? Even though James had not been allowed to leave his house very often in the past three months, the two always found a way to hang out.

When James and Neil were finally far enough away from the school and all the other students, James couldn't wait another second to tell Neil about the document. He described everything about the leather-bound pages he had found, and then told Neil the story of Hunter Wipley and the island, and of course the healing water.

"Are you serious?" Neil said, looking over at James and stopping in the middle of the street.

"I know it sounds stupid right, look just forget I even said anything okay," James said, feeling embarrassed that he had brought it up to begin with. He should have known Neil wouldn't understand.

"Stupid," exclaimed Neil, "No, it's not stupid man. Don't you remember my grandpa Pop used to research stuff like that all the time, he still believes in all kinds of so-called myths," Neil said, as James pulled him out of the middle of the street.

"So, you think this story could be true then?" James asked, still looking surprised.

"I don't know, maybe. My dad told me that my grandpa Pop used to work for the CIA and he researched all kinds of unexplained cases for them," Neil said.

"You're joking, Pop worked for the CIA?"

"Yeah seriously, he's retired now and has a bad hip and everything, but he'd probably go crazy if he knew you found a document with a story like that under your house."

"Well, don't think I'm crazy or anything," James slowly said, "but I was kind of thinking that if the document was real I might be able to use it to help my dad…. I mean don't get me wrong, I'm not sure how or anything but still…"

"Really, yeah it's, it's a bit out there but, hey if I were you I'd try just about anything at this point to help get my dad back too…" Neil said, shaking his head and looking sorry for James.

"I know, I don't think I can handle much more of this situation at home. Debra and Rex are getting meaner everyday. Have I told you she still hasn't taken me to visit my dad in the hospital?"

Neil stopped walking and looker over in disgust, "Still! Man, what's it been like two months?"

"Try three," James said, as he kicked a rock on the ground. "Listen, I called the hospital yesterday and found out he's in a coma now…"

"What! Are you serious?"

"Yeah, but you're not going to believe this, the nurse said he was asking about some document he had hidden in his office just before he passed out."

"Yeah, so?"

"So, I think it's the same document I found, it must be important if my dad had it hidden and was asking about it. Plus, remember I told you Rex and Debra have been looking around the house lately too. What if this document was what they were looking for?"

"Man that detective stuff your dad taught you is really paying off huh?"

"I don't know, I mean I think I just got lucky that's all. Anyway, I'm only doing this to try and find out what's going on. I figure my dad could die any day now, Neil, I need to do everything I can to help him."

"I know so, what are you going to do then, you got a plan or what?"

James looked confused for a second, "What do you mean?"

"You know with this document you found, it's has to be important, I mean you said that nurse told you your dad was asking about it. So, what are you going to do with it?"

James thought for a few seconds as they continued to walk. "Well, I guess I'd at least like to find out if it's real or not. You know, do some research on this guy Hunter Wipley and this town South Grove Harbor in Florida."

"Right, well then, why don't you bring it over tonight and we'll have Pop take a look at it. Man, I'm telling you he's like a genius when it comes to this stuff. He'll know whether it's real or not."

"All right," James said, gladly welcoming any kind of help, "I'll bring it over tonight then."

"Sounds good, you wait and see, man, sometimes this stuff can get really interesting. I've read some of Pop's research before and it's amazing how many strange things exist out there that people don't even know about or believe in."

"I had no idea you were interested in this kind of thing," James admitted.

"Oh yeah, I've always been a big fan of mysteries. I once did a science report on Bigfoot."

During the rest of the walk home James continued to be impressed by Neil's curiosity in the document. He continued asking James questions about the story and even knew a few facts of his own. James never thought Neil liked to learn about anything before, but it was nice to see him so interested in something for a change.

"So, what time do you think you'll be over tonight?" Neil asked, as they turned the corner that led down to James' house.

"Um, I was thinking around eight hopefully," James said, looking up the road at his house and then back at Neil.

"Okay, but no later then nine though, remember that's when Pop goes to bed. And by the way, how are you planning on getting out of that prison this time?" Neil jokingly asked.

"Same way I always do," James said with a grin, pointing over to a nearby car window. "Plus, by that time they'll both either be gone or passed out anyway."

Neil laughed and padded James on the back. "I'm sorry to hear about your dad," he said, as they stood on the side of the street and slapped each other five.

"Thanks, I'll see you tonight."

The boys both turned and walked in opposite directions now towards their separate houses.

As James approached his driveway, he walked around the line of tall bushes and saw Rex's dreaded truck they nicknamed 'The Bull', still sitting there in the driveway. His step-mother's car was gone, so he wasn't completely sure who, if anyone was home. *Please let them be gone*, he repeated in his head. As soon as he walked in the front door he was awestruck by how torn up the place was. It was the worst he had ever seen it. The once clean, organized home that James' father, Joe, worked so hard for was now a total disaster.

*Why would they do this*, James thought, as he carefully stepped around all the broken glass and unidentifiable objects? He felt a wave of anger come over him as he entered the kitchen and saw the armoire his father had bought for his mother was now broken. Where there had once been a pair of glass doors and china, were now small, broken pieces of glass and splintered wood. He couldn't believe it, there was no excuse for this excessive damage. He smelled and also noticed several empty beer cans and a bottle of vodka filled the trash can to the very brim. It almost seemed as if someone had broken in and robbed the place, or like someone went crazy trying to find something in the house.

James carefully navigated his way back to his room and opened the door. For the first few seconds he looked in, he thought he had gone to the wrong room, but then it hit him. Rex had also destroyed his room as well, it was a complete catastrophe. He felt a pawing at his leg and looked down only to see his scared little dog, Buddy, shaking nervously.

"It's okay, Buddy, it's over now," he mumbled, as he rubbed the dogs head. James looked up again at the room and felt completely shocked as he began to evaluate the damage. It really did look like a bomb had exploded in there. The clothes from his closet were all over the floor, along with bent and broken hangers, boxes of family pictures, and games. His posters of Albert Einstein and Ernest Hemmingway were torn off the wall, and his desk had been ransacked. James was almost speechless; the only words he managed to get out were a few well placed cuss words.

"Why would he do this, what does he want?" James finally blurted out. At that moment, he didn't care if anyone was home to hear him he had had enough. His mattress had been flipped off the bed and was now on the floor, along with papers, pens, and hats. Just about everything he owned had been rummaged through or thrown around. He couldn't believe it, if he hated Rex before, he simply despised him now. James was so shocked in fact that he had almost forgotten about the document hidden under his bed. Remembering it suddenly, he rushed over to the bed frame, which only had the box springs left on it, knelt down and looked underneath.

"No, no, no," he quickly exclaimed, sliding himself under and feeling around with both arms. "He took it, I can't believe it, that jerk took it. He could have taken anything else, but not this." He slowly pulled himself back out from under the bed and leaned up against the wooden frame, he was so angry he didn't know what to do. He took a few deep breaths, like his father had taught him, and instead of letting his emotions consume him he tried to calm down and think...

"Why would he want the document?" he asked himself, as the confusion set in.

Loads of questions raced throughout James' mind and mixed with the adrenaline that was pumping through his veins, he almost felt like he might pass out. He took more deep breaths and for the next ten minutes James sat there, propped up against half his bed in the middle of his destroyed room, and did nothing else but think of a way to get revenge. *I'll slash the tires on that stupid truck of his... No, I'll go break his new television and pour out all his alcohol...* James stopped himself right there. He knew none of these things would do any good, if anything they would only make things worse. He was over reacting, maybe even panicking. He needed to think straight, so he made himself calm down and from that moment on he decided to beat Rex at his own game. *Two can play this way...* He decided to still stick with the original plan that he and Neil had come up with for the night. That was to try and figure out as much as they could about the document, even if he didn't have it right now he could still remember it and describe most of it to Pop. Now that this had happened James was even more confident in the importance of the document. He had to get it back, but he knew he needed another plan. So, he decided he was going to clean up his room, and let Rex think it had not even bothered him; and then when the time was right, and Rex least expected it, he was going to steal the document back and then run away.

A moment later James got up, he put his bed back together, picked up most of the things off his floor, and reorganized his desk. He had just begun hanging his clothes back in the closet when he heard a tapping at his window. He dropped the clothes he was trying to hang and ran over to see who it was. Standing there in the front yard was Neil. He was looking through the window and around the room with a concerned look on his face. The look of shock soon changed to confusion as Neil gestured for James to open the window.

"What the heck happened to your room, it looks like a tornado hit it or something?"

"He took it," James blurted out uncontrollably.

"Took what?" Neil asked, still looking confused.

"He took the document, I had it hidden under my bed and he destroyed the house and my room and then stole it. He stole my dad's document from me can you believe that?"

"Are you serious—what, why would he do that?" Neil asked, continuing to survey the damage.

"That's the thing, I don't know why—I mean the document was hidden under the floor in my dad's office, how'd that idiot even know I had it?" James picked up a smashed plastic box that used to be his radio.

"I don't know, but man it really must to be important, huh? Why else would it get all this attention," Neil said, as James nodded. "We have to get it back, you know that right? I mean you should have heard Pop when I told him about it, he made me come over here right now and get you, that's why I'm here," Neil exclaimed.

"Well, I can still tell him a lot about it, since I've read it three times I have most of it memorized," James said, as he picked up some pictures off the floor. "You better believe after I get that document back I'm leaving here until my dad gets better and comes home," James announced.

Neil nodded his head in agreement. "We'll figure something out man, maybe you can stay at my house until then."

James grinned, he had been lucky to find such a good friend as Neil, and now he was beginning to realize it more than ever.

"So, your grandpa wants me to come over right now?" James asked, looking out the window at Neil.

"Yeah man, you should have seen him, he said go see if he can come over here right now. I tried to call, but nobody answered," Neil said, as he took out a candy bar from his pocket.

"Phone's missing," James mumbled, as he continued to clean up the mess.

"Well?" Neil mumbled, with a mouthful of melted chocolate.

"All right, I'm coming." James announced, figuring since Rex and his stepmother were not home yet that they'd most likely be out late. "Hey!" James yelled at Neil as he was walking away. He thought for a second, and then waved Neil to come back to the window.

"Listen, do you think we should look around here for the document first before we go?"

"What do you really think Rex would leave it around here right after stealing it?"

"I don't know, maybe he hid the pages in his truck or something," James quickly replied.

"Alright, we'll check 'The Bull', but I'm telling you man, if Rex shows up I'm out of here."

James agreed and then met Neil out front in the driveway. They both walked slowly towards 'The Bull' as if at any moment it might start up on its own and run them over. The truck's tires were twice as large as normal ones, and on the back of the truck was a picture of a bull's head tearing through a rebel flag. This was the reason they had given it the nickname they did. Even though Rex had been living there for over three months, James had never actually seen the inside of the large vehicle before. Still, he guessed it was probably dirty and smelled like booze, just like Rex did.

After the boys finally inched up along side of the truck they realized that it was simply too tall to see in. James reached up and tried the door handle, but it was locked. They both then tried jumping up beside the monster truck to get a look in, but this didn't work well either.

"All right," Neil said, after jumping up and down several times, "this isn't going to work. I'm going to have to lift you up, so you can look inside."

"Why don't I boost you?" James asked, while Neil stood with his hands clasped together giving him a stupid look.

"Oh, right." James said, understanding the look and then stepping into Neil's hands. Neil gave a couple groans as he lifted James up another three feet off the ground; as he went up James held onto the truck's large side mirror to help keep his balance.

"See anything?" Neil asked, continuing to strain.

"Uh, there's a couple old lamps and some vases and uh," James paused as he noticed a pair of boots and some hats that belonged to his father. "He's got some more of my dad's things in here," James exclaimed. "There's my dad's other watch too. Can you believe this?"

It took Neil a couple seconds to answer because he was straining so much, but he finally managed one word… "Document?" he grunted.

"No, I don't see it, you can let me—" but before James could finish his sentence he was already on the ground.

"Sorry," Neil gasped, as James barely caught himself, "you were, getting heavy…"

"I'm fine, but I didn't see the document anywhere."

"So, what are we gonna do now?" Neil said.

"What can we do?" James asked, kicking one of the over-sized tires. "I'll just start looking around the house and see what I can come up with, but for now let's go over to your place and talk to your grandpa; I can at least describe the document and see what he thinks."

"Sounds good," Neil said, wiping the sweat from his forehead. "I need something to drink anyway."

They made the short walk around the corner and down three houses. Neil's house was a large, two-story with red brick. Both his parents made good money and it showed. After they walked in the front door, they found Neil's mother, Judy, on the phone in the kitchen. There were paint buckets on top of drop cloths and tools on the floor.

"My parents are remodeling, making room for Pop." Neil explained to James, as he raided the refrigerator. Besides smelling like paint, the house was close to perfect condition. They seemed to have all new furniture, and there wasn't one thing out of place; this was partly due to the fact that Neil was an only child, just like James, and so there was never really any messes to clean up. James wished his house looked like this again; it reminded him of how his mother used to be.

Neil's father, Tim, was a lawyer, and was rarely ever home—his mother, Judy, on the other hand was a nurse and for the past year had been working part-time and taking care of Neil's grandpa Pop during her days off. Neil handed James a drink, as Judy finished her phone call and hung up. Afterwards, she said hello to James and gave him a big hug. Judy Kelly was a plus-sized woman, but had a very sweet voice and pretty face.

"Mom," Neil said, feeling embarrassed that she always hugged James.

"Oh I'm sorry, James," she said. "I'm just glad to see you. It's been a while and we were getting worried about you. Is everything all right over there at your house?"

James didn't mind the hug, but he didn't exactly know how to answer Judy's question.

"It's okay right now," he said, trying to sound convincing. He didn't like people feeling sorry for him, it made him feel uncomfortable.

"No it's not," Neil announced.

"I'll survive," James said, as his face got a bit red.

Sensing James' slight embarrassment Judy quickly chimed in. "Are you boys hungry, I can make you a sandwich I still got the turkey out?"

"No, I'm fine, thanks," James said.

"We don't have time, mom, we really just need to talk to Pop that's all," Neil explained, finishing off his drink.

"Well, he's been in the study all day working on some research project. I just got done taking him some food, so whatever you do make sure he eats it will you?" Judy said, as she quickly fixed another sandwich.

"Here, now you guys eat these or they'll go to waste. You're both still growing and need all you can get."

James and Neil both took a sandwich a piece, James then said goodbye to Judy as they walked to the other side of the house and down to where the study was.

James had met Neil's grandfather Pop only a couple times before; the man was always busy working on something and the boys were usually told not to disturb him. Neil knocked lightly on the double doors leading to the room, but no one answered. The room sounded quiet and looked dark, as Neil slowly pushed one of the doors the rest of the way open. James followed him into the room, and saw that there were bookcases from wall to wall; each reaching from the floor to the ceiling. The room was long and had several windows at the far wall with telescopes pointing out of each one of them. There was even a rolling ladder on each side of the room to reach books on the higher shelves.

As they both walked through the room and then stopped in front of a large desk with paper strew all over it, James could see on the other side the dark outline of Pop against an old, white, projection screen. There was a bright light in the room which was being produced by an old projector, and on the white screen Pop was watching there looked to be a documentary of some kind. As James watched the screen, he saw men in strange suits explaining something on a map. Neil called out to his grandpa several times as he approached him from behind. Pop couldn't seem to hear anything though, and it wasn't until Neil flipped on one of the desk lamps beside him that he finally got his attention.

"Judy, I told you I'm not hungry," Pop said, mistaking them for Neil's mother.

"No, grandpa, it's me, Neil. I brought James with me, remember?" Pop took the headphones he was wearing off and slowly turned around.

"Oh, yes, yes, I'm sorry boys—I thought you were your mother again. She's been trying to force-feed me all day. Oh," he said with a grin, "I see she already got you boys too."

James chuckled as he reached out and shook Pop's hand. "It's good to see you again, sir," he politely said to Pop.

"What's this sir business all about? You just call me Pop like everyone else, okay?"

"Okay sir, I mean, Pop," James said, and then grinned as the old man with the smooth silver beard grinned back. James had never noticed how defined Pop's face was before. He guessed he had to be in his late sixties or so, but his jaw line indicated a much younger man. His short, silver hair was somewhat wild, but matched his beard perfectly. His dark eyes seemed to command a certain respect that only develops after you've experienced the world and almost mastered it.

"Neil tells me you're a smart young man and a good detective, and that you've found a document you need some help with," Pop said, as he reached out for help getting up, and James and Neil both grabbed his arms and helped him to his feet.

"That's right," James said, after handing Pop his dark, wooden cane.

"Turn that off will you, Neil?" Pop said, as he took a firm hold of the cane and slowly made his way around the desk and over to a large, leather chair. Neil turned the projector off, then he and James followed Pop over to a sitting area where they both sat on a large couch across from Pop's chair.

"Okay, so tell me about this document?" Pop said, adjusting his glasses.

"Well, I found it under the floor in my dad's office," James explained. "It has a leather cover and two separate parts inside. The first part is just like an introduction to the second part which is this older, handwritten document that was supposedly written back in the early fifties by an explorer named Hunter Wipley," James explained. And then he continued telling Pop everything he could remember about the document. Pop listened closely, nodding every now and then, and after ten minutes James finished.

"Very interesting," Pop said, motioning Neil to come over to him. "I need you to go down to the end of that bookcase there," he said, pointing across the room. "I believe it's around the sixth row up; there should be a thick, black book with white lettering on the spine, you can't miss it. Will you bring that to me, please? I think there may be something in there that can help us."

As Neil searched for the book Pop began asking James questions about the document.

After a few minutes Neil announced he had found it, and then the rolling ladder slid out from under him and he fell.

"Still got it," he exclaimed, as James rushed over and helped him up. The book was indeed very large and its title said it all: 'Nautical Mishaps and Reports 1945-1955'.

James had a feeling he knew exactly what Pop was looking for, but didn't say anything. Instead, he just sat and watched anxiously while Pop read for a second and then turned the page.

"You said the document you found claimed this man Wipley disappeared on his boat in nineteen forty nine, correct?" Pop slowly asked.

"Um, yes, I believe so," James replied.

Pop then turned the pages a few at a time until he came to a section that caught his eye. His old hands shook somewhat as he read aloud what he had found.

"Now here we go...It says here that apparently on the date of May the 10th, 1949," he paused, and looked up. "I knew to look during the spring time because you said hurricane season," he explained, and then continued. "On that day there were several distress signals and reports taken, it must have been one hell of a storm... Anyway, this one particular report says a small, private ship, name unknown, owner a Mister Hunter Wipley, was reported as sending distress signals somewhere west of Loggerhead Island in the Gulf of Mexico. Here, James, come look at this spelling." Pops said, holding the book out for James to examine. He searched over the small print until he came to the line that Pop had just read. He couldn't believe it, but the name was right there: Hunter Wipley; the exact same one from the document. He reread it again, thinking there had to be some kind of mistake.

"It's the same," James softly said, "I can't believe it."

"Really, you're sure?" asked Neil, with a dumbfound look on his face, as he too leaned over and read the line.

"So, I guess this Wipley guy really did exist then, huh?" James asked.

"Apparently he did," Pop said, as he continued to look at the page.

"See, I told you Pop would know how to figure this out," Neil proudly said.

"Well, actually," Pop slowly said, as he shook his head, "I'm afraid all this does is open up another can of worms for us."

"What's that mean?" Neil said. Pop then went on to explain to James and Neil the history of the fountain of youth and healing water, and how it had been associated with the Garden of Eden, but eventually declared only to be a legend. "Yes, even Christopher Columbus himself had the idea of finding the magical water in the back of his mind when he went searching for another route to Asia, and that was five-hundred years ago."

"So, are you saying the story in the document that I found is made up?" James asked feeling confused now.

"I'm not sure, James, but I will tell you one thing, it completely intrigues me how a document with such a bold story would contain such a bizarre and uncommonly known fact like the one we have proved here today." The boys looked at Pop and then back at each other; Pop quickly picked up on their confusion.

"What I'm saying is how can the document you found be completely untrue if we've already found facts supporting it. This book of mine we found the information in was printed for navy use only; a very close friend of mine gave it to me so that I could add it to my collection of rare books. You see it would be very difficult for the author to know this detail about this man Wipley useless the story he is writing is in fact a true one." Pop then closed the book slowly and handed it to Neil to put back. James sat back down on the couch, still struggling with the thought that he no longer had the document because Rex had wrecked his room and stolen it. James wondered how he was going to find it again. He then explained this problem to Pop. He told him all about how Rex had been searching the house lately, looking for something, and then how he must have taken the document out from under his bed today. Neil then added the detail of James' father repeatedly asking for the pages he had hidden in his office just before slipping into a coma. It was a lot of information for Pop to receive all at once, and James could tell they might be overwhelming the intelligent man.

"Well boys, I've researched and seen a lot of unusual claims and myths throughout my career, and this document you found seems to be attracting quit a bit of attention. In my experience the only things that attract attention are things which usually have a significant value. I wish I could sit here and tell you for sure why this document is valuable but I simply don't know without doing more research. The problem is we can't continue this investigation without the evidence." Pop removed his glasses and looked at James. "Now, James you've done a remarkable job remembering most of the facts, but without all the facts, and the other things that come along with the actual object we will never know for sure if this story and document are real."

"What you're saying is we need to find that document again, right?" James said.

"Yes, I'm afraid so... I tell you what—I still have some time here before my doctor's appointment, let me run a few searches on the computer for you and show you exactly what we're getting ourselves into."

James and Neil watched while Pop searched the computer for other clues about the story's origin. He printed off page after page of information for James to read on the subject and history of the fountain of youth. When he tried searching for known documents claiming to have information on healing water the trail suddenly ended.

"Can't find anything about it?" Neil asked, now chewing on some candy he had found on Pop's desk.

"No, I'm afraid not. It would appear James that what you found may be one of a kind."

"Man, James, we really have to find that document," Neil said.

"I think the first opportunity we get we should search my house from top to bottom, and try to find it."

After both agreeing to this decision James realized what time it was and decided it best to head home. Before leaving, Pop gave him the information he had printed off so he could study it. He then shook James' hand again and smiled, "I really hope to be seeing you again soon, and I'm truly sorry to hear about your father. He will be in my prayers."

"Thank you," James said, he could tell Pop meant every word.

"And James, I want you to know I'll do whatever I can to help you figure all this out. I know how important it is at your age to have a father and if I can do anything else don't hesitate to let me know."

James nodded in appreciation. "Thanks Pop…I guess I just want to know why my father thinks this document's so important. I mean I know it sounds crazy but what if there really is something out there that could save his life?"

Pop chose his words carefully. "If you can retrieve this document again, you will have my full support in proving it to be real or not. That's all I can guarantee, I wish I could promise a miracle but those are very rare now-a-days, and we have to take this one step at a time."

James understood what Pop meant, and left that evening feeling hopeful again. He took comfort in knowing that he now had someone who believed in him and cared; someone who would help him figure it all out. Not only that but he had also found out that Hunter Wipley was in fact a real person and South Grove Harbor was a real town in Florida. Things really did seem to be pointing in one direction. Now all James needed to do was get that document back once and for all.

# Chapter Four
# One Step Closer to the Truth

    James had finished his last week of school with no real problems at home. Even though it was now officially summer break, he felt miserable. He had survived the last week unscathed by lying low and staying in his room. During this time, he had studied and read everything he could find about the fountain of youth. This was the next closest thing in comparison to the healing water, and he wanted to know everything he could about the myth. He learned that apparently during the sixteen century an explorer who sailed with Christopher Columbus named Ponce De Leon was the first one who searched for this mystical water in the new world. He traveled through the land now know as Florida, drinking every source of water he came to, but of course never found anything like it.

    There was one positive change that had occurred for James over the past week though. It seemed the arguments between Rex and Debra were almost non existent now; mostly due to the fact that Debra had been gone almost every night. At first, James was not sure whether this was a good or bad thing because it meant Rex was left alone with him all the time. But the strange thing was ever since the day he had trashed James' room and stolen the document he no longer bothered James. James even noticed he had quit tearing the house apart and seemed less angry. All he did now was wander around, watch TV, and drink beer. It almost seemed like Rex was waiting for something, but what?

The only real problem now with Rex always being there was that James never had a real chance to search for the document. He had been trapped in his room waiting day after day for an opportunity that never came. Luckily yesterday, while Rex was on the phone, James overheard the news he had been waiting for. He heard Rex say he was going to meet with someone tomorrow morning and again that evening. It was a good thing James knew this because he was really getting sick of being confined to his room. Rex hadn't left the house in literally over three days straight and it was killing James. He always felt paralyzed when Rex was there, and this weekend had been the worst one yet. James felt like he was getting stir crazy; and even though Rex wasn't bothering him like he had before, James knew not to take any chances. So, all he and Buddy did was stayed locked in his room, reading, making plans, and steering clear of the maniac in the next room over. James felt that if it wasn't for the late night escapes he and Buddy made out the window and over to Neil's house, that he might lose it and go crazy. He had never felt so impatient in his life. He wanted to know how his father was doing, he wanted the document back, he wanted to figure out if the document was real or not; but most of all he wanted his father back.

When it seemed like the next day might never come, finally, Monday morning rolled around. As soon as his alarm rang, James jumped out of bed, went over to the window and pulled up the blinds. *Thank God,* he thought, looking out at the sun shining on an empty driveway.

"Come on Buddy," he said, "we have to call Neil and find that document..." James got dressed and walked out into the kitchen. It had been over seventy-two hours since he had last been alone in the house, and he was more then happy to have the place to himself again. He immediately walked around looking for the phone to call Neil, but after ten minutes gave up and instead, he and Buddy ran down the street to Neil's house. He rang the doorbell and Neil's mother, Judy, answered it and invited him in; telling him that it was okay if Buddy followed too.

"Oh, it's so good to see you again, James," Judy said. "Neil and Pop told me what's been going on at your house and I think it's totally inappropriate... Neil's father and I talked about it last night and it was agreed that you should stay here until your father gets better."

James was overwhelmed; he didn't know what to say. "Thanks, Judy, I really appreciate it, but I'm not sure if that's such a good idea right now," he lied, thinking it was the best news he had heard all week, but knowing he couldn't leave the house yet, not until he recovered the document at least.

"No, now James, it's really no problem—that step-mother of yours and her boyfriend should be locked up for the way they've been treating you. Neil told me how Rex went through your room and stole some of your things. That's absolutely terrible, I thought about calling the police after he told me that. Have they done anything since, are you okay?" she asked, checking James' face for any signs of abuse.

"I'm fine, seriously Judy. And don't worry I'll consider the offer, I just don't want to...to leave Buddy there alone," James said. It was the only excuse he could think of and he knew once he found the document he would be more than happy to leave there.

"James, you know I love this little dog, he can stay here too you know that. Tim just had the backyard fenced in—actually, why don't you leave him here for the night to see how he takes to the new place," Judy persisted, as she held Buddy and petted him.

"Yeah sure, that's fine. I'll bring over his food later when Neil and I get back."

"Oh okay, that sounds great. I have to take Pop to his doctor's appointment in a few minutes so if you want you can go and wake Neil up, I know he's probably still asleep," Judy said.

"Alright, thanks again Judy, this all really means a lot to me," James said with a smile. On his way down the hall to Neil's room James saw Pop limping his way out of the study.

"Hey, good to see you, James," Pop said, as he turned around and leaned on his cane.

"Hey Pop, I was just on my way to wake Neil up, we're going to search my house for the document today. I don't know if Neil told you but I haven't been able to look for it yet because I've been trapped at home with Rex."

"Yes, I heard, Neil told me everything yesterday; he said you've been making some late night trips over whenever you can. I have to be honest James, we're beginning to worry about your situation over there. I know it's none of my business but I can't stand to see anyone treated badly."

"Come on Pop, we need to leave now or we're going to be late," Judy called from the other room.

"Well, I better get going. Good luck to you, I really hope you get that document back today. Make sure to come back by when you get done, I've been doing some more research and found a few things I think you need to see."

"Okay I will," James said.

A few moments later at the end of the hall James pushed open the door to Neil's room. He walked in and looked around the large space. Each wall had a poster of either a famous sports star or a model in a bathing suit. Along with football equipment on the floor, and a small miniature refrigerator beside his bed Neil had a large desk with a new computer sitting on it and a flat-screen television hanging above it on the wall. It had the typical disorganized look that Neil liked to call controlled chaos, but James knew was really only laziness. After stepping over a surfboard, James walked across the room and saw Neil spread out all over the bed. He had one leg off the edge on the opposite side and was laying at the wrong end with a pillow over his face.

"Hey, wake up Neil, come on," James said, removing the pillow from Neil's face.

"Sorry mom, but I don't feel good today, I think I'm too sick to go to school," Neil moaned as he pulled the blanket over his head.

"No, you idiot it's me—James," James laughed. "Come on schools out remember?" Neil sat up slowly and looked around; his hair was going in all directions and he still had a little drool on his mouth. James sat down at Neil's new oak desk and turned the computer on.

"What time is it anyway?" Neil asked as he tried to keep Buddy from licking his face.

"Uh, I think it's around eight, your mom and grandpa were getting ready to leave when I came in... I would have called but I couldn't find the phone. We need to hurry though because Rex just left and I don't know how long he's going to be gone."

"No, I know," Neil mumbled, and then rubbed his eyes and stood up to stretch. "I'll just be a few minutes, I'm going to go get ready."

"Good, I need to look up a few things anyway," James said, as he did some more research on the computer. He was amazed at the amount of information that popped up on the subject of legends, and as he searched he printed off everything he could find including: several explorers (all which had searched for the fountain of youth) maps, pictures, and even the origins of different myths and how they began. All he had had before were just a few old books from the library, and what Pop had given him.

"What else did ya find?" Neil asked, emerging back into the room, fully awake now and wearing a white Hawaiian party shirt.

"I'll tell you on the way, come on we need to hurry," James said.

During the walk back to James' house, he showed Neil a detailed map of South Grove Harbor in Florida. Having this map made the place seem that much more real to James, and gave him even more hope in the validity of the document.

As they walked, James and Neil went over the search plan they had devised a few nights earlier. Upon walking up the driveway to his house, James took a long look and noticed again how pathetic and different his house looked now than it had a year ago. At that time, the white brick exterior of the home looked immaculate, and the yard was tediously manicured to a point close to perfection. But after almost a year of neglect, caused entirely by the fact that Rex had sold most of James' father's lawn equipment, the large place now looked almost deserted. If it wasn't for James going out every week and push-mowing the yard, people would probably think it was waiting for demolition. Before entering the front door, James noticed the mailbox on the side of the house was overflowing with bills and mail. Apparently, nobody had brought it in for over a week.

"Look at all of this." James exclaimed, having to use both hands in order to carry it all in.

As soon as they got inside, Neil made his way downstairs to the basement and James went into his step-mother's bedroom just like they had agreed. The plan was simple: James would search the main floor and Neil the basement.

"Yell at me if you find anything," James called down the stairs, "and search through everything."

"Don't worry, I will!" Neil promised.

James went down the hall and quickly into Debra's spacious room. There he immediately began riffling through her tall dresser. He knew Rex had most of his things in boxes, but he still found a few articles of his clothing stuffed in the very bottom drawer. *Man, these stink*, James thought as he searched through the alcohol stained clothing. After he was sure nothing important was in the dresser, he moved on to the walk-in closet. His heart beat fast as he went through all the different shoe-boxes, he knew that Rex could show back up any minute and this made the situation very stressful. After the shoe-boxes gave up nothing, he searched everywhere else in the closet, but found nothing even slightly resembling the document. Back in the room now, he pulled several boxes out from underneath the bed. In one of these was a binder that contained all sorts of pictures and old letters. James flipped through them and realized they were ones that his father had sent to his real mother during the war. Debra must have not known they were under there or else James knew they wouldn't have still been there. He quickly read through a few and then put them back. He picked up several pictures of his mother when she was younger and smiled as he looked at them. She was a beautiful woman with straight light brown hair and innocent-looking, kind eyes. James felt he would give anything to still have her around, and he knew his father felt the exact same way.

As he reached back in to put the pictures away, James saw an old envelope at the bottom he had missed. He pulled it out and saw that it was addressed to his father, Joe Greene, but had no return address on it. He quickly opened the letter and after examining it for a minute he felt a sudden rush of excitement. James couldn't believe it, even though the letter was torn in half there was the name, Manny Jones, written right there at the end.

"Neil come up here quick, I found something!" James yelled. He couldn't believe it, Manny Jones and his father knew each other, this was amazing.

"Don't tell me you found it?" Neil said, as he came running into the bedroom.

"No, it's not that," James said, holding up the torn letter in one hand and the envelope in the other. "Do you know what this is?"

"Um, a torn piece of paper and an envelope," Neil sarcastically said, looking confused.

"Not just any piece of paper, it's a letter from Manny Jones to my dad," James exclaimed.

"Who's he?"

"Manny Jones, you know the guy I was telling you about from the document. He's real, this is unbelievable—he must have been one of my dad's old friends or something... Look at this," James said, and Neil leaned over and began reading with him.

"Check it out, he wrote something here to your dad about getting a tattoo, cool," Neil said, continuing to read the letter. "He says he got the aqua era symbol tattooed on the back of his hand to always remember his vow. Huh, I wonder what that looks like?"

James looked at what Neil was reading and reread the sentence.

"Oh yeah, it's like an ancient symbol for water or something," James explained.

"Really, how do you know that?"

"It's described in the document," James said, as he suddenly realized the importance of this discovery. "Do you realize what this means?" James said, as Neil shook his head. "It means Manny Jones is a real person, it means my father really was asking about Wipley's document in the hospital—this is huge, it's bigger than huge..."

"Oh man, you're right," said Neil, finally understanding the significance of the find. "So, that might mean that this story about the healing water could be real then, doesn't it?"

"I don't know, that's a pretty big assumption just because of a letter, but still, this is at least more confirmation that the document is legit... And it's another step forward, we have to show this to Pop," James said, folding the letter back up and putting it into the envelope and then in his pocket.

"Man, Pop's not going to believe this, more evidence." Neil exclaimed. "We really need to find that document, come on let's get back to it. I've already searched all the laundry room, found nothing but some dirty socks behind the dryer."

Over the next two hours, James and Neil searched the entire house from top to bottom. They looked in every drawer, every cabinet, and every place they could find. Finally, they both agreed that there was no way the document could still be in the house. It had apparently been taken somewhere else... But James did find the letter from Manny, and some more of his father's things, and even a gun that he was sure belonged to Rex, but still no document. He and Neil then began discussing different possibilities of where else the missing pages could be and that's when James mentioned Rex's truck again.

"He keeps everything else in there," James said, "It's like a giant safe on wheels."

"Yeah, but if it's in there I don't know how we'll ever get it out."

James shook his head in frustration. "You know none of this makes any sense...I mean what would Rex want with that document anyway?"

"That's what we've got to find out," Neil said. "Come on, let's go back to my house before somebody comes home."

During the walk back, James and Neil discussed the possibility of James moving over to Neil's house. James said as soon as he found the document he would, or on the other hand if the place got too dangerous he would then too. Once back at Neil's, the boys showed Pop the letter from Manny Jones and told him what they thought. Pop was as amazed by the letter as they were and said that it would most definitely help out once they got the document back. All three of them sat in Pop's study and went on for awhile discussing more possible hiding spots where Rex could be keeping the leather-bound document. In the back of James' mind, he kept worrying that he may never find it again.

At around one in the afternoon James decided to play it safe and reluctantly headed back home. He left Buddy's food on the way out, and promised everyone that he would either call or come back if things got too out of control.

After arriving home and realizing that still no one was there, James took another quick look around. He felt so close to having something he thought might help his father that there was no way he could let the idea go. No matter how crazy the story in the document seemed it still brought hope back into his otherwise hopeless situation. He even had Pop and Neil willing to offer help and support on his radical idea. He worried now that they might think he had made the whole thing up, since he still couldn't produce any real proof. *I found this letter though*, James told himself, *that's proof isn't it?* As he walked back down the hallway and entered his room, he couldn't help but blame himself for the situation. It was his own fault the document was stolen, he shouldn't have left it out in such a bad hiding spot like that, he told himself...

For the remainder of that evening, James passed the time by reading all the notes he had printed off of Neil's computer. He still felt bitter and up-set, but the letter he had found from Manny Jones really did help bring on a much needed boost to his spirits. If only now he could find that document. Before too long, he looked over and noticed it had gotten dark outside. He really wished he could walk out to the living room and just demand Rex to give him back the document. *Yeah right James, I'm sure that'll work*....A few minutes later he was shocked to hear his step-mother coming through the front door. She was yelling and cussing and James knew another fight was about to break out. He locked his door and within moments the argument escalated to what sounded like violence. Things seemed worse than ever this time and he really wanted to escape to Neil's. The only thing still holding him there was the hope and idea that he could find the document again, and with it he could possibly save his father's life.

# Chapter Five
# The Other Side of Town…

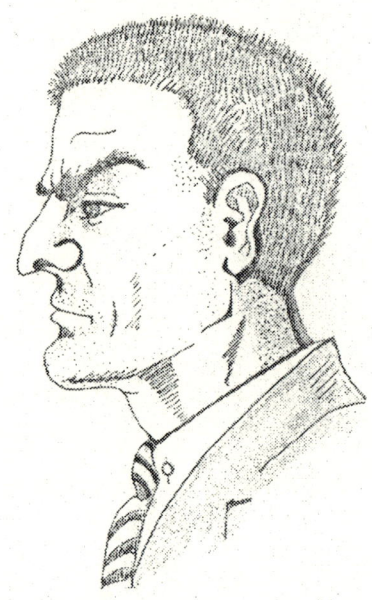

Around that same time on the other side of town in the back of a two story pawn shop, a group of four rough men were sitting around a green poker table playing cards. The room was all brick and filled with cigar smoke; electronic equipment was everywhere, along with glass cases full of jewelry and other high priced merchandise.

The men surrounding the table were drinking and smoking, as a large pile of money sat in the center and continued to grow. Bill Atwood, who was a thick, strong man with no hair and a big nose, was smoking a cigar and checking the recently dealt cards in his hand. He took a long puff of his illegal Cuban cigar and blew out a thick cloud of white smoke while the other men sat eyeing him closely.

"I'll raise," Bill said, with a dark voice, as he pushed more money into the pile.

"What are you doing Bill, trying to buy the pot again?" said an ugly, pale man sitting across from him.

Bill looked up and smiled; revealing dangerous eyes which were two different colors, one blue and one brown.

"Why don't you call me and find out, Scotty," Bill suggested, smashing his cigar out into a glass ashtray.

Scotty hesitated and then, with a shaky hand, pushed his money in.

The other two men quickly put down their cards and slowly pushed their chairs away from the table.

"What do you got, Billy?" Scotty mumbled, turning over his cards. The next second Bill exploded from the table and snatched up Scotty by both his arms. Bill then pummeled Scotty into the back wall and ripped open the inside pocket of his shirt, two hidden cards fell out as Scotty yelled and tried to fight back. His attempts were futile though as Bill had no problem restraining the frail man and as he did he slammed him into the wall several more times.

"You come to my place," Bill yelled, continuing the assault, "and try to cheat me, you ugly, slimy, little pig!" After the last blow was delivered Scotty's body went limp and he stopped struggling. Bill let go of him and the frail man crumbled to the ground, blood was leaking from his nose and his eyes were twitching.

"Get him outta here," Bill demanded, scoping up the money from the table and then walked over to a nearby sink. Bill's men picked up Scotty and heaved him outside in the alley behind the pawnshop.

"He was pulling those cards for the last few hands and you bozos didn't even see it. I waited for you two bums to pick up on it, but like always I have to do everything myself." Bill grabbed the phone with his scarred hands and punch in some numbers.

"It's me, listen I got the results on those pages you gave me, so bring the money and meet me at my shop," Bill grunted into the phone and then hung up. "You two go get that brief case from the safe and bring it up to my office, I'm expecting company."

The two men immediately did as they were told, walking over to a door and then down a set of stairs. Bill then strolled over to the front window and stared out with an amused look on his stern face. Making money had never been so easy.

A few minutes later and back on the other side of town, James heard the squealing of Rex's truck tires as he took off out of the driveway and down the road. James could hear his step-mother Debra in the kitchen crying. He soon heard the crying turn to sobbing, as the clanging of glass meant she was probably pouring another drink. James figured that they had just gotten into another argument, but this time Rex was the one who had left. He realized this was a rare opportunity to go out and talk with Debra alone. He thought maybe if he comforted her, she might let some information slip. It was a risky move, but he was getting desperate.

James opened the door to his bedroom, slowly peering out into the kitchen. He could only see part of the table, where Debra's hands held a bottle in one hand and a glass in the other. James stepped cautiously into the hallway and walked out to the table. His step-mother didn't even notice him standing there until he finally said her name.

"Debra?"

James' voice surprised her, she quickly looked up. "Oh, it's just you," she snapped, wiping her eyes clear. "What are you still doing up?"

"It's summer break remember, and it's only ten o'clock." James softly said, as his step-mother took another drink and pretended to look for a clock.

"Don't you have something you're supposed to be doing?" She snapped, her eyes showing no signs of sympathy or remorse. James shook his head and tried to be overly nice.

"Are you alright Deb?" James sincerely asked. "You know I think you'd feel better if we at least went up and seen my dad, don't you remember how happy we all use to be?" He pleaded, desperately trying to pull at her heart-strings. "And it's all just a matter of time before he gets better and—"

"Just leave me alone, and go to your room," she yelled as she jumped up knocked her glass off the table and rushed by James; leaving him standing there with his head down and broken glass at his feet. *What was I thinking, she's never going to change*, James thought, as he heard the door to her bedroom slam shut. Nothing was getting any better around there, if anything it was getting worse.

A few seconds later, as James turned around to walk back to his room, a ringing sound from somewhere in the kitchen went off. *Is that a cell phone?* James thought, as he looked down. He walked around the table and tried to locate the source of the noise. He moved a few things around as the phone rang yet again. He then looked down and there lying on the floor was a small black cell phone he had never seen before. He picked it up as it rang once more, he almost didn't answer it, but then as it rang for the fourth time he flipped it open. The voice on the other end was already speaking and sounded familiar and angry.

"What took you so long?" Rex barked. "Listen, I need you to go up to the attic and get that other briefcase, I forgot it."

James froze, *he must think I'm Debra*, he thought. James didn't say a word back, but instead just went, 'uh huh,' lightly into the phone.

"Are you listening to me?" Rex barked.

"Uh huh," James said a little louder this time.

"Alright, the case is in the floor safe, but don't let that punk know you're up there though. He's been snooping around again today I can tell. We can't risk letting him know anything, you got it?" Rex said.

James felt his heart jump after hearing these words. He didn't say anything back to Rex this time, due to the shock caused by what he had just heard. It was almost too much for his young mind to comprehend all at once. After a few seconds he heard Rex yelling about how much he hated cell phones, and James realized he must have thought the signal was cutting out and Debra couldn't hear him. He then heard Rex yell that if Debra could hear him he'd be back in an hour to pick up the briefcase and then he hung up.

James stayed rooted to the spot where he stood; the cell phone still up to his ear, and a look of complete shock on his face. He had just accidentally learned that something was hidden in the attic—*it's the document, it's got to be*, James thought. But he and Neil had checked up there… *But we never looked for a floor safe.* He now had some tough decisions to make; after all, this could be the answer he had been waiting for. So, should he take his chances and go up there now or wait? And if he was going to go investigate the attic now, how was he going to sneak up there without Debra seeing him? If in the last minute James felt he had just received a book-load of important information, then in the next two hours he would uncover an entire library's worth.

# Chapter Six
# A Deadly Deal

It was around eleven at night, and every light on the first floor of the pawn shop was shut off, the only sign of any life was coming from two large windows on the second floor; both of which were glowing brightly in the dark night. The street in front of the building was calm and vacant with lights reflecting off a few random puddles. Bill was sitting at his desk facing one of the large windows and looking down upon the street; like a ruthless king sitting atop his castle looking down on the village he ruled below.

Suddenly, headlights appeared down the street, Bill checked his watch and grinned. Within a few seconds, he saw a large truck pulling up out front. Rex parked and got out; he looked around cautiously and then hurried across the street with a thick envelope in his hand. A few moments later, Bill heard a knock on his back door downstairs. He yelled for his men to let the driver of the truck inside. Bill then slowly got up from his leather chair and walked over to the door at the top of the stairs. He opened the door just as Rex was getting ready to knock.

"Good timing," Rex nervously said, as he reached out and tried to shake Bill's hand, but instead of a handshake Bill gave him a cold stare. Bill then turned around and walked back across the large room. Rex followed and then sat down opposite of Bill in front of his huge, oak desk, which had the tinted windows behind it. Both men were larger than normal; in fact they might have even passed for brothers, Bill being the older and tougher of the two of course.

Bill finally proved he was human by pouring two glasses of whiskey and handing one to Rex.

"So," Rex said, after taking a gulp of the strong amber liquor, "Did you find the numbers?"

Bill didn't answer right away, instead he lit up a cigar and took a drag off of it.

"You know," Bill grumbled, "I don't usually do business with strangers."

Rex quickly sat up, "I thought Donnie told you about me?"

"He did. I just wanted to be perfectly clear that I'm doing this as a favor and not because I want to. That being the case I did find your numbers, they were microscopically encoded into several different pages of that document, but you've got a problem," Bill said his voice cold and sharp.

Rex looked concerned. "What kind of problem?"

"There's a page missing… You have an account number but only part of the pass code?"

"That worthless little punk," Rex said. "My girlfriend's step-kid had the document in his room, that's where I found it and I bet he's got the other page hidden somewhere else." Rex finished off his strong drink and looked furious.

"The account number is worthless without the pass-code," Bill explained, taking another puff off his cigar and leaning back in his chair. "Where did these pages come from anyway?"

Rex reached into his shirt pocket and took out a pack of cigarettes; he fumbled with his lighter for a second and dropped it. Before he could lean down to pick it up Bill had already flipped open his gold lighter and was holding out in front of Rex's face.

"Some guy got it at an auction or something, I don't know… So, if I get you that other page," Rex stammered, "will you finish the job for me?"

"Funny you should ask," Bill said, his eye's filled with revenge. "See, now that I know where the document came from I have a new condition."

"What, you want even more money now?"

"No, it's not only about the money anymore… Along with the cash I also want the document for myself. After of course I get you the pass code," Bill demanded.

Rex wiped sweat from his brow. "Let me get this straight, you want the money and the document? But how do I know you're not going to try and access the account on your own, I mean why else would you want the document?"

Bill grinned as he stood up and walked around the desk. "The past is never far from us, and it seems I've invested my time wisely in dealing with you, because now we both have something the other one desperately wants… That is how this business has survived for so long, compromises have to be made. And besides, I have my reasons for wanting the document, and those reasons are worth far more to me than money."

"Alright, well, since you want something else then I want something else too," Rex said with a villainous grin. Bill turned around and gestured for Rex to continue. "As you probably know the owner of this document also owns the account. The woman that is married to the owner of these items found out about this account a few months ago, and told me the only way we could collect the money from it is if he's dead…" Rex paused and took a drag off his cigarette. "So, since the tables have turned again I'd like you to take care of this little problem for me, and then you got yourself a deal."

Bill returned to his chair behind the desk and removed the case his men had brought up earlier. He sat it on the table and flipped the metal lid open. As he took out the document and looked up at Rex his blue and brown eyes flashed with the look of revenge again.

"It would be my pleasure to take care of this other problem," Bill said, as he handed the leather-bound document back to Rex.

"Are all these the account numbers?" Rex asked, as he looked at the long list of random numbers printed out on a paper inside the document.

"The account number and pass code are both fifty digits long," Bill said, leaning forward in his chair… "I wouldn't waste your time," he laughed, as Rex held the document up to the lamp and flipped through the pages, trying to see where the hidden number had come from. "There is only one instrument that can correctly extract the numbers from this document, and it's the same tool used to encode the numbers. Even with the strongest electron microscope you still couldn't see them."

"Then how do I know the numbers you gave me are real?" Rex said, as he flipped the document closed and put out his cigarette.

"You don't," Bill said, with a grin. "That's where trust comes into our little agreement. See, I have to trust you when you say you'll pay me the rest of my money tomorrow. And you have to trust that I have given you the correct numbers. Then, I trust you to give me the document and so on… It's a simple game really, with the only rule being that whoever breaks that trust first loses, and we both know what that means."

Rex felt his pistol still securely inside the waist of his pants; he nodded and slid a thick manila envelope full of money across the desk to Bill.

"That's the first half, I'll bring the rest tomorrow night…" Rex nervously said, as he stood up and looked around. "So, we have a deal then?"

"Let's hope so," Bill said, as he stood up and his two men from downstairs entered the room.

"Do you have any idea how long it might take to get rid of my problem in the hospital?" Rex quietly asked, as he leaned across the desk.

"I'll have my men take care of your little problem very soon; you just worry about getting me the other half of the money and that missing page." Bill nodded and then gestured for his men to escort Rex out.

A minute later Rex was back in his truck, he was covered in a nervous sweat and his heart was still pounding. There was a certain look in Bill's eyes that made people uncomfortable, the kind of look that you only acquire after you've hurt and terrorized many people. The only reason Rex hooked up with Bill was because he had run out of options and this was his last resort. It was well known that people who did business with Bill sometimes turned up missing, and it was these thoughts that plagued even Rex too.

"Get a grip, Rex," he told himself, as he drove in a hurry down towards the highway. "It's gonna be taken care of, and then you'll be rich again."

He drove with anger as he reached over and opened the glove box, taking out a bottle of vodka and his cell phone. While he was steering the huge truck on to the highway, he took a long drink out of the bottle and his eyes left the road for several seconds. The truck swerved suddenly as Rex jerked the wheel in order to avoid hitting an oncoming car in the left lane. He laughed again and then took another quick drink.

"I'm gonna get that little bastard," he grumbled as he threw the document inside the glove box and slammed it shut. A moment later a large green sign on the side of the highway read thirty miles to Brownwood, the town where James lived. Rex looked over at the sign and then pushed the gas petal down all the way, the truck backfired and then accelerated to seventy-five miles an hour. Suddenly, the cell phone in his pocket rang, he grabbed it and flipped it open.

"What?" he said, as he drove with one hand on the wheel now.

The voice on the other end seemed upset and worried.

"Hello, Rex can you hear me?"

"Yeah, what is it Debra? I'm on my way there right now!" he yelled.

"What? You're on your way here!" she exclaimed. "I thought you were going to drop that briefcase off?"

"I was remember, I told you I forgot it and to go up and grab it from the attic for me," he growled.

"You never told me that," she fired back.

"Forget it, I'll just take care of it when I get there!"

"Did you get the account numbers," she asked, her tone suddenly very persuasive.

"I got most of the numbers but you're not going to believe this, we're missing one of the pages so we don't have the full pass code. James must have hid a page somewhere else, so when I get there I'm going to rip him and that place apart until I find it."

"Don't worry I'm sure it's here somewhere," she said with an innocent tone.

Rex swerved again as he tried to take another drink out of his bottle, but instead spilled it on himself.

"It better be!" he roared, and then flipped the phone shut and threw it against the windshield. At the same time another green sign flew by the truck that read: You drink and drive, you lose.

Debra hung up the phone, and with a smirk on her face she opened her suitcase and quickly began packing. On the other end of the bed lay her purse, inside the black, leather bag was the missing page from the document; all folded up neatly and sealed inside a plastic baggie.

# Chapter Seven
# His Luckiest Night Yet

It had been over twenty minutes now since James had answered Debra's cell phone. During that time he had come up with a plan to find whatever it was in the attic that Rex had mistakenly told him about. It then took him another few minutes to convince himself to carrying out the plan; in the end it was his overwhelming desire to help his father that finally drove him to go through with it.

His first move was to stand outside the doorway to his step-mother's room, and listen to make sure she was either sleeping or at least staying put for a while. He listened and could hear her walking around. It sounded like she was pacing the floor or something. Then he heard the sound of metal hangers in the closet as they banged together. This sound was made several more times. He wondered what she was doing in there. *It doesn't matter just as long as it keeps her busy*, James thought.

After several more moments of eavesdropping, James decided the coast was clear, and quietly walked back down the hall, turned the corner, and went to the other end. He grabbed the string hanging down from the attic stairs and slowly pulled. The stairs creaked and popped as James unfolded the wooden contraption down to the floor. He looked back down towards his step-mothers' room and then up into the dark attic above.

"Well, here goes nothing," James said, once again feeling his nerves attack as he climbed to the top and flipped the lights on. He stood on the top step, looking around at all the cardboard boxes and pink insulation everywhere. He took the final step up and walked along the dirty, wooden floor, looking down as he went inspecting every inch for any signs of what Rex might have been talking about.

"Okay, floor safe, I need to find a floor safe," he whispered, as he took very small, quick steps back and forth scanning every area as he went. He noticed one particular board that was somewhat higher then the others, but after pulling on it several times he realized it wasn't coming up.

After several laps around, James decided to continue on his hands and knees, examining each board closely one by one now. The floor was littered with dust and James had to try hard to keep himself from sneezing several times, and even though it seemed quiet downstairs, he still paused every once and awhile to listen and make sure. The last thing he needed right now was to get caught searching for something he wasn't even supposed to know about.

James had ventured up to the attic with his father every year before for the past five years. He loved helping him get down the Christmas decorations and putting lights on the roof. As these memories surrounded him, he stopped searching for a moment and stared blankly at one of old boxes marked 'Christmas tree'. He was reminiscing the winter nights he and his father had worked together on making popcorn strings for the tree and roasting smores in the fireplace. James smiled as he remembered him and his father always having to untangle the giant ball of lights that seemed to keep getting bigger every year.

Sometime had passed now since James had climbed the crooked ladder up to the attic, but he was not sure how much. He looked around and for the first time realized exactly how large this room actually was, he worried he was beginning to run out of time. He shook his head in frustration as he stood up and walked back to the middle of the room.

"Where is it?" he quietly said to himself, standing and turning around in place with his arms up. He was just about to get down and check on Debra, to make sure she was still in her room, when suddenly he noticed a light at the other end of the hallway came on. James froze at the top of the stairs; he stood nervously and waited, listening to hear if anyone was coming. He then heard his step-mother's voice, it sounded like she was on the phone in her room. James listened closely, but could barely hear what she was saying. He kneeled down and stuck his head a little below the ceiling, which allowed him to clearly hear Debra as she told someone to hurry up and get there. James suddenly realized his plan was about to backfire, it wouldn't be long before Rex came home, and by the sounds of it he was already on his way. James' heart beat hard against the dusty floor as he laid and continued to listen to his step-mother. It sounded like she said something about the attic, and then something about Rex coming home early... *Wait a second*, James thought, *who is she talking to?*

Without any warning, Debra suddenly quit talking. He could tell by the sounds of things that he didn't have enough time to climb back down. So, instead he decided to pull up the stairs to the attic and hide somewhere. It took all his strength to begin lifting the wooden contraption, but after he got it going the springs kicked-in and all at once the stairs collapsed upwards in the ceiling; causing a somewhat loud bang, which James was sure his step-mother had to have heard.

"Oh, that's great James," he sarcastically said to himself, "now even the neighbors know where I am."

He scurried around for a few seconds looking for a good place to hide. After spotting one, behind a large cardboard box marked 'bedroom', he ran over and flipped the lights off. He then had to walk back to the spot in the dark, which wasn't easy considering it was in the far back corner where the roof sloped down low and nails stuck through. James moved methodically and was very careful as he made his way back to the hiding spot, only getting poked one time by a nail along the way. Behind the large box now, James crouched down in the dark and positioned himself out of sight; the spot was uncomfortable to say the least. He couldn't believe he had gotten himself into this situation, and apparently all for nothing.

With the lights off the attic was a very different place, almost scary. The wind outside howled against the roof, and James heard what he thought was a mouse running behind him. He stayed still though and waited, each minute felt more like an hour and after awhile he was beginning to think that no one was coming up there at all. *Maybe I overreacted,* he thought as he moved out from behind the box and stood up again. A moment later he heard voices downstairs and quickly crawled back behind the box. He stayed crouched down and listened closely. One of the voices was definitely his step-mother's, but the other he wasn't so sure about. He felt a rush of adrenaline as he heard the attic-stairs being pulled down from below. James held his breath as the stairs once again creaked and unfolded, he could barely contain his nervousness as he thought for sure he was going to get caught. After a few seconds the light in the attic was turned on, causing him to squint and look away for a couple seconds because of the sudden brightness.

"I know, that's why we have to hurry," his step-mother said in a panic-stricken tone, as she waited at the top of the stairs for whoever was behind her. James had gotten lucky he picked the spot he did because he had a small space in-between the wall and the box where he could look out, but no one could see in. He watched anxiously as Debra looked around and then walked to the opposite end of the attic.

"Come on, hurry it's over here," she said, as a thin, red-headed man James had never seen before entered the attic. James was completely at a loss for thoughts as he watched this strange man follow his step-mother to the opposite corner of the room. *What's she looking for*, he thought, when suddenly Debra and the strange man both went through some small door James never knew existed. *What's going on, where'd they go?* He stared intently through the crack, but was now only able to hear their faint voices. He couldn't make out what they were saying, but within thirty second they were back within view and now each carrying two, black briefcases.

"I thought you already had the document?" the red-headed man said, as he followed Debra to the stairs. James thought his ears were playing tricks on him; did he just hear the word document?

"Don't worry, I told you we have to take care of Rex first remember?" Debra soothingly replied, as she kissed the man. James looked away until he heard the sounds of them climbing back down the ladder. The wooden stairs then came flipping back up and smacked loudly into place again.

James couldn't believe what he had just witnessed; he knew Neil wasn't going to believe it either; and to tell the truth he wasn't even sure how he was going to explain any of it. The pile of unanswered questions seem to keep getting bigger by the minute, there was no way for him to predict what he was going to find out next. He only hoped that his step-mother and the stranger she was with, had just unknowingly left the document somewhere in that hidden room.

The question now though was: should he go over to the secret room right this instant and have a look inside, or stay hidden? It was once again another dilemma for James' young mind to ponder, as if he didn't already have enough.

"I bet that's where the floor-safe is," he told himself, as he waited behind the box in the dark again. He had no way of knowing when Rex was going to be home, and whom, if anyone was still in the house. *What would dad do right now*, he asked himself... *He'd go for it,* and just like that James got up and felt his way over to the other side of the attic.

Once there he began to search along the wall for an opening, and it didn't take him long before he noticed the faint outline of a small door. What made the job so easy was the fact that a light was coming from behind the door which in effect caused it's perimeter to glow like a thin, yellow line. Other than that the section of wall looked exactly like any other, with insulation and studs running every sixteen inches on center.

After James was sure he had both hands over the opening he pushed against it. The small camouflaged door slowly swung open and as it did the yellow light from inside cascaded out illuminating the dark attic. James looked around inside the secret room and was astounded at what he saw. The place was like a miniature museum, with antiques strewn about everywhere and paperwork all over the place. Most of the items were inside some sort of protective, clear boxes with labels attached to them. There was everything from jewelry, lamps, and paintings, to clothing, books and rugs—it was simply amazing.

As James walked further in and looked around, his mouth fell open and his imagination flourished with ideas. He went to take another step forward and when he did his foot kicked something from below. He looked down and noticed empty display cases all over the floor, their contents stolen out and most likely sold by Rex. As much as he wanted to be angry at that moment, his enchanted surroundings refused to let him be.

"Where did all of this come from?" He mumbled as his mind fired off all kinds of possible scenarios.

After the initial shock slowly wore off, he tore his attention downward to the floor again, searching for signs of this safe Rex had accidentally told him about. He walked behind an antique dresser and pulled over an old rug, but found nothing. Finally, as he kneeled down and looked behind a giant painting of a beach he saw it. The safe was nothing like what he had expected it to be. Instead, there was a metal handle and notched out grooves at both ends. He reached behind the painting and grabbed the handle. He pulled the lid off, set it to the side, and had a look in. Inside, he saw a metal-lined storage unit, but just as James had suspected it was empty.

"I think I know what was in here," James said, as he reached down in the safe and plucked out a crisp one hundred dollar bill that was stuck to one of its side. James figured the cash had apparently been left behind by Debra during her rush to flee. He hoped that the suitcases both Debra and the strange man had taken from the room contained only money; he prayed none of them had the document.

He replaced the safe's lid and stood up. Still hypnotized by the unusual collection surrounding him, James began examining a few of the items up close now. He came to a collection of old bank notes that read: United States Reserve Single Share, and wondered what the papers were. He checked the small white card attached to the outside of the glass case and found that it was a collection of deeds from an old railroad company of the eighteen hundreds. He read on and found out the collection was purchased on February 3rd, 1981 in Boston, Mass. Then, to his absolute amazement, he saw his father's name across from the line that read purchaser. Almost instantly it all became perfectly clear....*This was his father's collection, he was the one who went to all those auctions, he was Manny Jones friend, and he was the author of the introduction to Wipley's document.*

James had been on the right track all along. This was just the kind of break through in the research that he needed, and yet it all seemed so obvious now. He stood up and felt his enthusiasm shoot through the roof because of these new revelations. He still had no idea how any of it was connected, or why his father never told him about this before; but he did know, without any doubts now, that he was onto something very important, something that for some unknown reason was being kept secret and people desperately wanted.

James continued searching all over the mysterious room for any other clues that might help him figure things out, he had a feeling that whatever his stepmother had done tonight with that strange man was not what her and Rex had planned. James knew that things might escalate now to an even more dangerous level, and that meant he would have to escape to Neil's tonight with or without the document. Since they had already discussed this before he knew he would be welcomed, he just didn't think he would be forced to make the move so soon. After tonight though, it seemed as if things were going to be very different.

James didn't feel comfortable staying in the hidden room for very much longer. He knew it was only a matter of time before Rex would be home and he didn't want to be anywhere near the place when he found out what Debra had done. He was disappointed that he hadn't found the document still, but he was happy about all the new information he had uncovered, he knew it would help out somewhere along the way.

James carefully pulled the secret door closed behind him as he exited the room, and then he heard a loud noise downstairs. He stood perfectly still and listened… A few seconds later he heard it again. There was someone in the house, but whom? In the dark again, he carefully made his way back over to the stairs, out of nowhere a voice from below rang out like an alarm and hit James right in the heart.

"Yeah! I said I'll be right there, I need help finding this thing anyway," Rex boomed.

James instantly turned around and tried again to quietly rush back to his hiding spot behind the box. This time though he wasn't as careful and got poked twice by nails, as he tried hastily to feel around and position himself correctly again. His brown eyes peered nervously through the crack between the wall and the box, as he heard the stairs unfold and then saw the flash of bright light again as Rex flipped the switch. Rex didn't even look in James' direction as he marched directly over to the opposite corner where the small hidden door was. He shoved the door open with a powerful thrust and went in. Seconds later James heard him yelling and cussing as he undoubtedly discovered the safe to be empty. James then heard what he thought were the walls being punched and things being kicked. The next thing James knew Rex came ducking out of the small room with a look of pure rage on his face, his hands were bloody and he was continuing to yell and curse.

"I can't believe she did this," he yelled in-between cuss words, as he climbed back down the stairs. "I'm gonna find her and she's gonna pay I know that," he said, as he descended out of sight. The attic-stairs slammed back up in the ceiling so hard this time that the sound numbed James' ears. He was right again, it seemed that his step-mother had indeed double-crossed Rex for some reason, and by the look on Rex's face James couldn't help but feel somewhat relieved that he was up hidden away in the attic where Rex couldn't take things out on him. He didn't know exactly what was happening between Rex and Debra, but it seemed to involve this strange red-headed man, the document, and lots of money.

James went slowly back over and waited by the stairs again. While he did he thought about all the chances he had taken lately and how lucky he had gotten; it was almost as if someone was looking over him. It was a nice feeling, but it didn't last long, because like always James had another difficult decision to make right now—to either wait and play it safe in the attic, or go down and take his chances by trying to escape.

He waited for awhile until he couldn't hear any sound in the house at all. His heart pounded as he stood for the last few moments before he decided to take his chances and leave the attic. His plan was to grab a few things and then go directly over to Neil's; he couldn't wait to get out of this place once and for all. He knew that he'd be arriving without the document but he couldn't worry about that right now. As much as he wished he had found the mysterious pages again and would be able to show them to Pop and Neil, he knew they would still be happy to simply have him safe and there with them.

James took a deep breath and pushed down on the stairs. *Let him be gone, please.* It took only a second for the steps to unfold and come to rest on the carpet nine feet below. *So far so good*, James thought as he peered out of the attic and down into the hallway. The house sounded desolate, but James didn't want to take any chances, so he hurried and climbed down the ladder as quickly as possible. Once on the floor he carefully pushed the wooden stairs back up, holding the cord so they wouldn't slam this time. His heart was racing as he looked both ways down the hall and then moved carefully like a burglar towards his room. He was glad to see his bedroom door was left opened, and as soon as he rushed inside he turned and locked the door. He then went over and looked out the window and was deeply relieved to see that Rex's truck was gone.

"Thank God," he said, wondering how long he had until Rex would be back. With adrenaline pumping, he scurried around his room collecting clothes and stuffing them into a duffle-bag, he then ran back and checked out the window again. He almost felt paranoid and knew the sooner he got out of the house the better. Taking down a second bag from his closet James filled it with some of his father's belongings (hats, and some medals from when he was in the army, another watch, and a box of old pictures). He hoped that Neil would still be awake when he got there, and since there wasn't enough time to call he was just going to show up, he had no choice.

James strapped the two bags over his shoulders and then turned around and took one final look at his room. A place that for the past several months had kept him somewhat safe, but on the other hand had also begun to feel like a prison... With these mixed emotions behind him, he quietly and carefully made his way down the hall and to the front door. The image of his step-mother with that strange man flashed in his mind again. He had no idea who the man was or what Debra and he were doing together and this troubled him.

As James made his way out of the house and into the dark front yard, the feeling of freedom washed over him like a hot shower. It seemed as if this was the moment he had been waiting for, he was a prisoner in his own home no longer. As soon as this great sensation had filled him and suddenly it was gone; robbed away by the familiar and dreadful sounds of Rex's truck as it was coming towards the house. There was no way of mistaking it, he would be there any second and James had to hide. The roaring truck flew up just as James barely made it out of sight by diving behind the large row of bushes in the front yard. Rex came pulling into the driveway so fast that he actually hit the garage door and smashed it in. James' heart was racing hard as he pulled his bags through the bushes and watched Rex slowly backed up out of the garage, leaving the door mangled and the giant truck sideways in the driveway. James stayed kneeled down behind the tall bushes as he silently watched Rex talking on his cell phone in the truck. The window of the truck was rolled down slightly and James could hear him yelling.

"No, I don't know where she went but she's gone." Rex said, and then James saw him take a drink from a bottle. "No, I forgot to grab it!" he yelled. "But I'm willing to bet that she took that too... No, it doesn't matter, either way I've got the document and numbers right here, so if she wants to get in that account she'll need me," he announced as James inched closer with extreme curiosity.

"Alright Donnie. I'll be there," Rex said as he flipped his cigarette and jumped out of the truck. Rex was charging up to the front door when he suddenly stopped and looked over into the dark front yard. James held his breath and stayed perfectly still against the damp bushes. Like some killer in a horror movie Rex began walking towards the bushes. James could see the rage in his beady little eyes as he stalked the area. He was about half-way across the yard when his cell phone rang again.

"What?" he grunted into the phone. James didn't move a single muscle as he stared at Rex behind the bushes.

"No, I told you I need it tonight. What do you think this is a game?" Rex growled into the phone as he finally turned around, walked back over and went inside the house. James finally let out the deep breath he had been holding and slowly stood up. His relief was once again interrupted as he now watched lights inside the house begin turning on room by room. James didn't know for sure, but he figured Rex was probably looking for him. James looked back over at the truck as it sat idling roughly in the driveway. *The document's got to be in there*, he thought to himself as he remembered what Rex had said on the phone. He watched as the lights in the office came on. He could see Rex's shadow as he moved violently around in the room; James knew he didn't have much time. Even though every molecule of his body was against it, he knew he had to look in the truck one last time.

He sat his bags down and ran beside the bushes down to the driveway. He looked back over at the house in time to see the upstairs bedroom lights come on. He ran down the driveway and slowed to a walk beside the truck. Once at the driver side door he reached up, grabbed the handle and gave it a tug. The door opened slightly and at the same time the doom light switched on, illuminating the inside. After pulling himself up by the steering wheel and onto the seat he immediately began looking around. On the passenger side of the truck, there were two cases that looked like they were from the attic; each was empty, and neither had a label. James began tearing through papers and trash as he searched frantically for the document. *Come on, where is it?*

He was about ready to give up when he reached over and opened the glove box. There inside sat the leather-bound document, glowing like a work of art under the tiny glove box light. It was even more extraordinary than he had remembered it. The outside was now clean and almost looked polished, but there was no mistaking it.

James didn't hesitate for another second, he grabbed the document and then jumped down out of the truck; so much adrenaline was racing through his veins that he felt like he could fly. He ran along the back side of the bushes again to where he had left his bags. He couldn't believe his stroke of luck tonight, it was an amazing turn of events. He grabbed and shouldered his bags, then looked over through the bushes at his brightly lit house. The feeling was bittersweet; he finally had the document back, but he was leaving his home for God knows how long, maybe forever.

He turned and ran faster than ever before towards Neil's house. As he passed the corner of the street and cut through several yards he finally slowed to a brisk walk. With the duffle-bags digging into both his shoulders and the document held tightly in his hands he approached Neil's front porch with a smile. As the fear of being caught by Rex finally subsided, a strange feeling of freedom and the unknown seemed to consume him.

A moment later he was knocking on Neil's front door and trying to catch his breath. He looked back down the street at the side of his house one last time before Judy opened the door with a concerned smile and helped him in.

It had been the craziest day of James' life; his head and heart both felt exhausted with all the events that had taken place. James couldn't imagine what Rex was going to do once he realized that he and the document were gone. James didn't care though, he felt proud of himself tonight for many reasons. He had finally stood up and not allowed himself to pushed around anymore, he had outsmarted Rex and gotten the pages back, and he had taken control of his own life. Things he knew his father would also be proud of... But, if James had thought that today would bring an end to all his problems and discoveries, he was deeply mistaken. No, this was only the beginning of a long list of changes that were about to occur, changes and miracles.

After Judy got James something to drink she let Buddy inside to see him.
"He's been missing you all day," Judy said, as Buddy attacked James with licks and a wagging tail.
A few minutes later Neil came walking into the kitchen and saw James. "Hey, what's going on, are you alright?" he asked looking surprised and confused.
"Yeah, I'm fine, but you're not going to believe what I went through tonight," he said, and then held up the document in front of Neil.
"Is that, oh man you got it?" Neil stammered excitedly.
Judy soon said good night and told James to make himself at home. The boys immediately went back to Neil's room and began examining the document together. James went on telling Neil everything about his evening, as they continued marveling at the document with wide eyes. He couldn't remember the last time he had seen Neil so excited about anything. He kept repeating over and over again how real the pages looked, and how amazed Pop was going to be when he saw them.

An hour later, James was lying on an air mattress with Buddy beside Neil's bed. Even though they were both really tired, the discussion about the document and the events of that evening continued on for a while.
"What do you think was in the briefcases Debra and that guy took?" Neil asked, as he lay on his back and stared up at one of the pages inside the document.
"Money, I guess," James said. "At first I thought one of them had the document in it, but after hearing Rex in the driveway I knew that it had to be

in his truck… Can you believe that, we were right all along—it was in the truck's glove box?"

"What are you talking about we? It was all your idea from the start… Just like I've always told you, like it or not you're good at that detective stuff, just like your dad and grandpa."

"No I'm not. I seriously just got lucky that's all… Anybody could have done it," James modestly said.

"We have to make sure to tell Pop about all of this; I mean it's all he's been talking about for the past week. He keeps doing more and more research everyday, and he's always asking me if I've talked to you, and if you're still looking for the document. I can't wait to finally show him this thing so we can get down to work on it. You know this thing could be worth some serious dough."

James grinned, "You know I don't care about that."

"No, I know what you're hoping for. You really think this legend's true then don't you?" Neil asked, as he continued examining the pages.

"I believe there's a bunch of things out there that we don't know about. Good and bad," James explained.

"Well what do you think Rex and Debra wanted the pages for?"

"I don't know," James quickly said. "I told you she quit talking to me months ago. I just seen her up in the attic with that red-headed guy I've never seen before and that was it… Oh yeah, I almost forgot though—I did hear Rex say something about account numbers or something Debra needs him for. I'm not really sure what he meant, but I bet it has to have something to do with money, it always does."

Neil shook his head, "I'm just glad you're out of there man."

"Yeah, me too, now I just have to focus on helping my dad get better."

"Don't worry we will," Neil said, as he rolled over and handed the document to James who sat it on the desk above him.

"I still don't know what we're going to do?" James said, as he lay with his eyes closed and the reality of his situation setting in.

"What do you mean, you're gonna stay here with us and tomorrow me, you, and Pop are going to come up with a plan together. We're going to study that document and get to the bottom of all this," Neil said, as he yawned deeply. Within a few minutes both James and Neil were fast asleep. Neither one of them had any idea that just around the corner there waited a great adventure, one for the history books.

# Chapter Eight
# Research Is Power

The next morning came in a hurry since the boys had stayed up so late. It was almost nine o'clock and they were both still sound asleep as Pop came limping into the room, his wooden cane in one hand and a cup of coffee in the other.

"Come on boys, up and at 'em," he announced as Neil and James suddenly woke up, both looking startled.

Once Neil realized who it was he laid back down. "Oh, hey grandpa, we're getting up in just a minute," he mumbled.

"Good morning, Pop," James said, sitting up and rubbing his eyes.

"Hello James, sorry about waking you like this, its just Judy told me you had come over last night and I wanted to make sure you were okay—" Pop paused mid-sentence after spotting the document on Neil's desk. His eyes widened. "Is that what I think it is?" he asked, inching over closer to the leather-bound pages.

"Yeah, I found it last night completely by accident."

"There's no such thing as accidents," Pop automatically replied.

"What's that?" James said, looking confused.

"It wasn't an accident," Neil suddenly said, as he got up and went to his closet. "James is just a good detective that's all… See, I told you he'd be excited."

Pop nodded, his attention was completely consumed by the document.

"Go ahead," James said, as he noticed Pop's extreme curiosity. Pop leaned his cane against the desk and then carefully picked up the document. James thought he saw a look of shock come across his face; the same kind a child displays on Christmas morning. Pop flipped through the pages slowly and then stopped when he came to the older, handwritten section.

"This is marvelous, it's better than I could have ever imagined," Pop said, as his old dark eyes moved from top to bottom of each page, already studying it with respect.

"Pretty cool, huh?" Neil said, as they all three now stood around in a huddle and examined the pages together.

After several minutes of energetic discussion, Pop finally looked up from the document. "Oh, I almost forgot, Judy wanted me to bring you boys to the kitchen for breakfast before she leaves. She has to go to work soon, so we need to hurry. What do you say we eat then get to work on this thing right away?"

"Sounds good to me," James said with a grin. Waking up here was a pleasure compared to what he had been enduring at his house. James was more than grateful that Pop felt the same way he did about the document, he knew he couldn't wait to start researching it either and this made him feel hopeful again. The last two weeks were like an eternity, all he had done was worry about his father. It would be nice to finally start working on something productive for a change.

After quickly getting ready, James met Neil and Pop in the kitchen where Judy was standing at the stove cooking. She turned around and greeted the boys with a bright smile.

"Good morning boys," Judy said in a cheerful tone. "Did you sleep alright James, are you hungry?"

"Yeah starving," James said, as Judy brought over two plates to the table and filled them with eggs, some sausages and plenty of toast. She gave Pop a bowl of bran-flakes and a healthy shake, which he complained about for a while, but eventually ate and drank. Judy soon announced that she was off for work and would see everyone when she got home. James made sure to thank her several more times before she left.

While Neil finished his second helping of eggs and sausages, James told Pop all about what had happened at his house yesterday, and how he had found the secret room full of antiques. He also went over everything else that he had seen and heard in the attic, and how his step-mom had left with some stranger. Pop seemed to be just as confused by all of this as the boys were. He offered little advice on the matter and instead simply agreed with James that it had to be about money and that somehow the document played a key role, but he didn't know why.

After breakfast the three of them migrated to the study and immediately began research on the document. They started out by Pop reading over the old pages with a magnifying glass, while having the boys look up certain parts of what he had read on the computer. They also began searching for multiple books on the shelves Pop thought might help. He told the boys that he wanted to find out if there had ever been any documented reports of a man being lost at sea for five years and then returning.

"That kind of story would have to have been in a newspaper at some point," Pop announced, as they all went about the room working on their individual jobs.

Since they had found Wipley's disappearance documented in a book, it only made sense that they would be able to find his return too. But, this task proved to be very difficult since the town of South Grove Harbor didn't have a newspaper at that time, and Pop only had naval books from the thirties and the forties.

After almost two hours of reading articles in old newspapers and on the computer, they couldn't find any evidence to support the document's claim this time. Realizing they were spending too much time in one area, Pop moved on to locating all the islands in the Gulf of Mexico. He wanted to chart the directions and coordinates given in the document to see where they ended up on a map. Pop told James where to find the large rolled up map of the United States he had, and after retrieving it they spread the huge poster-sized map out on a large coffee table in the center of the room. Examining it closely, they discovered that there were islands of all shapes and sizes dotted around Florida and off the coast line in the Gulf. James read aloud the coordinates and directions from the document, as Pop and Neil made notations on the map. They soon found out that there were several small islands in the vicinity, but nothing in that exact spot. James didn't really expect to find anything on the map since it was plainly stated in the document to be an unknown island, but the information proved that at least the coordinates were charted correctly and in the area described.

The study session went on this way for another couple hours. Finally, Pop found some information about the disappearance of a man named Manny Jones from South Grove Harbor. James immediately rushed over and read what Pop had found.

"Look, it says here that he went out on a boating expedition and never returned… Just like Hunter Wipley, I can't believe it," James said, as he stared at the newspaper article on the computer screen. "It says that was ten years ago, that means the letter I found from him has to be even older than that."

"I don't get it," Neil said, as he looked up from the page.

"Neil, remember Manny Jones? He's the guy that vowed to solve the mystery—he's the one who wrote the letter to my dad," James explained, but Neil still looked puzzled. "You know the guy with the tattoo on the back of his hand."

"Oh okay, I get it, so that guy disappeared too?" Neil asked, as James nodded.

"Let me take a look at that letter again, James," Pop said.

James took the torn letter out from his wallet and handed it to Pop. They had looked it over several times already and it was easy to see that it didn't mention anything about the document whatsoever. All it basically said was that he hoped James' father, Joe, would come back down to Florida soon so they could do some fishing again.

"Do you ever remember your father going to Florida when you were little, James?" Pop asked, after reading the letter again.

"I'm not sure. I mean he was always traveling, so I guess it's possible he could have gone down there anytime."

"You see here in the document, it says that he and Manny had met when he was ten years old. That would make it nineteen-fifty-five."

"Okay, what's that mean?" James said not understanding what Pop was getting at.

"Well, if Wipley disappeared in forty-nine and was gone for five years then he would have been back in nineteen-fifty-four not fifty-five."

"Maybe my dad was mistaken about how old he was," James said.

"Yes, or maybe Manny was mistaken about the year Wipley disappeared." Pop explained, and James soon realized what he was implying.

"You think we're checking the wrong year don't you?" James quickly asked.

"There's only one way to find out," Pop said with a grin.

After making this adjustment they each began searching newspapers again, but this time from a year earlier and a year later than before. Like a puzzle piece that was missing there it was, a small article in the Florida Chronicle about a man by the name of Wipley who had been found in South Grove Harbor after being lost at sea. The year was nineteen fifty six, Pop was right, Manny had been off by a year and that meant Wipley had been gone for not five, but amazingly six years! The find proved further more the legitimacy of the document. There were still many unanswered questions, but James was beginning to see what Neil meant by Pop being a genius at this sort of research. He combed through pages of information as if they were sentences, he remembered dates and numbers like a computer, the man was wise beyond even his own years. As soon as James had finished reading the title of a particular column Pop was already on the next page of whatever he was reading, he was like a researching machine.

At around one that afternoon, they all took a break and moved into the kitchen for some lunch.

"I'm thinking about calling in a favor to get that document tested," Pop told the boys, as they all sat around the table eating peanut butter and jelly sandwiches.

"What will we do if it turns out the pages are real?" Neil asked, as he grabbed a handful of chips and put them into his sandwich.

"Well, James, what did you have in mind? It's your discovery?" Pop asked.

James thought for a few moments, he knew he had mentioned the idea of using the document as a guide to find the island and then seek out its healing water, but he was not sure how serious anyone took this idea.

"Um, well... I know it's a crazy idea and everything, but I'm still hoping that I might be able to go searching for this island. I don't know, maybe there really is something out there that could save my dad, but it's just no one knows about it." As soon as James finished he thought he had said too much. Pop and Neil both nodded slowly but the look on their faces seemed uncertain.

"I don't think it's crazy," Neil finally said, as he continued nodding. "Yeah, I think there are all sorts of things out there that people haven't discovered yet."

"I know that for a fact," Pop suddenly chimed in. "But James, I want you to understand that I've investigated hundreds of other claims that were never proven. In fact most of these legends are just that, there stories, something interesting to talk about."

James had a feeling he knew exactly what Pop was trying to get at. He knew he was getting his hopes up too high already, but he had to follow his gut-feeling on this.

"I know I shouldn't believe in a story like this, I just, I guess I just want to know there's a place out there like this. A place that can help save my father, a place where miracles are real."

"I know, and believe me I do too. Look at me, I'm sixty-nine years old, grey headed, and I walk with a cane—how do you think this story sounds to me?" Both Neil and James looked at Pop's cane. "Exactly, and I know your father's in bad condition, and I don't agree with a lot of things that happen in this world. Bad things shouldn't happen to good people. I believe we're all too young to be in the condition we're in and I'd give just about anything to find a cure for all these problems. But like I said before, we'll go as far as we can to figure out if there is an unknown answer like this out there, and if indeed there is one I promise you we will find it." Pop looked directly at James, smiled and nodded. "But you have to promise me that if we learn the document is in anyway untrue, we will all put our hopes back into the medical field for an answer."

James nodded his head in agreement; he knew Pop was already helping prepare him for what would most likely happen. Somewhere in the back of James' mind though he had a voice telling him that the legend was real, but on the other hand he figured it was just false hope and probably a matter of time before they proved the document to be fiction. Either way, he still thought it best to enjoy the hope while it lasted.

Later that afternoon as more facts began to pile up, James noticed Pop was becoming more and more convinced that the document was real; so convinced in fact, that he even decided to make that call to have the document tested. Since he had retired from the CIA Pop still knew certain people that had access to equipment and restricted information that the average person could only dream about or see in the movies. One of those people was a young woman by the name of Cori Nichols. She was a thirty-two year old natural beauty who had graduated from Oxford with a PHD in forensic science. She had joined the CIA as a scientist and worked with Pop for over five years, during which time she had become one of Pop's favorite protégés. Not only was she smarter than most of the men in her department, Pop said, she was also friendlier. Her expertise was used by the CIA in many ways, but mainly to prove currency to be real and to find and track down counterfeiters. Pop was hoping that she might be able to run some standard tests on the document, tests that would further prove its worth. This was all news to James, but apparently there were in fact several procedures that could be done to prove if a document was authentic or not.

After Pop dialed the number, James listened closely to the conversation he was having. It had taken several minutes of security clearance before he was even able to speak with Miss Nichols at work. James was still telling himself not to let his expectations grow too high. He was thinking about what Neil had told him the night before, about how Pop had become a bit of a myth hunter after he retired. Neil said Pop was always looking for the next so-called miracle. Still, James felt that all this excitement was a perfect distraction from his utterly nonexistent and dangerous home life; and anyway what would be better right now than a miracle?

After Pop hung up the phone he looked over at the boys and smiled.

"It's all worked out, she agreed to test the document for fingerprints and carbon-dating tomorrow, but if anyone finds out what we're doing they'll probably send me to the loony bin and tell you boys that I was crazy for helping you. We need to keep all of this a secret okay... In fact we'll need to wait until Judy goes to work tomorrow before we can even begin to get ready."

"Get ready for what?" Neil asked, as he brought over another book for Pop.

"We're going to the take the document to Miss Nichols in Atlanta tomorrow. Just think if she can tell us the age of these older pages then we'll be even closer to the truth. Not to mention all the other things she can find out... Did you know we can actually pinpoint the time and place where a certain ink or paper was manufactured? If it matches closely with the dates and place given in the document it would certainly satisfy my doubts in the authenticity of these pages?"

Both James and Neil looked at each other in amazement; their imaginations took over as they discussed the possibilities of what might come from proving this document to be true. James spoke of nothing else but saving his father, while Neil said that they were all going to be famous. Seeing the boys so excited only fueled Pop's motivation to prove the document's worth. He still made it perfectly clear that this was only a research project and that they wouldn't go chasing rainbows until they knew for sure the document was what it claimed to be.

That night after Neil's father, Tim, arrived home, they all sat down for dinner and it was agreed that James would be staying there indefinitely or at least until his father recovered. The Kelly's had of course known about James' situation for awhile and were more than happy to help him out of it.

Dinner ended sooner then expected when Neil's father realized what time it was and had to leave for his plane to New York. He gave the boys both a pat on the back and kissed Judy goodbye, he then instructed his father, Pop, to take his medicine and do his exercises.

"We don't need you falling again, Dad" Tim said. "Now, I should be back by the beginning of the week, so I'll see you then," he said and then disappeared out the door.

That night the boys and Pop took a break from the document; instead of searching through books they watched a movie and ate popcorn in the living room. The movie was titled: The Lost Fountain of Youth. Pop had Judy drive to two different movie stores just to find it. James and Neil would have normally not wanted to watch an old, black and white movie, but once Pop told them that it was about the fountain of youth, they begged Judy to rent it for them.

The next morning Pop once again woke both the boys, who had both fallen asleep on the living room floor. Judy had already left for work and Pop told the boys she would be back at around three that afternoon so they needed to hurry and leave soon.

"That should give us just enough time to meet with Miss Nichols and get back before Judy gets home," Pop explained. "I've got my car in the garage, but we're going to have to stop and fill up the tank because we have about a hundred miles ahead of us… I figure we should make it there and back by two if I speed a little."

After getting ready, James and Neil grabbed a bag of chips and several cans of soda for the road, around that time James noticed Neil looked uncharacteristically nervous.

"What's wrong with you?" James asked, as he put the document inside a thick briefcase Pop had given him.

"Oh nothing," Neil said, watching Pop drink coffee out on the porch.

"What is it, come on I can tell something's wrong."

"Well, you see," Neil said, looking around, "Pop hasn't exactly driven in awhile."

"What do mean awhile?" James asked, looking out the front window at Pop.

"Um, I don't know, I think it's been about two years or so. My parents said he's kind of a hazard behind the wheel now," Neil slowly said.

The boys both looked at each other and then back at Pop as he came limping through the front door whistling with a cup of coffee in one hand and his cane in the other. "You boys about ready then?" he asked.

"Yeah, how about you James?" Neil asked in an unsure tone.

"Yep, let's go," James said, having complete confidence in Pop's abilities.

After the boys helped Pop into the driver's seat, Neil got up front and James rode in back. The dark blue Cadillac still looked brand new, and after Pop slowly backed the large four-door car out of the garage he aimed it towards the road and took off. *I can't believe we're going to get the document tested*, James thought. *If this thing turns out to be real I wonder what we're really going to do next.*

They stopped a few miles down the road and had the gas tank filled, James chuckled as he saw that Neil still had his fingers crossed. After another few miles they finally made their way over to the highway and headed south. Pop made a few unpredictable lane changes at first, almost running a small hybrid car off the road, but then after that he seemed to get back into the old routine and drove fairly well. After about an hour and a half ride, Neil took out a large road map and tried figuring out exactly how far away they were from the exit.

"The map's up side down Neil," James said from the back seat.

"Oh yeah," Neil said, turning the map around.

"The street's called Easton Avenue," Pop kept repeating as Neil and James scanned over the map.

"Look at that, it says legend," Neil announced, pointing to the box at the bottom of the map and trying to make the sound of scary music.

James shook his head at Neil. "There's Easton Avenue right there."

"So, that means we're about ten miles away," Neil said, using his fingers to measure out the distance. James nodded and adjusted the baseball cap he was wearing that his father had bought for him last year.

## HEALING WATER

"We're meeting Miss Nichols at her house which is down the street from the lab," Pop said, and then handed James a piece of paper with directions and the address on it.

At around eleven o'clock the dark blue Cadillac was less then a mile from Miss Nichol's residence. As they drove through the streets of Atlanta, Pop pointed out different landmarks for the boys to look at. They saw office buildings of all sizes, along with apartments, condos, and small houses. The city was booming with people and traffic, and James and Neil couldn't quit calling each others attention over to different things on each side of the road.

"You boys don't get out of town much do you?" Pop joked, as he made the final turn and entered the condo's parking lot where Miss Nichols lived. James and Neil helped Pop out of the car and then gave him his cane. They all walked inside the condo building and began looking for the correct door.

"Look for the letter C," Pop said, as the boys walked from door to door searching. The building was large and had many floors, there were two elevators at the back of the lobby, but Pop insisted that she lived on the first floor.

"You're right, I found it," Neil called out, pointing to the last door on the right side of the wide hallway.

"All right," Pop said, "now you guys be on your best behavior, this young lady is doing us a big favor here." The boys nodded as Pop rang the doorbell. Within a few moments a stunning woman with curly auburn colored hair was standing in front of them hugging Pop and gesturing for them to come in.

"Hello Mr. Kelly, how have you been? I haven't seen you in forever, please come in sit down," Miss Nichols said, all the while being stared at by both the boys.

"Getting older but doing pretty good, how about you, you haven't changed one bit have you?" Pop said with a smile, as he sat down at the small kitchen table. The boys also both sat down at the table, as James put the briefcase on the floor beside the chair and looked around. The place was small but very clean. It smelled like fresh flowers and as James turned his attention back to Miss Nichols he realized he would have never guessed her to be a scientist. *More like a model or actress*, he thought. Her eyes were very blue and almost seemed to glow, her skin was light and reminded James of porcelain. He had been staring at her for so long that when Pop introduced him he didn't hear anything and simply sat there.

"James," Neil said, nudging his chair. "Pop's introducing you."

James quickly came to, "Oh, hi," he said, smiling, "I'm James Greene."

"Hello James," she said with a smile as they shook hands.

Pop wasted no time getting down to business, he explained what he wanted the document tested for, but not why. Miss Nichols didn't ask many questions as she wrote down the short list that included the age and source of the paper and ink, along with a fingerprint dusting of a few random pages. Pop knew she only needed a few pages to actually run the tests, he told the boys that whatever was on one page was probably on all the rest. He had James give Miss Nichols two pages from the older document, which she took and sealed in a plastic container.

"It'll take at least twenty-four hours before I get the results back," Miss Nichols explained, as she went and got drinks for everyone.

"What time is it?" Pop asked, as James checked his father's old watch.

"It's eleven-thirty," James replied. A minute later Miss Nichols emerged carrying four cups of tea that smelled like the fresh flowers James had noticed earlier.

"So, let's see," she said after looking at the two old pages James had handed her, "why is it you want these pages tested anyway?"

Pop grinned for a second, "The boys and I are working on a small project."

"Are you going to tell me which myth you're trying to prove this time?" Miss Nichols asked with a smirk.

Pop laughed, "You'll probably be able to figure that out from the pages we gave you to test… They were found by James here in his father's office, they look authentic to me but you're the expert, that's why we came to you."

"You do remember that everything you have me test usually turns out to ruin your projects right?" Miss Nichols said.

"Yes, but I've got a strange feeling about this one," Pop said, as James and Neil nodded seriously in agreement.

The statement Miss Nichols had jokingly said worried James. *What if these tests prove the document to be a fake? A document someone made to look old and fool people. No way*, James thought, *they have to be real, even my dad thinks they are.*

Over the next hour they continued to visit with Miss Nichols and talked about all the different myths and adventures Pop had investigated. James was amazed at how much he had actually done and all the places he had gone. He had no idea that Pop had become senior intelligence officer for the 'X' section of the CIA. James didn't exactly know what that meant but he figured he had a good idea.

It was sometime after twelve when Pop announced they had to be getting back.

He gave Miss Nichols a hug and thanked her again for her help. She then smiled at James as he also told her goodbye, James couldn't resist smiling back. Neil quickly finished off his last cookie he was eating and then with crumbs falling off his party shirt he shook Miss Nichols hand and said goodbye.

During the walk back to the car, James imagined himself being old enough to date Miss Nichols, she was a stunning woman and smart too. He then thought about the fact that she was going to be the same woman that would either tell them the pages were real and keep his hopes of saving his dad alive, or would prove that they were fake and crush those same hopes.

During the drive back, Pop drove almost flawlessly and stayed in the fast lane for most of the time. Neil complained about being hungry, and James studied the document in the back seat. They arrived home an hour before Judy, and while Pop and James tried to park the Cadillac in the exact same spot, Neil got out and ran inside the house. After finally parking the car, James helped Pop back to his study and then found Neil in the kitchen on the phone.

"Thanks for helping Pop in," Neil said, after hanging the phone up. "I just ordered us a large cheese pizza it's on its way."

James shook his head, "We were wondering why you took off like that," he said sitting down on the barstool beside Neil. "Hey, what'd you think about Miss Nichols?"

Neil grinned, "I don't know, she seemed nice I guess, I just didn't think that Pop worked with people so young. I mean I always imagined him in some big office with a bunch of old guys who had beards and smoked pipes just like him."

James nodded, "Yeah, I admit she's not what I expected either."

"Wait a second, you like her don't you?" Neil said, as he pointed at James and laughed.

"What, no, I just meant she seems smart that's all," he quickly explained as Neil gave him a playful shove.

"Yeah, whatever man, I saw the way you were staring at her, let me guess you were just admiring the size of her brains," Neil joked, opening a bag of chips.

"All right whatever, but seriously, what do think she's gonna find out about the document?" James said, trying to change the subject.

Neil threw a handful of chips in his mouth, "I don't know," he mumbled, "but if Pop trusts her she's gotta be good."

James hadn't thought about it that way but Neil was right—this would be the deciding factor there was no doubt about it. Over the next five minutes James and Neil sat and talked about what Pop would have in store for them if the document was real.

"I'm telling you James, he will seriously take us to search for that island, I'm not kidding. He's done this kind of research for like thirty years, why wouldn't he want to do it now?"

"Because," James said, "he's older now and I just don't think he'd be up for some kind of wild adventure out on the ocean at his age. You see the way he depends on that cane."

"Boys, come here," Pop called from the study. James and Neil both hurried to the room and over to the desk where Pop was sitting.

"Look at this," he said, as he showed them a documentary he had found online about a group of researchers who searched Egypt for some fountain that locals claimed healed the sick. They all sat around the computer screen and watched as the video played. It was filmed with handheld cameras and had the look of a home movie. It showed two older American researchers named John Surface and Todd Moore, traveling through the desert in search of some small village known as Yolo. They rode in all-terrain jeeps and had two local guides directing them. They ended up in some small village with all stone huts and found a very old chief they said could lead them to this special water. Just as the old chief was walking with them through the village and down into a small valley, the door bell rang. Neil quickly jumped up, "Pizza guy's here, pause it will you Pop?"

Pop stopped the video and turned to James, "he never misses a meal does he?" he joked.

"No he doesn't..." James laughed.

Suddenly they heard Neil yelling something from the front porch. The tone of his voice sounded very serious and almost scared.

"What's he yelling about?" Pop asked.

"He's yelling come here," James answered, as he jumped up and ran towards the front door. As he approached the door he looked through the side window and saw Neil and the delivery kid standing and looking over at something in horror. He dashed out onto the porch and looked over. In a flash of orange flames, he saw it. At first, his brain couldn't comprehend what he was looking at, but after a few seconds he realized what it was, his house.

"It's your house James!" Neil yelled, looking over and suddenly noticing James. "What should we do?" he exclaimed, as James stared down the street and watched the fire engulf the second floor. "What do we do?" Neil repeated.

"Uh, I think you should probably call the fire department," the young delivery driver said, as he stood holding the pizza.

James stood in a silent daze as Neil rushed by him and ran to get the phone, by the time he found it and ran back, dialing numbers along the way, he stopped; the sounds of sirens told him that the fire department had already been called. The look on James' face displayed his feelings perfectly, his mouth was gaped slightly and his eyes were fixed to the horrible scene... Somewhere behind him the delivery guy was asking to be paid, but James barely heard him. His mind had slipped off into some kind of rare trance, he couldn't speak, he only stared as the blaze roared on out of control. There were now multiple fire trucks and ambulances in front of his house; James looked all around in the street, searching for any signs of his step-mother or Rex. He could see that their vehicles were not in the driveway and even though he was worried that he might be seen, James couldn't help but walk out to the sidewalk and get a closer look. The sirens from the truck blared loudly as Neil followed right behind him, he then grabbed James by the arm when he tried to continue towards his burning house.

"What are you doing?" Neil asked, as James struggled for a moment and then gave up, realizing there was nothing he could do.

"It's all burning," he mumbled in disbelief, still watching as several firefighters doused the flames with water.

"What's happened?" Pop shouted from the porch, standing with his cane and trying to see what was going on.

"James' house is on fire," Neil yelled, as he attempted to walk James back to the porch.

"Do you see anybody James, what happened?" Pop asked.

"No, I don't, I don't know," James softly said, never taking his eyes off the inferno.

Two hours eventually went by before the firemen finally managed to completely stamp out all the flames. It was obvious to everyone that James' home was completely destroyed; besides the back wall the only thing left recognizable was the front porch. James, Neil, Pop, and Judy stood in silence on the front lawn as light clouds of smoke continued to rise from the wet black pile of wood that used to be his home. Small groups of firemen were still left working in the street, winding up water hoses and putting equipment back on their truck.

"I'm so sorry James, is there anything I can do?" Judy asked, putting her arm around James and hugging him.

"No, I'll be fine, thanks," James struggled to say, thinking how lucky he was to have Neil and his family's support.

The rest of that evening James spent talking with Pop in the study. Pop offered his wisdom and tried hard to help James cope with his latest, most traumatic experience.

"You know I had a feeling my luck would eventually run out again, I knew it was only a matter of time before something bad happened... It's just, my dad loved that house so much, we moved in there when I was little, and he told me that if something ever happened to him I would always have it," James said with his head down.

At that same moment Neil came walking into the study, wearing a red robe and slippers. He didn't interrupt James and Pop, but instead sat down quietly across from them and began setting up the chess board on Pop's game table.

"I was thinking," Pop said, as James looked up, "how would you feel about going to visit your father tomorrow in the hospital?"

James sat back and ran his fingers through his thick dark hair pondering the question. "I don't know, I mean yeah, of course I want to, it's just I haven't seen him in months and he's in a coma now? I don't know how I'm gonna react to seeing him like that," James confessed.

"People in a coma just look like they're sleeping, don't they Pop?" Neil said.

"Yes, I guess that would be one way of describing it," Pop admitted. "But still even though it is peaceful the more important thing to remember is that people in a coma rarely feel any pain. I remember when my father Ronald became sick, I took comfort in knowing that they were able to keep him comfortable, he didn't feel any pain or have to suffer like so many other people do. You have to always remember to look at the positive side of everything boys; it'll make a huge difference in your life." Pop reached out for his cane and James helped him up.

"It's getting late and I need to be going to bed… James, you think about it and let me know if you want to go tomorrow. I'll wake you boys up in the morning, so don't stay up too late now, you hear?"

After Pop went off to bed, Neil and James played a few games of chess. James won the first game in under ten minutes, the second game turned out to be a draw, and the third one was won by James in only eight moves.

"Are you sure you've never played chess before?" Neil asked, as they put away the chess pieces and then headed off to bed.

"No, I've seriously never played before… It's just beginner's luck anyway, it'll go away soon like it always does."

"What's that supposed to mean?" Neil asked, as he climbed into his bed and James lay down with Buddy on the air mattress.

"It means I'm cursed with bad luck, I mean look at what's been happening to me lately. My dad's sick, our house burnt down, what else could go wrong?"

"You're not cursed, you've just been dealt a couple bad hands lately that's all…"

James stayed quiet as he stared up at the ceiling deep in thought.

"Look," Neil finally said, "we know Rex did it. Pop said he's going to call the police tomorrow and report him. He'll be put away for this, and then you won't have to worry about him anymore. I know that doesn't bring your house back, but still."

"No, you're right," James slowly sighed. "I guess I'm just getting stressed out about all this, it's starting to get to me, that's all."

"Well, why don't we go see your dad tomorrow? I know it's not cool he's sick, but at least you can still see him again… I seriously think it might help," Neil said.

James pulled Buddy closer and yawned. "You're probably right, I'll let Pop know in the morning."

# Chapter Nine
# The Graveyard Shift

While James and Neil slept soundly that night, James' step-mother, Debra, sat waiting for someone in a small diner on the outskirts of town. The diner was nearly empty at this time of night; the only people left there was a waitress and two old truck drivers who were getting ready to leave. A bright red neon sign flashed the phrase, 'open-24 hours' in the front window, and was the only clue from the highway that indicated the place's existence. In the booth next to Debra was the same strange red-headed man James had seen in the attic.

Debra and the man each had empty mugs of what used to be coffee in front of them; they spoke quietly as they stared outside, both showing signs of nervousness.

"Would you like a refill?" the waitress sighed halfheartedly.

"No, we're fine," Debra quickly snapped, as she eyed an approaching vehicle with intense curiosity.

The dark sedan's lights flashed in the window and then disappeared as the car parked out of sight, a minute later a large burly man appeared at the door; the same dangerous man that Rex had met with a few nights earlier. As he entered the diner, Debra noticed the dark suit he wore looked as if it contained enough fabric for at least two men. His walk was powerful and as he sat down the booth's wooden frame creaked under his enormous weight. The waitress seemed nervous as she approached and took his order. He demanded coffee, and then with precision directed his cold stare across the booth; revealing those same strange blue and brown eyes.

"Where is Rex?" Bill grumbled, clasping his hands tightly on the table, "he owes me money we had a deal."

Debra smiled sardonically, "I don't know where he is, but I do know that he doesn't have your money," she said with a roguish grin.

Bill's expression became angrier. "Then why did you call me here?" he demanded.

"I have a business proposal for you," she said quietly. "I want you to finish the job that Rex hired you to do."

"I don't do business with strangers, it has a tendency to get messy too often," he growled. "Take today for example, I had to burn down a perfectly good home, I'm glad to see you weren't in it," Bill said as he turned his attention towards the man beside Debra.

Just then the waitress approached carrying Bill's coffee, she carefully set the mug down and backed away quickly, as if she were feeding a wild animal. Bill picked up the mug with his huge scarred hand, took a drink and then returned it to the table, "And who might you be, you look familiar?"

The red-headed man looked over at Debra, but didn't answer.

"He's a friend of mine, don't worry he's harmless," Debra quickly said.

"A friend, well it seems like you got a lot of friends don't you?"

"I have a lot of enemies too," Debra said, as she flashed her cunning green eyes at Bill and smiled. "Why don't you go wait in the car honey," she said to the strange man, who immediately got up and walked out of the diner as commanded.

"A woman who calls the shots, I like that," Bill said, as he smoothed down his thick dark mustache with his thumb.

"I'll tell you what I'd like, and that's for you to finish the job." Debra said again.

Bill sipped his cup of coffee, "I told you sweetheart, I don't work with strangers."

"I thought you might say that," Debra said, taking out a piece of paper from her bag and sliding it to Bill's side of the table. "Now we're not strangers anymore," she said, "And, I'll also pay you to have Rex found and dealt with, which I assume you were already going to do anyway."

Bill eyed the paper casually; it had copies of Debra's driver's license, social security card, and passport on it.

"And, so you know they're real," she said, flipping open her bag and pulling out all the originals.

Bill seemed slightly amused by this act, but barely compared the items. He knew that anyone dumb enough to try and con him would be hunted down and made to pay in one way or another. Still, he always liked to avoid those hassles whenever possible, and the idea of being paid to enforce his rules was tempting.

"Well, you have really thought this through haven't you, I like that… But I have a feeling this isn't all you had in mind is it?" Bill asked.

Debra pulled out a shiny computer disk and handed it to Bill.

"This should explain everything," she said, "it will only play once though, so pay attention, but don't worry I kept it short and sweet."

Bill hesitated taking the disk. "How'd you know I'd agree to do this?"

Ignoring Bill's question Debra went on. "Here's the first half of the payment, I'm sure you'll find it to be more than your usual," she handed Bill a large envelope. "And as soon as the jobs are done you will get the second half delivered to you."

Bill took the money and looked mildly impressed, "I assume your husband is still in the same hospital?"

"Yes, he is, so, we have a deal then?" she asked with a mischievous smile.

"Almost, but first I seem to recall getting account numbers off some document for Rex. The funny thing is that there was a page missing, one that had a pass code on it."

"What are you trying to say?" Debra asked.

"I want that document," Bill demanded, "And I want half of whatever you're getting from that account."

"That's fine, but I don't have the document. Why do you think I came to you," Debra asked.

"So, where is it then?"

"The last message I got from Rex said that he was going to hunt me and my husband's son down, because he knew I took the money and James took the document... So, I would guess that somehow my step-son, James, has it, the problem is I have no idea where he is right now."

"Okay, so, let me get this straight, I get rid of your husband in the hospital, I get rid of Rex and I have to hunt down some kid for the document... This seems like an awful lot of trouble, I don't really know if it's worth it."

"Well believe me, it'll be well worth it because once my husband's gone and I have the account number and pass code we'll both be splitting ten million dollars, and you can have that little document too... Now, how's that sound?" Debra asked.

The waitress once again approached the table, after setting the check down she quickly collected the three mugs and was gone.

"I'll tell you like I told Rex, this verbal contract is not easily broken, if it is the price doubles, no exceptions. And if you and your new boyfriend out there decide to take off and fly to Spain or something I will find you, I always do," Bill said, picking up the disk, paper, and money.

"I don't think this should take very long, but finding that kid might not be so easy?" Bill said, sliding out of the booth.

"He couldn't have gone far, he's only fifteen years old... And you'll know exactly what he looks like after you visit his father," Debra said. "Don't worry it's all on the disk I gave you."

Bill grunted a laugh and then leaned over to Debra's side of the booth. "When you're powerful you never have to worry. And don't you worry, I'll be in touch, so remember what I said," Bill reminded her and then walked away.

# Chapter Ten
# Security

The arrival of morning the next day was accompanied by the sound of thunder. The sky was swirling with an army of light and dark clouds of various sizes. The sun's rays tried hard to cut through the dullness, but failed miserably. The result was a dark grey day that seemed as if it might last forever. Pop was sitting in the living room watching the morning news report about the upcoming storm as Judy came rushing through.

"Oh, I'm going to be late for work if I don't get going now," she said, searching the closet and pulling out an umbrella. "Pop, will you and the boys be all right fixing your own breakfast today?" She asked fumbling with her car keys.

"We'll be fine, you just be careful driving in this mess. They say it's supposed to storm like this all day."

"Don't worry I will, now if you guys need anything, anything at all don't hesitate to call me, you know where the number is, right?"

"Will you stop already, we'll be fine." Pop said looking somewhat irritated as he scratched his white beard after Judy kissed him on the cheek.

"Good bye, love you," she said, walking out the door and into the garage.

Around that same time James rolled over too far and hit his knee on the wooden leg of Neil's bed, the sudden pain caused him to wake. He rubbed his knee and then his eyes as he heard the first loud crack of thunder. He looked over out the window and watched as blankets of rain began to fall. A few minutes later, he was in the kitchen pouring a glass of milk, and then giving Buddy some more dog food. In the next room over, James noticed that the television was on so he wandered in and found Pop still sitting there in the recliner watching the news. Pop looked over and grinned at the sleepy-looking James; his dark hair was standing up in back, he had a milk mustache, and the pajamas of Neil's he was wearing were entirely too big on him.

"Good morning there James, did the storm wake you?" Pop asked.

"Kind of, why is it a bad one?" James asked, wiping the milk from his face and looking over at the weather station, which was showing a radar picture of the state with different shades of red moving over most of it.

"It's just another thunderstorm," Pop said, "nothing serious."

James sat down in the chair next to Pop and took another drink of milk. "Hey Pop, I was thinking, if it's still okay I'd like to take you up on that offer to go see my dad today," James gradually smiled.

"Of course it's okay, we'll get ready and go there this morning. You know I really think this'll be good for you," Pop said, adjusting his glasses. "Have you ever heard the phrase—there's nothing to fear, but fear itself?"

"Didn't Theodore Roosevelt say that?" James asked.

Pop nodded. "That's right, and it's the kind of advice you should live by."

Neil woke up a half hour later after Pop began cooking bacon and set off the smoke alarm. The only way James managed to stop the annoying beeping was to stand on a stool and remove the batteries from the device. To everyone's surprise though, breakfast turned out to be really good, and as the three of them sat in the study and ate the omelets, Pop looked up directions to the hospital and James wrote them down. He was completely surprised to find out that this new hospital was actually only about an hour away, and not the three or four as he had previously thought. Of course his step-mother, Debra, was the one who originally told him this and used it as one of her many excuses not to take James to visit his father. Naturally, James was angered by this lie, but he didn't express any of this to Neil or Pop because he didn't want to look gullible. Still, it bothered him to know that all along his father had been a lot closer than he had known.

Pop estimated the drive would take a little over an hour and said if they hurried that they could probably make it there by ten. This time Neil sat in back, he was wearing one of his trademark Hawaiian shirts again and snacking on a bag of popcorn. James meanwhile rode shotgun and sported one his father's favorite old baseball caps and a pair of jeans; his young face looked excited and nervous as he studied the directions and tried to imagine how his father might look. Pop on the other hand was busy adjusting the windshield wipers as he backed the huge Cadillac out of the driveway and onto the wet road. The rain still continued to pour but the sound of thunder had dissipated significantly. There were now large gaps in the clouds where the sun shined through, and Neil was the first to spot a small rainbow directly ahead of the car.

As they drove, the three of them held an extended conversation about the document and how great it would be to have been an explorer like Christopher Columbus or Hunter Wipley. Pop told them that he had finished watching the documentary on the healing water in Egypt that they had started the other night. And it turned out that some one had actually flooded the fountain in the small town with antibiotics and that was what had caused all the positive effects.

"Hey, are you going to call that lady who did the tests on the pages for us today?" Neil asked.

"Maybe later today if she doesn't call first, but remember she said that it'd take around a day or so, and I don't want to rush her since she's doing us a favor," Pop explained, as he steered over into the fast lane. James knew it was good to be patient, but he agreed with Neil. He was tired of waiting and he wanted to start getting some answers right now. He didn't know how much time his father had left, and if these healing waters did exist he wanted to find them as soon as possible. In his young mind, he even told himself that he would go searching for the island without Pop and Neil if he had to.

The rest of the drive flew by and at around ten they were all looking out the windows for the correct exit number.

"Did you read that last number?" Pop asked the boys, as he squinted and wiped the windshield with his handkerchief.

"It was thirty-seven," Neil exclaimed, with his nose pressed up against the side window.

"That's the one we need," James said, double checking the directions.

"Okay then, we're almost there," Pop announced.

"I still can't believe it's been so long since I last seen my dad," James softly said, staring out the window and remembering his father telling him during the drive to the hospital that everything was going to be fine and that when he got better he'd start teaching James how to drive.

The hospital was located only a few miles from the exit and before James knew it he was walking through the parking garage and up to the automatic double doors of the five story building. Once inside James looked around the spacious lobby for the information desk. It wasn't hard to spot the large suspended sign that read: Community North Hospital Help Desk, and as he did he pointed Pop in the right direction and they began walking towards it. Neil was left behind because he was too busy gawking around at the amazing architecture of the place, and hadn't noticed James and Pop had left.

"Man, look at this place," Neil said, pointing up at the curved steel beams that ran hundreds of feet across the ceiling. Full sized trees lined the front wall which was made entirely of tempered glass. The trees were surrounded by steel grates at their bases and each rose thirty to forty feet high, with branches reaching out towards the window in the direction of the sun. This lobby was anything but ordinary, and it took Neil a few more seconds of admiration before he finally realized that James and Pop had walked away.

*Look at that waterfall*, James thought, as he watch water pour down a huge artificial rock-wall; unlike Neil though he was looking for anything to distract him from his nervous thoughts. The nurses at the information desk first offered Pop a wheelchair, thinking that he was being admitted, but then after a brief explanation they apologized and looked up what room James' father was in.

"Okay a Mr. Greene, let's see, yes here it is, room thirty-five on the third floor. Now, all you'll need is some visitor passes, so may I ask your relation to Mr. Greene?"

"I'm his son," said James nervously with a grin. The older woman behind the desk smiled and handed James a pen.

"Okay dear, you'll just need to sign in here, and then put this sticker on for me."

Pop and Neil also signed in as friends of James' father and were both given visitor stickers too. The three of them stuck the white passes to their shirts and then walked down the long hallway, stopping at the end in front of a set of elevators. James noticed the further away from the lobby they got the more the place became like every other hospital he had ever been in: the same white tile floors, along with bright fluorescent lights, and of course the same typical sterile smell they all have.

As the elevator doors opened, Pop struggled to walk off by himself, but insisted on doing it without any help though; lately he had been trying to prove to everyone and himself that he was getting stronger and didn't always need his cane, but the opposite of that was the truth. As they walked down a large hallway on the third floor, James looked through the glass windows and into the rooms on each side, noticing all the differences between patients: some were white, others black, some with family and friends at their bedsides, others all alone, men, women, even children. But yet, all with one thing in common, they were all sick and needed help. A group of nurses and doctors quickly rushed past James, Pop, and Neil as they all walked towards a sign at the end of the hall that read: Intensive Care Unit.

As they neared the end of the hallway James kept rubbing his hands together, trying to rid them of the clamminess being produced by his nerves. He thought of all the things that bothered him about hospitals and started listing them to Neil.

"I hate the way they kept them so cold, and the smell, don't they all smell like this, and the way everyone looked sick under all these fluorescent bulbs," James stopped.

"You're right man, you do look weird," Neil joked.

"But they save lives," James said, as it dawned on him that he would go through anything in order to see his father again; and even though they didn't say so, he knew Pop and Neil understood this.

When they reached the doors at the end of the hall the three of them showed their passes to the woman at the nurse's station and the double doors were automatically opened. Inside this part of the hospital things were suddenly very quiet. James could only hear whispers now, and every once in awhile echoes of a television or radio, he couldn't be sure which. The rooms in this section were much larger and only on the left side of the hall. Taking up the right side was a huge nurse's station, where doctors and nurses were talking on phones, typing on computers, and looking at charts. None of them seemed to notice

James, Pop, or Neil as they stood in the middle of the hallway looking lost. James couldn't find room numbers on the walls anywhere, and felt uncomfortable peeking in stranger's rooms. Eventually, Pop motioned for them to wait there, as he walked over to one of the stations and got a young woman's attention. James and Neil stood on the other side of the hall and watched as the young woman said something to Pop and then pointed him down yet another hallway. James felt a sudden rush of anxiety, as Pop walked back over shaking his head.

"She said we're on the wrong side, I guess this is the north wing and we need to be in the east," Pop said.

James shook his head slightly, the anticipation was killing him; he just wanted to see his dad already and stop this worrying. As James turned to follow Pop, he ran face first into a stocky man with a dark beard. The impact almost knocked James completely down, but at the last second he was able to brace himself against the wall. The man continued on his way past James without saying a word.

"You okay?" Neil asked, as he rushed over and helped James up. "Yeah, excuse us!" he called down to the rough man, who still didn't respond.

"What happened?" Pop asked, as he watched the man continue down the hall and disappear around the corner.

"Nothing, I'm okay," James promised, brushing himself off and pointing to the door. "Come on, let's just go."

The three of them walked back to the end of the hall and this time turned left. They approached and walked through yet another set of double doors and entered a much smaller section of the hospital. Here there were only eight rooms and as James began checking each room's number, he once again noticed the large man that had ran into him.

"Look James, there's that guy again," Neil said.

"Who cares?" James said, as the man walked into one of the rooms.

James looked over and noticed Pop was still staring at the man with the beard who had just entered the hospital room.

"Pop, it's no big deal seriously," James assured him again.

"No, it's not that, I just noticed something alarming," Pop said, as he waved the boys to follow him and quickly limped over to the nurse's station.

"Listen to me carefully you two," Pop suddenly said, "and do as I tell you."

"What's wrong?" James said, seeing that Pop looked very uneasy about something he had seen.

"This may be more serious then I thought... Hello?" Pop called. "We need some help over here!"

A few seconds later a heavy man rushed over. "Are you okay, sir?"

"Maybe, but I need to know where a patient of yours by the name of Joe Greene is, he could be in danger," Pop quickly said.

James looked startled. "What's going on Pop, what are you talking about?"

"Listen James, when we were sent to the wrong room I saw that same man that just ran into you, I didn't notice it at first, but I believe now he's carrying a gun. It's just a hunch, but it seems to me that he's looking for the same person we are." Pop quickly tried to explain. "Remember, you said it yourself, James, Rex would probably do just about anything to get that document back, especially if the thing's worth money. You guys just stay with me and do what I say."

James and Neil looked nervously at each other as the man behind the desk heard what Pop said and looked concerned. "Mr. Greene was moved this morning to room thirty-two, why, what is this all about, should I call security?"

"Where is that room?" Pop demanded, ignoring the man's question. The heavy-set man stood up and pointed to the same room that the large man with the beard had just gone into only a minute before. They all three looked over in confusion as they watched a nurse leave that room and pull the door closed behind her.

"I think you should call security now, tell them to get up here immediately," Pop demanded. After hearing this, James quickly added everything up and suddenly realized what Pop was suggesting, he then took off running towards the room.

"No, James wait!" Pop shouted, as Neil took off after him.

James got to the closed door and tried to open it, but it was locked, he looked in the small rectangular window and saw the curtain up around the hospital bed and the large man standing at the end of the bed.

"James, what's going on, what are you doing?" Neil asked, trying to hold on to James and get his attention.

"That guy's after my dad," James exclaimed, as he sidestepped Neil and then kicked at the door, trying desperately to get in.

The banging on the door not only got the guys attention, but before James and Neil knew it a gun shot rang out and ripped through the wooden door, barely missing James' arm.

"He's got a gun!" Neil shouted, as he and James immediately ducked out of the way and everyone started to scream and run for the exits. At the same time two security officers came rushing into the wing and ran up to the locked door. The security guards both drew their guns. "No, stop my dad's in there," James shouted, as he grabbed one of the guards' arms. It took Pop and Neil both to get James back and out of the way. A few seconds later one of the guards took out a set of keys and tried to unlock the door. James struggled again to free himself as Pop and Neil held him.

"We have to stop him," James exclaimed.

"It's all right," Pop pleaded. "They're getting ready to go in."

After hearing this, James stopped struggling and watched as the guards attempted to reason with the gunman inside.

"Put down your weapon and come out with your hands up," the guard yelled. "We will not harm you."

At the same time, Pop moved them all over to the wall about five feet back from the side of the door. Then another two security guards arrived and tried to get them to leave.

"I'm not going anywhere," James insisted, as one of the guards tried to motion for them to leave. "That's my dad in there."

"You stay where you are then and don't any of you move." The guard demanded, as he moved slowly forward to where the other three guards were. All four of the guards had their guns drawn now, and one finally found the right key and unlocked the door.

"Don't come any closer," a booming voice yelled from inside the room.

"Okay, alright, what is it you want?" one of the guards asked.

"I'm leaving this hospital, dead or alive!" the man inside yelled.

"Stay calm," Pop said, seeming to read James' mind as he reacted to this comment. "Stay close to the wall, I think there getting ready to go in."

"How do we know you haven't hurt him already?" The security guard asked as he made a hand motion to one of the other guards and then crouched down and moved forward. James felt all the adrenaline in his blood starting to make him dizzy, he thought about how he had lost his mother when he was young and how now he was about to lose his father too. *Why is all this happening now?* The whole scene in front of him seemed surreal as he watched a second guard also crouch down and slowly open the door.

"Are you still with us?" One of the guards on the outside of the room shouted, but there was no response. The two guards that were crouched down then hastily made their move into the room, a few seconds later there was lots of yelling.

"Go, go, go," one of the guards on the outside commanded.

The two remaining guards then rushed in and for a few tense moments there was a lot of confusion and more shouting, "clear here, closet clear, bed clear," and then, "he's gone out the window!" yelled one of the guards. James moved forward and stood to the side of the doorway.

"He's outside moving down the ledge!" the guard shouted. "You two take the stairs down and cover the grounds out front, Larry, you stay here and call for help, I'm going out after him."

Before anyone could grab him James rushed into the room. "Is my dad okay?" he asked, as he moved quickly to the end of hospital bed and saw that his father had been injured.

"You can't be in here," one of the guards said, "come on son they're gonna take care of him now, you have to wait outside." He moved James back despite his struggles to stay; Pop and Neil also grabbed him and helped move him back out of the room.

"No, how is he, is he alive?" James strained, as they finally pulled him back outside into the hallway.

The guard inside was on the phone asking for help as James explained to Pop and Neil what he had seen. "He's been shot," James mumbled in disbelief, "he's hurt."

"Did you see his face?" Pop asked, still holding James tightly by the shoulders.

"What, what do you mean?"

"I mean are you sure it was him?" Pop said, as James tried to remember what he had just seen.

"No, I don't know, I mean, I didn't look at his face, why?"

"They said he had been moved to a different room remember?" Pop hastily explained. "It's very possible that it may not be him, James," Pop said.

The double doors opened again and several nurses and doctors came rushing through.

"Are you all alright?" asked one of the nurses as the rest of the group entered the room.

"Yes, we're fine physically, but we need to know who that man is in there."

The nurse looked confused, so Pop quickly explained.

"Okay, okay," the nurse said, as she immediately understood and rushed in the room to find out. She hurried back out again with the patient's chart. "The patient's name is Greene, Jeff Greene."

James instantly felt relief; Pop had been right about everything. The nurse smiled for a split second, and then hurried back in to help.

"So, where's James' dad then?" Neil asked, still looking shocked by what had just taken place.

"I think I know right where he is," Pop said, leading the boys back through the double doors.

A loud speaker in the hallway suddenly came to life as they walked and announced that the hospital was on lock down and no one would be allowed to enter or leave.

"Do you think they caught the guy yet?" Neil asked.

"He couldn't have gotten far," Pop said, looking completely in control again. "Remember he's thirty feet off the ground; they should be able to catch him he's got nowhere to go but down."

Pop turned right and went back to the same hall that they came from the first time.

"Wait, you think my dad's in the first room they told us about?" James asked.

"Didn't you hear what the nurse told us that poor guy's name was, Jeff Greene. That's so close to your father's name it wouldn't surprise me if they had switched up the room numbers in the computer... That mistake might have just saved your father's life."

"But why would anyone want to hurt my dad?" James asked as they all turned the corner and went back to the north wing.

"I'm not sure James, like I said if this document is worth something then you'd be amazed by what greed does to people, especially people like Rex. Statistic's say the number one reason for murder is money, there's no doubt about that." Pop stopped walking and looked up. "This is it, come on boys let's hurry," he said limping quickly down the hall.

Pop walked up to the first desk they came to and hit it with his cane, trying to get someone's attention. A nurse rushed over and Pop quickly explained what he thought had happened.

Five minutes after Pop's explanation, a large group of policemen and detectives had arrived and were taking statements. They informed everybody that the gunman was still on the loose and had somehow managed to elude hospital security. The detectives promised that with the information they now had that they would be able to hunt down the man and bring him to justice. They also guaranteed James that his father would be protected at all cost. In order to do this, they moved James' father to a private room on the fifth floor and posted an armed guard outside his door.

By the time everything had settled down, it was a little after noon and James, Pop and Neil were all sitting outside of his father's private room waiting to go in. A nurse came by a few minutes earlier and informed them that the man who had been shot was in critical condition, but would most likely live. It was a huge relief to all of them since it could have just as easily been James' father.

A few minutes later, James was finally allowed into his father's large, protected room. He nervously approached the hospital bed and looked down at his father. He looked fine to James as he laid there with his eyes closed, it was just like Neil had described, he looked like he was in nothing more than a deep sleep and that's all. He didn't even look sick. James remembered what the doctors had told him earlier about his father's body functions starting to slow. They said that even though they were still clueless about what exactly was wrong with him, they were working around the clock to figure it out.

With tears building up in his eyes, James stood over his father's hospital bed and prayed. He then took off his father's favorite baseball cap and set it beside him in the bed. All kinds of memories flashed through his mind, as he looked around at all the complicated equipment required to monitor his father's condition. A machine softly beeped every second indicating his heart beat and respiration. James sat down beside his father and looked at his face. He seemed peaceful and exactly the way James had remembered him. He then took his father's hand, closed his eyes, and bowed his head.

"Dad, I promise I'm going to help you get better, no matter what I have to do. I'm going to make you proud of me…" He looked back up and with tears on his face he told his father he loved him, and then said good bye.

Before leaving, the head of the hospital actually met with James, Pop, and Neil and promised to keep them updated on any changes with James' father's condition. He also vowed to step up security around the building and update their visiting protocol. Pop made sure they had the phone number and address where James could be reached and told them to call regardless of time, day or night.

When they finally left the hospital, it was obvious just how hungry and exhausted everyone was because no one spoke much as they walked through the parking lot and piled back into the car. James still felt good about making the trip even though it had turned out to been so traumatic. He massaged his temples as he tried to put all the negative events of late behind him. This was helped out by the weather which had changed from the dark stormy day it had been before, to a bright sunny one now.

"I can't believe we got shot at today," Neil said. "Man James, I swear you've had the craziest week ever. You know you probably saved that guy's life when you kicked at that door?" Neil said, patting James on the back.

"I don't know about that, it's nothing you wouldn't have done," James said, looking at the hospital one last time as they drove off. "To tell you the truth I don't know how much more of this stress I can take, I mean it's getting to me."

"Things will get better, James," Pop said. "There's a reason for everything that happens. These times of struggle only make us stronger; and you have to always keep your head up. Now I admit that sometimes when it rains it pours and it seems that everyone and everything is against you, but those are the times that define us. We're measured by what we do then: either run away and hide or face our troubles and become stronger."

Pop had once again opened James' mind and helped him see the big picture; James was beginning to think of Pop as a mentor and knew that he was going to continue to need his help if he was going to get through this trying time in his life.

Pop stayed quiet during the drive home as he sorted out everything that had been happening around this document. It seemed to be drawing an awful lot of attention, both positive and negative. He knew that something this important couldn't possibly be a fake, but he didn't say anything to the boys. He would simply wait for the phone call he knew was coming from Cori Nichols and hope the boys didn't realize the danger they all might be facing now.

# Chapter Eleven
# Patience Is a Virtue

That evening, after arriving home from the hospital an hour before Judy again, the boys and Pop fixed something to eat and all tried to relax. Naturally, they continued to discuss and come to terms with the incident at the hospital and what it all might mean. Pop must have been able to tell the continuing conversation of the event was bothering, James so to take his mind off of it he suggested they all get back to researching the document. James was glad Pop did this because now he felt even more determined to figure out whether the pages were real or not. He believed it was the only chance he had for helping his father; and by the looks of things at the hospital there was nothing else they could do but wait and hope he recovered on his own. *I don't want to put my hope in the hands of strangers,* James thought as he read over the document again. Neil was running around looking up certain details of Wipley's story as Pop checked out more information on the computer. They had quickly become a sort of well oiled research machine. James reading aloud the document and Neil trying to find books about different things it mentioned. Pop sorting through countless numbers of articles and maps trying to find anything at all that might help in their quest to find the truth.

A few hours later, after Judy arrived home late, she told them that Neil's father, Tim, had called and said that he would be home from his business trip in a week and that he wanted Pop to go out hunting and fishing with him when he did. Before turning in that night, Pop told the boys that once Tim returned home it'd be a lot harder to move forward with their research, so they needed to get as much done in the next few days as possible.

That night James and Neil both had trouble sleeping as they continued to talk about what they had seen happen at the hospital today. James was of course still concerned about his father's safety but Neil reminded him that security at the hospital had been heightened drastically now and that he would be fine. Finally after exhaustion overcame him, he fell into a deep sleep.

At seven a.m. the next morning, the sun was shining brightly, but Pop had been awake since dawn; trying to get in some more research on the document before Judy woke up. He was doing an elaborate search on the computer when he was interrupted by her calling his name from the living room.

"Pop, come on it's time for your exercises, I know you're in there," Judy called.

James and Neil woke after hearing this announcement and looked over.

"What's she talking about?" James mumbled.

Neil sat up and look around, "What's today, Wednesday?" he quickly asked.

"Yeah, why?" James moaned.

"I forgot, it's my mom's day off today," Neil said.

"So, what's that mean?"

"So, we're not going to be able to do any research with Pop because she's going to follow him around all day and bother him with exercises."

James looked confused. "What do mean?"

"Oh, she takes Wednesdays off so she can make my grandpa do these exercises and eat these special meals, it's supposed to help him, but he hates it… I bet he forgot she'd even be home today."

"What are we going to do then?" James asked as he stood up and stretched.

Neil grinned. "Don't worry, Pop's smart he'll figure something out, and if not then we'll do some studying on our own."

James knew this was probably the first and only time he would ever hear Neil say something like this. He grinned and thought, *these pages have to be special, even Neil wants to study them.*

An hour later, while Pop was stuck doing his exercises, the boys sat in the study by themselves and continued doing research alone. James was on the computer trying to finish the list of all the different islands in the Gulf of Mexico when he opened Pop's desk to find a pen, but instead found an old report Pop had done on Area 51. It was just sitting there in the drawer with a stamp that said declassified on it. James looked at it for a few seconds before he showed it to Neil.

"Look at this Neil…" He said, handing the folder across the desk, "is this the kind of thing Pop really did?"

"Oh yeah, I told you he's always researched myths and believed in them. He's been to this place in Arizona, Area 51, searching for UFO's, he's gone to the Bermuda Triangle, he's even been to Egypt and examined the great pyramids for the government—Yep, he did all that stuff when he worked for the CIA, but now he does it for himself. He said he'll never stop searching for answers just because he's retired." Neil looked back at the door to the study and then over at James. "He's done all sorts of stuff since he's lived here too, but he doesn't tell anyone except me."

James wondered why Pop continued to research these kinds of things if he had never actually proven any of them.

"Has he ever found any of these myths to be true?" James asked, as he found folder after folder of strange assignments.

"I'm not really sure, but he still gets these letters and faxes all the time that ask him to go investigate stuff, so he has to have done something right... I think he's always wanted to live like an adventurer you know; that's why he's collected all these books and believes in your dad's document so much."

Over the next few hours they both worked on separate parts of the document, then James and Neil began taking turns reading it aloud to each other, trying to see if they had missed any important detail or clue that might help them. After awhile they began to discuss what would happen if they actually found the healing-water. Again, James told Neil how serious he was about going to look for the island that the document claimed held the water. He said he knew it could save his father and he thought they should go find it. This comment seemed to almost worry Neil and he showed some concern that James might be getting his hopes up too high.

"I don't think it hurts to believe in something," James told Neil. "It's better than sitting around doing nothing, right?"

"No, you're right," Neil finally agreed. "I know it's better than nothing, I just don't want you to get let down if it turns out this story is made up."

James nodded. "At this point, I don't think I can get any lower," he said with a grin. "Hey, everybody used to believe the earth was flat remember? It took people who believed in something different to go out and prove that it was round, but before that I bet it too had been an ancient myth," James said, still trying to prove his point.

"Alright, alright, I said I'm on your side now," Neil said. "If you really believe this story is real and that there's water out there that can heal your dad then you know I'll be right behind you on your trip to find it."

"Thanks, I've just been feeling the stress of everything lately and the document seems to relieve some of that you know… But still you're right, I shouldn't put all my eggs in one basket," James admitted.

After lunch the day began to go by more slowly for the boys. Judy and Pop had left for another doctor's appointment, and the boys felt like they had already gone over almost every detail of the hundred page document they could. They were now sitting out on the front porch talking and taking a break. The whole time all they did was speculate what the test results of the document might be. Pop's friend, Cori Nichols, was supposed to call later that day with the results, and the suspense was driving the boys crazy. After awhile though they made themselves go back into the study and again crack open the books. Summer break was beginning to feel more like the school year with every passing minute. They had pulled down and read through so many books that there were gaps in the shelves all over the place, not to mention all the print outs of maps and articles they had found on the internet. The place looked like a library that had been in an earthquake. James had been on the computer so much lately his eyes seemed to be permanently red. Hour after hour crept by until eventually Judy called for the boys to come have dinner.

They welcomed the break with open arms and as they ate their cheeseburgers and the boys watched Pop with curiosity as he sat at the table and stared at his brown glass of vegetable drink. James could tell that he had just about had enough of his so called healthy day.

"It looks thick," Neil joked, as Pop swirled the glass in his hand.

"What are you trying to do to me, Judy?" Pop asked.

"What color would you say that is?" Neil said, continuing to mock the drink.

"Oh stop it Neil, leave your grandfather alone. It's not that bad, Pop, just try it," Judy said, taking a cookie off Neil's plate and putting it on James'.

"This is why you never want to get old boys," Pop said, watching as Judy walked out of the room and went to answer the phone.

"It might be Miss Nichols," Neil said, as he walked over to the other room and began listening to see who it was.

"James, help me out here will you?" Pop said. James went over and helped him to his feet. Pop then proceeded to walk to the sink and dump the brownish liquid in his glass out. James then helped him spray the sink out and get back over with the empty glass to his seat at the table.

After listening for another few moments to his mom's conversation, Neil finally came back to the table looking disappointed. "It's just one of your doctors, Pop."

Pop shook his head. "Can you believe we let them practice medicine on us? Well not anymore, I'm done being a pincushion," he said, as Judy walked back in and stood with her hands on her hips.

"That was Doctor Howler's office Pop, they said you cancelled another one of your appointments, why are

Pop shook his head. "They practice medicine, and can you believe we let them practice on us? Well not anymore, I'm done being a pin-cushion," he said, as Judy walked back in.

"That was Doctor Howler's office Pop, they said you cancelled another one of your appointments, why are you fighting this so much now?" Judy asked, and then noticed that his vegetable filled glass was empty. "See, that wasn't so bad now was it?" She said with a smile, as she took the glass to the sink and Pop winked at James.

"I hope you don't think this is over mister," Judy told Pop. "I'm going to call tomorrow and reschedule your appointment somewhere else you hear me?"

Pop nodded to Judy and then grinned at James, who grinned back. He figured that since Pop was as old as he was he should be the one who decides what he eats and drinks, and if he should go to the doctors or not. He knew Judy was just trying to do the right thing, but James figured that Pop had made it over sixty years now, so he shouldn't have to do anything that he didn't want to do.

The rest of that evening passed uneventfully. James and Neil watched some TV and tired to ignore the sounds of Pop as Judy pulled and twisted on him some more during another one of his therapy sessions. James wondered how something that sounded so painful could actually relieve pain. By night time, the boys had camped out beside one of the phones and were waiting impatiently for Miss Nichol's call. They were playing a game of chess in the study, but it was tough to concentrate with their thoughts completely elsewhere.

Suddenly, the door to the study came open, and for the first time all day Pop came limping in with his cane. The boys were more than glad to see him.

## HEALING WATER

"Hey Pop," the boys called out.

Pop turned on several over head lights as he made his way to the leather chair and sat down across the game table from the boys. James looked around and with all the extra lights on noticed that the study was a total mess, he knew it was mostly due to all their researching sessions of late, but still the place looked ridiculous. There were books laid open on almost every surface in the room and parts of the floor. Sheets and sheets of paper were piled on top of all the furniture; all of which included information about or relating to the fountain of youth.

"Has she called yet?" Neil asked, soon after Pop sat down.

Pop looked tired as he adjusted his glasses, "No, not yet. I'm thinking about calling her in the morning if she doesn't call tonight."

Neil got out a deck of playing cards and began shuffling.

"So, how's the research been going today?" Pop asked

"Well, we've made a list of all the known islands in the Gulf of Mexico, and we did a few more searches for Manny Jones but couldn't find anything new... It's like he dropped off the face of the planet or something," James said.

"You up for a quick game of cards Pop?" Neil asked, looking over at the door.

"Sure, I know I could go for a change of pace. Poker sound alright?" Pop asked.

James smirked. "Uh, I don't know how to play that," he said, turning his baseball cap around backwards.

"It's easy man, Pop taught me when I was like five," Neil said, looking over and seeing his mother in the doorway.

"Are you forgetting something?" Judy called out to Pop.

"What is it now?" Pop asked.

"Your medicine, remember?" Judy said, shaking her head and walking in. "See this is why I worry about you." James helped get Pop to his feet and watched as he limped back out of the room again with Judy.

"He'll be back in a few minutes boys," she said. "What are you guys doing in here anyway, this place is a mess," she asked Pop as they left the room together.

Ten minutes later, as they boys sat impatiently waiting for Pop to return, Neil got up and headed for the door. "Man, where is he?" he complained.

James stood up too and was about to follow when Pop emerge and slowly reentered the room by himself.

"What took so long, you okay-do you need some help?" Neil asked.

Pop smiled, "No, I'm doing a lot better now," he replied, in a pleasant tone.

James wondered what kind of medicine Pop took that made him feel better so quickly. James then thought Pop was acting a little strange, he couldn't tell what it was but something was definitely different about him.

"What's up with you, why are you grinning?" Neil asked.

But Pop didn't say anything; he just went to his desk, opened a drawer and pulled out his pipe. James and Neil both stayed standing and watched as Pop puffed away.

"Come on Pop, what's going on?" Neil asked again, as Pop casually limped over to the wall and pulled the painting with the safe behind it towards him, the large art piece swung on its hinges revealing a steel box in the wall behind it. He turned the combination lock several times until the thick door gave way and slowly creaked opened.

"I thought we were going to play a game," Neil protested, as he and James stared back at each other. "What are you doing that for?"

Pop ignored Neil's questions as he reached in and retrieved the document from inside. "Do you know what we have here?" he finally said, as he walked back to his desk and held the document up.

"Yeah, we've seen it like a hundred times," Neil grumbled.

"Yes, but before now you didn't know it was real did you? Miss Nichols from the lab just called," Pop said, nodding his head as they all three stared at each other.

"So, what'd she say?" James quickly asked.

Pop sat the document down and opened it. "Well, she has not gotten all of the results back yet, but, what she did find out so far is excellent news... Apparently, we got ourselves an original here boys," he said with a smile.

Neil looked over at James, and then back at Pop. "What do you mean an original?" he asked.

"I mean, the pages match the timeline exactly, they are in fact fifty years old. And it seems that the ink used to write on them was even older. She says the ink's chemical make-up is only produced by one American company and it's in Florida." Pop held the document up to the light and studied it closely. "She also said that these older pages must have been subjected to a high humidity climate because she found microscopic water damage over most the surfaces."

"What's all that mean?" Neil said.

James grinned slightly, "Florida," he said. "Remember, that's where Wipley lived and where he would have written the story."

"So, it's true then, I mean this really is a document written by Hunter Wipley?" Neil asked, standing upright and looking down at the leather-bound pages.

"I believe it is, of course we have to continue researching it, and since Miss Nichols has not gotten back the fingerprint results yet we still don't know who else has handled this thing; and then we also need to try and find a writing sample of Wipley's and have the two analyzed." Pop paused, he could tell by the looks on the boys faces that they were hoping for a much more aggressive approach to investigating the legend now. They had been doing research for days, and he could tell they expected more. James felt that his father didn't have time for more research. He really just wanted to take the document and follow it's directions to the island, then he'd really know for sure if there's water that could help save his father's life or not. *I think we have done all the research we can,* James thought, maybe Pop didn't see it the same way he did; maybe Pop was just humoring him this whole time in order to keep his hopes alive.

As Pop realized that the news was less exciting to the boys than to him, and that they were let down with the idea of more research, he considered the alternative.

"Alright boys, what's going on? I can tell there's something on your minds."

James and Neil looked at each other, neither one wanted to break the news that they were tired of research and wanted to go after the myth like Wipley did. James took his hat off and sat it on the desk. He looked over at Pop and nodded.

"I think it's great news… So, what's our next step?" he asked, feeling that he owed Pop the respect of following his intuitions.

"Now, I know it's not the conclusive news you were both hoping for, but it still moves us one step closer to the truth."

"So, what's our next step," Neil asked, "head down to the library for some more research," he sarcastically said.

"What do you think James?" Pop asked, ignoring Neil's question.

"I don't know," James said, "I guess I was just hoping that if we found out this document was real then maybe it could help my dad somehow. You know ever since I found those pages I felt like I had discovered something extra special. I don't know why, but it was like a light flashed on in my head and told me it's okay to believe in this story because it was real. I argued with myself for days and thought I was just being stupid and desperate but after awhile, and especially now, I realize that I do believe and I want to go see if I'm right, and if Wipley was right."

As soon as James said this the room got quiet, he knew this was the only way to be sure that everyone understood his intentions.

Pop took another look at the older pages. "That's what I was hoping for too. See, ever since I first laid eyes on the document I knew you had something special here. I've been hoping to prove one of these myths for a long time now, and what better reason to do that than to save a person's life," Pop said, looking up at James. "You boys have given me the last chance I have at doing something like this, and I just want to be sure we do it right. I don't want to fail again that's all."

If it wasn't clear what the boy's hopes were before, it was definitely clear now. Follow the documents directions, find the island, and maybe even save James' dad.

"We understand what you're saying Pop," Neil respectfully said, taking the words out of James' mouth. "So, what do we want to do next: find some writing samples, go back over the document, look up some scientific stuff of water?"

"Yeah," James said with an accepting smile, "what should we do next, Pop?"

Pop suddenly realized that even though the boys wished to go out there and try to prove this legend, they were showing respect and still allowing Pop to be the great leader that he had always been. Even if that meant staying put and doing more research, then that's what they'd do. This revelation lifted Pop's spirits and he knew now what they were going to do. He could tell with everything that had happened over the last couple days that James not only needed but deserved a chance; something that would recharge his hopes again and maybe even change his and his father's life.

"Well boys," Pop said, picking up the document and smiling. "I think I'm convinced enough."

"What do you mean convinced?" Neil said, looking from James to Pop.

"Well, I think we've done enough research, and I'm not getting any younger, so I say let's go."

James heard Pop speak these words, but thought that maybe he had misheard or misunderstood him.

"What exactly are you saying?" James ask, looking back from Neil to Pop and then at the document.

"I'm saying let's go prove this document and find that island," Pop announced, as he got to his feet by himself and took another puff off his pipe.

"You really want to?" Neil excitedly asked.

"Yes, yes I do…Now we shouldn't assume we'll find anything of course," Pop reminded them. "We're just going to consider this an extravagant vacation, one that may hopefully lead to a new discovery."

"No problem," Neil said. "We know this might not work out, but James taught me that it's better to believe in something than nothing at all."

"That's right," Pop announced. "People may think it's crazy, but remember that's the same thing they thought about people who said the world was round," Pop said, and Neil looked over at James and they both laughed.

Later that night at a little after midnight, Pop was sound asleep but the boys were still wide awake; both sitting on the new bunk bed entranced in energetic chitchat over the prospect of the upcoming journey.

"Can you believe we're going to do this?" Neil said, as he munched on a brownie.

"I know it's crazy, but I'm wondering how he thinks we're going to pull all this off?" James asked, stealing half of Neil's brownie.

"Don't worry he'll figure it out, I told ya he's done this kind of thing before," Neil took another bite off the brownie. "So, what do you thinks gonna happen when we get out there?" Neil mumbled with brownie still in his mouth.

"I haven't even thought that far ahead yet, I mean how are we going to leave anyway, what are your parents going to say?"

"Man, I told you not to worry about it Pop's going to take care of it, seriously he'll figure out something."

James reached over and grabbed a piece of paper with a road map of Florida on it.

"All right look at this, we have to get all the way down to the coast and then what, I don't think they have flights to any of these tiny islands, I mean there's not even a name for some of them, so what are supposed to do?" James asked, seeming overwhelmed.

"I know we have some planning to do and we're going to do it. Here have another brownie," Neil said.

"No, I'm fine," James said, now looking at another paper with a map of the Gulf of Mexico on it. "I guess I just never expected to really try and do this you know, I've imagined it over and over, but I never actually thought we would," he explained.

"You still want to go though, right?"

"Yeah, but it's more of a need than a want," James said, yawning widely.

"We better get to sleep man, I bet we're going to have a busy day tomorrow."

# Chapter Twelve
# Planning the Adventure

The next morning's dawn was clear and blue with the look of a perfectly normal day; but with this dawn came the abnormal energy of Pop as he woke the boys.

"Morning boys," he said, walking through the room with his cane and pulling open the blinds. "Come on let's go, let's go—you talked me into this, so let's get to it. We have a lot of planning to do today."

James sat up and stretched, he had never seen Pop this energetic and mobile before.

"That means you too," Pop said, leaning over without his cane and tapping on Neil, which caused him to rolled over and almost fall out of bed.

"Okay, okay," Neil moaned, "I'm getting up, let's go."

Pop turned around and grabbed his cane. "Better not press my luck," he said to James as he grinned. "So, what time did you boys get to sleep anyway?" he asked, as he checked out one of the maps strewn about on Neil's desk.

"We stayed up for awhile talking about the trip, well, actually more like worrying about it," Neil said under his breath, while trying to fix his crazy looking bed-head.

"Well, we certainly do have a lot to figure out, and that means I'm going to need all the help I can get. So, after you two get something to eat meet me in the study, we have some planning to do".

The boys were quickly getting ready when Neil offered James one of his party shirts; a bright yellow one. James politely declined and threw back on his same old jeans and plain grey t-shirt. He then went to the kitchen and got a glass of orange juice from the fridge and fixed a bowl of cereal. As James entered the study he found Pop sitting at his desk talking on the phone. James walked in with his bowl of cereal and looked around, immediately noticing the study was completely clean now; book shelves perfectly stocked, floors swept, even the leather furniture looked waxed. James figured Pop must have been up for hours already with everything that was done. Besides cleaning the study, James also noticed Pop had already taken down detailed notes from the document, made several phone calls, and was now off the phone and on the computer, searching for upcoming weather conditions in Florida.

"You've been busy huh?" James asked, looking at all the color-coded notes on the huge desk.

"Well, I thought it would be best since we really only have a few days to come up with this plan and make all the arrangements," Pop said, printing out a seven day forecast for the southern part of America.

"I was the one who was doing the worrying last night," James suddenly admitted, as he sat down across from Pop at the desk.

Pop looked over the top of his glasses. "That's why I woke up so early this morning, I can't stand to worry; I've always felt that the only way to combat that feeling is to take care of everything early and make sure you have a good plan."

"I feel the same way," James said, shaking his head, "but Neil never worries."

Pop spun around in his rolling chair and reloaded the printer with paper, "Ignorance is bliss I guess." They both laughed and then looked up to see Neil walking into the room.

"What's so funny?" Neil asked, carrying a plate with four donuts and a glass of milk. "What—what is it?"

"Nothing," James chuckled, "you wouldn't understand."

Neil shook his head and walked up to the desk; he too noticed all the work Pop had already done.

"So, what else do we need to figure out?" Neil asked.

"Everything," Pop said, "I've taken all the notes I can find in the document on where the island is, but how and when we're getting there is a different story."

"So, are we going to try and go soon?" Neil asked, as he looked down at several pages of flight information, which all included: prices, times, dates, and different airlines.

"I think it would be best to go before your father gets back. It'll be a lot easier to convince only Judy that we're all three taking a summer vacation for a few days. If Tim is home he'll insist on going with us because of my health, and we can't have either of them knowing what we're really doing… I just think it'll be a whole lot easier if we left before he gets back on Monday," Pop explained, and then took a sip from his coffee mug.

Neil took a bite off one of his powdered donuts, "where are we going to tell them we're going?" he mumbled.

"Florida of course; it's the best idea since we're actually going there anyway. I just need you, Neil, to bug your mother into letting you two go with me."

Neil chugged down a drink of milk, "I think I can handle that," he said, as he wiped milk off his face.

"Good, now what do you think of this?" Pop asked, handing James a piece of paper with a detailed plan on it.

"I thought you said you didn't have any of this figured out," Neil exclaimed, looking over James' shoulder at the typed page.

"That's only a rough draft," Pop said, focusing back on the computer screen.

James read the schedule Pop had come up with, which on the left side had times and dates, and on the right side locations. He briefly imagined each part of the trip; first the plane ride to Florida and then the drive to South Grove harbor and the marina, a place he had been imagining for what felt like years. Then, James daydreamed about being off on a boat ride to the unknown island, a place he pictured to be lush with vegetation and beautiful. According to the page James was reading, he should be standing on this island by five o'clock in the afternoon on Sunday. It sounded too good to be true. But after a certain point, the plan on the page became very vague and didn't really explain or cover the trip back.

"This looks good to me," James said, handing it over to Neil. "But what do you think we should do once we get on the island?"

"I don't really know yet, that's where the plan becomes, for many reasons, obsolete," Pop said, turning back towards James. "Since we don't know how large the place is and we don't know where to look, I couldn't come up with any kind of timeline."

"Well," James said, picking up the notes Pop had taken from the document off the desk, "what else does it say in here? I thought I remembered reading something about where the water was located." He continued flipping though Pop's notes for the part he was referring to.

"Are you talking about the page where Wipley describes the cliffs?" Pop asked.

"Yeah, here it is, it says the hundred foot cliffs that are never without the sun."

"Never without sun, what is that supposed to mean?" Neil asked. "It never gets dark there?"

"No, I think it probably means the cliffs face the south, that's the only direction that gets sunlight all day, right?" James said, continuing to read more of Pop's notes.

"You know," Pop said, reaching for his cane and struggling to his feet, "you just might have something there, James, I never thought of it that way before, that's good, well done. Why don't you see if you can find anymore clues, I have to go take my medicine. I'll be right back."

Pop left the study and James continued to read over the notes. Neil had finished his donuts and was now looking over the notes too.

"See, I told you Pop would be taking care of everything, he's the most organized person in the world," Neil said, as he took Pop's seat and rolled back up to the computer.

"I know I can't believe how much he's gotten done already," James said, as he suddenly realized something and looked up.

"What?" Neil asked, noticing James' change in position.

"Well, how do suppose we're going to pay for all this?" James asked. "I mean there's airplane tickets, food, renting a boat, that stuff isn't cheap it's—"

"Don't worry, Pop has plenty of money, remember he retired from the CIA and he lives here. He's always trying to give my parents money, but they never take it. I remember one time when I went to the bank with him and seen his receipt, dude, it had like a nine with a bunch of zeros behind it," Neil quietly said.

"I don't know how I'll feel about Pop paying my way, I'm already staying here with you guys, and that makes me feel bad enough."

"What are you talking about, my parents love having you here, and Pop probably feel like he owes you one anyway for giving him such a cool project to work on." Neil grinned widely. "Heck, before you came over here with that document Pop was bored to death, I mean you should have seen him after you came over that first night and told him about those pages, I hadn't seen him that excited in a long time."

James nodded. "All right, but after we get back I'm going to figure out a way to pay him back, him and your parents both," James said.

"What about me?" Neil laughed, as James shook his head. "Just kidding, anyway when we get back your dad's gonna owe you one."

James smiled, "Yeah, he will won't he?"

After Pop returned to the study, he assigned each one of them a specific job to do. James was responsible for finding a place where they could rent a boat and guide, Neil was stuck with making a list of the gear and items they'd need to get for the trip, and Pop concentrated on finding the best flight.

After two hours of planning; which included a couple arguments and some complaining (mostly from Neil) the three ate a quick lunch and once again returned to the study. They spent the next couple hours going over details of the plan and making suggestions. Pop had found them a flight that left on Saturday morning at eight, departing from Atlanta International and going to Fort Myers, Florida. The fight would take less than an hour and put them fifty miles or so from South Grove Harbor. Pop had mentioned that he'd rather take a taxi to the harbor then rent a car. Of course, James was fine with pretty much any decisions, considering he never thought he would ever actually be going on this trip in the first place.

"Well, that's it," James said, after hanging up the phone. "I've called every place we can find and the soonest boat guide we can get is on Sunday morning at nine," he announced, handing the list of businesses to Pop.

"Perkins Boat Tours, huh, what else did they say, anything about restrictions?"

"No, not really, the guy on the phone seemed really laid back. He said that he charges by the day, but that he'd basically take us wherever we wanted to go, as long as we pay the fee upfront everyday."

"How big of a boat is it, is it a schooner?" Neil asked.

"I don't know, he didn't say," said James.

"I doubt it's a sailboat Neil, probably more like a fishing boat," Pop guessed, adjusting his glasses and reading the notes James had taken. "Well, this looks okay to me. Now all we need is a hotel room for the weekend. Neil, why don't you look up some hotels in the area and make us a reservation," he pointed at Neil like a general commanding his troops. "We'll just have the taxi take us from the airport to the hotel on Saturday, and that'll give us some time to explore South Grove Harbor then."

James nodded, "I was hoping we'd get to do that," he said, as he sat on the leather couch and looked over the actual document, which Pop had gotten out of the safe after lunch. He was still trying to find any clues as to where this healing water was supposedly located on the island. The document gave the exact location to where the island was in the Gulf (25 degrees north by 88 degrees west, which Pop said just about anyone with a boat and compass could find) but nothing about the location of the healing water once on the island. *Does it flow like a river through the middle of the island,* James thought, *is it a tiny creek, or maybe a waterfall, or some kind of pond or something?*

As another half-hour passed, James stayed quiet and continued pondering these questions, searching over the document for answers. Pop was across the room, sitting in front of the large coffee table putting together the final plan. Neil was still at the computer printing off all the hotel information he had finally put together.

The scene in the study went on this way until four in the afternoon, and that's when Pop announced he was finished with the rest of the plan, and asked the boys to gather around the table to help him arrange and double check everything.

"Okay, let's see," Pop said, gathering all the notes and papers they had printed off the computer. "What are these?" he asked Neil as he set down another page.

"This is the hotel I think we should stay at, its call The White Rooks Inn and it's in South Grove," Neil said.

"Alright then, we got the hotel here, the flight information here, and the boat rental papers here. Now what am I forgetting?" he asked, shuffling through the pages.

"I think that about covers it," James said, looking at the weather information for the region again. "Oh yeah, what about the list of supplies we need for the trip?"

"That's right, what'd you find out Neil?" Pop asked, stapling another page.

"Actually I found quit a bit of help on the internet, this page shows what to take on a Caribbean cruise, so I thought that'd be perfect for us. And then you know, we can just add some extra clothes and stuff and then we should be good." He handed Pop and James each a copy of the list.

"This doesn't look bad," Pop said, reading down the long list. "Nice work boys, I think we're all just about set here."

James looked at his watch, it felt like they had been in the study for weeks. "It's almost five," he said, reminding Pop that Judy would be home anytime now.

"Oh really, I should start making those calls then," Pop said, quickly retrieving his glasses and scooping up his cane.

The next twenty minutes was a mad dash of multiple phone calls and exchanging of information. Neil dialed the phone to each place and would then hand it to Pop who would make the arrangements. James meanwhile wrote down confirmation numbers and other things as Pop announced them. The process went smoothly, and just as Pop finished reserving them three airline tickets, Judy came walking in the front door home from work. Pop and the boys hurried and put the plan, document, and all the notes into the safe and locked it.

"Hello, I'm home, I brought dinner," Judy called from the kitchen.

Neil was the first to exit the study, just as the smell of chicken began to fill the air. That evening they all sat around the table and ate slowly for once. James was more than relieved to have everything planned and ready to go. He still couldn't believe they were actually going to do this at all. He was filled with enthusiasm, as he grabbed another chicken leg and some gravy for his mashed potatoes.

The subject around the table couldn't have been more different than James' thoughts. Judy told everyone that she had spoken with Tim, Neil's father, on the phone and that he would be home on Sunday not Monday like he had originally thought. She then went on about her crazy day at work, and how bad traffic had gotten. James was eating his dinner and pretending to listen, but was really wondering how and when Pop was going to bring up the idea of the trip to Judy. They were almost done eating and tomorrow was Friday. *He's not going to bring it up the day before we leave is he*? James asked himself.

"And then," Judy said, as James came to and suddenly began listening again. "I told her that there was no way that I could work all five days next week because I have to stay home with you on Tuesdays. Can you believe that, this is a woman who just got back from vacation two months ago, and now she wants to take another week off? I swear, people these days are getting so lazy," she said, and then took a quick drink of her wine. Neil and James didn't say anything to this, but instead just smiled, Pop on the other hand looked mildly concerned.

"I'm sorry, I know I shouldn't complain so much," Judy said, seeming to read Pop's facial expression.

"No, you're right," Pop said. "People in this country are changing, it's just," he paused and looked down.

"What is it Pop?" Judy asked.

"Well, I feel bad because I know you would have moved up already into that position you wanted at work if you could start going full time, so, I've been thinking," he said, spooning up another bite of broccoli. "I was thinking that maybe I'd just hire a nurse to come once a week and do my therapy."

James watched as the look on Judy's face changed from confusion to concern.

"What, no Pop, now I've told you some of those people will end up leaving you worse off than when you started. They're under paid and angry, and who knows maybe they'd give you the wrong medicine or something. No, I won't have it," she demanded.

James was waiting to see where Pop was going with all this.

"I don't know, Judy, I was even thinking about moving to one of those retirement homes," Pop softly said, with a sad expression on his face as he poked at his green beans.

James couldn't believe how good of an actor he was, he really did seem upset.

"I refuse to let you move to one of those places, Tim and I want to make sure you're doing okay, and we love that you're here, right boys?" she implored.

"Yeah," Neil and James said in unison.

"I don't know, I just feel like I need my own place or something," Pop said. "I haven't left this house in weeks," he complained, and James and Neil had to fight to keep from laughing.

"Oh dear," Judy said, "I know you haven't and I'm sorry Pop. Maybe next week we can go out and do something, or better yet maybe you need a—"

"A vacation," Neil exclaimed, and James almost fell out of his chair.

"Well," Judy slowly said, as James adjusted himself correctly back into his seat. "That's actually not a bad idea."

"Yeah, and we can go with him," Neil excitedly said.

James couldn't believe what he was hearing; Neil was going to blow the whole thing.

"Now boys, I'm sure your grandpa doesn't want you bugging him on a vacation."

"You know, I don't think that's such a bad idea actually," Pop said. "I wouldn't mind going down to Florida this time a year."

"I heard the fishing is excellent in the summer," James added with a grin, figuring he would fan the flames some too…

"You hear that Judy, the boys want to go with me. You know, this is exactly the kind of thing I've been needing. Come to think of it, I just received something in the mail about vacationing for five days in Fort Myers Beach; it looked like a heck of deal."

Judy was smiling now that Pop sounded happy, James was thoroughly impressed by Pop's tactics, his performance would have fooled just about anyone.

"Okay," Judy said, with a smile. "Yeah why not, I know all of you could use a bit of a break from everything that's been going on lately."

When everyone had finished eating, Neil ran to the study and grabbed a coupon he had printed off the internet, he ran back into the kitchen and showed Pop who showed Judy. James was amazed that he had found a coupon so quickly that expired on Sunday. Judy really had no choice but to agree to the trip, especially after she saw how excited Pop was about the idea.

That night James and Neil basically laughed themselves to sleep. Pop made sure to explain to them before they went up to bed that he didn't condone lying, but said that desperate times called for desperate measures. When Neil had finally quit laughing he fell asleep, but James lay awake for awhile and pictured his father waking up from the coma healthy and smiling.

# Chapter Thirteen
# Flight Time

As the next morning rolled around Pop and the boys all slept in until nine, afterwards they got up, went out to eat, and then over to the superstore to pick up some of the supplies. They divided up the list and found most of the items on it; they also picked out some of their favorite snacks and beverages to bring as well. The stuff that they didn't get on the list, Pop said they'd pick up after they got down to Florida. Back at home they reviewed the plan once again, printed off their airline tickets, and double-checked their luggage. When Judy got home from work that day she brought in a couple more bags of things she had picked up for them to take, including: sun block, travel size toiletries, and of course more food. Now they each had three bags a piece, two for clothes and supplies, and a third smaller bag containing only edibles. Neil joked that if they happened to get marooned on a deserted island they could still survive for weeks. Pop didn't find the remark very amusing in front of Judy, but he still grinned.

That night, Judy ran around the house for an hour making sure they had everything; she kept saying that she couldn't believe they were going to Florida without her, and that she was going to miss them all very much. They promised to call everyday and to take plenty of pictures. Pop never even asked whether or not she had told Tim where they were going. James figured he probably thought it best not to bring up the subject if she didn't.

As night approached they all decided to turn in early, and just like he figured, James had trouble falling asleep. He kept worrying that they wouldn't even be able to find the island, and that it was all just some huge mistake. *What are we doing*, he thought as he tossed and turned, *this is totally insane, are we seriously going to try and find some island and then search it for magical healing water?* How could a man as intelligent and educated as Pop believe in such a thing, it was ludicrous he told himself. *Maybe this is all just a waste of time, maybe I've bitten off more than I can chew.* This evaluation went on for what seemed like most of the night; James continued to wrestle with his doubting mind until eventually passing out from real exhaustion.

"Hey, James, come on wake up," a tired voice said, and James slowly opened his sleepy eyes. Instantly, bright light filled them and caused him to squint, the light was coming from the lamp beside the bed, looking over he could tell that it was still dark outside the window.

"What time is it?" James said, shielding his eyes.

"It's like five-thirty. Pop woke me up and said we should start getting ready soon."

James lay back again and pulled the blanket over his head.

"Wake me up when you get out of the shower," James mumbled, as he began to fall back asleep. It only seemed like two seconds had gone by before Neil was calling his name again. "James, James, hey come on it's almost six," Neil repeated.

"Okay, I'm up" James moaned.

Neil walked over and began dragging his luggage to the door as James sat up and shook his head.

"Oh, man," James said, as he stood up.

"What's up with you?" Neil asked. "Aren't you excited?"

"Huh, yeah, I'm just tired… I didn't sleep much last night," he explained, pulling his luggage over to the doorway beside Neil's.

"You were up worrying again weren't you?" Neil said. "Look man, it's gonna be fine, I mean what's the worst that could happen, just like you said, even if it turns out to only be a myth at least we tried to do something great and save your dad, right? It's better than doing nothing at all," he said, as he took a look at himself in the mirror. "Anyway, how often do you get to go on a real adventure like this, I mean we got an old document to follow and everything!"

"I know, I know," James said, pulling over his other two bags. "It's a once in a lifetime thing, but aren't you a little concerned? I mean we are going to search for an unknown island out in the ocean?"

Neil laughed, "Heck yeah I'm concerned, I seriously had a dream last night that—"

"You boys up?" Pop yelled from down the hallway.

"Yes, we'll be ready in a few minutes," Neil yelled back. "James you better hurry up and take a shower, Pop said the taxi will be here at six thirty."

James rushed to the bathroom and started to clean up. The idea of what they were about to embark on hit him even harder as the warm water splashed on his face, waking him fully and bringing his senses quickly to life.

*I'm going to be in the Gulf of Mexico tomorrow*, he kept thinking... *On an island, searching for water that heals people...this is craziness.*

The next thing James knew he, Pop, and Neil were in the back seat of a yellow taxi cab on their way to the airport. The trunk of the taxi was not large enough for all their bags so they had to put two of them in the front passenger seat. The taxi and its foreign driver had a strange odor to them, and Neil kept making goofy faces at James like he was dying because of it. Meanwhile, the sun had come out enough for Pop to begin reading his morning newspaper. He put his glasses on and flipped through the pages until he found the weather section.

"It looks like it's supposed to be hot today in Florida boys," Pop announced as he flipped to the next page.

"What's it say about tomorrow?" James asked.

"Over the next few days it shows clear skies and high temperatures, basically the same as today. Here's the satellite picture," Pop said, pointing to a colored graphic of the southeastern part of America. "This symbol indicates a storm coming in from the Atlantic around Monday or so, but it should die down after it hits land fall and dissipate to merely rain by the time it gets to us," he said, looking up suddenly as the taxi swerved, barely missing a truck that was changing lanes.

"You imbecile, idiot!" The taxi driver yelled, honking his horn as Pop shook his head. "Well, are you boys ready for all this?" he proudly asked.

"I'm excited, but I don't know about James," Neil confessed with a smirk.

"Really, well what seems to be the problem?" Pop asked, looking up from his paper and removing his glasses.

"Nothing serious, I just get nervous before flying," James lied, while giving Neil a dirty look.

Pop saw straight through the front James was trying to put up.

"I know exactly how you're feeling," Pop confessed. "I feel nervous every time I go after something important too, and this time it's even worse. It's completely normal to be anxious; its true there really is a lot riding on this trip. I've been sleeping less and less everyday this past week. Planning all this out, knowing how important all of it is... And it's all riding on yet another myth which most people have never even heard of," Pop said, pausing for a second and thinking. "Do you know how many people looked at me differently after they found out that I was traveling to Jerusalem in search of the Holy Grail? They thought I was going crazy, even my best friend called me a loony and said I was naive, and this was a guy that I worked with for over twenty years. He eventually stopped taking my calls all together and totally abandoned me because of my strange hobby. See, most people don't like the idea of things that are unknown because it means that they don't know something. People like this usually hate imagination and only believe in things that can be proven scientifically, things they can touch and see, most have no faith, no faith at all. They believe only in man and his creations. And yet, I have always thought and felt like there were mysteries that whoever created us didn't want us to understand, and it was these things that would help us and remind us that once we too were created."

James understood and agreed with Pop's speech, but didn't say anything. Instead, he simply nodded his head and enjoyed the relief of knowing that Pop had such a profound explanation for the trip and that, in fact, he did realize the extremely high odds against them being successful. But what James gathered Pop meant was that he didn't care about the facts, he was throwing caution to the wind again and going against the odds in hopes of proving a miracle. Pop was being a kid again and that was all James needed to understand; he knew now that it was okay to go against the crowd every once in a while, maybe even healthy.

The cab turned off the exit and into the airport at a little after seven, it pulled up to gate B and after scraping the curb came to a stop. The boys each climbed out of opposite sides of the car, and immediately James heard Neil take in a huge breath of air, as if he had been holding his breath for the entire ride there. James walked around to the trunk and got Pop's cane as Neil helped him out of the car. Afterwards, they all collected their luggage and put most of it on a trolley; the two smaller bags that wouldn't fit James and Neil had to carry.

It was a long walk through the terminal and as they went James looked around constantly; he had never seen so many suitcases in one place before. Each hallway was long and crowed with people walking and standing in lines at the front of forty-foot long desks. Between these desks there were long windows, all displaying different views of the vast runway system below. In some windows, James could see planes parked and connected to retractable hallways leading back to the airport. He noticed some terminals had restaurants, shops, and even a barber shop (which he could have used since his hair was down past his eyes now and had to be pushed to the side and out of the way all the time).

As the boys pulled the trolley and followed Pop, they had a little trouble keeping up with him because of his eagerness. He was moving along easily on the concrete floor and you would have barely noticed that he was using a cane. James and Neil talked excitedly as they turned down another hallway. As they passed a group of people, Neil told a good looking blonde woman that he was going to find the fountain of youth. James put his head down and laughed as they finally slowed and eventually stopped in back of a ten person line. The line led to one of the long desks and snaked back and forth in-between metal poles that were all attached to one another with a black band that looked like a seat belt.

They moved up slowly in line, and each time they did Neil would moo softly like a cow. Halfway through the line Pop checked his watch and James saw that it was twenty-five after seven. They had a half-hour until their flight at eight, and James' stomach was growling, he hoped that they were going to have enough time to get some breakfast before they left, and he could tell by Neil's blank stare at the food court that he was thinking the same. It took another five minutes until they got to the front of the line and after Pop showed several pieces of identification the woman behind the counter took all the luggage and printed them three more tickets and they were done. Pop agreed they could stop by Melick's Muffins and all get a snack before heading to their gate. Neil ordered two giant poppy-seed muffins and a soda, while James and Pop both got blueberry muffins and orange juices.

It was a short walk afterwards to gate B-14, and after going through the metal detectors they all sat down and waited for the flight to begin boarding. Neil was concentrating on his breakfast as James took a bite off his own warm muffin and watched two men filling the plane with fuel outside the window in front of him. They looked like large ants compared to the gigantic aircraft, and James found it hard to believe that this huge vehicle on these tiny wheels would be able to move people anywhere on the ground, let alone fly them through the air. The thing had to be longer than two buses, and the engines were these massive round tubes that looked liked overgrown, electric-razor blades. James had seen planes in the movies of course, but since his father also had a fear of heights he and James had never actually taken one anywhere before. This made James' hobby a bit tough to pursue, but he figured it was just another problem for him to solve.

"How much do you think that planes weigh?" James asked Pop, who was re-examining his newspaper and drinking his orange juice.

"Oh, let's see, I believe they're somewhere in the neighborhood of two-hundred tons," Pop said, looking up at the plane with James. "It's amazing isn't it, just think in one hour that machine will lift off, climb to twenty-thousand feet in the air and return to earth almost three-hundred miles away from here."

"How fast does it go?" Neil mumbled through a bite of his second muffin.

"Well, do the math. If Fort Myers is three-hundred miles away and it takes an hour to get there then how fast would we be going?" Pop asked, as Neil shook his head and looked to James for help.

"Three-hundred miles an hour, Neil," James casually said.

Ten minutes later James watched the men pack up the fuel truck and drive away. A woman then came on the loud speaker and made an announcement. "Flight one-twenty-two departing for Fort Myers, Florida at eight a.m. will be boarding rows one through ten in a few minutes. Please have your boarding passes out and carry on luggage with you as you board, thank you."

"Here's your tickets boys," Pop said, handing Neil and James each a white pass with their names on it.

"You ready for this?" Neil asked, bouncing around in his seat excitedly, and waving his ticket in front of James.

"Yes, now quit it," chuckled James, as he pushed Neil's hand away.

"Just easin' the tension baby," Neil said, quoting yet another movie.

James watched as people began standing and collecting their bags, children and other personal objects. A little while later another announcement was made, this one informing everyone that boarding would commence now. People immediately walked over and formed a single file line leading to a woman who sat behind a computer with a scanner in hand. James looked down at his ticket and read that he was in row fifteen, he checked with Pop and Neil to make sure they were all sitting together and then went back to watching the people in line. It looked like a fairly simple process, and once rows eleven through twenty one were called James found out that indeed it was—you just hand your ticket to the woman, she scans it, your information comes up then she rips the ticket along the perforated line and hands the smaller part back to you. *So far so good*, James thought.

The tunnel leading to the plane seemed fairly sturdy, and as James crossed the threshold into the plane he looked to his left and marveled at the cockpit for a few brief seconds; there were an endless number of knobs and buttons spread out along a wide wrap around console that surrounded the pilots. He turned back to the right now and followed Pop down the far left aisle. There were seven rows of seats going straight back, two on both sides and three in the middle. After passing through to the second section, Pop found their specific row and James helped him in. During the check in procedure, Pop had declined a handicapped seat, explaining sarcastically that the he used the cane merely to get attention. He did however take the aisle seat in case he had to get up this would make things a lot easier on all of them. James got the window seat and as he sat down he looked out, he saw yet another plane going down the runway and then take off into the air.

"Check it out," Neil said, as he leaned over James and pointed at the large plane as it quickly gained altitude and banked to the right. "You all right with the window seat?" he asked James as he was buckling his seat-belt.

"Yeah, I was hoping I would get it," James said, trying not to let his nervousness show.

"Good, cause there's no way I'd sit there, it always makes me sick to look out the window when we're flying," Neil said, shaking his head "especially when it gets bumpy."

"Bumpy, what do you mean bumpy?"

"Oh, not to worry, James," Pop said, "it's perfectly normal to encounter air pockets that cause the plane to shift a little during flight. It's usually nothing more then what you feel when riding a Ferris-wheel."

"I think I'll be fine then," James said, as he looked back out the window and watched another small jet taking off. He definitely wasn't worried about getting sick, he had always been good at riding carnival rides and rollercoaster's, it was actually one of the very few things that didn't affect him. The real thing he was worrying about was how this colossal piece of metal was going to leave the ground and not come crashing back to earth. He kept telling himself that people had been flying planes for a long time, something like a hundred years now. *They've got it down to a science by now*, James reassured himself.

As soon as the rest of the passengers boarded, which took another twenty minutes, James watched two flight attendants close the door to the plane and then he heard the captain's voice crackle over the loud speaker, announcing that they would be taxiing to the runway shortly. *Here we go, it's going to be fine—just remember we're doing this for dad,* James told himself.

Soon the plane was in motion; it was being pushed backwards by a miniature truck with a long pole that was connected to the plane's front wheels. By using this connection the truck was able to steer and move the huge aircraft slowly backwards and into position. After it finished, the engines of the plane kicked on and began vibrating the seats slightly. James held tight onto the armrest, but tried to keep a relaxed look on his face so Neil wouldn't make fun of him. He noticed Pop had a headset on and already seemed to be dozing off. *How can he sleep now?*

Gradually, the noise from the engines got louder as the plane began to creep forward under its own power for the first time. It was gaining momentum quickly and bouncing up and down a little as it made its way down the runway. Neil looked the other way while James watched out the window as the ground below moved by faster and quickly became blurry. A moment later he felt a sudden burst of extreme power that pushed him back in his seat. Gravity was still fighting hard to keep the plane grounded as it broke one hundred miles an hour and shuttered slightly. James held on even tighter still, as he wondered how much more runway they had left and how much faster they needed to go. Without warning, the front end of the plane tilted up and rose off the runway, as if it was doing a wheelie. Then, suddenly, the shaking stopped and the noise from the tires disappeared. James opened his eyes and saw that they had indeed left the ground. The only sound now came from the engines which were still winding strongly as the aircraft rose gradually towards the sky.

"See," Neil said, "nothing to it."

"Yeah, not too bad," James lied, as the plane continued to climb and then banked its wings towards the south.

Over the next twenty minutes James' ears popped over and over again. One minute he could hear perfectly clear and then the next everything sounded far away, or like he was under water. Neil gave him a piece of gum which helped the problem but didn't completely solve it. Eventually, the captain came back on and announced that they had reached their altitude of twenty-thousand-feet, and he was turning off the seat belt sign. The stewardesses then made their ways up and down each aisle with a wheeled-cart that held food and drinks. Pop politely declined anything and went back to sleep. But of course, Neil asked for two cans of coke and some peanuts; while James just had a sprite, which he hoped would calm his stomach.

Over the remainder of the flight, Neil and James held brief conversations about everything from Florida to the other people on the plane; particularly one good looking young woman seated a row in front and across from them. Neil kept going on about how she was the kind of girl that he was going to marry. James was laughing at him when the plane suddenly dropped violently.

"Whoa, see, I told you," Neil quietly said, as the plane dropped again. Of course this stressed James out, but it didn't make him sick; Neil on the other hand was a different story. He had put his head down and was taking deep breaths as the plane jerked again; James figured that if it hadn't been for the second announcement by the captain that they would be descending now, Neil would have probably lost his lunch.

"We're almost there," James calmly said, trying to reassure Neil and himself.

"I'll be all right now," Neil said. "We're on our way down right?"

"Yeah, that's what it looks like," James said, looking out the window as they descended through another dense, white cloud.

As the plane continued downward it stabilized and became almost perfectly still. Pop stirred a little and then woke up and took off his headset.

"You boys okay?" he asked, sitting up and checking his watch.

"I'm all right," James said, as Pop looked over and examined Neil, who still had his head down and looked quit pale now. "But he's feeling sick," James explained, seeing Pop's reaction.

"I'll be fine," Neil said. "Just have to keep my eyes closed until we're on the ground again."

"Oh man that's too bad because that girl you like is looking back here right now," James joked, as Neil couldn't resist and slowly opened one eye.

"Got ya," James laughed, as Neil closed his eye again and shook his head.

"Now that's funny," Pop said as he and James chuckled.

"Laugh it up guys, but don't worry I'll get you both back," Neil promised, as the plane shook once again. "Come on," Neil grumbled.

"We'll be on the ground in five minutes," Pop reassured him.

James stayed glued to the window for the next five minutes. He watched as the tiny colored dots below were slowly revealed to be cars, houses, trees and even people. The ground looked like a bunch of rectangles and squares all put together, each one was a different size and either some shade of green or brown. The lower they got the more detail James could see, and before too long he could read billboards and eventually he knew they couldn't be much more then a couple hundred feet above the ground. The airplanes engines had gone quiet now and the only noise came from the landing gear as it was lowered into position; afterwards it felt and sounded like they were simply gliding towards the runway at Fort Myers Airport. Pop was looking over Neil and out the small window with James, as the ground came even closer and moved by in a blur. Then the grass below instantly turned into concrete as a tall, bobbed wire fence quickly went by, James realized that they were now over the runway. The next second he heard and felt the tires touch down and the plane's engines rev up again, this time in reverse, slowing the plane considerably. Neil opened his eyes and looked over at James.

"You alright," James asked.

"Are we on the ground?" he asked, refusing to look out the window.

"Yep, we're here," James said, watching Neil's face resume normal color as he looked over at the pretty girl again and smiled.

# Chapter Fourteen
# The Real South Grove Harbor

    Once they had left the plane, James and Neil waited beside a large metal carousel for the rest of their luggage to come down. Neil said he was feeling normal again, but he kept missing their bags. It took two more passes around before James was able to grab them all. Afterwards, they both packed everything on another trolley and then followed Pop to the elevator. After going down a floor they walked through a long hallway and then exited the airport. The bright sun was the first thing James noticed as they all walked out to the curb and waited for a taxi. Neil was still so dazed from the plane ride that he didn't even notice the same pretty girl from their flight standing right beside him on the sidewalk. James didn't notice the girl either because he was busy staring up at the sky admiring the exceptional weather. Along with the abundant warm sunshine, there was a light breeze that caused the temperature to feel almost perfect. He watched as palm trees out far ahead swayed lazily in the wind and white seagulls glided freely over head; the place pretty much felt like a foreign country to him. As he continued his evaluation, Pop stood on the curb and was attempting to hail a cab with his cane. The roads in front of the airport were full of buses, cars, and taxis; the horn from one of these vehicles was what caused James to return from his blissful observations. He then immediately noticed the pretty girl standing right beside Neil. Unlike James though, Neil had apparently not come back from his daze yet, because as he stood staring into space he reached up and was about to pick his nose.

"Neil!" James called out, causing Neil to turn away from the girl.

"What man?" he asked, with his finger almost in his nose.

James hastily moved over and grabbed Neil's arm. "Look," he quietly said, motioning with his hand toward the girl who appeared to be with her mother.

Neil put his hand down, slowly looked over and caught eyes with the girl. She smiled and then looked away as her mother turned around.

"How long has she been there?" Neil quietly asked, after he turned back towards James again.

"I'm not sure, I just now noticed her."

"Oh, do you think I should say hi?" Neil said, looking over again and making eye contact with the girl as he adjusted the collar on his party shirt.

James nodded. "Why not?"

Neil hesitated for a couple seconds, "what's she doing now?"

"She's leaving," James said, as Neil turned around and watched the girl and her mother move forward towards a taxi that had just pulled up.

"Bye," Neil said, waving at the girl as she smiled and waved back.

"Did you see that she—"

"Let's go boys," Pop announced, as he limped forward with his cane and approached a second taxi that had pulled up for them. Neil didn't move as he watched the girl of his dreams drive off. "I'll never see her again will I?"

"If it's meant to be you will," James told him.

During the drive to the hotel the boys and Pop talked excitedly almost the entire time. Pop pointed out different landmarks along the way and provided an array of interesting facts to go along with each of them.

"Did you know you can run an engine on coconut oil?" Pop informed them.

"No way," Neil exclaimed, looking back out the side window of the taxi at a coconut tree. "Look at that, James," he suddenly said, pointing at a billboard with a picture of a giant Florida marlin on it that read: Florida, where the fishermen don't have to lie.

"Those are in the water down here?" James asked, looking at the sword-faced fish with its dangerous-looking spiny fin on its back.

"Oh yeah, they're all over these waters, along with lots of other unusual creatures known only to this region as well," Pop said.

It was around eleven-thirty that morning when the driver finally told them that they were at the White Rooks Inn Hotel.

"This isn't it," Pop said, looking out at two, round tower-like buildings, each made out of all white stones and standing some hundred feet tall.

"Yes it is, don't worry we're at the right place," Neil reassured them.

But James wasn't so sure either, the place looked nothing like the picture Neil had shown them, and after they got out all of their stuff from the taxi and looked around, he realized that he wasn't even sure if this place was a hotel at all.

"Isn't this place cool?" Neil asked, as James and Pop looked up at the strange buildings, each of which was connected at the bottom with what appeared to be a lobby area of some sort.

"What is this supposed to be, a lighthouse?" Pop curiously asked.

"Yeah, it's the two oldest lighthouses in Florida, they turned them into one big hotel," Neil announced, as they all stood in the front of the towers and looked around. "I wanted to surprise you guys so that's why I didn't tell you. Isn't this awesome though?" He exclaimed, while James looked to the side of the structure and out over the rocky cliffs, which dropped off to the ocean far below.

"This is great and all" Pop confessed, "but I can't believe I didn't see this place when I was researching the town."

"Yeah, I know I was kind of worried about that, but when I found out that this place wasn't actually part of the South Grove I knew you wouldn't find it."

"So, if we're not in South Grove, then where are we?" James quickly asked, as he continued to survey his unique surroundings.

Pop began riffling through one of the bags on the luggage rack.

"Um, I'm not exactly sure but I know it's not far," Neil said, as Pop finally produced a map from one of the bags and began figuring out exactly where they were.

"Does Fox hill sound right?" Pop asked.

"Yeah, that's it," Neil answered confidently, as James rolled his eyes.

"According to this map, South Grove Harbor should be due east of here, that way," Pop said, pointing down to the right of the towers. "It looks like it's only about a mile or so away."

"See, it's not that far," Neil said, "and look at this view."

"Yes, it's breath-taking," James sarcastically said, as he grabbed the luggage cart and pushed it towards the front doors. He was impressed by the set up of the place, but he felt a little irritated that Neil was treating this more like a vacation then an attempt to save his father. *It's no big deal, he's just being Neil*, James eventually told himself. *He's been more than supportive this whole time.*

"You know, we may actually be able to see the harbor from up there," Pop said, gesturing towards the top of the light houses as they all walked in.

As he passed through the double doors, James was instantly hit by a blast of cool ocean air; he looked up and noticed several large windows and skylights all wide open on the back wall. As he walked further in, he became surrounded by the smell of sun-screen and salt, and saw telescopes pointing out the back windows in front of them. There were also large wooden columns along the walls leading down both sides of the lobby to a glass desk that was protruding out of a short stone wall.

"This hotel is sweet huh? Hey, look over there," Neil said, pointing at a gigantic glass incased light that had apparently been used at the top of one of the towers a long time ago.

"What did this place set me back?" Pop joked, looking through the case at the five foot tall light.

Neil laughed. "Don't worry, since you have a government ID we got a discount."

"Do we get to choose our rooms?" James asked, hoping they would be able to look out from the top floor and see South Grove Harbor like Pop had suggested.

"I requested the top floor for both the rooms, but they couldn't guarantee them," Neil explained; and by the looks of all the people walking around the lobby James could see why. The place was packed with travelers; most of them looked around Pop's age. He actually hadn't seen one kid since they had entered the building.

When they got back to the glass desk and rang the bell a broad, thick man appeared from the back. "Welcome to the White Rooks Inn, I'm Michael how can I help you, sir?"

"Yes, I believe we have a reservation, the last name's Kelly," Pop said, pulling out his wallet. The man behind the desk did not seem like he belonged there at all. He was tough and if you had to guess you would have thought him to be a navy seal, or secret service agent of some kind. James figured with his hair shaved as short as it was the man had to have been in the military at one time or another. Still, despite the man's abrasive exterior he was surprisingly kind, and after quickly looking up their reservation, he then summonsed a bell hop from the room behind him. A second man quickly appeared from the back, and to everyone's astonishment he looked identical to the first, definitely a twin brother. He came around the counter and greeted them with a smile.

"I'd like you to meet my brother, Nick, he'll be taking your bags up for you," the gentleman behind the desk politely informed them.

"This is a very interesting place," Pop said, as he continued to look around the place. "What a great idea to turn two lighthouses into a hotel."

"Yes sir, we're sure proud it. These lighthouses have been in our family for almost a hundred years."

"Really," Pop said, sounding impressed. "So, you two run the hotel then?"

"Yes sir, as soon as Nick and I finished our time in the army we came back home to take over the business for my father. His health was declining, but he made us promise not to sell the place, so here we are."

"Well, it really is amazing, the boys and I are looking forward to doing some sight seeing from our room."

"That shouldn't be a problem, you've got two of the best rooms in the house. Now, don't hesitate to call if you need anything, Nick and I are always around here somewhere."

Pop said thanks as the other brother took the luggage cart and wheeled it away. "Let's see, Mr. Kelly, your rooms are both on the top floor as requested, so if you'd turn to the right and follow me to the elevator we can go up."

"Come on boys," Pop said, as James and Neil were looking through one of the many telescopes that were built into the floor and pointing out different windows towards the ocean far below.

"What floor are we on?" Neil excitedly asked, as they all got into the elevator.

"Your rooms are right next to each other on the ninth floor," Nick said.

The ride up to the top floor seemed to take a while, but finally the doors reopened and Nick pushed the luggage cart forward with ease, as James and Neil walked out and looked down a very short narrow hallway that had only two doors on each side and a long window at the end.

"You can just take it all to one room," Pop said, "We'll sort it out later."

"Yes sir, here we are then," the man said, opening the second door on the right and handing Pop both room keys. "Will there be anything else," he asked, after pushing the cart into the room.

"No, that's fine thank you," Pop said, handing the man a generous tip.

Neil rushed into the room and went over to another long window. "Look at this," he exclaimed. James walked over and looked out, the view from up here was unbelievable, and as he looked down and over the beach to the east he saw a tiny collection of docks, houses, and boats.

"Pop come here," James said, "I think you were right."

Pop limped over and looked out the window.

"You think that's South Grove Harbor," James asked, pointing over to the very right side of the long window.

"It has to be," Pop said, as he stood with the boys and gazed in awe. "I guess we'll find out for sure here shortly after we clean up and head down there for some lunch."

"See, and you were worried James," Neil said.

"No, you did okay, Neil, this place is nice," James admitted.

"I wonder how old these lighthouses are." Neil asked, as he picked up a brochure off the nearby desk.

"Come on we can find out all the details later, let's get ready so we can start exploring the town," Pop said.

By the time everyone was done cleaning up and unpacking, Pop had already called down to the front desk and found out that they didn't need a taxi because the hotel provided a shuttle bus that could take them anywhere within a ten mile radius.

"It says here that this place was built in nineteen-hundred and one?" Neil said, as he read from the brochure on the elevator ride back down.

"What a good idea, to turn this place into a hotel," James said.

"Oh absolutely... I bet since modern technology keeps ships from running a ground now these lighthouses became obsolete."

"You're exactly right, Pop," Neil said. "It says that here in the brochure too. It also says that the reason there were two lighthouses built was because it took several hours to change a burnt out light and Rock Shore Peninsula is one of the busiest and most dangerous passes for ships in the world. Whoa, so they were so worried they built two separate towers, that's crazy huh?"

"Yeah, but did it work?" Pop asked as the elevator slowly came to a stop.

"Hold on I'm looking—After the construction only two ships have gone a ground and sank and both of those were due to hurricanes… That's pretty good, two ships in over a hundred years."

As Neil continued to read off facts about the interesting lighthouse hotel, James couldn't help but feel anxious to get down to South Grove, even though he had seen it he wanted to be sure it actually existed. As they stood out in front of the hotel waiting for the shuttle bus, James felt impatience creeping up again. This whole experience was completely new and out of character for him. He had always been reserved and patient up until recently. He didn't feel like he was handling all this stress very well, but he was slowly learning that he needed to if he wanted to succeed at anything. It seemed like every place he went to required some kind of adventure to get there; even a small town less than two miles away.

Finally, after another minute of waiting, a long white van pulled up in front of them and James and Neil helped Pop in and then they jumped in back. The driver was a small old man with a dark outfit and hat. He looked like the typical chauffeur and acted like one too.

"And where are you fine young gentlemen off to today?" he inquired.

"Is that South Grove Harbor down east of the hotel there, we thought we seen it from the top floor of the hotel," Pop said.

"Yes it is, and yes you did, especially on a clear day like this. You know they say ships could see the lights on top of those towers from over twenty miles away, yes sir they did," the driver said. "So, South Grove Harbor then?" he said as Pop nodded.

The van left the parking lot and turned left; it then went down a long hill for about a mile before turning left again onto a windy road. This road was much narrower than the last and had small white houses scattered around on each side of it. When the road straightened back out the ocean was not more then fifty feet from the left side of the van. James knew they had finally entered the town of South Grove because he saw a small wooden sign on the side of the road that said so. Within a hundred yards of the sign there now appeared a row of buildings, some larger than others, but all with signs above them: Mike's Restaurant and Deli, The Great Outdoors bait and tackle shop, and The Shoppers Corner Store, which looked like it carried groceries. There was basically everything that any other small town had, the only difference being

## HEALING WATER

that these buildings were all very old and lined up in one long connected row. They all looked like they had been repainted dozens of times, and looking at them reminded James of a painting that had been left out in the rain so that all its colors had ran together.

As continued slowly down the road, James looked back to the left and saw docks now with boats of all kind tied to them. Some larger than others, and a few sailboats, but most of them looked to be used for fishing. Men were working all around on the docks, some cleaning the boats, others organizing nets and ropes; and still others standing and talking to one and other. The place almost looked like it had been forgotten by time or something, it was amazing. This was basically the exact kind of place James had been imagining all along... He stared at one of the longest docks and pictured Wipley's beat up boat as it came floating in towards the shore that day fifty years ago. He couldn't believe it had all taken place right here in this very town. The place he had been learning and reading about for a countless number of hours now.

As they continued slowly down the road, the driver pointed out different places to eat and tourist attractions. Everyone in the van was so preoccupied looking around that no one had heard the driver when he asked them where they would like to be dropped off at.

"Is this okay here sir?" the man repeated a little louder this time.

"Oh, I'm sorry," Pop said. "So, where did you say is the best place to eat?"

"The Lobster Spot's got the best seafood around," he said.

"What do you think boys?" Pop asked, looking back at James and Neil who were still in awe of the place.

"Sounds good," Neil said.

"Yeah, sounds good," James repeated, enjoying the relief he felt as he looked around the town and thought of it as a halfway point and yet another confirmation of the document's validity.

The driver pulled the van into a small parking lot and turned around.

"It's just around the corner there on the right," he said. "Here's the hotel's number you can give them a call when you're ready to be picked up."

"Okay thank you very much, we've been looking forward to coming here for awhile," Pop said, handing the driver a tip.

"This little town has some history I know that, I'm surprised you have even heard of it though, most people that come to Florida usually stay in one of the cities. The ones that come down here usually do because of the hotel," the driver said.

"Well, we thought it'd be nice to explore off the beaten path a little. By the way do you know where a boat guide named Perkins lives out here, I thought we might go out on the ocean tomorrow," Pop said.

"I'm sure you mean Walter, he's the only one that does that sort of thing— yeah, his place is down past town a little. About what time were you thinking of going out tomorrow?" the driver asked, as James and Neil got out of the van.

"I was thinking sometime in the morning," Pop explained.

"That shouldn't be a problem, just give the desk a call in the morning and I'll be able to run you back over here."

"Well, I thank you kindly and I'll give you a call when we're done," Pop said, opening the door and getting out with help from Neil and James.

As they walked in front of the row of buildings, James wanted to ask everyone they passed if they had ever heard of the legend of Hunter Wipley before. He didn't though because Pop had instructed both he and Neil not to ask anyone about the story. He didn't think it was such a good idea if people knew exactly why it was they were down there, and James understood how crazy the whole thing sounded, so he kept it to himself.

"This town is just like I pictured it," he told Pop and Neil as they entered the front door of the restaurant. That afternoon James, Pop, and Neil had one of the best seafood dinners ever. The waitress was kind enough to tell them stories about South Harbor but, to James dismay, none of them were about Hunter Wipley. James figured that it was probably so long ago that nobody remembered the tale. He could tell Neil was just dying to ask someone, but like always they both did as Pop had instructed.

Afterwards, they all walked around the town and then along the shoreline. The sun was beginning its long descent downward and the sky had a deep red and orange color to it. Sea gulls glided above the small waves and James could see rocks of all sizes covering the land below the lighthouse hotel; the rocky shore line jetted far out to sea and then slowly disappeared. Everything seemed pretty much normal about the town despite its antique appearance. The people were friendly and with all the water that surrounded the place it was easy to imagine why an explorer like Wipley would choose such a secluded place like this to live. As the sun finally began to be swallowed by the horizon, Pop made the call back to the hotel so they could send the van for them. Everything was going according to plan so far with great results, but they would soon all realize that something's you just can't plan for.

# Chapter Fifteen
# The Problem Before the Plan

    Back at the hotel now, James and Neil boarded the elevator with Pop limping closely behind. A few moments later and as the doors were starting to close, Michael, the front desk clerk, hit the call button on the wall which caused the doors to instantly retract.
    "Sorry, Mr. Kelly," he said, "but I promised to inform you that you received several phone calls from your daughter-in-law, Judy, and a Miss Nichols?" He looked up from the piece of paper he was reading. "They both wanted you to call them back as soon as possible and wanted me to deliver the messages to you personally."
    "Thanks Mike," Pop said, handing the man they had become friendly with a tip and taking the paper.

As soon as the elevator doors closed Neil looked over and tried to read the note in Pop's hand. "The lady from the lab called huh, well, what'd she say?" he excitedly asked.

"It only says what times the calls were received and from what number. It does looks like Miss Nichols called several times though. I'm guessing she must have gotten the fingerprint results back from the document... When we get back up to the room why don't you go ahead and call your mother while I call Miss Nichols."

"Why do I have to call mom, she's going to talk my ear off," Neil stubbornly said.

"I'll call Judy," James interrupted.

He was so excited to hear Miss Nichols had called that he wanted to make sure Pop could call her back immediately. Once the elevator reached the ninth floor Pop limped into the hall and over to his room alone. James could tell Pop was just as anxious as he was to hear the news, and as he continued on down the hall he hoped the phone call to Miss Nichols wouldn't take too long. He also secretly wished that somehow the phone lines would accidentally become crossed and he would be the one who got to talk with her. *Yeah right, like that's ever going to happen.*

As James and Neil continued down to their room and entered, Neil plopped down at the foot of the bed and flipped on the TV, while James walked over to the table and picked up the phone. He punched in the number to Neil's house and waited. It began ringing and as it did Neil gave him an appreciative thumbs up and mouthed the word, 'Thanks'.

"Hi Judy, yeah it's James..." he said, as Judy greeted him softly. "Yes, everyone's fine down here, Pop's in the other room making a phone call and Neil is..." James paused and looked over at Neil who was pointing at the bathroom. "Neil's in the bathroom... Uh-hu, yeah, it's great down here we're having a lot of fun, uh-hu, okay... I will... Thanks, you too bye," James finished and hung up the phone. During the call, he had thought Judy sounded different, not like her usual cheery self.

"Thanks a lot, you just saved me a half-hour long phone call. So, what'd she say? I can't believe she didn't bug you anymore than that," Neil said.

"Um, that's the thing; she kind of sounded upset," James said, as he walked over and sat down at the end of the other bed.

"Really, did she say anything's wrong?" Neil looked over and asked.

*HEALING WATER*

James furrowed his brow. "No, she just asked how we were doing and told me to have Pop call her back as soon as possible."

"That's weird, I wonder what she wants to talk to Pop about. Why didn't she just tell you whatever it is and have you tell Pop?" Neil said.

"I don't know, maybe it's something personal?"

For the next twenty minutes the boys sat and watched TV quietly as they waited for Pop to come tell them what it was Miss Nichols had found out about the document.

"Man, what's taking him so long?" Neil finally said, glancing at the door.

"You know Pop, he's probably writing everything down and asking all sorts of questions," James said.

Only moments later there was a light knock at the door. James jumped up as the door slowly opened and Pop came limping in, his cane in hand and a look of mild uncertainty on his face.

"So, what'd she find out?" Neil asked, as he stood up and joined James and Pop at the table they had both gathered around.

"Well," Pop said, after sitting down and taking out another piece of paper. "She said that she was only able to positively identify two individual sets of finger prints from the document samples we gave her. She did find several other prints, most likely including ours', but she said these were the only two that came up in the worldwide database."

James didn't really care about the details this time, he just wanted answers.

"Who are the two people? Do we know them?" Neil impatiently asked, taking the words out of James' mouth.

"Just put it this way, the results are puzzling to say the least. It seems the first set matches a dangerous criminal by the name of Bill Atwood; he's a known murderer that's been on the run from the authorities for years." Pop paused as he noticed the concerned look on the boys' faces. "Now we have no way of knowing how old these prints are so there's no reason to be alarmed... This man Atwood could have handled the document years ago."

"But you're saying this could have been in the hands of some maniac and now we have it," Neil said, suddenly looking worried.

"Calm down Neil, we're almost grown ups we have to be able to handle this kind of situation sooner or later," James said. "You're tough anyway, what do you have to worry about?"

"Yeah, I guess you're right," Neil said, looking down at himself proudly.

"Thank you James." Pop said.

"Okay, what about the other set of prints?" James asked.

"It matched with your step-mother's boyfriend, Rex Hanson," Pop said, as he handed over the notes he had written to James. "This is his correct full name, right?"

"Yes, that's it, Rex D. Hanson," James said, as he thought about the results.

"That's it, she found some murderer's and Rex's fingerprints on the document? We knew half of that already." Neil disappointingly said.

"That's not all of it, apparently when she was doing the fingerprint scan the ultraviolet laser revealed something strange. An encoded pattern of microscopic numbers was inscribed within the document. At least, she believes they're numbers, the printing is so tiny in fact that even under the CIA's strongest electron microscope Miss Nichols was still unable to read them all. She did say however that this kind of inscription is usually numeric."

"What do the number's mean?" James asked, as he thought out loud.

"She didn't know for sure, but she said they might be part of some kind of a code, she found them running through the middle of only one out of the two pages we gave her though."

"Hidden numbers inside the document, that's weird," Neil said.

"It's not unheard of, actually scientist have been able to print an entire copy of the Bible on one single grain of rice for years—it's called laser inscription. But this seems to be even more advanced than that. This document seems to keep getting more mysterious with every new thing we find out about it," Pop said, as he shook his head and looked down at the notes he had just taken. "That along with this Bill Atwood character makes it all the more complicated still, I just don't know what to think…"

"Oh yeah," James remembered, "Judy wanted you to call her back as soon as possible, she said it's important."

"Anything specific?"

"No, but I thought she sounded upset," James said.

Pop immediately picked up the phone on the desk and dialed, as James and Neil got up and walked back over to the beds. They ignored Pop's conversation as they continued quietly discussing the latest information concerning the document.

"What do you think the hidden numbers are?" Neil asked.

"I have no idea, but it has to have something to do with my father."

"Who do you think this other guy is, what was his name Bill something?"

"Bill Atwood," James said, as he paused. "I don't know, I've never heard of him before, but think about it—how many people probably had their hands on those pages? They're over fifty years old; we were lucky Miss Nichols got any matches off of them at all."

James looked over at Pop and for the first time noticed he was speaking very quietly into the phone and had his back turned away from them.

"So, anyway what time are we supposed to meet that boat guide tomorrow?" Neil enthusiastically asked, as he sat up and faced James.

"At nine in the morning," James answered, as he eyed Pop curiously again.

While James listened to Neil go on about what he thought they were going to find tomorrow, he kept looking over at Pop who now sounded upset as he spoke in hushed tones with Judy on the phone. James silently got Neil's attention and nodded towards Pop who had turned in his chair all the way around and was now whispering again. Neil gave James a sideways look and they both quit talking as they tried to hear what he was saying. A minute later, Pop hung up the phone, but instead of turning around he stayed staring out the window in silence. James and Neil both looked at each other and put their hands up in confusion.

"What'd she want to tell you Pop, is something wrong?" Neil finally asked.

Pop hesitated and then turned around to face the boys, he scratched his white beard and slowly shook his head. James could tell he had bad news. *Oh no, what now?* James thought.

"Why don't you boys come over here," Pop said. "I've got something to tell you."

James and Neil got up and walked over to the table. They pulled up the two other chairs again and both eyed Pop intensely.

"Is everything all right?" Neil asked again.

"No, not really. Judy has just informed me of some disturbing news," he said pausing and looking up at James. "I'm afraid your step-mother's boyfriend, Rex, was brutally murdered last night James."

James froze, his face filled with shocked as his mind raced to comprehend what Pop had just said.

"Wh—what do you mean—Are you sure, I mean how does she know?" James rambled as his heart rate increased.

"She found out when she was watching the news last night. She said she saw something about a local murder of a man whose name was Rex Hanson…

She wasn't completely sure it was him until they showed a picture of Rex on the screen. After that, she knew it was the same man who lived with you," Pop paused, as James shook his head.

"I don't understand," James said.

Everyone was quiet for a moment as the reality of the event set in, then Pop apprehensively went on. "There's more," he said.

"What, what do mean more?" asked James.

"The police have a suspect in Rex's murder," Pop announced.

"Who did it?" Neil asked, his eyes widening with interest.

"They believe it was Bill Atwood," Pop said.

As soon as the words hit James' ears he realized who Pop was referring to, *the other man who left his fingerprints on the document*, he thought, *but could it really be the same person?*

"Is it, is it the same guy?" James asked

"We can't be sure yet," Pop said.

"What guy, who are you guys talking about, who's Bill?" Neil interrupted.

"I'm not sure why, but I believe somehow this is all connected," Pop continued.

"Who are you guys talking about?" Neil forcefully asked again.

"The guy with the other set of fingerprints on the document, remember Bill Atwood," James finally explained, as he picked up the piece of paper Pop had written on and showed it to Neil.

"Oh, that guy! No way, see I knew it," Neil exclaimed, as he finally realized what was going on.

James thought for a quick moment. "Hold on a second Neil, let me get this straight, Rex was murdered last night and they think this guy Bill Atwood did it? How do you know it's the same guy whose fingerprints are on the document?"

"Well, it seems like an awfully big coincidence doesn't it? And, didn't you say Rex had a lot of criminal friends just like him?" Pop asked, as he grabbed his cane and stood up.

"Yes, but I didn't think they were this dangerous."

"Let me ask you a question James, you never once heard Rex speak about a man named Bill before did you?" Pop asked.

James thought for awhile, "I don't think so…" he said, as he paced around the room and racked his brain. Suddenly, and for no particular reason at all, something came to him, like a flash of lightning the memory surfaced. "No, wait a minute, that's right," he exclaimed. "Remember when I told you guys that I answered my step-mom's cell phone and Rex accidentally told me about that floor-safe in the attic?" Both Pop and Neil nodded. "Well, before he hung up he said that he was going to meet somebody named Bill, and pick up some results," James said, as he stopped and remembered the conversation again.

"Are you sure?" Pop asked.

"Yeah, without a doubt because I remember thinking, who is Bill and what is Rex talking about."

"See what I mean, there's no way all of this is merely a coincidence. Rex and this Bill Atwood must have worked together somehow; whatever the case maybe we'll find out soon enough." Pop hastily limped over to the door.

"Hey, where are you going?" Neil asked.

"I just thought of something, I need to make another call I'll be right back," Pop said, as he closed the door behind him.

"What the heck's going on?" Neil asked, looking overwhelmed and worried.

"I don't know, but this is getting out of hand. Do you realize what this will mean if Pop's right?"

"What do you mean?"

"I mean if this guy Bill Atwood is the same one from both the document and the murder of Rex."

"What will it mean?"

"It might mean exactly what you were saying earlier; he could be after the document for some reason…"

Neil sat down on the bed again, "Oh man come on, are you serious?"

"Yes, I'm serious, look at the facts Neil… My house was torched, Debra's missing, and Rex is dead."

"Someone also tried to attack your father," Neil said, looking more worried with every passing second.

"Exactly, like Pop said this is probably all connected somehow, and that somehow could be the document."

Neil looked really concerned now as he and James ran through the facts again. It was clearly obvious that in someway all these events were in fact connected, but how and why was another story…

Before long Pop reappeared into the room, startling both the boys as he did. He rushed over and sat down at the table, rubbing his head anxiously as he contemplated the best way to deliver the rest of the bad news. With James and Neil waiting quietly, he finally told them.

"It is the same man, I'm afraid we were right. Miss Nichols just confirmed it. She had no way of knowing Rex was living with you, James, so in effect she had no reason to inform us that he was murdered. After I explained the situation to her, it didn't take long to match the prints and prove we were correct in our suspicions." Pop shook his head, "she will be faxing a mug shot picture of Bill Atwood over to the hotel, along with all the information the FBI has on him... She said he's been wanted by the police for over three years now and for a multitude of crimes. She's also checking up on the murder of Rex for us to see what else if anything investigators have found out," Pop explained.

"So, what do we do now?" Neil asked.

Pop stood up and limped over to the window again, he looked down at the dark ocean below. "Stick to the plan like always... That's really the only thing we can do."

James watched as Pop stared out across the vast dark sea. The smart old man looked worried and was having trouble hiding it. His worries had just increased tenfold with the idea of this killer Bill Atwood being connected to the document. He didn't tell the boys but Miss Nichols had also told him on the phone that when the police found Rex he was still barely alive and had whispered the phrase, 'Atwood wanted the pages'. The detectives of course had no idea what this meant, but it was how they came to the conclusion that Atwood had murdered Rex. That and they also had some DNA evidence. Miss Nichols also said that like Pop she thought it might somehow all be connected to the document. She promised to keep him informed and updated on any other new information that came out, and said tomorrow she was going to work on Rex's case some more.

*What's wrong with Pop, look at him—he knows something else and isn't telling us,* James thought as they all discussed the situation some more.

After another intense hour of conversation, covering everything again from the fingerprints found by Miss Nichols, to Rex's murder, and the encoded numbers on the document, Pop still secretly concluded this killer, Bill Atwood, might be coming for the document and thus for them too. At first, he kept this theory to himself because he didn't want to upset the boys anymore than they already were, but he didn't want to take any chances either. *James has been through enough lately,* Pop thought, *I shouldn't worry him with more problems tonight.* But he soon changed his mind though when he realized that James may have already come to this conclusion on his own.

"I think the guy who tried to attack my dad in the hospital is probably the same one who killed Rex, it all seems to be connected somehow, just like you said before, Pop," James said, as they all sat around in front of the table again.

"Well, I didn't want to bring it up tonight but I agree and I believe that we may be in some kind of danger here, I'm not sure to what extent but—"

James interrupted. "You don't have to say anymore, Neil and I already discussed it when you were on the phone, we understand what's going on," he said, figuring that he would relieve Pop the burden of trying to comfort them.

"We know if this Bill guy is after the document then he might be after us too," Neil said.

Pop felt relieved. "You're right, and I am concerned for our safety, but I don't want you boys dwelling on this and worrying about it. The last thing we want to do is let this hinder our main goal of the trip. We could all be jumping to conclusions here, I just can't say for sure."

James nodded. "We understand, so what do we do then?"

"We're going to take a few precautions just to be safe. For example, we'll move to another hotel tomorrow and stay out even longer on the ocean where it will be almost impossible for anyone to locate us."

"So, we stay out on the water and move to different hotels until they catch this psycho," Neil repeated, mainly to reassure himself.

"I think that's our best bet, and like I said before this is all just a precaution, we don't know any of this for sure so try not to let it worry you, okay?"

Pop felt grateful that the boys had acknowledged this possible threat so maturely; it also relieved a lot of stress on him knowing that they had been informed of the situation. He just hoped now that this knowledge would protect and not panic them.

It was getting late that night and James could tell, he looked down at his father's watch and saw that it was after ten. Suddenly, the phone rang. Pop reached over and instinctively picked up the receiver. "Hello, yes... Okay... Yes, thank you," he said and then hung up. "That was Michael from the front desk; he said they received the fax for us that Miss Nichols sent over, we can pick it up at the desk anytime."

"We'll go down and get it," James quickly said, attempting to prove that he and Neil were not going to be scared by the recent revelations.

"Yeah, we'll go down," Neil slowly said, seeming a little less confident than James.

"Okay, but straight there and straight back, don't forget there's a stairwell at the other end of the hall here if you don't want to wait on that slow elevator."

"Right, well, we'll be right back then," Neil said.

James and Neil left the room and stood at the end of the hall waiting for the elevator. Neil was trying to show some courage but apparently no enthusiasm.

"I'm not walking down nine flights of stairs, you volunteered me to go but I never agreed to take the stairs," Neil protested.

"I know, I already said we'll wait for the elevator."

"Oh sorry, I'm just a little tense."

James grinned. "Welcome to the club."

During the elevator ride down even James seemed to get a bit nervous. When they arrived on the first floor and the doors opened, they both hesitated to step out, but after a few seconds James finally broke the stand off and walked forward into the lobby. Neil followed close behind and surveyed their surrounding carefully. Every person walking around the hotel now seemed like a potential enemy. They arrived at the front desk and after Michael greeted them he handed James the fax.

"Look, she sent three pages of information on this guy," James said, as they made their way back over to the elevators.

"Okay, come on we'll check it out on our way back up," Neil quickly said.

"Alright, I'm coming," James said, as Neil rushed him forward.

During the ride back up, the boys examined the first page together; it contained some basic information and had a grainy black and white mug shot of Bill Atwood on it.

"So, that's the guy whose fingerprints are on the document," Neil asked, as he and James stared at the small, blurry photo.

"Yeah, and the guy who we think killed Rex. Look it says Bill Atwood right here along with his description… He has black hair and blue and brown eyes, what?" James said, checking the photograph again.

Neil also looked closely at the small face on the page. "If he has two different colored eyes you can't tell, this picture is terrible, I can't even tell what he looks like, that could be a grizzly bear for all we know…"

"Well, it does say here he's six-two and weights two-hundred and fifty pounds," James read.

"It says he's been charged with attempted murder twice and is mentally unstable. I wonder what this guy was doing with the document to begin with; I mean how'd he know about it and why would he want it?" Neil asked.

"Those are the same questions I asked when Rex stole it from my room, and I still don't know the answers, but I'm willing to bet they are the same," James said, as the elevator doors opened.

The boys hastily returned to the room and showed Pop the fax. The second and third pages of which contained the rest of Bill Atwood's history. As Pop was reviewing them he noticed something unusual. "So, that's what Miss Nichols was talking about."

"What is it, what'd she say?" James asked, as he looked over and saw Pop closely checking over all three of the pages.

"There's no history on Bill Atwood before the age of thirty, here have a look."

James took the pages and read through them. "You're right, it only goes back to when he was thirty. Look, it says here that the individual's birth place cannot be determined and background deemed incomplete. What do you think that means?" James asked.

"Maybe he didn't get into any trouble before then," Neil speculated.

"No, that's not it because Miss Nichols specifically told me to check out his background information. This must have been why… Huh, so we got a man that began life at the age of thirty, doesn't make any sense."

"It says no other records of any kind could be located on suspect before nineteen-seventy-nine," James informed them, as he continued to study the pages.

"So, he just appeared out of thin air, huh, maybe he's a ghost?" Neil joked.

Eventually, after Pop had combed through ever other detail of the fax, he decided to put everything that did not pertain to the original plan away.

"I know this is going to be an ongoing situation and naturally there's no way of ignoring it, but I want us to all focus on the real reason we're down here. Like I've told you both it never does any good to worry, we have addressed the problem and now the best thing we can all do is keep our eyes and ears open and wait for Miss Nichols to call with any further updates on the case. Okay? So, where are we at for tomorrow James, what time do we need to schedule that shuttle bus to pick us up?"

"Around eight or nine, the boat guide said he'd be there, but I think I'll give him a call in the morning just to make sure."

"Good idea," Pop said, as he yawned, "let's double-check everything and then get ready to go to sleep. I don't know about you two but it's been a long day and I'm tired."

After going over the plan and making the necessary arrangements for tomorrow, Pop told the boys good-night and went to his room. That night, Neil kept waking James up every time he heard any little noise, he did this several times until James threatened to leave the room. Finally after one in the morning, they both fell asleep and stayed asleep. They would need all the rest they could get, because tomorrow was going to be the longest day of both their lives.

# Chapter Sixteen
# The Hunt for Wipley's Island

The alarm clock shined 6:29 a.m. in bright red numbers in between the two hotel beds; James laid asleep in one and Neil snoring in the other. A moment later the numbers on the clock changed to 6:30 while simultaneously triggering the alarm.

"Shut it off," Neil moaned as the alarm clock continued to ring loudly. He rolled over slowly on the bed, opened one eye and noticed James was gone. "Where's James, oh no Pop!" Neil shouted, sitting up in a panic and looking all around.

"I'm right here," James said, as he walked out of the bathroom, "calm down."

"Oh, sorry about that," Neil said, as he silenced the alarm clock and rolled back over in the bed.

Within a few minutes, Pop limped into the boys' room dressed and ready to go. He made his way directly over to the small coffee pot in the corner and began preparing some Joe.

"It's time to get up boys you heard the alarm let's go, we have a big day ahead of us," Pop said, as he put his glasses on and began filling the coffee maker up with water. He then limped back over to the door and reopened it; there on the floor now at his feet was a fresh newspaper that had apparently just been delivered. James grinned as he watched Pop slide the paper inside the room with his cane, and then try to balance it up to his hand. *You can't say he doesn't try*, James thought, as he got up and grabbed the paper for Pop.

"Thank you, James... I didn't want to test it this early," Pop joked, as he patted his bad hip and sat down at the table over by the window. The sun was already producing light that reflected off the ocean far below. It was such an amazing view that it even drew Pop's attention away from the paper, which didn't happen that often. The sunlight quickly made its way up and across the room to Neil's bed, annoying him just enough to wake him back up. While Neil got up to get ready, bad mouthing the sun under his breath along his walk to the bathroom; James was busy on the floor going through his bag looking for the number to the boat guide. *Here it is, Walter Perkins*, he thought, as he took the paper over and dialed the number. It took six rings, but finally a man answer.

"Walt's boat rental," the man said with a scratchy, pirate-like voice.

"Yes, hello, I just wanted to confirm that we have a reservation for today," James said, rubbing his sleepy eyes in the bright sun.

"Last name Kelly?"

"Yes, that's it," James said.

"I got three of you in total and you've booked up a tour for eight hours?" the man asked.

"Um, actually we were wondering if it might be possible to stay out longer on the water, is that possible?"

"Aye, as long as you pay the two hundred dollar fee up front we can stay out as long as you like sonny," the old man said with a laugh. "But, it gets a little cold at night for the tourists."

"Okay, well we'll be there around eight this morning then, if that's still all right?"

"No problem, you just come on down to the end of the docks and you'll find me around here somewhere."

"We'll be there, thanks a lot sir," James politely said.

"Don't mention it, I'll see you all soon now."

James hung up and looked over at Pop who was busy organizing the last of the supplies and drinking his cup of coffee.

"He said he'll be waiting for us and after we pay the fee we can stay out as long as we like," James announced.

"Good, now you boys get something to eat real quickly, and then help me take down these bags," Pop elatedly said.

James felt his usual strange mix of different emotions again this morning. This time it was excitement and nervousness all wrapped up together and fighting in his stomach. He ate a cinnamon roll and had a cup of water, hoping it might help settle things down again. After everyone was ready, the boys assisted Pop in gathering all the supplies and packing the cooler, then they headed out the door and down the narrow hall.

"This is it man, can you believe it!" Neil exclaimed, his excitement boiling over. "We're about to go on an adventure like real explorers."

"I know it's pretty cool, I just hope everything goes all right," James muttered, as he helped carry the bags onto the elevator.

"Remember, don't worry, we need to focus on the task at hand now," Pop encouragingly said, as he put on his light khaki hat that matched his pants.

"Nice hat Pop," Neil beamed, slipping on a pair of sunglasses and buttoning up his white party shirt. James was still in clothing straits, so he had cut off a pair of cargo pants and made them into shorts, he wore that along with another grey t-shirt.

After making their way through the lobby, they emerged and saw that the van was already there waiting on them. They packed everything in and then took off in the same direction as yesterday. James still found it very hard to believe that in less then five minutes they would be at Walt's boat rental and then would soon be heading out on the ocean in search of Wipley's island. The whole plan was mind-boggling to say the least.

The same old man from yesterday was once again driving the shuttle-bus and said he knew exactly where Walt's place was.

"Yeah, Walt's a real good guy; he's been working these waters for all his life. I'd say you couldn't find a better set of sea hands anywhere else in Florida." The bus driver reported, as he turned the wheel and began driving them through South Grove Harbor again.

James noticed that everything looked about the same in the small town as it had yesterday. Men still lined the docks working on their boats, and the stores on the right had their doors opened again; while people walked up and down the sidewalks enjoying the warm weather and shopping. It was quickly becoming another gorgeous day out, with hardly any clouds in the sky and another light breeze. James watched out the left side of the van as the ocean waves came rolling into the harbor and then hit the shoreline and made splash after splash. At a little before eight, they pulled into a small driveway leading up to a blue all plaster building which had a large, wooden sign in the side window that read: Walt's Boat Rental, in dull red letters. As the van came to a complete stop, James was still fighting with his nerves, but the breakfast he'd eaten had helped.

He just wanted everything to go perfectly, but knew this was not the way life usually went for him, and that's what always bothered him. That coupled with the news about this killer, Bill Atwood, was enough to disturb and worry anyone. Still, he tried his best to put these thoughts in the back of his mind, like Pop had instructed him to do. He told himself not to worry, and that what they were about to do was not impossible. *This island is out there somewhere, we just have to find it,* he told himself.

After James and Neil helped Pop from the van, the driver left and they all walked up to the old house and went in. Bells hanging from the door chimed as they bounced back and forth against a dusty screen. Inside, there were stuffed fish on most of the walls and boat motors and equipment all over the floor. The smell of salt-water filled the large room as they all looked around and waited at a small counter to the left. James looked down a wide hallway to the right and noticed that there was furniture and what looked like part of a kitchen at the end. He realized the man's business must also be his home as well.

"Come on out back here, through the screen door!" a scratchy voice suddenly called out from behind the building.

James and Neil followed as Pop limped over and pushed open another old door. Below them now was the dark, wet wood of a long dock. James looked around and saw two boats tied to thick posts on opposite sides, both about thirty feet out. Each of the boats looked old and their colors had faded substantially from the sun. James could tell that they were fishing boats because neither of them had sails and they each had large outboard motors attached to the backs of them.

"Hello there," a voice called out from inside the larger boat on the right.

## HEALING WATER

"Hi," Pop said, as they all three looked over and saw a rugged, middle-aged man lying on his back working on some electrical equipment under the steering wheel.

"This damn relay switch keeps going out. I have to change it at least once a week, should only take me another minute or so," the man assured them.

"No problem, take your time," Pop kindly replied.

As they waited, James noticed two, old, blurry tattoos on both of the man's forearms. He also had a thick goatee that was a dark shade of red; along with his hair which was average length and looked blown dried by a strong wind. James could tell by his rough, scarred up hands that Walt was no stranger to hard work.

"He's got a silver tooth," Neil whispered to James as they began walking along and evaluating the long white and blue boat. It was easy to tell that this boat had seen better days; there were some dents around the bottom of it and one of the glass windows above the driver's seat was missing. The vessel had an upper and lower deck with a metal railing stretching around its entire length. As they got to the front, James saw a section of railing was bent out and looked like a silver boomerang now. The waves moved the heavy boat up and down, and as they did it pulled hard on the two thick ropes that tied it to the old dock, causing even it to sway in a rhythmic way. *Its floating fine enough*, James thought, *that's all that really matters right?*

"Hey," Neil whispered, "this is almost like the boat from Jaws, huh?"

"Yeah, remember what happens to that boat?" James reminded him, as he saw the man inside suddenly stand up. "Come on Neil, he's done."

"Sorry about that, it's nice to meet you my name's Walt," he said, in his raspy, pirate-like voice. He wore an old blue t-shirt and dark cargo pants and had to be at least six feet tall; James figured he looked around fifty years old, but was still extremely fit.

"Hello, I'm Pop and this is James and Neil," Pop said, shaking hands with the man as James and Neil did the same.

"I had to use a cane once too," Walt told Pop, as he helped him aboard the boat with ease, "Yeah, got me leg wrapped around an anchor line as it was being released, broke it here in three places... Doc said I'd never walk tha same again, that was ten years ago. Ha, proved' em wrong didn't I?" he proudly said, as he walked with a slight limp to the front of the boat.

"I like this guy," Neil told James with a grin.

Over the next twenty minutes, and after getting all the supplies aboard, Walt went over some basic rules and explained things about the boat. Pop then told Walt how he wanted to take James and Neil out somewhere around Loggerhead Island for some fishing.

"The great Gulf of Mexico, yeah I love this part of the ocean. It's not the most popular but I think it's the best place to live in tha world." Walt announced.

Pop nodded, "I did some fishing out here a few years back and it was the best time I've ever had. Thought I'd take these boys out and show them what I've been talking about for all these years."

*Here we go*, James thought. He knew that the island Pop had mentioned to Walt was within twenty miles or so to the where the document claimed the island with the healing water was. He also knew that Pop had a plan of how to search for the actual island without coming out and saying what exactly it was they were doing. He figured it would probably sound a little too crazy, especially to an experienced man like Walt who had most likely heard it all. Pop and the boys had briefly gone over the plan again before leaving the hotel and the idea was to let Pop handle it, and to just be polite.

After Pop finished explaining where it was he wanted to try and find this particular fishing spot, Walt untied the ropes from the dock and they were ready to go. Pop took the seat directly behind Walt, while James and Neil sat on the bench seat in back. James felt the cool ocean breeze gliding past as his heart hammered with anticipation. Soon, the boat's motors were engaged and running, the twin engines vibrated the metal boat and churned the water behind them with great power. Walt then pulled the throttle back and reversed out away from the dock, he then pushed the lever forward and the engines engaged and moved the boat easily along. It didn't take them very long to escape the small cove and begin cruising out into the Gulf. Neil wouldn't quit bouncing around beside James as he looked around everywhere and pointed at everything. Walt stayed standing as he steered the craft and navigated with an advanced digital compass mounted on the large console in front of him. James finally got up and sat on the left side of the boat in one of the two fishing chairs.

"Good idea," Neil said, as he followed him and sat in the other.

James looked out over the wavy surface and watched as they passed beach-front property and all kinds of other boats on the water. A sail boat glided easily past in the opposite direction, with its colorful array of sails flapping around in the wind like a giant flag from some unknown country. Some time later, Neil jumped up and pointed at a large cruise ship that was docked along the Florida Keys, he said something, but it fell on deaf ears because of the noise from the engines. James nodded anyway and went back to enjoying the pleasant ride.

After chopping along at around twenty knots for almost an hour, James figured they must be out past all the normal routes now because there were virtually no ships or boats around anymore. He could still see one tiny sail boat off in the distance, but it was fading fast. Neil jumped up again and checked the boat's speed which had stayed the same so far. It seemed funny to James that Neil got so sick on the plane yet he was perfectly fine on a boat, which constantly went up and down as it encountered each wave. As they passed by a large, white buoy James saw a brown seal resting peacefully on its base, and a speed restriction symbol painted on its sides; realizing at once that this was the reason why Walt had kept the speed the same so far. He figured it wouldn't be long before he pushed the throttle down and they went faster.

It was almost ten-thirty now and the sun was about two-thirds of the way up in the blue sky, James felt its powerful rays starting to penetrate his light skin already. He had heard the sun down here was stronger but he had no idea it was this hot. Pop had already gotten out some sun block and applied it to his face. Soon James took the bottle and did the same. Since it was hard to have a decent conversation over the sound of the two engines, James just sat watching the ocean and thinking most of the time about what the island might look like. When he wasn't picturing the island in his head, James was praying silently to himself that there would even be an island.

As they passed by yet another buoy, this one with no numbers, Walt did exactly as James thought he would and pushed the throttle down. The front end of the boat immediately lifted up and they took off faster now as the engines revved and spit water out everywhere. They had covered over seventy miles so far and were now heading south west at around thirty-five knots. They were completely surrounded by water with no land in sight; it had been this way for the last half an hour. It was an eerie feeling to James as he looked around and saw nothing but miles and miles of deep, Blue Ocean. The boat continued to push its way through the waves as James looked over and noticed Neil digging through his bag of snacks. Realizing how hungry he was, he too grabbed his bag from under the seat. James looked up and laughed at Neil as he saw that he had bright orange fingers from eating his cheese popcorn.

This entire time, Pop had been reclining peacefully in his chair with a pair of tinted glasses on and an unfolded map in his lap. He also has a compass that was built into his watch that he checked frequently and a pair of binoculars that at the moment was being used as a paperweight to hold down the map. James reached into his bag of snacks and got out some chips and a banana. He was peeling the banana when Walt turned the engines' power down and looked around.

"We're about five miles from tha Dry Tortugas National Park now, we can either swing around south of it and get a great view or continue north of it and make better time," Walt loudly announced, as he took a drink from the large mug he had beside his seat.

"I'd like to make it in the least amount of time possible," Pop said, looking down at his map. "Last time I was here it took me two days to find that fishing spot, but I know I'll remember it when I see it, and I promised these boys we'd find it," Pop said, and then smiled as Neil and James both nodded their heads in agreement.

"We'll find her," Walt said, taking another drink from his mug and wiping off his goatee, "I'll see if I can't bump it up a few more knots and get us out there by Loggerhead in less than an hour."

"Sounds good," Pop said, as he looked down and checked the map.

James finished his banana but decided not to have any chips; with the suspense and excitement that were filling his stomach there really wasn't any more room for food. He scanned out over the water in the direction where Pop said the first island of the Tortugas should be, and watched the horizon patiently while the boat continued zipping over the waves. Soon the outline of land appeared, it was a dark dot at first, but slowly grew bigger and bigger as Walt turned the boat to the right and pointed over towards the land.

"That's part of Tortugas National Park Islands," Walt shouted. "This here is Bush Key Island!"

James watched as trees along the shore of the island came into focus, he saw birds flying all around it and beautiful plants of all kinds with lush green leaves and flowers. The sand on the beach was pure white and James couldn't imagine anything much more inspiring than this. It was like something out of a dream.

They cruised along side of the round island about one hundred yards out. There were no clearings in the thick brush or trees that would enable James to see further in, but this view alone was breath-taking enough; and James thought that this feeling must have been close to what Columbus had felt whenever he first laid eyes on the Americas. How great it must have been to discover, above all, a new land!

As quickly as they had come upon the island, and they were already gone past it. James looked back and watched as it slowly faded. It grew smaller and smaller until eventually it was swallowed up by the massive ocean again. James looked around the boat and noticed Pop was searching over the map constantly now. Pop looked at his watch and then took his pencil and marked a spot on the large detailed map. Walt reached over and pulled the throttle back up, the motors immediately slowed as he stood up and looked around. James suddenly realized that they must be getting close to Loggerhead Island. He looked at the clock on the display board beside the steering wheel and read that it was a little after twelve, it had taken them almost three and a half hours to get this far out.

Walt then aimed the boat slightly to the left as they continued forward to the south. Everyone was watching for the first sight of land again, it had almost become like a game of some kind. After a little while, Neil jumped up and spotted the second island.

"There it is," he yelled, pointing with a smile on his face as James looked over and saw a small green strip of land coming into view.

A few minutes later they were idling along closely to its beach. James noticed that this island was even bigger than the first one. He noted that even though Bush Key was long it wasn't nearly as wide as Loggerhead. *I wondered how big the island is we're looking for,* he thought, *it can't be very big if it's so unknown.* As he looked out and realized how enormous the sea actually was, the idea of such a place existing now seemed to be even more plausible. *If the earth is seventy percent water and it took us this long to find all of it, why couldn't there still be places in the ocean no one else has found yet?* It seemed like a logical question, and one he hoped would soon become rhetorical.

James got out his binoculars from one of the bags; he knew that they would definitely come in handy during this phase of the trip. Finally, Walt shut the motors off completely; the sudden silence was stunning and it took a moment for James' ears to fully adjust. He watched as Pop studied his surroundings and made pencil marks on the map again.

"Alright mate, I think it'd be best if we circled around tha island starting a quarter mile out and gettin wider with every pass," Walt consulted.

"Okay, I know I'll remember the fishing spot when I see it... I think I've even got some coordinates around here somewhere," Pop said, pretending to search his pockets. "Yes, here we go," he said, pulling out a folded piece of paper and reading off the numbers to Walt. James had the real numbers memorized and knew Pop did too. He realized that when Pop didn't give the exact location it had to have something to do with his strategy. James figured calling out the exact coordinates of the island and then going straight to it would have probably been a little too obvious; he knew Pop wanted it to sort of look like an accident if and when they found the island.

"Is there anything that stands out about this location?" Walt curiosity asked.

"I thought I mentioned there's a small sand bar that runs up and down the area," Pop said, never looking up from the map.

"Really?" Walt surprisingly said. "Well, now I got to see this, lord knows a sand bar out this far would have to be quite a spot."

"That's what I've been telling these boys, it's like something sent from heaven and the fish just congregated there all the time. I caught a five foot marlin out here last time, that fish had almost a three foot long sword-head on it," Pop said, looking out at the ocean as if he was remembering the epic battle.

"Well, I'm all set up for any kind of fishin, so ya just let me know. I'll start around these coordinates and we'll work our way around tha area, sound all right?" Walt asked.

"Yes, that sounds fine," Pop remarked. "You boys keep your binoculars close now, and call it out if you see anything."

James and Neil both nodded as they strapped their binoculars around their necks. Walt started the engines back up and hit the throttle again. The front end of the boat rose up this time so high that James couldn't see over it for a few seconds, slowly it came back down and leveled off. Loggerhead Island seemed almost even more beautiful than the Tortugas Park Islands, but James paid very little attention to it since he was now completely focus on finding the unknown island from the document.

The reality of what he was doing did not actually set in until around the time when he first looked through the binoculars. For some reason, it was then that everything dawned on him. He once again felt overwhelmed with excitement

## HEALING WATER

and energy as he scanned along the ocean for another island. Walt turned the boat again to the left and then straightened it out. They skimmed over the water with ease, but the waves made it somewhat difficult not to hit yourself in the face with the binoculars, which by the sounds of it Neil had already done a few times.

"Ouch," Neil exclaimed, as he looked over at James and rubbed his right eye.

"This seems to be around the area," Walt yelled to Pop over the engines as they slowed down some. James, Neil, and Pop all had their binoculars up now and were looking in every direction. Walt kept the boat cruising around at ten knots or so in an elongated circle pattern. James couldn't have found a better guide for this trip; Walt was easy-going and very patient. He seemed to be at home on the water and the role fit him to a 'T'.

This system of searching went on for over an hour before Pop finally asked Walt to go out west about a mile further. James knew that now they would have to be very close to the exact latitude and longitude given in the document. James gave Neil a nod as if to say this is it, and Neil immediately understood and gestured for him to come to the back of the boat.

"We're really that close huh?" Neil asked James, as he leaned over towards him.

"We have to be, I'm almost positive that we're near the coordinates given in the document. Just keep your eyes peeled," James said, over the noise of the engines.

James and Neil, along with Pop, looked all over the ocean for the next hour as Walt cruised along slowly in another oblong circle. James looked up and even saw Walt searching the horizon with his binoculars every once in awhile. But, to their disappointment, no one spotted anything resembling land.

Some time after two o'clock Pop decided they should stop for lunch. Walt cut the engines again so they could all get a bite to eat and use the restroom. Everyone welcomed the break with open arms, the boys especially, they had no idea how much being out on the ocean actually took out of you. Walt was the last one to go down into the galley of the boat and as he did Pop leaned over and got the boys' attention.

"You're doing a good job guys. We just have to stay patient, it's out there even if these coordinates aren't perfect they at least put us in the right vicinity. We'll all keep looking and have Walt continue to move around in different areas. I've marked all the locations so far so we won't have to worry about back tracking any," Pop said, as James looked down and examined the small circled areas Pop had drawn on the map each one connected by a line indicating the route taken to get there. James couldn't believe it, they had barely covered any area on the map at all. He was still having trouble grasping just how huge the ocean really was; this map was yet another stunning reminder of how daunting the task was that lay ahead. He remembered learning in school that water covered seventy percent of the earth, but until now it had not had any impact whatsoever on his life.

"Do you think we should look farther out?" James quietly suggested to Pop. "Remember Wipley said in the pages that his compass went haywire when he was around eighty five degrees west and twenty-seven degrees north. Since the document's final statement as to the location was different maybe it's somewhere in between the two.

"That's exactly what I was thinking," Pop said.

"Yeah, me too," Neil said, and James looked over at him and grinned.

"Anybody up for some coffee?" Walt suddenly called from below.

Neil looked around as James shook his head. "Pop does, but that's it," he yelled back down.

At two-thirty in the afternoon they returned to the search, and all continued watching the horizon for the next two hours. Everyone stayed focused out to sea the entire time, but the work was beginning to grow monotonous. As the clock reached five p.m. James tasted the first faintest hint of failure arising and hated it. Neil had taken to eating snacks with one hand while holding up his binoculars with the other. Pop meanwhile continued his detailed mapping of the searched areas; James looked over at the maps every now and then, and saw that it was peppered with dozens of small circles and many lines. They had covered basically the entire area where the document said the island was, and no one had seen even the slightest bit of land since Loggerhead Island; it seemed there was nothing out this far but ocean. Walt slowed down again and seemed to be picking up on the defeated feeling going around the boat.

"We got 'bout three more hours of the daylight left—do you want to keep looking and go back in tha dark or not?" Walt said, "I don't mind it either way," he assured Pop.

"Let's head north some, then we'll search in circles to the east and slowly make our way back to South Grove," Pop said.

"Aye then," Walt throatily said.

James ripped open a can of soda, foam dripped down the sides of the red can as the boat rocked back and forth with the waves. He felt like his energy was getting low so he opened a candy bar and took a bite; above all he wanted to stay focused and optimistic. *It's okay; it's still the first day,* he told himself, as he argued with his conscience that kept telling him they were looking for something that didn't exist. Nevertheless, to keep his spirits high he kept returning to the thought of possibly helping his father. This was more than enough to keep him motivated and searching the sea.

As evening began to take shape, the sun almost seemed like a tyrant now. Hanging there, blazing its rays through the sky and onto the boat relentlessly. Even though it was after four in the evening, it still felt like it was burning right through the multiple layers of SPF 40 sun block James had rubbed on. He wished that at least a few clouds would make their way out and help block the burning, yellow nuisance. James could already feel that his neck, face, and arms were burnt. Either way he knew neither he, nor Pop, or Neil were going to give up this easily; no matter how sun burnt or tired they got, if the island was out there they were going to find it.

Once James had finished his can of soda and candy bar, he felt the sugar re-energize him and he went back to searching the ocean with new found hope. He told himself that at any moment now he was going to turn his head one way or another and see a small island. He and Neil began working together as a team now, with one on the right side of the boat and the other on the left. They both looked from side to side, and with Pop in back it made a three person watch tower that they felt nothing could get by. Walt was still steering the boat around in large elliptical circles as the search continued on.

Eventually, as the evening stretched out and gave way to a deep red sun set, they all realized they were not going to find the island today. They were finally forced to give completely up after the sun made its way so low on the horizon that no one could see very well any more. Walt got out a couple flash lights and handed them to James and Neil.

"They only shine 'bout forty feet out, but they'll bounce right off a sand bar," Walt explained, as Neil pointed his around and tried to continue the search. James was impressed that Neil had stayed so devoted despite their failure; he knew he truly wanted to help James do this no matter how long it took. James on the other hand was becoming less enthusiastic with each passing minute.

"I think we should call it a night boys," Pop finally announced, squinting as he looked out over the dark, choppy ocean water. "We'll come back tomorrow and try it again... If not we'll just be wasting our time out here in the dark...What do you think Walt?"

"Aye, you're probably right there, Pop," Walt said, as he sat down and flipped a button that turned lights on in front of the boat.

"Well, that's it for today," Neil said to James as they sat back down in the rear of the boat.

"I'm starting to worry this isn't going to work out like I thought it would," James admitted as he felt the cool breeze now rushing past his sun-burnt skin.

"Man, look at him," Neil said as he nodded over at Pop who was still examining the map with his small flashlight. He checked his compass and GPS watch and then made another mark. "He's not going to give up that easily and neither am I... Heck, I didn't think we'd find it on the first day anyway."

"You seriously didn't?" James asked.

"No, I figured we'd probably have to come out here for at least a few days."

"But what about the document and the exact coordinates, I mean it didn't work out, we looked there—so where do we search at tomorrow?"

"Everywhere around that area, Pop knows where else we need to go," Neil confidently said.

*Maybe Neil's right*, James thought, *Rome wasn't built in a day, right?* He let this thought set in as he stared out at the ocean waves ahead of the boat. The lights lit up the very tops of them as they rolled along sideways for what seemed like forever. It was completely dark now and James couldn't see more than a couple feet in front of him. He tried to look out and find the Tortugas islands again as they cruised by but it was impossible. He was not even sure where they were, so instead he began looking up at the sky.

"Look at that," James said to Neil, pointing up at the black abyss that seemed larger and closer than ever. It looked just like a black velvet sheet with hundreds of diamonds spread out randomly all across it.

"That's awesome," Neil shouted. "Look, there's the big dipper!"

Night time on the ocean is a very strange and vastly unfamiliar place. James could see how easily it would have been to get lost and think you're somewhere else. It was a very dream-like feeling to be riding across the water in the dark, and it made goose bumps appear several times on James' arms. Walt wasn't lying when he said it got cold at night; the difference in temperature from the day to the night was like, well, day and night…

By the time eleven o'clock rolled around, Pop and the boys were just about out of it. Walt told them that if you're not used to being out on the water all day it can take everything out of you and it certainly had.

"It doesn't seem like much work, but it can really be the hardest of kinds," Walt said, above the noise of the engines, as James and Neil fought to keep their eyes opened. "That sun reflects off the water and drains you of all fluids; you guys will probably sleep like babies tonight, yes sir, you'll wake up every couple hours crying." Walt joked, and Pop laughed while the boys barely chuckled.

Being tired and sun-burnt was not the only problem either, along with that their muscles were also sore from bouncing around all day. Now James understood why back in the old days sailing across the ocean was so hard and dangerous. He leaned back against the seat and felt his eyes starting to close; the air almost felt good now as they cruised along in the darkness atop of what looked like a sheet of black ice. As he watched the pitch black pass he was beginning to think they were lost. A moment later, he saw lights on the shoreline and immediately sat up.

"Hey, we're back," he told Neil who was lying sideway on top of his backpack.

"What, really?" Neil said, as he looked around. After a little while of cruising through the marina they finally arrived at the docks.

"I hope you gentlemen had a good time, hopefully tomorrow we'll have better luck at finding that spot you're looking for. I know you're tired so I'll drive ya back up to the hotel so you don't have to wait on that van," Walt said, as they all collected their things from the boat. Even though Walt was a man of few words James felt that he was a genuinely nice person. The kind you don't find very often these days.

"Thank you Walt," Pop said.

"What time should I expect you all tomorrow?" Walt asked. "I'll tell you what, here's my home number you just tell me a time and I'll pick ya up."

"You don't have to do that," Pop said, after they all got off the boat.

"No, I insist, haven't had polite tourists down here in a while and you and your boys are good company, I respect that," Walt said.

"Thank you, we enjoyed it, you're a true professional…" Pop said. "How does seven o'clock sound?"

"That's fine, just fine...."

James and Neil were dragging their feet as they walked along the dock to Walt's truck.

"You know I might know a trick or two that could help us find that sandbar of yours tomorrow," Walt suddenly announced after they had packed up the truck and was on the back to the hotel.

"We're open to suggestions," Pop said.

"All right, well if you need anything else, anything at all you don't hesitate to call. Not many people know this town like I do."

"Okay, we will," Pop promised.

James and Neil waved as Walt pulled out of the hotel parking lot and drove off. They gathered their bags and followed Pop into the hotel. Before going to the elevator Pop stopped by the front desk this time to check for messages. There were two again one from Judy and one from Miss Nichols, they both said to call back as soon as possible.

"It's like déjà-vu," Neil said, as they staggered into the elevator.

The elevator bell sounded for the ninth time and the doors opened. The boys followed Pop to their room and went in, they were all so tired that no one noticed the doors on the left hand side of the hall were both standing wide open and their frames were partially damaged.

As soon as James and Neil walked into the room, they both collapsed on the bed while Pop sat down at the desk and picked up the phone. The room was quiet as Pop made his first call to Miss Nichols—even though it was midnight the message said to call her back regardless of the time. James lay on the bed with his eyes closed, but he could still hear Pop's telephone conversation.

"Hello, yeah it's Pop... Yes...okay what is it?" Pop said as he turned towards the desk with the phone to his ear. "Are you sure... I will, don't worry... Okay, I'll call you back, thanks, bye."

James opened his eyes and sat up. The tone in Pop's low leveled voice sounded troubling.

"What's wrong?" James asked, as Pop lifted the receiver again.

"Hold on a second, James," he said as he pressed one button. "Michael this is Mr. Kelly... I don't think so, but I need to know if there is anyone else staying up on the ninth floor now besides us?" Pop asked in a very hushed voice. There was a long pause, "Okay, well, I think you better send him up now, we might have a problem."

James looked over and saw Neil passed out on the other bed. Fear flooded into his body like an electric tsunami. "What is it Pop, what's wrong?" he asked again.

Pop grabbed his cane and got to his feet, he quietly limped over to James, "Miss Nichols just informed me that the police have tracked Bill Atwood down to Florida, she thinks the same thing we do and she said they believe he may be in the Fort Myers area. I've told Michael at the front desk about our situation."

James' face turned pale. "What situation, what do you mean, how'd Bill know—"

"I have no idea," Pop interrupted, "but we need to get Neil and get out of here right now… Just try and stay calm, I'm going to call Walt, you wake Neil and pack only the essentials."

James couldn't believe what he was hearing. He had escaped one dangerous environment to only replace it with another. *Why me*, he thought as he carefully shook Neil awake.

"Shhh, you need to get up we have to leave," James whispered.

"Why, what's wrong?"

"I don't have time to explain just help me pack come on."

While James and Neil hastily packed, Pop was busy on the phone with Walt. James could tell Pop was asking him for help, and luckily for them Walt was true to his word, he was indeed a good man. They had all learned on the boat that Walt had a wife once, but she died and they never had any kids. Fishing had become his life and he lived a simple one at that. If anyone would help them out of a situation like this it would have to be a man like Walt.

Before Pop could even finish explaining their dilemma, Walt had already agreed to help out and said he would be there in a five minutes to get them.

"You boys almost ready?" Pop asked, as he grabbed his cane and pushed himself up.

"Will someone tell me what's going on?" Neil said, as they heard the elevator doors opening and then heard voices in the hall.

"Get over here both of you now," Pop softly demanded, as he quickly limped over to the door and looked out the peephole.

The voices in the hall way grew louder and suddenly there was a thump in the other hotel room Pop had rented.

"Stay back, I think something's going on," Pop said, the concerned look on his face said a thousand words.

It was incredible, it appeared their worst fear had come true; somehow Bill Atwood had tracked them down. It sounded like he was in the next room over, Pop's room!

"What's happening?" James asked, as he and Neil stood behind Pop as he watched out the peep hole.

"I'm not sure I can't see anyone," Pop quietly said.

James and Neil stood tired and shaking nervously with bags strapped around both their shoulders.

"We can't just stand here, we need to go," Neil frantically said.

Pop put his hand up. "We go at the wrong time and—"

Without warning a loud crash rang out. It almost sounded like whoever was in Pop's room was trying to come through the wall.

"Okay, remember the stairwell—we're going to make a break for it on three," Pop quickly explained, "Out and to the right, ready, one, two, three."

As soon as Pop pulled the door opened and limped out, two men from the next room over burst out into the hallway, just as the elevator door opened and Michael and his brother emerged and engaged the two men. Pop was moving amazingly fast, as he led the way down the hall and away from the violence. As James followed closely behind Neil, he looked back just in time to see the two men trying to fight off Michael and his brother. One had a pistol, but was on the ground grappling with Michael and losing. The other larger man was trying to elude and get around Michael's brother and for a split second James looked back and locked eyes with the vicious man. A split second later and Pop was at the stairwell door yelling for the boys to go. James whipped around and followed Neil in, his senses heightened tenfold by the adrenaline coursing through his veins.

"I want those pages!" James heard one of the men yell from behind him, the voice echoed down the concrete stairwell as the door slammed shut behind Pop. Within a couple seconds, the noise from the fighting soon faded, and now all they could hear were their own footsteps and heavy breathing as they all three raced for their lives down floor after floor.

"Is he coming, is he behind us?" Neil gasped as he turned another corner and ran down another section of steps.

Suddenly something dawned on James. "I saw him, he had, two different colored, eyes," he panted, as they all continued to run. "We were right, it was him!"

"Just keep moving, come on boys!" Pop shouted, as he limped in pain behind them. "We're almost there."

The stairs ended on the main floor and out to a door which opened to the far side of the building and outside.

"Come on follow me," Pop gasped, as he suddenly changed directions and almost went down from over straining his hip. "Ow!" he yelled, as James and Neil rushed over and grabbed him.

"You okay Pop?" Neil shouted, as he and James helped him up.

"Just get me to the parking lot that way. Walt should be waiting for us."

The boys had two bags on their backs and Pop hanging over each of their shoulders. They were tired, sunburned and scared to death, but adrenaline is an amazing chemical during these fight or flight situations. They managed to drag Pop around the building and into the parking lot in front. As soon as James spotted Walt standing outside his truck with a shotgun in hand he felt relieved.

"Over here, Walt! Help!" he yelled out as Walt put the gun in back and rushed over.

"What happened to him is he hurt badly?" Walt asked, as he took James' place and grabbed Pop.

"No, I'll be all right, it's just my hip," Pop strained.

Walt and Neil helped Pop into the front of the truck, as James threw the bags in and jumped in back. Once they were all in, Walt took off and left the parking lot in a hurry.

"Don't go straight to your house, drive around and make sure we're not being followed please," Pop woefully said, as he clinched his hip in pain.

Neil leaned forward, "Are you sure you're all right?"

"I'll be fine, don't worry about me," Pop dismissively said.

"Nobody will be able to follow us through here," Walt announced, as he turned off and went down some dirt road into a wooded area. "Is everyone else all right? Did they get the guy?"

"We don't know," Pop said, "the last thing we saw was the brothers who own the hotel fighting Bill, thank God for those guys."

"You think they'll be okay?" James asked. "I saw a gun in that one guy's hand."

Pop craned his head around. "They were both in the army they can handle themselves, plus Michael told me he was calling the police before he came up."

"Closest police station is about twenty miles from here," Walt said, "That's why most people who live out here usually have the background those brothers from the hotel do."

"You boys sure you're all right?" Pop asked again. "I never expected this to get out of hand like it did... If I would have known it was going to escalate so quickly I would have been better prepared for you guys," he disappointingly said, as if he had let James and Neil down.

"We're okay, seriously, I just can't believe he found us," James said.

"What'd the guy look like, what else did you see?" Neil asked James.

"I think I saw Bill, but it was only for a second. Did you hear what he yelled?" James asked, as he watched the dark trees pass by the truck.

Neil nodded. "Yeah, I thought he said something about the pages, didn't he?"

"I think so... And the thing is we don't even have them."

"That's one thing we did right," Pop said, as he held his hip tight. "But I guess it wouldn't have made a difference either way though. This madman thinks we have those pages and seems to be willing to do anything to get them."

Walt made another sudden turn to the left and the truck went down another deserted, back road. Over the next half an hour, Pop explained most of their situation to Walt as they drove. He never asked a single question, but said he believed they were good people and he would continue to help them despite the danger.

"That's what people should do for each other," Walt said. "I'd hope someone would be willing to help me if I was in trouble."

By one in the morning, Pop and Walt finally decided it was safe enough to head back to Walt's house. After they got there, Walt and Pop locked the place down and the four of them camped out in the basement living room beside the fireplace Walt had lit. As the fire warmed the room, Pop went on explaining almost everything else to Walt. He told him what they were really doing down in South Grove Harbor. He left out most of the details, but told him the most important parts, about the document and how they were trying to save James' father. Walt was the most understanding anyone could have ever been about the situation. He still didn't say much, but only had one question, and that was: what else could he do to help? Pop and the boys assured Walt that he had already helped and would be most grateful if he would just continue to take them exploring in the gulf for this island.

"I've always been a skeptic myself, but I have to admit there's plenty of water and things out there that I still have not seen. If an island like tha one in your story did exist, the Gulf of Mexico would be a perfect hiding spot for it," Walt admitted.

The conversation eventually went back to the attack at the hotel. Each one described their own separate version of the events, but they were all very similar.

"It seems to me like they were there waiting for us," Pop said. "Either they went through both rooms before we got back and probably thought we had the document on us, or maybe they planned on waiting for one of us to enter that other room alone," he speculated, as he sat with ice packs around his hip.

"I think we got lucky," James said, as he sat beside the fire and tried to put the scene behind him.

"Well, you boys try and get some rest; Walt and I are going to check on things at the hotel. Don't worry we're not going to leave, just stay down here and get some sleep."

As it got later into the night and the boys laid on the floor in front of the fire on blankets Walt had brought down, it didn't take long before they both began dozing off. They were so exhausted, and that mixed with the warmth at their feet and the solid basement walls surrounding them allowed them to feel relaxed enough to finally both fall into deep sleep. They were once again all safe and sound, at least for now. But tomorrow would change everyone's lives forever.

# Chapter Seventeen
# Search and Protect

By the next morning, everything that had happened the night before seemed like a terrible nightmare to James and nothing more. He figured it was just severe fatigue that had triggered a complex hallucination, and that was all. But after he rolled over and opened his eyes, he quickly realized he was wrong. *It was real*, he thought as he heard Pop and Walt upstairs talking. He decided to get up and go see what was going on, he was still concerned about what else occurred at the hotel after they left. He hoped they had caught the men who tried to attack them, but most of all he hoped the two brothers at the hotel who saved them were all right.

He felt better now that he had slept but his skin was still tight and very pink. He left Neil snoring on the floor and walked up the wooden steps to the kitchen. There, he immediately saw Walt and Pop sitting at the small metal table drinking coffee and going over several maps. James said hello and walked over to the table. He must have looked stiff because both Pop and Walt asked how he was doing at the same time.

"I'm fine, just a little sun burnt and sore that's all," James said, as Walt made his way over and opened a cabinet. He then walked over and handed him some old looking bottle with red liquid in it.

"Here take a teaspoon of this, it helps the worst kind of aches and pains," Walt said.

James walked to the sink and poured a little in the cap, he drank it quickly. "Ugh, tastes like licorice," he exclaimed, as Pop and Walt chuckled.

"So, what happened after we left the hotel did you go back up there last night?" James curiously asked as Walt handed him a glass of water.

"No, actually after you guys fell asleep we called up there."

"So, what exactly happened, did they get the guy's or what?"

"Well, the police said Bill escaped, but they promised he won't get far," Pop said.

"What, are you serious?" James asked, looking shocked

"I'm afraid so, they have a manhunt going on right now for him, and the detective I spoke with said that after we went down the stairs, Bill was able to fight off both the brothers and made it down the stairs too. They said they chased him but that once he got outside he jumped into a car that was waiting on the side of the hotel and took off. The good news is that he left his gun and some blood behind. The police are running a DNA test on it to see if it's a match from Rex's murder."

"Did you tell them it has to?" James asked.

"Yes I did, and Miss Nichols has informed the detectives about our situation. But they still have to prove the allegations, so we're just waiting on the DNA results and then they'll know for sure."

James shook his head and let it all soak in; as usual it was a lot of information to grasp especially at such an early hour.

"By the way, I called the hospital and checked on your father again."

James quickly looked up. "How is he?" he asked with hope in his eyes.

"Still unconscious, but the nurse said his vital signs were not well; apparently they're having trouble keeping his heart rate stable."

"Really, did they say why?" James slowly asked. Pop shook his head, James could tell that it was not looking good for his father still.

"I'm sorry James, I don't know what to say… The nurse I spoke with said she would have someone call us back tonight with an update. I didn't even want to tell you any of this, but I figured it's best you know the truth."

James nodded. "Thanks for calling and checking on him Pop," he said softly.

Pop put his arm around James. "You're doing everything you can, James, I know things must almost look impossible right now, but you're strong and you'll fight through this, I know it."

"I know how you must be feeling," Walt announced, as he stood and cooked eggs in front of an old stove. "When my mother was sick I felt like my whole world was falling apart. I know I would have done anything to help her."

James respected Pop and Walt's compassion. He knew they wouldn't lower their guards like this for many people. *They're right*, James thought, *I have to keep fighting if I want to make a difference.*

"Thanks for the support, without it I know I'd be sitting in the hospital right now doing nothing," James said.

"Hey, you want to look over the search plan we made out for the day," Pop said, trying to help take James' mind off the bad news; which seemed to never end.

"Yeah sure," James said with a grin.

"Good-man," Pop said, "good-man…Now that Walt knows what our real goal is he thinks it's best if we start here." Pop said, as he pointed out a spot on the map to the west of where they had been searching yesterday.

"There's an underwater shelf that runs along that area," Walt said, as he drank his coffee, "It's the kind of thing islands are created on top of. There's several tiny places scattered around there, places that are uninhabited and have never been researched."

That all made sense to James and also boosted his confidence. He knew they needed all the help they could get and it didn't get much better than Walt.

Twenty minutes later, after waking Neil up and filling him in on everything, they all ate breakfast and watched a news report on TV about the incident at the hotel. It was very brief, but showed Michael and his brother being interviewed by police after the attack.

"Look," Neil said, as he pointed at the small TV. "They're both all right. Man, those are some tough guys."

"We owe them a debt of gratitude, if it wasn't for their help…" Pop said, as his thoughts trailed off and he realized he didn't even need to say anymore.

After breakfast, they all hurried and got ready for another long day of searching on the water. By seven-thirty they were back on the ocean and heading almost due west. Neil acted nervous all morning, and it wasn't until they were completely out of sight of the land that he felt truly safe and turned back into his normal goofy self again. Pop was in the same seat as yesterday, and had his map out along with another older map of Walt's which was topographical. James noticed that this morning there was a light dew in the air still and it was a little foggy. Walt had the throttle down and the boat was cutting through the waves effortlessly. James had on his father's sunglasses and a captain's hat which Walt let him borrow to protect against the sun. Neil was in his usual cargo shorts, flip-flops, and this time an autographed Don Johnson button up t-shirt. The morale was high despite the fact that less then ten hours ago they were almost attacked by a mad-man who wanted the document for unknown reasons. This entire time the document had been safely left at home in Pop's safe while they carried copies of the hundred or so pages. Walt was extremely impressed with the story but said he had never heard of Wipley of the legend.

As the sun rose and covered the boat in heat, an optimism and energy filled James. He sat quietly and waited as they cruised back out to sea. Time flew by and before he knew it Walt had the throttle down again and they were speeding out to the predetermined location. Within an hour, everyone was looking around and searching for any signs of a small island. The same style of searching continued again today with binoculars and mapping of the areas.

Around noon, the energy of everyone had died down some and was replaced with hunger. The four stopped some hundred miles off the coast of Florida and ate lunch. The medicine Walt had given James really helped with his soreness, in fact, he had almost completely forgotten about it. The sun was not as bright this Monday afternoon, and James noticed small clouds had begun to fill the sky. There was also a light breeze that seemed to be picking up. Walt had on the radio that was announcing weather conditions as they all sat and ate. There had not been nearly as many boats out today. James was beginning to wonder if anyone ever traveled through these waters, because it didn't seem like it.

"Look what's that?" Neil said, as he stood on the side of the boat and ate his hoagie.

James looked over and into the clear water, there he saw a long slender fish with a spear like head.

"That's a salt-water barracuda, they're actually quite dangerous and rare for these waters." Walt explained, as he turned the radio down and started the engines back up.

They returned to the task of searching and for the next two hours they saw nothing but open water. Finally at around two in the afternoon, Neil called out land and James jumped to his feet, Pop turned so quickly in his chair that he almost fell. Walt turned the boat and aimed it at the tiny solid mass. He eased the throttle down a little further until the wake behind the boat changed forms and was now only one long white line. As they got closer and closer to the unidentified land, the excitement in the boat grew.

"That's it, I know it is!" yelled Neil as he and James kneeled beside each other on the seat and held up their binoculars. The boat bounced up and down as they skimmed along the surface of the water. Pop kept looking down at the map and then at his compass trying to judge the distance.

"That thing looks tiny," James exclaimed. "What's our position?" he asked Pop who called out, "we're a little over a mile west from the original point in the document."

When the land mass finally came into full view the excitement tapered off and then diminished. This island was little more than an extra large sand bar. No one said anything for a moment as Walt pulled the boat up next to the sandy surface. It was long and narrow and had some plant life growing on it and a few trees, but you couldn't even have built a small house on the tiny patch of land. Never the less, even though it was a let down, it somehow seemed to recharge the hopes of everyone aboard the boat.

As the search continued and evening began to develop, James saw a huge wall of dark-grayish clouds moving towards them. It looked the same way he was starting to feel, and that was terrible… Walt turned the engines off and was tuning the weather radio again and listening closely. The waves had become much larger than usual and were now rocking the boat hard from side to side. Even Pop had turned his full attention to the radio and was waiting for an update.

'Repeating the National Weather Service has issued a severe storm warning in the Gulf Coast region effective from now until one a.m. All ocean going vessels are advised to return to port and residence to stay inside and away from all windows… At three twenty one eastern standard time National Service radar indicated a large storm quickly forming off the east coast of

Florida and moving west into the Gulf region, this storm has estimated winds of approximately sixty miles per hour and is moving in a north to north-westerly line at approximately twenty-five miles per hour.'

"That storms' coming out of nowhere and it's moving in our direction," Walt said looking over wildly at Pop.

"That's unbelievable, we checked an hour ago and it was a little rain shower over Cuba, have you ever known a storm to rise up so quickly?" Pop asked, looking back over at the dark wall of clouds that were covering the horizon.

"I've seen hurricanes swell up in under a day and become deadly, but this storm has developed out of nothing. If we want to try and outrun it back to the harbor we're going to have to leave immediately and really put the throttle down," Walt said, also looking out at the sky.

James and Neil were sitting at the back of the boat and looking through their binoculars.

"I can see lightning," Neil announced.

"Yeah, me too, I can't believe this, what are we going to do?" James asked Pop.

At that moment a huge wave lifted the boat up high and dropped it hard back on the water.

"Holy crap," Neil exclaimed, as Walt started the engines and steered the boat around so they took the next large wave head on.

"Look at these waves," Walt said. "That storm must be a bad one…"

"What do you suggest we do?" Pop asked, trying to control the tone of his voice.

"If it was up to me, I'd say we should head for Key Island, the national park's got shelters and if we hurry we can beat the storm there… I just don't want us racing across these waves and not making it back to the harbor in time. I don't know if you've ever been on the water in a storm but I don't recommend it," Walt announced. Pop and James looked at one and other and nodded.

"Let's go to Key Island, we'll wait the storm out there and then head back out."

"All right then," Walt said, as he turned back around and pushed the throttle forward. "Everyone hold on to their seats and stay alert, things could get rough."

"Oh great," Neil said, as he and James grabbed the rails along the back and held tight. The boat took off and the front end rose up as it usually did, but this time it hit a large wave and became airborne for a second. The frame shuttered as it smacked back down and accelerated forward. The front end came back level and Walt angled the boat sideways a little so that they were going slowly up and over the wave instead of straight through them. James watched to make sure Pop was all right and noticed he had actually clicked the fisherman's seat belt together and was now attached to the chair. They ran up and over wave after wave as James held tight beside Neil and watched the sunny sky slowly becoming dark and cloud covered. The sunny calm day was quickly turning to a dark, wild one.

There were bright lightning bursts that exploded in the direction that they were traveling towards. Walt had said that they were only ten miles from Key Island but James couldn't even see it yet. He thought that each wave seemed to be bigger than the last, and as they sped up the mounts of rolling water the boat struggled up and then came rushing back down. Finally, Key Island came into view and Neil pointed anxiously at the sky which was now a dark grey, and the storm looked to be approaching the island from as far away as they were. James knew since they were moving twice as fast that they would get there first but it still made everyone a little nervous. Walt stood holding the steering wheel with one hand and the top of the window frame with the other. It felt like they were on some kind of giant bull that bucked in slow motion and then paused and bucked again. Almost twenty minutes had passed and now James could see the island perfectly clear. The trees surrounding it leaned sideways as strong winds blew against them.

"We're going to come around and dock on the east side," Walt yelled out as he turned the boat back into the waves. They hit head on now and slammed the boat over and over again. All the coolers and objects on the floor flew up and then came back down as they blasted through another monster wave. James spotted a row of docks just as cold rain started to fall. He grabbed a shirt out of his bag and handed Pop one. Neil draped a hooded sweatshirt over his head as the boat lunged forward and slowed. Walt took his sunglasses off and wiped the windshield with a towel as he sat down and steered the boat in between two long docks. They sputtered up closer to the island and James heard thunder crashing in the distance. After getting as close to shore as he could, Walt slowed the boat and put it in neutral, he hurried over and threw ropes onto the dock. James and Neil helped Pop to his feet and then stored their supplies below deck. The rain was pouring harder as they all climbed off the boat and hurried down the dock. Pop was still suffering from the stress he had put on his weak hip from yesterday so he could only limp so fast. After walking on shore, everyone looked around but didn't see any sign of a shelter. The place was desolate and seemed to be deserted. The four of them continued in to the dense tree line and then stopped. Walt looked around hastily and put down his bag.

"I'm going to run in and have a look around, I'll be back, you guys stay here." They watched Walt journey slowly into the jungle as the rain got even worse.

"What are we going to do if there's no shelter?" Neil loudly asked, quivering in the hard rain.

"I'm not sure, go back to the boat I guess and try to find shelter on the other island, it's only a mile away," Pop said, as they all stood together.

The wind began to whip through the trees even faster and James heard a crack and then a tree broke and fell somewhere in the woods behind them. It was becoming harder to see and his clothes were completely soaked. He tried to keep himself from shivering but the wind was just too much on top of the rain.

"I'm freezing," Neil said, trying to look into the woods. "Where's Walt?"

"He'll be back soon," Pop said, trying to comfort them.

James noticed that not even he could fight off his body's attempts to shake. As minutes slowly crept by, the storm increased its assault even more. James and Neil were struggling to hold up Pop as rain came in from the side now, hitting them all in the face. Just as a huge lighting bolt struck down somewhere along the coast Walt reappeared. His pants were muddy from the knees down and he had cuts and scrapes on his arms and face.

"I couldn't find anything, I don't understand it," he shouted, as he breathed heavily. "We'll have to go back to the boat and try for the other island."

Everyone immediately took off in a brisk walk for the boat. James and Neil were helping Pop along as he leaned on his cane and struggled to keep up pace. The waves hitting the shore were huge and loud, as they rolled over and slammed the sandy beach relentlessly. The boat rocked and heaved heavily as the four boarded it with difficulty. Walt pointed the boys and Pop into the hull as he removed the ropes and pulled the top up over the driver's seat, locking the dome into place.

"Oh man, that was terrible," Neil exclaimed, as they all dried off with towels. James had been down in this part of the boat several times to use the small bathroom but it had never sounded like this before. With the waves cracking against the hull every few seconds, they produced a deep booming noise and knocked things off the shelves. There was a small table and a bench seat which was all bolted down to the boat and that is where they all sat. James heard Walt increase the engines' power as yet another lightning bolt exploded forcefully somewhere close.

"Do you think Walt's okay up there?" Neil asked.

"He's been doing this all his life, I'm sure he's seen a storm or two," Pop said, as he dried his head with a towel.

James walked over to the steps and looked up through a small window on the door leading out. Rain was splashing against it so hard he could barely make out the dark outline of Walt. He wiped off the water from the glass and noticed the dome over the driver's seat where Walt was standing.

"He's underneath some kind of canopy, but it still looks rough," James announced.

"Oh yeah, he's got that dome he was telling me about, let me see," Neil said, walking up to the steps. Suddenly, the boat turned sideways and fell hard; knocking Neil down. He smacked his head hard against the metal wall.

"Neil! Are you okay?" James shouted as he turned around and rushed down to help him.

"What happened?" Pop asked, moving over and attempting to get up as another wave hit the boat and knocked him back in his seat.

"He hit his head," James said, looking over at Pop and then back at Neil's bleeding head.

"Can you drag him over here?" Pop said.

James grabbed a hold of Neil's sweatshirt and began pulling him backwards.

"Neil can you hear me…Neil wake up." James said as he managed to get him over to where Pop was sitting.

"Now, just prop his head up with something and get me that first aid kit," Pop instructed James. "And be careful!"

James did exactly what Pop asked over the next sixty seconds; he covered the cut on the back of Neil's head and applied pressure. The fall had caused a deep gash and knocked him unconscious. The lifelessness in Neil's body reminded James of his father.

"Is he going to be okay?" James kept asking.

"He'll come to in a minute," Pop said. "It's probably just a mild concussion… Come on Neil, come on." He fanned Neil's face with his towel.

Ten seconds later Neil opened his eyes. "What happened, where am I?" he said, looking startled and trying to sit up as the boat tossed them around on the floor.

"Just stay there you fell and hit your head, you're in Walt's boat remember?" Pop asked. The boat went up and hit the water hard again as the sound of rain got louder on the upper deck.

"Oh yeah, we're in a storm," Neil slowly said, looking up at James.

"I think it'd be best if we all stayed seated until Walt gets us to the other island, it shouldn't be much longer," Pop said.

James stayed on the floor with Neil who had his head propped up and a bandage around it. Pop sat close by on the bench and looked nervous as more and more time passed. It had been over ten minutes since they had left Key Island and now James realized that something must be wrong.

"I think I should check on Walt," James finally said, as the boat slammed down against the ocean again and Neil moaned. Pop was leaning down holding onto Neil also as he checked his watch and looked over at the steps going up to the deck.

"Maybe you should," he said to James. "Just be careful, please."

James got to his feet and walked over to the steps, he held the railing as he pulled himself up to the door leading out. The small window was being peppered so hard with rain that James thought it might break. He hesitated and then pushed it open. The wind took the door and lifted it up so hard that it pulled James out of the hull. He landed hard on the deck above with the door still in his hand. He looked around quickly and evaluated the situation. The rain seemed to be coming from all directions as a wave crashed over the top of the boat and water rushed down and hit James in the face. It was cool and salty and James almost lost his grip on the door as the boat went back down and gained momentum. *Are we sinking, what's going on*, he thought, as he searched and finally saw Walt still standing at the wheel looking desperate. His hair was soaking wet as water easily penetrated the light metal dome over him. Walt was looking around everywhere and then looked down at his compass and noticed James.

"Hey, what are you doing?" Walt yelled as another wave came over the top of the boat and James braced for the impact. This time the water hit him with such force that he lost his grip on the door and began sliding backwards towards the back of the boat.

"Got ya," Walt said, as he snagged James by the collar of his sweatshirt and pulled him back up. "Come on!" he shouted as he rushed back under the dome.

"Thanks!" James yelled, as he and Walt struggled to stand behind the wheel. "Where are we Walt?"

"I don't know! Lost my compass because of all the water inside the console! I've been circling for the last ten minutes hoping to spot the… Hold on!" Walt said, as another wave hit the front of the boat and rushed over. James looked down at the door which had lucky been slammed shut by the wind, and watched as the wave rushed over it and to the back of the boat.

"This is hurricane-like conditions, we need to find land immediately but I can't see anything," Walt yelled as he spun the wheel back and forth trying to avoid the waves head on.

"Should we call for help?" James asked, holding onto the seat behind them and trying not to fall.

"No one could find us in this, I'm just going to keep circling and hope I spot something soon… Tell Pop to check my radio down there and see if there are—hold on!"

The boat lunged up quickly and came back down hard against another wave.

"Son-of-a—oh no, you need to get down there now!" Walt yelled, as James got down and crawled to the door on the floor. He pulled it open and slipped inside just as another wave hit and rushed over the deck. He shut the door behind him and latched it just in time before water ran over top of it again. He held the rail again as he rocked side to side and walked back to where Pop and Neil were.

"What's going on up there?" Pop asked, leaning forward and holding Neil's head.

"Walt's compass is not working right, something about all the water, but he said he couldn't see anyway, so he's going to keep circling until he sees land," James explained.

"Does it look real bad?" Neil mumbled in a strange tone as he blinked very slowly, apparently still effected from the injury.

"The waves are rushing over the front of the boat; it almost knocked me all the way to the back. He said it's hurricane like conditions."

"Oh no, that's it we're going to sink," Neil exclaimed, and then closed his eyes as they got hit by another wave.

"No, we're not, you stay still," Pop commanded. "Walt knows what he's doing."

"We are lost though," James said. "Pop, he asked me to see if you would check the radio for any news about the storm's size."

James stood up and quickly snagged a small handheld radio that hung from a wire off the wall. He handed it to Pop and took over applying pressure to Neil's head with the large bandage. Pop turned the radio on and adjusted the knob. Very few stations came in; and the ones they could find didn't provide any helpful information.

"Do you think I should take him your compass?" James asked.

"It may not do much good now considering he has no idea where we are, although—"

Just then the boat smashed hard against another wave and turned sideways. Neil slid along the floor towards the wall as Pop fell over, just before Neil hit the wall of the boat James grabbed him. Pop kept himself from falling by holding onto the edge of the table.

"We're going to die!" Neil yelled hysterically.

The boat made another lunge in the opposite direction and then hit something hard. The crash sent James and Neil both along the floor and under the table, Pop slid into the corner and hit hard. James was stuck behind and under the table as Neil landed on top of him. He closed his eyes and waited for water to come rushing in, but it never did. Everything was silent except for the rain which had slowed some and was now at a normal level. The boat was suddenly motionless and felt solid again. James slowly opened his eyes and sat up. Neil was beside him and looked asleep. The room around them was a catastrophe. Clothes, food, and supplies were everywhere. James sat and listened, there was no sound of the motors, no more thunder, nothing except rain. Pop finally lifted himself back up and looked around and then down at James.

"What happened?" Pop asked as he looked around stunned.

"I don't know," James said, as he crawled out from under the table and got to his feet. "It's like the storm disappeared or something."

"That's impossible, we must be in the eye," Pop said. "Where's Neil?"

James kneeled down and examined Neil, he seemed to be breathing and his heart was definitely beating.

"He's okay," James said, looking over suddenly as the door to the deck flew open.

"You guys okay?" Walt yelled as he staggered down the steps.

"What happened, where are we?" James asked, as Neil came to.

"What's going on?" Neil mumbled.

"It's alright, we're okay," Walt announced. "I don't know how and I can't explain it but we've run aground on land somewhere. A huge wave picked us up and slammed us on top of this place. When I got back to my feet the tail end of tha storm had pasted, it's unbelievable"

Pop reached out and Walt helped him up. "Do you know where we are?" Pop asked, as he leaned down and checked on Neil.

"No idea, compass and GPS are down. I tried the radio but got nothing but static," Walt explained. "It seems as if we've run aground somewhere, on an island I believe."

"Did you say we're on an island?" James asked, as he felt a strange excitement he couldn't explain.

"Yes, and it's like no place I've ever seen before," Walt said, still looking shocked by what had just transpired. One minute the boat was about to be capsized by the storm, and then it was placed safely on top of a beach and the storm was gone; it was simply unexplainable.

# Chapter Eighteen
# The Place of Miracles

James was still standing in amazement, as Walt and Pop helped Neil back up on the bench. Without saying a word, James walked over to the steps and went up to the deck door. When he pushed the door open, he was sprinkled with very light drops of rain on his face. He emerged from the hull of the boat and was amazed by what he saw. Walt was right, they had been washed up on land and were now about ten feet inland on a beach somewhere. James looked up and down the shoreline and marveled at the bluish-white sand. It was without a doubt the most beautiful and awe inspiring place he had ever seen. He looked out behind them and to both sides and knew this had to be an island. He walked over to the back of the boat and looked down. The beach was riddled with shells of all different colors; pink, blue, white, even a few red ones. There was something different about this place. As James climbed down the ladder and off the boat, he reached down and picked up a handful of sand. It felt like silk as it slid through his fingers. He looked out at the ocean and saw the skies on one side were light blue again, he looked in the other direction and watched the dark clouds of the storm sailing further and further away. It had completely quit raining, and as the sun hit the shallow water just off the beach it turned a light green color. James walked up the beach a little and looked in through the thick palm and coconut trees. The plants within were brilliantly colored as well, and he felt a peacefulness as he stared at them. He estimated that this island had to be small because now that he was on the ground he could see each side from where he stood, of course he had no idea how long it was, but something told him he needed to find out. A minute later, James looked over and watched Pop, Neil, and Walt walk out together onto the deck of the boat. Neil was walking on his own now with a bandage wrapped around his head and fastened. Pop leaned against his cane as he gazed out towards James.

"Hey, look at this place," James said, as he ran over and climbed back up on the boat. "Pop, check the compass on your watch will you."

Pop hit a button on his watch and looked up, "This can't be right," he said, as he pressed the button again and checked one of the maps.

"Why, what's it say?" James asked again.

"It looks like we're two hundred meters north of the tropic of cancer," Pop mumbled.

"What's that mean?" Neil asked, as he looked around and still seemed a bit dazed.

"It means we're in the same spot the document said the island would be, but we were there, or, here yesterday, we searched this location... There was no island, this watch must have gotten water logged or something," Pop said, as he shook his wrist and looked around.

"Maybe it's right," James softly said, more to himself than anybody else.

"Ain't that something," Walt said. "A real life mystery and I'm a part of it."

James and Walt help Pop and Neil down the ladder and onto the beach. There was silence for a long while as everyone looked around and marveled at the place while they studied it in their own ways.

"What should we do?" James finally asked, as he looked over at Pop who was holding a bright pink shell and examining it closely.

"This place is special," Pop said to no one in particular.

"I know, so what's the plan?" James asked.

"Uh... I think we should do what Hunter Wipley did," Pop said, now gazing down into the bluish white colored sand.

"What do you mean, go explore the island," James asked, staring into the jungle.

"Precisely," Pop simply said.

The four of them all sat down on the beach and quickly devised a simple plan. It was decided that they should stick together, since Pop had the bad hip and Neil, the concussion. Walt would lead the way with Pop and James behind them watching Neil. James looked at Pop's watch and read that it was four-thirty; he was relieved to know that they still had several hours if not more of sunlight. He had a strange feeling it would be more than enough time. The foursome walked up to the scattered tree line and in through an opening between two tall tropical trees. James watched as a colorful bird flew overhead from one branch to another. It felt like every one of his five senses were being positively affected by this strange place in a way they had never been before. The ground was covered in a soft, short grass, and wild flowers and plants were growing sporadically everywhere. Walt and Pop walked slowly in a straight line as James stayed close to Neil and followed them

"This is where I wanna live," Neil said, as he looked around.

James could tell the excitement of all this was overpowering Neil's recent injury.

"It's like something out of a dream isn't it," James said.

"That's exactly what I was thinking, but I had to stop because my head hurt."

The trees in the inner part of the island began to become less dense as they progressed further inward. They had been walking for ten minutes when Walt stopped. "Did you hear that… It sounds like a person's voice."

"I don't hear anything," Neil said.

"Shh, I hear it too just listen," James said.

They all four stood still and listened, the sound of a person's voice in the distance could be heard but they couldn't figure out from which direction the sound was coming. James was positive that it was coming from the right but Neil argued the voice was more towards the left, and Pop and Walt could not decide either way. Eventually it was agreed that since the island was larger than they had anticipated they would pair up and go in both directions. Walt and Neil would go to the left and James and Pop to the right. Everyone agreed and understood that they were to walk in as straight of a line as possible and meet back up in this same spot (which Walt marked by leaving his red bandana tied to a tree) in no longer than two hours.

As each pair then separated and continued on in their own direction, James soon realized that it was a little harder to help Pop through the jungle than it had been with Neil. He didn't mind though, he was so full of excitement and energy that he felt he could have carried Pop if he had to. James looked back and could still see Walt and Neil going in a straight line away from them. Neil looked back too and waved. A little while later when James looked back again they were gone, replaced instead by thick plants and trees.

"What do you think about this place?" Pop asked, as James helped him around a large rock.

"I don't know what to think, I'm afraid if I say too much I'm going to ruin it or wake up from a dream I'm in or something," James confessed.

"Even though I don't understand how it happened, how we got here, it's almost like I don't want to know…It's a relief but it's strange though because I've always wanted to know everything, it's been like a…"

"A bad habit," James finished.

"Exactly," said Pop with a grin.

For a while they continued forward through the island jungle without talking. They both felt comfortable enough just simply looking around at all the bright colors and smelling the freshest flowers you could ever imagine. The climate was cool but not cold; the sun displayed complex patters of sunlight on the ground and made the droplets of rain left by the storm twinkle like tiny diamonds. Up ahead, James heard the sound of the voices again and he and Pop stopped and looked at each another.

"I think you were right," Pop finally said, looking back as the sound of the voice echoed over the island again. "We're getting closer."

"Come on, let's keep going," James said.

They had to navigate more slowly now since the jungle had become increasingly denser. The trees and plants had not only multiplied, but they also seemed larger in size. After they had gone another quarter mile or so in, the trees and plants had become almost twice as large as normal.

"Look at this," James said as he reach down with both hands and picked up a coconut that was the size of a basketball.

"That's twice as large as it should be," Pop said, as James handed him the huge coconut. "These trees are massive, look at all of them."

"This is just like the island Hunter Wipley described in the document. This may be it Pop, can you believe it?"

Pop put his hand on James' shoulder, "I believe good things happen to good people," he said with a smile, as another sound came echoing through the jungle.

"That sounds really close," James said, grabbing Pop and helping him move forward between two huge palm trees.

"We've got to be careful," Pop said, as he pointed at another prehistoric sized coconut. "If one of those things hits you in the head you'll look worse than Neil.

"That's not possible," James joked, and they both laughed.

Over the next ten minutes, their journey towards the noise and through the jungle became even more crowded with the unusually large trees and plants. James and Pop struggled to find a clearing they could both fit through. After James helped Pop over a row of gigantic flowers and around a few trees, he turned to walk and stopped. What he saw ahead of him almost caused him to faint. They had come to the edge of a large cliff that dropped off seventy feet to a small tear-shaped lagoon down below. James watched as a dark completed woman wrapped herself in a light colored cloth of some kind. Her hair was dark brown and she looked very healthy and happy. James' mind exploded with thoughts as Pop slowly emerged beside him and looked down. Neither of them made a sound for over a minute. The only noise came from a splash in the shimmering blue water below. James stood speechless as his and Pop's attention instantly became drawn to a dark completed man who was emerging from beneath the water and was being helped out by the beautiful woman. The similar pair laughed so freely and innocently that they almost sounded like children. Pop looked over at James and nodded his head, his eyes were bright as he quietly whispered two words. "It's real."

James then looked to the left and noticed a narrow path worn down in the grass along the ledge that sloped down and went around to a small hill on the other side of the lagoon.

"What do you think we should do?" James quietly asked, pointing out the path to the Pop.

"Let's do what we came here to do," Pop said, turning James around and following him along the path. James' heart raced as a thousand thoughts flooded into his mind. It was a dream come true, he felt like he was having an out of body experience, like it was all too much for his mind and senses to handle. As they walked carefully down the path, James periodically looked over to make sure the island couple was still there. They had walked back to a small area with a fire and what looked like woven blankets, and were sitting together. James couldn't hear if they were talking or not and was wondering what language they might speak. The angle of the path became greater as James and Pop approached the turn. Large plants were the only thing separating them from the cliff which had now lessened in height by half. After another minute, they were over on the top of the hill behind the lagoon; just above and looking down on the couple.

"What do we do now?" James whispered to Pop as they watched the couple laughing.

"We say hello," Pop said, instinctively walking forward and waving. "Hello there," he announced in a friendly voice.

The couple looked over and stood up; James was amazed to see them smiling. He followed Pop down the small hill and studied the two people as they got closer. They both looked like brother and sister, with the same dark brown hair and perfectly clear olive colored skin. James estimated their age to be in the mid-twenties. They both wore a light colored fabric of some kind; it was woven together perfectly and wrapped around the women like a dress, the man's looked more like a short-sleeved robe.

"Hi," Pop said, reaching his hand out, "I'm Pop, and this is, James."

The island man smiled and reached out clasping Pop's hand with both his. He smiled and did the same with James. The woman came closer and kissed both James and Pop on the cheek. Neither one said anything but instead only smiled and made a hand gesture to follow them. James and Pop looked at each other for a second; neither of them said a word as they followed behind the couple. They were lead around the lagoon which had steam rising from its surface and small bubbles emitting from it depths. James stared longingly at the beautiful, dark blue colored water and wondered if it was the healing water his father so desperately needed. They walked for a couple hundred feet into the jungle again until coming to a small hut made of wood and woven together with what looked like the same material the couple's clothing was made of. The square structure looked very sturdy, and James noticed four large trees on all its corners that were connected to the hut as if they were part of it. There was a round opening in the front with a huge woven covering spanning over it. The island couple stopped and the man said something in another language that James had never heard. He said it again and then James heard a man inside say something back. The couple pulled the fabric from one side of the opening and gestured for Pop and James to enter. James smiled and then helped Pop in.

Once inside, James saw candlelight and smelled burning wood. Across from him, he noticed a slim, white man who had a golden tan, his hair was gray and wild but his face looked middle aged and almost young.

"Come in, come on, don't be shy, I've been expecting someone for a long time now," the man kindly said.

"What do you mean someone?" Pop asked as the man stood up and reached out his hand.

"Well, I didn't know who would come, but I knew someone would find that document one day and follow its directions here."

"Are you saying you're, you're Hunter Wipley?" James said very slowly, with his mouth hanging open in amazement.

"Yes, that's right, I am he. Were you the one who found it?" Wipley asked, as James shook his hand vigorously.

"Yes sir, I did. I'm James Greene," James said as he and Pop sat down across the small fire from Wipley.

"We've come a long way to find this place, my name's Poplar Kelly, you can call me Pop."

Wipley smiled and with a stick he stirred at the orange fire which had a metal kettle simmering above it, his light blue eyes flashed brilliantly in the light as smoke lightly rose up and out a small slit in the top of the hut.

"If you don't mind me asking, where did you find the document young man?" Wipley asked, as he stood up and removed the kettle from above the fire.

"Um, well, it was actually my father's... See after he was admitted to the hospital I went in his office and noticed a loose board in the floor and that's when I found the document hidden underneath it."

"There was a prologue added before your story that mentioned you had died," Pop suddenly said.

"I wondered what people would think once I left and came back here to stay for good. I didn't tell anyone I was leaving but I left that document to my only son hoping he would understand and come to find me. After the first few years passed, I knew he didn't believe it, and then after ten years, I completely gave up hope. Still... I always hoped someone would read those pages and come looking for me and this place," Wipley said with a smile.

"So, how old are you exactly?" Pop said as Wipley handed him and James a cup with some strange tea inside."

"Oh, let's see…ninety-eight, I believe," he said with a chuckle. "I just had a birthday last week."

James tried to control his mind but questions continued to fill it to the brim, even Pop seemed overwhelmed and didn't know what to say.

"Why do you stay here, and how did this place become like this?" Pop finally asked.

"It's the last truly natural place left on earth. Every plant and tree on this island lives twice as long, and as you've probably noticed around the lagoon here they grow twice as large as normal. Did you not read the report I wrote?" Wipley said, as he sat back down.

"Is the document all true?" Pop bluntly asked.

Wipley sipped his tea and grinned. "It has been so far has it not?"

James and Pop stared at Wipley with curiosity so great that they didn't even need to ask another question Wipley just began explaining things.

"When I first found this island as the document explains I spent several years here, doing scientific tests and trying to understand how such a place could exist. Eventually I came to the conclusion that it didn't matter how but why…" Wipley said, seeing the confusion grow in James' and Pop's faces. "See, I lived my entire life by all the rules, I was merely surviving and that was it. I lived like a robot and was too afraid to take any chances. After forty years of living as a research scientist, I finally decided to do what I always wanted to do and that was to travel and explore the world. No one in South Grove Harbor even knew where I had come from, they just assumed I had been an explorer my whole life, but the truth is that on my second day out to sea I was caught in a hurricane and ended up on this island."

"So, it was completely by accident?" James asked.

"That's right, I had never even been out on the ocean by myself before; so you can probably imagine my feelings when on my second trip out I almost died and ended up crashing and becoming marooned on some unknown island."

"That's kind of what happened to us," James said.

"What do you mean; I thought you followed the document?"

"We did but we couldn't find it; then a huge storm came out of nowhere and blew our boat up on the shore of this island," James exclaimed, as he took another quick sip of the tea.

Wipley stood back up. "That's amazing," he said, walking around on the grass covered floor. "You're saying that you went to the coordinates I wrote down and there was no island?"

"No, nothing at all just ocean… Oh, and a small sand bar," James said.

"Who are the people that brought us here," Pop asked.

"They are part of a small village that was here when I landed on the island."

"They're the ones who gave you the water," James said, remembering the story in the document.

"Oh, the water," Wipley slowly said as he smiled. "One of the few great gifts left on this earth. It's the source of all life and yet has been changed and transformed into what we now know. But not this water… No this water is still pure."

"But no one knows about it," James said, looking over at Pop and then back at Wipley as he stood beside a long hammock.

"I don't believe most people deserve the water, I'm not trying to sound selfish but I truly believe now that if you are meant to find this place then you will find it; just like you have."

"Then how did you manage to find it again for the second time?" Pop quickly asked.

"I didn't," Wipley said, "I had the man that brought you over here with me. He lives close to me and is one of my friends here on the island. He's also one of the first men who found me after I crashed into the island."

"But what about the people watching from the docks, there was nothing about another person being with you," James curiously asked.

"He stayed aboard my boat and waited for me to return."

"What did you go back to the mainland for anyway?" Pop asked.

"I wanted to meet my son and leave the document for him, I hoped he would believe me but just like everyone else he didn't… Do you know how it was your father came to acquire the document?" Wipley asked, as he sat down beside James.

"My father bought it at an auction," James softly said, realizing that this information would probably hurt Wipley.

"He sold my collection then," Wipley asked, his strong face showing vulnerability for the first time.

"I'm sorry," James slowly said, feeling bad for telling him.

"No, I'm glad you told me the truth. I wouldn't accept any less from men who were also blessed with finding this place."

Wipley looked at James and then at Pop's cane, "Come with me, you can tell me why you're really here along the way."

James and Pop got up and followed Wipley out of the hut. They noticed he moved like a man half his age. As they all left the hut, James saw that the sun was beginning to hang lower in the sky and the jungle now felt even more mysterious. Wipley helped with Pop as they walked back down the same way they had come before. During the short walk, James told him about his father and how he hoped the water might save his life.

"They don't know why he's sick?" Wipley asked, as the lagoon appeared ahead of them.

"No, not really; he's been in a coma for months now and he's getting worse... Do you think...? Will this water heal him if he drinks it?" James asked.

"I honestly don't know James, but I can tell you this—in the next five minutes, Pop here will no longer need help from anyone when walking, or this silly cane," Wipley announced.

Pop didn't say a word as they walked back down to the lagoon. James had a feeling he was worried when they got there it might all be dried up, or that it wouldn't work on him or something. And James had worries himself for that matter; he kept wondering how Wipley could be so sure the water would help Pop but not his dad. He didn't ask though as they came back down the small hill and approached the dark blue, tear-shaped lagoon. It had become considerably cooler now, but James could still easily see steam and bubbles rising from the water's surface. They walked up to the edge and stopped. James looked down at the perfectly mirrored imagine of himself in the water. His hair was everywhere and the sun burn had already turned into a light tan, the freckles on his nose were more noticeable now than ever. He grinned at Pop in the water as he hesitated to move closer to the lagoon.

"What do I drink from, my hands?" Pop turned to Wipley and asked.

"Drink... No, you do not drink; you have to submerge yourself completely in the water." Wipley said, and James instantly understood why he had been unsure if it would help his father. All this time James had been under the assumption that you simply drank of the water and you would be healed, at least that's how all the stories he had read went; he had never heard anything about submerging yourself in the water before. Now he realized why the island couple was swimming in the lagoon earlier.

"How many times do you have to swim in it to become healed?" James asked, as Pop slowly approached the water's edge.

"I've only been in once," Wipley replied. "The villagers only go in once and no one has ever died before the age of one hundred and thirty."

"Then why was the couple who brought us up to you swimming in it?"

"It was their first time," Wipley happily said.

Pop finally threw his cane to the side and limped slowly down the thick grassy bank. He didn't remove a single article of clothing as he entered the lagoon.

"It's so warm," Pop exclaimed, as he continued in up to his waist. "It feels like a million hands massaging every muscle in my legs," he said, and then laughed as he became chest deep. He then turned around hesitated and went under. A few seconds later, he resurfaced and James noticed his face looked a little younger; he didn't look totally different, just more like completely refreshed. It was as if life had been breathed back into him.

"I feel… I feel wonderful!" Pop excitedly called out, as he swam around for a moment, splashing water and laughing like a kid. It looked exactly like what the island couple was doing when James had seen and heard them in the lagoon. After a few more minutes, Pop swam to the bank and walked out of the water. James watched closely as he took his first step on land, and then another, and another. Pop looked up and smiled.

"There's no pain, no limp. It's doesn't hurt anymore, I can't believe it—It's a miracle!" He exclaimed, as he laughed and continued testing his newly healed body out.

"Are you serious, you really feel better?" James asked in disbelief.

"Better, I feel absolutely amazing, it's like I've been completely renewed!"

Wipley laughed. "It never gets old witnessing a miracle, I can tell you that much."

"It's real," Pop exclaimed, as he put his arms up in victory. "The water heals, it really heals, we found it James!"

James couldn't have been happier for Pop. After a short time of excitement and celebration, Pop realized that the next order of business needed to be addressed; and that was what to do about James' father's situation.

"How are we going to take back enough to submerge him?" James asked. "A bath tube holds like eighty gallons, we don't have anything big enough to take back that much."

Wipley and Pop sat on the bank and discussed different options, as James paced back and forth anxiously. Wipley had no problems sharing the healing water with his new friends, in fact he wanted to help them, he just did not know how.

"So, no one's ever tried drinking the water?" James finally asked, looking closely at the marble blue surface.

"Not that I know of, the people here do not speak much about the water, they have their own understanding of the world and that's a very simple one." Wipley said, as he walked over beside James and looked down onto the surface, staring at his own reflection and then at James'. "I've lived here long enough to learn their simple language and understand that these people have had very little to no contact with the outside world. Before me, they said that only two other men had found this island in the past several hundred years. I was told that they crashed here the same way I did, but that they soon fixed their ship and left without ever exploring the island. When I tried to explain to the island people that this water was unlike anything else in the world, they didn't understand. See, they have never been affected by illness or disease before; this place is…it's pure in some way I don't think our world will ever be."

*Well, that's it then,* James thought, *the best chance I have is to just take some of the water with me and hope it works.* By what he had just witnessed happen with Pop, he was feeling more than a little confident in the water's powers.

"It looks like we're going to have to take what we can with us, so we can get back to your father as quickly as possible," Pop said.

"I agree," James added.

Questions and conversation went on for awhile longer, with Pop continuously walking around James and Wipley.

"Exactly how many people are there on this island, is there a village nearby?" Pop inquired, as he finally stopped and stretched his newly healed body.

"There really isn't a village as you would imagine it, families live freely throughout the island in groups, but if I had to guess I'd estimate their numbers to be around a few hundred or so."

"Are you going to stay here forever?" James asked, turning towards Wipley.

"I am, it's the kind of place I've longed for my entire life, James… It's simple… It's just you and nature, I know how that must sound to a young man like yourself, who lives in such a modern world with computers and cell phones, but maybe one day when you get a bit older you'll understand."

But James already understood what Wipley meant, he had wished many times to be left alone and not bothered by the world or the people in it. The only difference was that James didn't want to run away from his problems, he wanted to fix them. He knew that he still had a life to live and he wanted to know what he might be able to make out of it. Great people have come from the world, and he wanted to be one of them; he knew his father would be proud of him for coming this far and believing in himself when it would have been so easy to doubt everything and give up.

"James," Pop said, looking at his watch. "It's almost six, we've been gone for over two hours, Walt and Neil are probably waiting for us. Here, help me get out the bottle so we can fill it up," Pop said.

"Doesn't look like we're going to be able to bring back very much," James said, as he removed a small plastic container with a snap on lid.

"Come follow me, I have a large canteen you may take with you, it's the only thing I have that will safely hold water for an extended period of time, but you can have it," Wipley told James. They all hurried back along the path again and into Wipley's hut.

"It'll be dusk in less than two hours and after that it won't be easy to navigate through the jungle. Do you think you can make it back to your boat before then?" Wipley asked, as he opened an old trunk and pulled out a metal canteen about the size of a football.

"We will only if we leave now," Pop said.

"It's been a pleasure meeting you both, and I truly hope the water provides at least one more miracle for you," Wipley said, shaking hands with James and smiling, his light blue eyes reinforcing his words.

"Thank you sir, I'll never forget this," James softly said, his thoughts escaping him now when he had so many only moments before.

"Thanks again," Pop said, shaking Wipley's hand. "You and your document have saved several lives today."

"Good luck, gentlemen," Wipley called out, as James and Pop set off back down the path towards the lagoon.

Shortly after they approached the water's edge, James unscrewed the cap from the canteen and submerged it in the blue liquid. He looked over at Pop with a dazed look on his face; one that needed a morale boost.

"It's going to work," Pop confidently said.

"You really think so?"

"It has to, look at me, and that's with the water touching the outside of the body," Pop said, as James screwed the cap back on tight and stood up. Pop always seemed to know the right things to say during these times. So, James told himself to believe in him once again.

"Alright, let's go," James said, taking one final gaze out across the lagoon.

The walk back through the jungle quickly turned into a brisk jog. Pop was moving around as well, if not better, than James now. He moved around trees and plants with great ease, and took long strides that would have previously been impossible. Before long, James was out of breath and the strap connected to the canteen bottle was rubbing his neck raw. He took it off and decided to carry it under his arm as they continued in a straight line back through the jungle. As Pop checked his watch for the time and direction, James looked behind them and saw that the sun was touching the horizon. Its rays displayed every spider web and insect for fifty feet in front of them.

"It's seven o'clock, we have less than an hour—we need to keep moving," Pop said, as he continued leading the way.

After awhile, and just as James thought he was going to have to stop and take a break, they heard Neil's voice.

"Hey, over here, hey you guys…Walt come on I found them!"

James slowed to a walk now as he and Pop went over and greeted Neil and Walt.

"Where have you guys been we were about to come looking for you? What's that under your arm," Neil quickly said, pointing to the canteen.

"We found it," James said; as he tried to catch his breath.

"What?" Neil asked, noticing Pop was standing without his cane.

"We found it, it's all true," James repeated.

"What's he talking about Pop, where's your cane?" Neil asked, looking stunned. Walt was also staring at James and Pop, apparently looking for an answer too.

"We found the healing water, just like the document said it's all true." Pop said, but it was easy to tell by the looks on Walt and Neil's face that they wanted a more detailed explanation. "Look we don't have time to explain everything right now, we need to get back to the boat and get to shore as soon as possible so that we can get this water to James' father… It's the main reason we did all this remember?" Pop hastily said, as he turned and led the way.

"What—wait a minute, how'd it happen?" Neil asked again, as he lagged behind.

"I got in the water and it healed me, now come on," Pop repeated. "We'll tell you all about it on the way back."

Pop stayed good to his word and during the trek back, James and he both told the entire story. They were then bombarded with questions, mostly from Neil, but even Walt was in disbelief and had a hard time containing his amazement. James knew Walt understood how important it was for him to get back to his father now as quickly as possible, but he could tell Walt wanted to see this lagoon for himself. So, once they finally reached the shore line and found the boat, James carefully opened the canteen and allowed Walt to look at the light blue liquid resting along the rim. Neither Walt nor Neil could believe that this strange liquid was water; still they had no choice but to accept the amazing tale.

As they all emerged out of the jungle and onto the beach dusk had set in. As luck would have it, there was once again large waves hitting the island and smacking into the boat that rested up in the sand with its propellers out of water. The problem now was that the sand underneath the fishing vessel had become so wet that it caused the boat to sink fairly deep into the beach. With each passing wave this problem got even worse as the water rolled back and took out a little more sand from under the hull.

"How are we supposed to get the boat back into the water, it's sinking into the sand?" Neil asked, as they all stood at the front of the vessel and evaluated the situation.

"What do you think?" Pop asked Walt, as he walked into the waves along the back. He stood knee deep in water as waves rolled in and hit against the back end of the boat.

"The only thing we can do is start up tha engines and put'em in reverse. Then hope a big enough wave comes in to cover tha propellers so we can back out," Walt said. "We better hurry up though, the ocean usually calms down at night and if it does we'll never get this thing out of the sand by ourselves."

Everyone quickly climbed aboard and Walt positioned himself at the wheel again as Pop and the boys stood at the back. All three of them watched as the waves came in, and they were set to tell Walt when to accelerate backwards. The plan was to give it a lot of gas when the water was deepest around the propellers; they hoped it would be enough to pull them back into the ocean. Walt started the engines and kept it in neutral as he revved them up a bit. James watched as waves rolled in and hit the back of the boat, each one barely covering the propellers for less than a few seconds.

"Okay, I'm engaging the propellers, tell me when to hit it," Walt shouted, as he pulled the throttle back.

James watched as both propellers began to slowly turn tossing up sand and quickly digging out two ruts in which water filled as a wave recessed back into the ocean. As the next wave built up and came in all three of them yelled, 'Now!' and Walt pulled the throttle back to full power. Instantly, water rushed up and around the propellers as they trashed and threw more sand violently up everywhere. The boat shook and vibrated but didn't move an inch. Walt pushed the throttle back forward and the engines quieted and slowed again. He had explained that with the props of the engines completely out of water they could potentially burn up and break if he kept them at full power for too long. Obviously, no one wanted that to happen so for the next wave after everyone yelled 'Now!' and the same thing happened they all yelled, 'Stop!' as soon as the wave was gone. They repeated this sequence several times, and each time the boat would rock and vibrate violently, but there just wasn't enough water to propel the boat backwards off the sand.

Walt then decided to turn the wheel at the same time as he revved the engines and this actually lifted the boat a little and pulled it sideways a few inches. He did this a few more times until eventually they had moved a foot to the right where there was less of an incline on the shore and waves came up farther. This little adjustment meant the propellers got another second or so under the water and were now able to slightly pull the boat backwards. As another wave rolled up, the propellers spun viciously and they moved another half inch towards the ocean. After several more attempts, they began to move backwards more and more with each wave. Without warning, James smelled something burning and looked over as one of the engines began to lightly smoke.

"That engine's smoking," Neil yelled, as another big wave came in and covered the propellers.

"Now," Pop and James yelled to Walt who hit the throttle again and turned the wheel. The engines moved to the side and the propellers chopped hard into the shallow water. James felt the boat lunge backwards slowly again, like some kind of giant turtle. The engine closest to him was now producing thicker dark smoke.

## HEALING WATER

"The engines getting too hot," Neil yelled. "Shut it off."

Walt looked back at the engine but continued to keep the throttle down and turn the wheel.

"Walt," Pop finally shouted, as the other engine began to also smoke and the prop sizzled red hot from the friction of being out of water. For the next few seconds, James watched in a panic as Walt left the motors at full power and smoke and water flew up all around him. Pop and Neil were watching in horror when suddenly the boat lifted and accelerated quickly backwards, throwing everyone forward with great force. As James held tight onto the back rail, he noticed the sounds of the propellers became muffled and the prop sizzled as it finally went under the salty water. The boat continued backwards and into the oncoming waves which caused for a bumpy departure.

"Yeah, we did it!" Neil yelled, as Walt shook his head and Pop and James looked at each other in relief.

"Another close one," Pop said, as Walt turned the boat around and slowed the engines some.

"I knew she could do it," Walt announced as Pop and the boys took their seats. "How do those engines look now?" he asked, as he squinted towards the back.

"The one on the left is not smoking at all but the one on the right is a little," Neil reported.

"They should be all right now that they're in the water," Walt said.

"Looks like water saves the day again," James joked, feeling overcome with joy.

Pop handed Walt his watch with the compass on it, as they began plotting a course for the way back. In no time at all it had become completely dark out and was another beautiful cool night on the ocean. Everyone took their seats again, as James and Pop continued trying to tell the rest of the story over the noise of the engines. Eventually they all settled in and quietly relaxed though. James was very tired, but still more excited than he had ever been in his life.

The rest of the journey back was completely uneventful and would have been boring if not for the fact that James had in his possession healing water from an unknown island. That was quite enough to produce excitement almost the entire way, which in total took a little over five hours. Pop and Walt tried to take note of where exactly they had been, but in the dark and with only a small compass this task was difficult, to say the least.

After arriving back at the docks at around midnight, Pop helped Walt tie up the boat and then everyone went inside Walt's house. They had discussed it and it was decided that they would leave as early as possible the next morning. Pop explained that even if they were able to somehow get back to the hospital tonight it would probably be closed anyway. James agreed and after Walt offered to drive them to the airport tomorrow, they all sat down in the kitchen and began to eat and unwind. Even though they were all tired, the conversation stayed lively and was almost non-stop. The tale of meeting Hunter Wipley had already turned into a great one and the way James and Pop described it was like watching a movie. Walt and Neil were simply speechless to hear about everything and to see Pop walk around with no cane. What had started out as a dangerous unlucky day and turned into the night of a lifetime. After they finished eating and talking, Walt put a few logs on the fireplace, stuffed some newspapers down under them, and lit a fire. The flames quickly produced lots of warmth, and illuminated the room nicely. For awhile, they all continued sitting around relaxing and talking, but it didn't take long before they decided it was time to start getting ready for bed. The next thing anyone knew there was a loud knock at the front door.

# Chapter Nineteen
# A Complete Circle

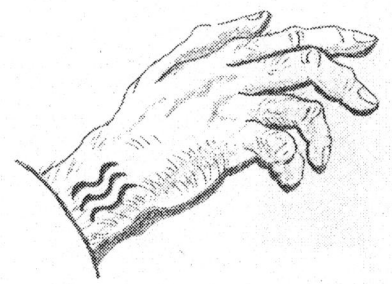

Everyone froze. No one made a move or spoke for a few seconds, and then there was another loud knock at the door.

"Pop, you and the boys go back into the bedroom; any sign of a problem don't hesitate to call for help." Walt quietly said, as he stood up and cautiously walked over to the door. The boys followed Pop and stood together in the hallway as they heard Walt unlock the door and open it. James could hear another voice beside Walt's and it sounded female.

"Hey Pop, you got a visitor," Walt called from the living room.

James walked around the corner behind Pop and Neil and saw Cori Nichols standing in the doorway. *I can't believe she left the lab and came all the way down here*, James thought. She looked like a woman on a mission, with a briefcase in one hand and a cell phone in the other. Her hair was pulled back and her cheeks were a bit flushed, but she looked just as elegant as ever.

"I've been trying to call," she said, sounding exhausted.

"What are you doing here; I told you we're fine you didn't need to come down here?" Pop stiffly said.

"You knew I couldn't let some maniac stalk you down—what, is it a pride thing now? Too stubborn to allow a woman help out, is that why you haven't been answering the phone?" she asked, smiling at James and waving. "Do you know how tough it was for me to find this place in the dark?"

"Are you sure you got the right phone number, because we've been back for awhile now and the phone hasn't rang once," Pop said, offering Miss Nichols a seat beside him on the couch which she politely ignored.

"That's interesting," Walt said, standing in the kitchen with the phone in his hand. "The phone's dead."

"I'm sorry, Cori Nichols this is Walt Perkins, the best boat captain in Florida," Pop said. "Do you often have problems with the phone service down here, Walt?"

"Hi, nice to meet you," Walt said, walking over and shaking Cori's hand. "No, never had the phone go out before…"

"Huh, that is strange," Pop said.

"Yes, it is, and that's why I came because this seems to be getting a little too strange and dangerous for you and everyone else involved. Whenever you called me last night and told me about what happened at that hotel I knew I had to come down here as soon as I could and talk you into coming home. It's too dangerous for you to be running around down here chasing another one of your crazy myths with this man, Bill Atwood, on the loose, especially with these kids."

"Hey, we're not kids," Neil quickly pointed out.

"I'm sorry, young men… Its just, if anything ever happened to you and I had the ability to prevent it, I'd never forgive myself. Plus, the CIA is breathing down my neck wanting information since they know I've been in contact with you about this case… You need to come back with me before this guy tracks you down again," she finished.

"Alright, we'll go back with you," Pop calmly said.

Miss Nichols looked stunned. "You will?"

"Yes, you're right anyway it's getting too dangerous… So when do we leave?" Pop asked, as he rubbed his beard.

"The first flight out leaves at five a.m., that's in six hours. I have my rental car outside we can take it and be back tomorrow at around six."

"It's settled then," Pop said, as he looked down at the briefcase. "Just out of curiosity is there anything else you've found out about this guy, Bill Atwood?"

Miss Nichols finally sat down beside Pop and opened the briefcase.

"That's actually the other reason I came down here, so I could show you this. I'm sure you realized that on the information I faxed over to you there was no history on Bill Atwood before the age of thirty," she said, opening the briefcase on her lap and shuffling through several papers.

"Yes, we noticed that," Pop said. "So what's the deal?"

"Well, take a look, apparently there was a man missing in the first town that this man," she flipped over the mug shot of Bill Atwood, "Bill Atwood shows up in... Take a guess at what his name was?" She asked as she showed Pop a copy from an old newspaper clipping. "One Bill Atwood, the same exact name as our murderer."

"What do you think this guy killed the original Bill Atwood and then took over his life or something?" Pop asked, sounding confused as the boys gathered around and took a look.

"Not me, this is the FBI's file on the suspect. See this paper doesn't say that this other Bill Atwood was murdered, but that he had simply been missing for several months. This paper is ten years old, exactly the right time line...Now, I did some research on this guy and found out that he had no real family, no close friends, not much of anything. In fact, he stayed inside his house almost all the time and lived on disability; nobody really even knew who this guy was. Apparently, the only reason anyone got suspicious about his whereabouts at all was because newspapers started piling up on his doorstep and his bills stopped being paid." She showed Pop another article, "after all this happened suddenly he shows back up again, but somehow looks strangely different than before... He claimed to have gotten plastic surgery in an attempt to change his life, oh yeah and he claimed he was gone on vacation for the two months he was missing, but I don't believe it. I mean who goes on vacation for that long after not leaving the house in years. It just doesn't add up. After I read this story, it all seemed fairly obvious to me that something wasn't right."

No one said anything for a few moments as they all sat and pondered her theory.

"What would he want someone else's name and life for?" Neil suddenly asked. "Couldn't he just change his name and move?"

Miss Nichols smiled. "If you changed your name legally and moved away people would still be able to track you down because your original name always stays attached to your new name. It's designed that way so people can't commit crimes and then just change their names... But, if you take over someone else's name and their life then it's like your original one never existed. You could have done anything before, and afterwards it's like it never happened," she explained, as she continued to sort through the papers and then handed Pop another one from her briefcase.

"So the question still remains," Pop said. "Who was this Bill Atwood during the first thirty years of his life, and why would he go through all this trouble to change identities if he was just going to start committing crimes again?"

Miss Nichols shook her head. "That's what bothers me about this case," she said, as Pop and the boys studied the newspaper articles again.

James continued listening as he thought about everything Miss Nichols had said. He felt more nervous now about being there than ever before; and even though he had the canteen safely sealed up and hidden he still worried about their safety. He remembered the crazed look in the guy's face at the hotel and he never wanted to be that close to him again.

"So, this guy's got like two identities?" Neil asked James, as they sat across from Pop and Miss Nichols.

"That's what it looks like," James said, turning his attention back to the other side of the room. Pop had gotten up and was checking out something with Walt when Miss Nichols noticed that he was walking without his cane.

"Hey, where's your cane?" she curiously asked.

"Uh, my physical therapy has really made a difference, I don't have to use it all the time now," Pop said.

"Uh-huh, I'm glad to hear that," she said, with a sly look on her face. "Anyway, I need to double check the airline tickets for tomorrow, when we get back I'll make all the necessary arrangements so we can catch this guy," she said, giving Pop another look as he walked around in front of the fire. "I was thinking maybe you should come back into the office and help out a little on this case."

"I might have to," Pop said, as he sat down again. "This guy's not going to give up I can tell you that much. In fact, I think we better take shifts tonight Walt, if you don't mind—you know sit up and keep an eye out on the place."

Miss Nichols looked satisfied by this comment and James realized that Pop was no longer acting, everyone was truly concerned.

"No problem, I'll just put a few more logs on the fire and sit up here in the living room tonight. I don't sleep much anymore anyway…"

"Well, I'll stay up too then," Pop said, "Cori, after you're done on the computer why don't you and the boys head downstairs and get some sleep. There's a couch down there and the boys can take the floor."

At around two in the morning the boys and Miss Nichols went down to the basement to get some sleep. Miss Nichols had reserved them all airline tickets home and they would have to leave Walt's in three hours. James was exhausted but still very happy. As he laid there on the floor with Neil, he felt safe and sound knowing Pop and Walt were upstairs guarding the place once again. Before closing his eyes, James took a quick look across the room at the couch where Miss Nichols lay. He knew she must really care about Pop to come all this way in order to talk him into coming home. James also knew why Pop had not told her what they had found yet, because before Miss Nichols had shown up Pop instructed everyone to keep the news to themselves until they decided what exactly to do. James thought Pop probably figured she had enough on her mind right now with this killer on the loose, and that he would explain everything to her tomorrow. Even with the evidence, I'm sure telling someone you found water that can heal isn't something you should jump into lightly.

As James continued to replay the day in his head he unknowingly fell asleep… The next thing James knew he was startled awake by the sounds of voices upstairs. Suddenly, all the lights in Walt's house went out.

"Hey, wake up," Pop called from upstairs, as Miss Nichols sat up.

"What is it Pop?" she called back.

"You and the boys stay down there, we think someone cut the power," he said, as the small fire at James' feet sent waves of dim light up the dark steps.

"Oh man, why does this keep happening to us?" Neil quietly said. James could see by his wide eyes that Neil was scared; and he was too for that matter. The boys joined Miss Nichols on the sofa and all sat perfectly still, listening to what was happening on the main floor.

"Walt, can you see the neighbor's house, are the lights off over there too?" Pop asked, as he walked across the room and looked out the kitchen window.

At the top of the stairs James heard Walt's voice. "No, it looks like their lights are still on… Here take this."

"What's going on?" Neil asked James since he was closest to the stairs.

"Nothing, they're checking out the windows," James answered, as he watched the faint outline of someone upstairs walking by. Without saying anything, Miss Nichols quietly got up and went over to the bottom of the stairs.

"You two stay there," she quietly demanded.

The next thing anyone knew there was a loud bang, which sounded like a rock hitting the house.

"What was that?" Neil said.

"Shhh," Miss Nichols whispered, as James watched her standing nervously now on the first step, staring up at the floor of the living room. The next thing James knew he heard glass breaking in different places upstairs. Then it went quiet again, no one moved, no said a word, no one even breathed.

"They're coming through the windows!" Walt suddenly yelled, as Miss Nichols went a couple more steps up and then stopped. James had already gotten to his feet and was now trying to advance around her.

"They may need our help," James said, as his heart pounded and he heard banging and things being broken.

"Stop him, he's got a—" someone yelled, and James jumped back as gunshots rang out. Two more loud explosions drove Miss Nichols and him back down the stairs as the struggle upstairs continued. James and Neil were both now at the bottom of the stairs looking to go up, but Miss Nichols put her arms out and blocked them from going around her.

"He's over there!" James heard Pop yell.

"Behind you... No!"

Another loud gun blast emanated from the living room. With each shot there was a bright light that illuminated the room above the stairs for a split second. White smoke trickled down the top of the steps and the smell of gunpowder filled the house.

"He's running, don't let him," someone shouted, and then James heard two men yell in pain.

"Agh!—No, he's there—stop, no!"

It was finally too much for James to take, he had to do something. He quickly ducked Miss Nichol's arm and started running up the steps.

"James, no!" Miss Nichols yelled, trying to grab him by the back of the shirt but missing. He got to the top step and the scene revealed before him was like one from a movie. Two men lay motionless on the floor as the fire produced light against only one side of their faces. Pop was standing over one of them with a gun in his hand, and Walt was on the ground by the kitchen, trying to stand up, but James could tell he was hurt badly.

"Don't try to get up," Pop said, as he rushed over to Walt. "Cori! Get up here, hurry."

James rushed over and helped Pop turn Walt over to his back, that's when he saw the blood leaking from his chest.

"You're going to be fine," Pop reassured Walt.

"We got 'em didn't we?" he asked, as he strained to breathe and looked around.

"Yeah, we got them," Pop said, as Miss Nichols ran over.

"Oh no, okay um, keep pressure on the wound and I'll go get help," she said, as she looked around at the scene.

"Just run over to the neighbor's and call nine-one-one," Pop said, as he held a small blanket from the couch over Walt's chest.

"Oh, I'll be right back," Miss Nichols said in a panic stricken tone.

"Tell them Walt's boat tours in South Grove Harbor," James stammered.

"You're going to be okay, help is coming," Pop reassured Walt as he and James kneeled down around him and held his head up and the blanket against his chest wound.

"I got him," Walt said, still holding a grin through untold amounts of pain. "I got him for ya kid," he told James.

James went to get up, "I'm going to get the water—"

"Don't," Walt shouted, and then coughed. "Don't you dare kid. I lived my life; I'd never forgive myself if you wasted that stuff on me… I've always wanted to go out like a hero anyway," Walt softly said, as James kneeled back down beside him.

"You're one of the great ones," James told him as he held his hand.

"You too kid." Walt very softly said. "You helped a bitter, old man like me believe in something again. Now ya go and save your father for me, aye?"

"I will," James promised. "I will."

The next few minutes that passed seemed like days. Pop continued holding the blanket tight against Walt's chest as James and Neil tried to keep him talking.

"I'm getting tired," Walt quietly said, as the sound of sirens finally rang out in the distance and Miss Nichols stood in the doorway trying not to cry.

Pop looked down. "You hear that Walt, they're almost…" But it was too late, Walt Perkins had closed his eyes and breathed his last breath.

"No, not him, Pop," James whispered, as he looked up at Pop with tears in his eyes.

"I'm sorry James," Pop said, as he looked down and wept.

When the ambulance finally arrived a minute later, it was confirmed that Walt was gone. Pop told the detectives that during the assault he was knocked down and Walt had taken on both armed men by himself and it was then that he became fatally wounded. After the police searched the crime scene, they found several items on Bill Atwood's body and showed them to Miss Nichols. Pop was standing out in the driveway getting some fresh air when she came out to show him what they had found. James was sitting on the porch listening to Neil give his statement to the police when he noticed Miss Nichols carrying something over to Pop. He instantly thought he recognized the item as it reflected off the headlights of a nearby police car, so he jumped up and walked over to where Pop and Miss Nichols were standing.

"What is that?" James asked, as Pop held and looked at the evidence.

"Not sure, detectives found it on Atwood's body, thought maybe you two might know," Miss Nichols said.

Pop and James examined the torn page together. "It looks like a letter or something," James said, as he continued examining it. Very soon afterwards a thought struck him. "It almost looks like the missing half of the letter I found," James told Pop, as he checked his pockets and eventually pulled out the envelope with the letter he had stumbled upon in his father's room under the bed.

"Let's see," Pop said, holding the two torn pieces up to each other. To their complete astonishment the two halves basically fit. "This is very strange... Why would Bill have this on him?" Pop said and then paused, as he and James looked at each other, apparently both thinking deeply.

"Did the police find anything else on Bill?" Pop suddenly asked Miss Nichols.

"Yes, they also found some money, a computer disk and a cell phone," she said, showing Pop all the items separated inside individual plastic evidence bags.

"What's that?" James asked, pointing to a small folder Miss Nichols was holding.

"This, oh, just some standard pictures of the body forensics takes for the purpose of the case," she explained. Pop looked curiously up from the missing page he was still reading.

"Anything unusual on the photographs?" Pop asked, as he adjusted him glasses.

Miss Nichols opened the bag and took out a few pictures. She flipped through them and then handed them to Pop. "Nothing that I can tell, here you can have a look though."

Pop took the pictures and began examining them. Even though James never wanted to see Bill Atwood again, dead or alive, he couldn't help but take a look. As Pop held out one of the photos under the headlights, James saw Bill's large body stretched out on the hardwood floor with one arm still reaching out making a fist, as if forever frozen in anger. Just before James looked away, he saw something very peculiar that caught his attention.

"Wait a second," he said, as Pop went on to the next photo. "Go back one."

"Did you see something?" Pop asked, as he took out the last picture again and he and James studied it closely.

"What is that?" James said, as he pointed at something on the back of Bill's fist.

Pop looked closely at the odd image. "Did he have a tattoo?" he asked Miss Nichols.

"Um, yes, I believe so, he had several, why?"

James quickly looked at Pop. "The letter!" he exclaimed.

"What did this tattoo look like?" Pop asked Miss Nichols; since the picture they were looking at was from too far away to see the marking clearly.

"I'm not sure, there's a close up of it in here somewhere," she said, as she took the rest of the pictures out and sorted through them until she found the right one. "Here it is, it looks like some kind of weird design or something."

Pop took the picture and he and James stared at the close up shot of Bill's fist. There in dark black ink were three wavy lines one on top of the other, creating the ancient symbol for a water source. An epiphany instantly erupted in James' mind, like a thousand voices all screaming one name.

"Are you thinking what I'm thinking? Could it really be him?" James asked, his heart jumping inside his chest.

"What exactly is going on here Pop?" Miss Nichols asked, as she stood with her hands on her hips looking impatient and confused.

"It has to be him," Pop said, as he looked back and forth from the page to the picture.

It was astounding but the answer had been right behind them the whole time. Tracking them down, following them, and then trying to attack them.

"We know who Bill Atwood really is," Pop finally announced.

Miss Nichols eyes lit up like fireworks. "You do?"

"Yes, we believe his real name is Manny Jones," Pop said.

"And, who is he?"

"He's a man that was obsessed with the story in that document we had you test. Apparently, he was so obsessed that he was willing to do anything to get it back." Pop explained.

"Just like we thought," Miss Nichols said. "This explains it, I have to make a call."

"I can't believe this," James mumbled, as he held the picture lower under the headlights of the emergency vehicles. "I still can't believe that man in there is Manny Jones, I mean how could it have happened? He was friends with my father at one time?"

Pop knew he couldn't answer that question. So, instead he went back to studying the missing half of the letter to try and find another clue as to how this happened.

Miss Nichols was busy making a phone call now, as James also went back to reading the missing half of the letter. The bottom half of the page didn't say much, in fact, it didn't really make any sense at all. It was dotted with half finished sentences and illegible, angry handwriting. A few moments of silence passed, and then Pop stopped trying to make sense of the page and looked up.

"Well, it looks like the only one who can answer the rest of our questions is most likely going to be your father, James," Pop confessed, as Miss Nichols hung up her phone and walked back over.

"Okay, I just got off the phone with my boss and he wants you to explain everything you know to the detectives here, because I still don't understand very much of it. And he expects a full report on Monday to send to the FBI," Miss Nichols said.

"Come on we'll explain everything we know," Pop said. "After all we do have a plane to catch in a few hours."

"Hey guys, what's going on," Neil asked, walking out to the driveway and taking a look at the pictures in Pops hands. "What is that stuff?"

"It's what they found on Bill, I mean Manny," James said.

"What do you mean, Manny who?" Neil asked.

"Come on you'll find out in a minute, you're not going to believe this," James said, still with a bewildered look on his face.

*HEALING WATER*

Miss Nichols and Neil listened as James and Pop explained everything they could to the authorities and were then escorted by police to the airport. It was already four in the morning by the time they got there. The officers stayed with them all until they boarded the plane at around six. By this time everyone was so tired and worn out that they all fell asleep within ten minutes of being on the plane. James didn't really even notice the take off or landing, and Neil didn't feel sick at all as he snored lightly and leaned against Pop's shoulder. Once the plane had landed and taxied to the correct terminal, Pop woke the tired boys and they all exited the plane. James waited anxiously at the gate for them to bring out his specially protected package with the canteen in it, and when they did he perked up a bit at the thought of seeing his father and hopefully saving his life. As they walked through the airport and then out to the parking garage, where Miss Nichols had left her car, James could feel his nerves bothering him again. This was really it, in the next hour he would know whether all of his effort was in vain or not, it was the moment James had been imagining ever since he had first read the document.

"Are you ready for this?" Pop asked, as he insisted on driving and got into to Miss Nichol's car.

"I think so," James said, as he sat the case with the healing water down on the seat in between himself and Neil.

During the car ride to the hospital, Pop told the shortened version of what had taken place on the island to a disbelieving Miss Nichols. He told her the truth about how his hip became healed, but her scientific background was keeping her from believing the story. The boys also swore to the account and then James even showed her the water. She was speechless for a full minute as she realized that they were all being serious. She sat in the passenger seat examining the water in the canteen with intense curiosity. The dark-bluish water inside the metal can had a smooth, almost glass-like texture.

"There has to be a scientific explanation for all this," she finally said.

"Maybe so, but the myth is real," Pop said, "and we want to thank you for all your help in proving it."

"Help, I just thought I was being a good friend. I never knew you were actually going to go try and find this place. No, wait, I take that back. I guess I figured you would just be satisfied with the news I gave you and leave it at that," Miss Nichols confessed.

Pop laughed, "I thought you knew me better than that. It has been my lifelong dream to discover something like this."

Miss Nichols carefully handed the canteen back to James. "So, let me guess you're going to take this water and try to heal James' father with it?"

"That's the plan," Pop confidently said.

"If this works do you understand what that will mean? It'll be the most important substance in the world," she exclaimed.

"We're not sure if we're going to expose this find to the world yet," Pop said.

"Well, why wouldn't you, if this works it could save a countless number of lives?"

Pop steered the small car off the highway exit ramp and onto the northbound lane heading towards the hospital.

"Like I said, we're not sure what to do yet. We've decided to take it one step at a time," Pop said, as he gestured to the back seat and a worried-looking James.

"Oh, I see," Miss Nichols softly said, realizing that Pop was still not sure if their plan was actually going to work at all.

Neil was leaning up against the window napping as they drove over a speed bump and into the hospital parking lot. His head bounced up and hit the window which startled him awake.

"Ouch... Man, where are we?" Neil mumbled, as he looked over at James and yawned.

"We're in the hospital parking lot," James said, as Pop pulled the car into a parking spot on the ground level of the garage.

"Alright, let's do this," Neil said, sitting up and suddenly looking wide awake.

James didn't feel or look tired anymore either; he had too much adrenaline coursing through his veins to allow him to feel the way he normally would after only a couple hours of sleep. But before anyone got out of the car, Pop once again went over the plan they had come up with the night before. Since they knew it would be virtually impossible to get anyone to believe that this shiny blue liquid in the canteen was actually healing water, they had no choice but to come up with a way in which to secretly administer the water to James' father without anyone knowing. The irony of the whole situation had become painfully obvious to everyone, it seems the very same protection Joe Greene needed to keep him from being harmed, might actually now keep him from being helped as well.

"Okay guys, listen up," Pop said. "Once inside we're going to distract the guards while James administers some of the water to his father. We're going to be looking out for any nurses or hospital personnel and on my signal Neil you stand in front of James while he does it. Is that all clear?"

"We got it Pop, don't worry you're going to make James more nervous than he already is," Neil said.

"That's not possible," James said, zipping the canteen up in his duffle bag underneath flowers they had picked up in the airport.

Miss Nichols turned around and smiled at James. "Don't worry," she calmly said, her bright blue eyes seemed to cause his anxiousness to melt away. "You're going to do fine James, and here, I think I have something that might help," Miss Nichols said, as she opened her purse and looked around until she found and handed James what looked like a large eye dropper. "It'll be a lot easier to dispense the water to your father using this. Just drip a few drops in his mouth at a time and his body should naturally swallow it."

"Thanks, I was kind of worried about how I was going to do that," James admitted.

They all got out of the car and walked over to one of the side entrances. Certain security measures had been updated in the hospital since the incident with the gun man, they worried these things might hinder their plan. For instance, now you had to have one of the new gold visitor wrist bands in order to access the elevator or the doors to the stairs. Without this band you could not get off the first floor, but to get one required identification and a fingerprint scan.

Everything went fine though, and Pop lead the way after they had all cleared the process and received wristbands. James watched Pop as he stepped across the threshold into the elevator this time with absolute ease. Remembering how much he struggled before with this task and seeing him do it now really brought on some much needed reassurance.

"How have you been feeling, Pop?" James asked as they all walked down one of the main hallways on the third floor. He was curious to know what else if anything had been affected by the healing water Pop had swam in.

"I feel great, I really do. Not only does my hip feel better, but somehow I feel lighter and younger than before," he explained, as they all turned down a hallway on the right and approached a group of nurses behind a three-sided desk.

"Hello, how may I help you?" a young nurse asked, looking up from the paperwork she was filing.

James stepped forward slightly. "Hello, I'm here to visit my father," he said nervously.

"Okay, and his name?" she asked with a smile.

"Uh, Joe Greene, he was brought to this floor over a week ago," James said, looking down the hall and noticing a security guard.

"He has a secure room," Pop told the nurse.

"Yes, that's right, Mr. Greene... He is just down the hallway there, go through the double doors and then talk to the guard on the left."

"Um, do you know how he's doing?" James slowly asked.

The nurse hit a few more buttons on the computer and then looked up. "He's in about the same condition, he's just not responding to the new treatment. I'm sorry, I'm afraid it's going to take some time before we know anything for certain."

"Thanks," James softly said.

"Thanks again," Pop said, as he patted James on the back and led the way down the hall. On the other side of the double doors sat a stocky black security guard in an all black uniform with a silver badge on his chest.

"Need to see your visitor tags," the security guard said. His African accent was strong and after he stood up with a scanner in hand he moved it over each wrist-band and then led them down to a room on the right.

"Only one of you can go in at a time," the man said in a serious tone.

"Excuse me," said Miss Nichols, taking out her CIA badge and giving the man a close up inspection of it. "It's the young man's father; I don't think it's too much to ask if he and his best friend go in together, now is it?"

The man looked at the badge and then at Miss Nichol's pretty face. James thought there's no way anyone could say no to a woman with that much authority and beauty.

"Okay, but just this once then... Hey, what's in the bag there?"

"Flowers," James immediately answered, unzipping the bag slightly until the man could see the tops of the yellow lilacs. "They're his favorite."

"Go ahead then," he said. "Hey...sorry about your dad, kid."

James nodded, and then he and Neil walked through another door and into the small room on the right. James felt the temperature drop a few degrees and heard the sound of the machines as they constantly monitored all of his father's vital signs. Neil stayed behind James as he approached the curtain that was surrounding the hospital bed. He could see the outline of his dad's legs but that was it. He reached out and pulled the curtain back until there was enough room to walk in. He looked down at his father's face and noticed it looked weak. He saw no emotion, no movement, nothing. It appeared as if he was merely sleeping, but James knew better.

"I don't think we're going to need Pop's plan," Neil quietly said to James, as he looked over and saw that there was really no way anyone could see in through the curtain.

"No, I guess not, but we still need to be careful," James said, as he took his father's hand. "Come on dad, let this work."

"It's going to work," Neil said, already checking on the door to the room.

"Okay, let's do it… Hand me that canteen Neil," James nervously said.

Neil opened the duffle bag all the way, and underneath the flowers and some clothes was the metal canteen. He took it out and carefully handed it over to James. James took it and slowly unscrewed the top. The fluorescent light in the hospital room caused the water to shine a light blue color now, as James took and poured some into a small plastic cup. He handed the canteen back to Neil as he continued his job of look out. For a couple seconds they both stared at the cup in James hand. The water just looked so pure, and for some reason the light blue color seemed natural and right.

"Here goes nothing," James said.

"It's going to work, it has to," Neil repeated.

James took out the dropper Miss Nichols had given him and dipped it into the cup. After filling the dropper completely up with the light blue water he put it to his father's lifeless mouth; he paused for a brief moment as his hand shook.

"Careful," Neil said.

James nodded and very delicately slipped the dropper into his father's mouth ever so slightly. He squeezed the plastic top and watched as the light blue water ran from the dropper into his father. It took several seconds for tiny amounts of the liquid to go down, but before long James had administered the entire cup and filled a second one. James repeated the same procedure as Neil continued to keep watch on the door. The second cup went down even easier and faster than the first.

"How much are you going to give him?" Neil asked, and suddenly there was a knock at the door. James quickly handed Neil the dropper and wiped his father's mouth.

"The nurse needs to administer some medicine to your father, you'll have to leave the room for a few minutes," the guard announced, as Neil pulled out the flowers from the duffle bag and handed them to James who hastily put them on the table beside his father's bed.

"Okay, we're coming," Neil said, as he zipped up the bag and James took his father's hand.

"Please let it work," he softly prayed, and then let go and followed Neil out of the room.

"You can come back in twenty minutes or so, I should be done by then." The nurse said, as she walked into the room and smiled.

Miss Nichols and Pop were sitting across from the guard's desk on a bench; they both stood up and looked at James with great interest as he and Neil approached.

"Why don't we go down to the cafeteria and get something to drink while we wait, huh boys?" Pop said, and James nodded.

"Alright," Neil said, "I'm starving anyway."

"Would you like anything sir?" Miss Nichols asked the guard.

"A cup of coffee would be great," he said, sitting back down behind the desk and hitting a button that automatically opened the double doors.

"We'll be back," Pop said, as they walked out into the hallway. No one said a word until the doors to the elevator closed in front of them.

"So, how'd it go in there?" Pop calmly asked.

"Not bad, James gave him two cups of the water," Neil said.

"Was it difficult to do with him in that condition?" Pop asked.

"No, it actually went pretty smoothly. I poured a little in at a time and his body seemed to swallow it naturally, just like you said," James told Miss Nichols.

"That guard scared us though," Neil said.

"I know, sorry about that. We tried to keep the nurse occupied with questions about your father for as long as possible… I couldn't believe it when she showed up a few minute after you two went in," Pop said.

"How are you feeling James, you look a little flushed?" Miss Nichols asked.

James looked up and pushed his dark hair to the side. "I'm okay, I was just wondering if I gave him enough, I mean, how are we supposed to know how long to wait. What if nothing happens," James said, as he adjusted the duffle bag hanging from his shoulder and stepped off the elevator.

But before anyone could answer James, they were suddenly surrounded by people. He and Pop led the way through the crowded cafeteria which almost seemed like a maze.

"I think we'll know what step to take next by the time we get back up there," Pop told James as they walked around a group of cash registers with workers standing behind them. "I wouldn't worry too much, we've gotten this far haven't we?"

James nodded in agreement as he dodged several small children as they ran past with drinks. The place was full of noise and more people then he had seen in the whole hospital. Some were standing in line to get food, others sitting down at tables eating, James noticed everyone had on some kind of uniform. Whether it was a blue pair of scrubs, or an apron with a hat, or a suit and tie, everyone had their own specific uniform for whatever job they performed in the place.

James and Neil walked over to a line of refrigerators against the wall that contained drinks of all kinds. James didn't really feel hungry, but his mouth was dry so he decided to get a drink of something.

"Pop's right you know," Neil said, as he surveyed the drinks. "We've come so far already. If you would have told me that we were going to find a hidden island and this healing water during summer break I would have laughed and called you crazy." Neil then grabbed two bottles of chocolate milk.

"You and everybody else," James said, as he shook his bottle of orange juice.

"Exactly, but you got me and Pop to believe," Neil said.

"That wasn't very hard," James laughed.

"Yeah, I guess we're all regular old myth detectives now, huh?"

Pop and Neil both ended up getting a plate of pancakes and eggs, Miss Nichols bought a water and small salad, and James finally picked up a banana so no one would complain. They found a booth in the far corner of the large room and all sat down to eat.

"Are you sure you don't want anything else to eat?" Pop asked James.

"Yeah, I'm fine thanks," James said, as he peeled his banana and took a small bite.

"I know it's hard to believe," Miss Nichols suddenly said, after a minute or so of silence. "But I know how you're feeling. Well, not exactly how, but I can definitely relate. See two years ago, my mom had open heart surgery and the doctor said she had a fifty-fifty chance of making it. The procedure took four hours and the entire time all I did was pace back and forth in the waiting room and bite my nails… And then after they came out and told me everything went well during the surgery, they said it would still take up to another two days to know if her body was going to accept the new heart or not… Let me tell you, those were the longest two days of my life."

James took another drink of his juice. "So, is she all right?"

"Yes, she's doing great now—actually she turns sixty tomorrow," Miss Nichols said with a smile. James smiled back and then looked down at his father's watch. It had been a little over ten minutes since they had given the water to his father. He put his opposite hand over the watch and remembered the look on his father's face when James' real mother gave it to him so long ago. He could not believe that ten years had already passed since her death. He knew she would have protested what he had done to try and save his father, but he also knew that she would have probably done it too as a last resort to save him. She would have done anything for his father, and James could never imagine two other people loving each other more than his mom and dad did.

"James, hey, are you listening?" Neil said, for the second time.

"What?" James asked, as he finally made himself return from his deep memories.

"I asked you what the first thing is you want to do with your dad after he's better?"

James paused for a few seconds, he had never really thought about it until now. "Uh, I don't really know," he confessed.

"Oh, come on man, think of something," Neil begged.

"Um, well, I think we need to find a new place to live," James said, "and I've always wanted to build something with my dad."

"Wait a minute, the first thing you want to do is build a house?" Neil said.

"Yeah, why not… Of course, I'd have to talk him into it, but yeah that'd be great."

"Okay, but if you're building a house then I'm helping," Neil said, as he took another bite of his eggs and patted James on the back.

It was ten o'clock by the time they had all finished in the cafeteria. James stood tense as they all waited for the elevator to come back down. He could tell that everyone else was anxious too because no one was saying anything. When the elevator bell rang and the door opened James noticed that nobody moved, a few moments went by before James finally led the way into the elevator. He knew this gesture was out of respect, but it made him even more nervous to see them all acting in this strange way. The ride back up to the third floor actually seemed like it took longer than the one at the White Rooks Inn hotel. When the bell finally rang for the third time, James again led the group out and down the hallway. His pace was normal at first, but began to slow as he turned the corner and saw the double doors leading to his father's room. Noticing James' apprehensive behavior, Pop stepped up and urged him on.

"Remember no matter what be strong, James," Pop quietly said, and James nodded and continued down the hall. Once they got to the nurses station everyone immediately noticed that no one was there.

"Hey, where is everybody?" Neil curiously asked, looking around along with everyone else. "How are we supposed to get through the doors if no one's here?"

"They're all in the next room over," Pop announced, looking through one of the square glass windows in the double doors. "Hello!" he called out, as he knocked on the window. "Can you let us in please, we have visitor passes," Pop informed someone on the other side, as he held up his wristband in the small window.

James' heart and mind were racing with worries and questions: *What is everyone doing in there? What happened to my dad, is he better, is he worse?* Just as he rushed over beside Pop and tried to get a look through the small window, the double doors automatically opened and James saw all sorts of nurses and doctors scrambling around in the hallway talking excitedly. As he watched the mayhem continue, visions of his father reacting negatively to the water he had given him flashed in his mind. He quickly shook himself free from this pessimistic vision and navigated himself through and around the small groups of people, trying desperately to get to his father's room. After he got around one last nurse, he saw the same African security guard standing in the doorway. James approached the guard and looked around him into the room; he saw a group of doctors and nurses surrounding his father's bed.

"What's going on, what happened?" James exclaimed, as Pop, Miss Nichols, and Neil finally caught up and crowded in behind him, all trying to get a look at the scene inside the room.

"Your father woke up a few minutes ago, the doctors are checking him out but they think he's fine," the guard said with a smile.

As soon as these words left the guard's mouth, James felt a feeling he had never experienced in his whole life. It was the most abundant amount of happiness that any one person could feel at any one time. It rushed over and through him like a fast, warm breeze.

"Are you serious?" James exclaimed, turning towards Neil and Pop. "Did you hear that guys?" He grabbed both of them and they all hugged.

"He's okay, James, he's okay!" Neil shouted, as James laughed and turned back around to face the guard.

"Can I see him, can I?" James quickly asked, as every muscle in his body felt magnetized to the spot where his father was laying.

"Um, excuse me, Doctor Brankly," the guard said. "Sorry, but Mr. Greene's son is here and would like to see his father."

The silver haired doctor flipped the chart he was holding closed and looked at James.

"Yes, of course he can," the doctor said, and James rushed forward, almost knocking down a short nurse who was trying to leave. After he squeezed in between two other nurses at the foot of the bed, he saw his father. He was sitting up and talking to one of the other doctors when he suddenly looked over and saw James.

"James, oh my boy, come here," he said, with the biggest smile any person could possible achieve. James rushed up and grabbed his father tight around the chest. They hugged each other for twenty seconds in silence.

"I never thought you were going to wake up dad," James finally said.

"I know, they told me everything," Joe said.

"How are you feeling, are you okay?" James quickly asked, as he looked over his father.

"That's the funny thing, I've never felt better in my life," Joe happily replied. "I want to get up right now, but they said I won't be able to walk without help for a few days. Guess I've been out for a while huh?"

"Excuse me, Mr. Greene, it appears all your vitals seem to be stabilizing, we're going to continue monitoring you for the next few days and if everything checks out then you should be able to go home by the beginning of next week."

"Thank you Doc, hey, I'd like you to meet my son, James," Joe said, as he patted James on the back.

"Hello," James said, as he shook the doctor's hand. "Um, do you know what caused my dad to wake up from the coma?"

The doctor looked up over his small glasses. "Well, sometimes these things just naturally work their course and then they're gone. The body is an amazing machine, and when you're dealing with an unknown problem like what your father had, and then you add in a coma which is an unpredictable state to begin with, then that question gets almost impossible to answer," the doctor said. "Yes, it's amazing but these complicated machines do happen to fix themselves sometimes… Makes it hard to believe the body is made up of eighty percent water, huh?"

"I believe it," James said, as he sat down on the bed and gave his father another hug. It was the single greatest moment of his young life.

James and his father sat together talking excitedly for the next ten minutes as the crowd around them slowly diminished. Pop, Neil, and Miss Nichols were still standing in the doorway with the guard watching and waiting for James to call them in.

"So, what's been going on at home lately, and where's Debra? Is that her waiting to come in?" Joe asked, noticing everyone standing in the doorway.

"Um, well, I hate to tell you this dad, but she left and… I really don't know where she is," James said.

"How long ago did this happen?"

"About a week ago, I think… I've been staying at Neil's house ever since," James said, as he stood up and pulled a chair over next to the bed and sat down facing his father. "Listen Dad," he said slowly, looking over at Pop and then back at his dad. "There's a lot of things that happened while you were here, it's all pretty complicated so I think it would be easier if I had some help explaining it, is that alright with you?"

"What do mean, help from who?" Joe asked, looking over again at the doorway.

"Do you remember Neil's grandpa Pop?"

"Yes, of course," Joe said, "why?"

James waved Pop over, and Neil and Miss Nichols followed; they all stood at the foot of the bed and said hello.

"Dad, you know Pop and Neil, but this is Cori Nichols she used to work with Pop and she really helped us out," James said.

"Nice to meet you," Joe slowly said, looking somewhat confused as he shook hands with Miss Nichols. "Helped you out with what?" he asked, turning back towards James.

"I told my dad I wanted you guys to help me explain everything to him," James announced.

"Explain what, James?" Joe asked again, looking more concerned now than curious.

"Um, James, I think it would be best if we took it one step at a time here, you know, give your father a chance to get back in the swing of things before we get into explaining everything," Pop said.

"He will want to know everything now, I'm telling you," James said, knowing how his father was when it came to secrets.

"With all due respect, Pop, I don't like waiting to hear bad news, so if you don't mind could you please explain to me exactly what it is you're all talking about?" Joe said, as he buttoned up the rest of his plaid dress shirt.

"Why are you getting dressed?" James asked.

"The nurses are coming back in here later to get me up and take me to get a few final tests," Joe explained. "Now stop trying to change the subject, what's going on, what happened with Debra?"

"I told you dad, she left… And then someone, burnt, down, our house," James said very slowly.

"What, how'd that happen, did anybody get hurt?" Joe exclaimed.

"Alright settle down, Joe, we'll explain everything," Pop said, pulling up two chairs for himself and Miss Nichols. "But you need to hear the entire story first before you ask any questions, because we have questions too… Agreed?" Pop asked.

"Okay, okay, what can I say—you took care of my son I'll do anything you ask me too… So go ahead, I'm listening," Joe sincerely said, as he adjusted the mechanical hospital bed further up and waited.

Over the next hour, James and Pop explained almost everything; Neil and Miss Nichols even added bits and pieces of what they could, as they tried to help explain things. Joe sat quietly for awhile and listened as the story was told. His eyes seemed to keep getting bigger with each passing sentence. Eventually, when James told him about meeting Hunter Wipley on the island he couldn't contain himself any longer.

"Wait a second, hold on…" he said, looking stunned. "You're trying to tell me that you actually found the hidden island from the document and met Hunter Wipley?" he asked, in an unbelieving tone.

"He's telling you the truth, Joe," Pop said, as Joe looked over at Miss Nichols.

"Surely, you don't believe this stuff too?" he asked.

"I'm sorry, I hate to admit it," she confessed, "but as crazy as it sounds, I really do believe they found something extraordinary out there. Pop's now able to walk without a cane, you woke up almost immediately after being in a coma."

Joe put his head in his hands and leaned forward in disbelief. After a few seconds of silence, he looked up again.

"Do you realize we searched twelve hours a day for over two weeks in that Ocean; we followed the document's instructions precisely every time and never found anything remotely similar to that island, nothing at all." Joe finished, and then adjusted the bed again until it finally reached its maximum upright position.

"You and Manny Jones?" Neil quickly asked.

"Yes... Manny Jones... See, after I bought that document at an auction, Manny talked me into staying down in Florida with him, he swore up and down that after we found that island we'd both be rich and famous just like we had always talked about. I have to admit after I stumbled across the document, I did begin to believe the story could be true. But after the fifteenth day out at sea in Manny's boat, I was ready to give up. We hadn't found one thing that backed up the document and I was sun burnt, seasick, and ready to go home; but Manny refused to head back to shore. He was like a man obsessed; he just wouldn't give up... We eventually got into a serious fight over it the next night and I forced him to take me back in—He swore we would never be friends again and that he was going to found that island by himself, and then I'd regret it when he was rich and I wasn't...And before I got off the boat I secretly took the document with me, in hopes that without it he would forget the location and maybe give up, but I doubted it—still, I had to do something, I felt like it was my fault for buying the collection in the first place. He would have never gone crazy if I hadn't called him and told him about it. He would have eventually realized that the story was not true and given up."

"But, dad, it wasn't made up, it's the truth, that document was real, Hunter Wipley's real, the healing water is real," James repeated.

"Here, why don't you just show it to him?" Neil said, handing the duffel bag to James.

"Let me guess, you have some of the water in there?" Joe sarcastically said.

"Yes, we brought some of the water back and gave it to you forty minutes ago," James said, as he unzipped the bag and pulled out the metal canteen.

James got a cup from the bedside table and poured a little of the shiny, light blue water into it. James' father took the cup and examined the strange water.

"What'd you guys do put food coloring in this water or something?" Joe asked with a grin.

"No, dad, we didn't, it's the water from the island," James stubbornly said. "How do you think you woke up and are now suddenly healed after you've been so sick for the past five months?"

"You heard the doctors, sometimes people just get better," Joe said, still looking closely at the water in the cup.

"Look, Joe," Pop said, as he got up and walked around and then balanced on each leg perfectly.

"Where's your cane?" Joe asked.

"I don't need it anymore," Pop said, "the water healed me too."

The room filled with silence for several seconds as Joe's mind processed this revelation. After five seconds, Joe finally shook his head and grinned.

"You guys are really being serious aren't you?"

"Yes, dad, we found the island, it's real," James said.

"My God... Do you know what this means... It's...It's, I don't even know what to say," Joe quietly said, as he shook his head again and stared at the water in the cup.

"Then just tell us about the hidden numbers on the document, dad," James asked.

Joe didn't respond for a few seconds. "Numbers...ah yes, the numbers. I had those secretly printed on the document, but wait a second—how did you know about them?"

"Miss Nichols tested the document and found them," James said. "So, what are they?"

"I guess I don't have any reason not to tell you this now, it seems that the secret has been exposed by Debra anyway... The numbers are to a very important account our family has had for years. See, after I quit the antique business I took all my profits, along with most of my other antiques, and opened what is known as a Fort account; it's the most secure place anyone can keep anything... They told me that there could be only one copy of the account number printed and that it had to be on something inconspicuous, but still important to me. I couldn't think of anything that fit that description better than that document of Wipley's... So, I took it in and the company secretly encoded the one hundred digit account and pass code on it by printing ten different numbers on ten different pages.

James looked confused along with everyone else in the room, Joe noticing this continued to explain. "I know it all sounds a bit extreme but you have to understand, after owning the detective company I've seen people have their money stolen from every kind of account except for this one. I had to be sure that it would be protected no matter what. I wanted to provide for our family for generations to come, it was my life's goal."

"Well then how did Debra know about it?" James asked.

"It all happened after I became sick… I thought I was going to die, and I figured I could trust her to use the money and take care of you, James. I told her about the document, but I didn't tell her where it was. I figured I would have you tell me if she started acting suspicious and searching around the house for something, and it would have worked, but the plan backfired after I slipped into the coma before I could explain things to you… It's easy to see now what a dumb plan that was, but at the time I was so sick, I guess I just wasn't thinking clearly, I only wanted to make sure that you would be taken care of," Joe said, reaching out and taking James' hand. "I thought she was one of the good ones like your mother, but apparently I was wrong. So, did she ever get the account numbers?"

James shook his head. "No, she didn't, but there is still a page missing from the document. And I did call up here, dad, and I wanted to tell you what she was doing, but then when I found out you were in a coma I knew it was—"

"It's okay, James," Joe interrupted. "After all, you still did the right thing; you protected everything for us, and you saved my life, what else could a father ask for out of a son."

"But I didn't really save everything," James said, in a low tone. "The house remember?"

Joe smiled. "That's the least of my concerns right now James, we can always rebuild. Plus the most valuable things from the family business weren't in the house anyway, everything's still safely stored in the account, and the most valuable thing of all is right here with me," he reassured James with another hug.

James instantly felt relieved, losing the house was one of the other huge worries he had weighting on his mind this whole time. Things seemed to be working out better than he could have ever expected.

"What about Manny Jones, how does he fit into all of this Joe?" Pop asked.

"Well, I never told James this before, but after I took the document and left Florida I guess Manny went crazy. He tracked me down and sent threatening letters and said if I didn't come back and help him solve the mystery that he would hunt me and my family down. James was very young then and I didn't know what to do, so we moved several times and eventually he disappeared and I figured he had finally given up."

Suddenly the door to the room opened and two nurses came walking in, the older one was pushing a wheel chair.

"Are you still feeling okay, Mr. Greene?" the younger of the two nurses asked.

"I feel great, thank you," Joe said, as he turned to the side on his own and with the help of James and one of the nurses stood up. He was about to sit down in the wheelchair when he took a step to the side of it.

"Dad, what are you doing, the wheelchair is over here?" James said.

"Wait a second, I think I can walk by myself," Joe said, as he took his arms out from behind the nurse and James' necks and took a couple steps forward.

"Mr. Greene, the doctor advised you not to—"

"I know, but he said I wouldn't be able to walk, not that I shouldn't," Joe interrupted, as he began to pace slowly around the room.

"Be careful, dad," James advised, as everyone watched Joe in amazement as he strolled back and forth across the room and then began bending at the waist and stretching.

"I'm fine, James, actually I feel great, it's like I've completely gotten all my strength back again," he said, as continued to stretch and looked over at the duffel bag. It was then Joe Greene finally believed the water had truly healed him

The nurses were so shocked that they ran out and got Joe's doctors right away. No one had ever seen anyone get up after being bed ridden for six months and just start walking around so easily. The doctors were baffled too, as they examined Joe's muscles and found no deterioration at all. Afterwards, they ran a few more blood tests and were even more puzzled by the results, which showed Joe being healthier than most men half his age. If Joe didn't believe the water had healed him before, he had no doubts about it now.

An hour later, and against doctor's wishes, Joe Greene signed himself out of the hospital. While he was getting dressed and his things together in the room

James, Pop, Neil, and Miss Nichols waited outside in the hallway for him. It was there that they all decided not to bring up anything else about what happened with Manny Jones yet. James worried this might upset his father even more and he already had Debra's betrayal to think about. Even though there were still a few unanswered questions, Pop made it clear that they should leave it up to James to decide when to ask about them.

After Joe was dressed, everyone walked together through the hospital and towards the parking lot. It was a euphoric time for everyone, as they all made small talk about the beautiful weather and normal things again.

"I called us a cab and rented us a room at the Lazor Hotel downtown, I told the hospital where we are staying just in case," Joe told everyone, as they all continued down the hallway leading to the parking lot.

"Do you think you should stay one more night here, dad, you know just to be safe?" James asked.

"You heard what they said; I'm healthier now than I've probably ever been. I'll be fine, but if it makes you feel any better they said they're going to send a nurse over to the hotel tonight to check on me," Joe nodded and grinned.

"That's really nice of them," Miss Nichols said, taking out her cell phone and turning it back on.

"So, we're all meeting at eight o'clock tonight for dinner then, right, my treat?" Joe asked.

"That's fine, I'm sure you two still have a lot of catching up to do." Pop said, as everyone walked out the automatic doors leading to the parking lot. After a few minutes more of light conversation, James saw a yellow taxi cab pulling up off the curb directly in front of them.

"Well, I guess I'll see ya later then man," Neil said to James, as they slapped each other five.

"Yeah, I'll call you from the hotel," James said. "Hey Neil, thanks again."

"Goodbye, nice meeting you," Miss Nichols said to Joe. "I'm so glad you're doing better; you know James here really is a great person."

"I know I'm a lucky father," Joe said, and James pretended he didn't hear the compliments because he didn't want Miss Nichols to see him blush. "So, you're coming to dinner tonight too, right?" Joe kindly asked.

Miss Nichols smiled and as she checked her phone again, her light curly hair had become bushy from all the traveling, but she still looked beautiful. "I might,

I have to check with work about some things," she said with a smile as she shook hands with Joe. "But, I'm sure I'll see you again soon, hopefully under better circumstances. I still can't believe what happened."

"Yeah I know I'm still trying to comprehend it all," Joe said with a smile. "Well, I hope to see you there, and it was very nice meeting you."

"Yeah, thanks for everything," James told Miss Nichols, as he stood beside his father and shook her hand with a smile, his face and dark hair looking exactly like his father's; the resemblance was remarkable and impossible not to notice. Joe shook hands with Pop and James gave him a hug.

"Thanks again, Pop, for helping me out, and teaching me everything," James respectfully said.

"I think you're the one who taught me," Pop replied with a wink, his old blue eyes twinkled with new life and energy.

"See you soon guys," James called out, as he and Joe climbed into the taxi.

"Bye, be careful," Neil yelled, pointing and making goofy faces at the taxi driver.

James stared out the side window of the taxi and watched Pop and Neil walking with Miss Nichols towards her car. He realized then just how much he owed all of them. They had helped save his father, they had believed in him, and most importantly they had stood by his side through everything. And now that James had his father back he truly felt happy again, the last time he could remember feeling this way was back when his mother was still alive; he knew she was looking down on him smiling right now. The world had never looked quite so kind to James, and he now had proof that miracles were real and that good people still existed.

But there still were some questions that remained in his thoughts, like: Where did Debra go, and who was the strange man she left with… James had yet to tell his dad about this or about what happened with Manny Jones. He didn't want to ruin his first day back with more negative talk, but he remembered what his father had told Pop about wanting to know the bad news as soon as possible. So, against his new feelings of happiness James decided to tell his dad the rest of the facts after they got to the hotel. He had no idea that in less than twenty-four hours all the rest of the questions his father couldn't answer would also be answered as well.

# Chapter Twenty
# Greed and Forgiveness

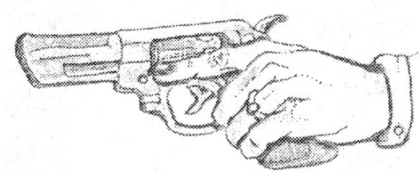

    During the rest of the drive to the hotel James made sure to talk only about the good things that had happened while his father was in the hospital. He told him all about the giant coconuts he and Pop had found on the island, and about how Pop had started running around and laughing like a kid after he had been healed in the lagoon. Soon they were both exchanging information and talking like they had always done.
    James learned that in fact his father had been an antique buyer during his first five years after college before taking over the family business. He told James about the company that hired him, and how he got to travel around the world and go to hundreds of auctions for them. He then told James that during this time he learned that the real money was in the antique business; so he and a close friend invested together and created a company. He said that two years later it was worth millions. He explained the reason why he had never told James any of this before was because he didn't want him to grow up being spoiled like most rich kids, who ended up never working and depending on their parents for the rest of their lives. Instead, he wanted James to be strong and independent, but to also know that he could always look to his father for real help. James had become like this despite the fact that he knew his father was wealthy. He was too smart not to understand the benefits of supporting and providing for yourself. James was also deeply relieved that his father did not

always want to be a detective either. But, the strange thing is that now the idea was beginning to grow on him, especially since the skills basically saved his father's life.

When they arrived at the hotel, James was still telling his father how Pop had tricked Judy into believing that they were all going to Florida on vacation. Joe laughed as James reenacted Pop that night at the dinner table when he told Judy the reason why he wanted to go.

"He looked like this, dad," James said, as he hunched up his shoulders and stuck out his lower lip. "And he said, 'I just don't know what I'm living for anymore, Judy,' you should have been there it was really funny," James said. He and his father both laughed hard after James' great impersonation. A second later, the cab door flew open and the driver was standing on the sidewalk in front of the Lazor Hotel. They had both been laughing so hard that neither of them noticed him.

"Your bags sir," the bald driver said.

"Oh, I'm sorry," Joe said, getting out of the taxi and giving the man a bill from his wallet. "Thank you."

James followed his father out of the taxi and looked at the tall skyscraper-like hotel.

"This place is huge dad, what'd you want to stay here for?" he asked.

"Yeah, I thought we should celebrate, it's not everyday you get brought back from the dead," Joe joked, as he and James laughed and walked into the building and up to a long, marble front desk.

After they were shown to their spacious suite on the first floor, which contained a kitchen, living room and bedroom, James asked his father to sit down because he needed to tell him a few more important things.

"I thought you already told me everything," Joe said, getting a bottle of water from the fridge and sitting down at the table beside James with a suspicious look on his face.

"Well, Pop left it up to me to decide when to tell you the rest, and I thought you should hear it now rather than later…"

"Alright, I'm listening," Joe slowly said.

"Uh, well, the first thing is that before Debra left she was hanging out with this mean guy named Rex, she even let this guy move into the house, dad," James said.

Joe's face turned a bit flushed. "I had a feeling she had been talking to someone else, but I guess I just didn't want to admit it to myself," he told James.

"I understand... But this guy was a total jerk though, he stole and used your stuff, he threatened me, and I know he was working with Debra at first to try and steal the document."

"What do you mean at first?" Joe quickly asked. "What happened?"

"See, after I found the document, this guy, Rex, stole it from my room. Then a few nights later I found out that they had stuff hidden in the attic. So, I went up there hoping to find the document, but instead I watched Debra come up there and go into that secret room."

Joe looked surprised. "I had that room built to keep some of my personal antiques in, but I never told her about it," he said, leaning forward and putting his hand over his forehead in frustration. "I can't believe I trusted her... Oh well, I guess it doesn't matter now though does it?"

"No, it doesn't" James agreed, "but the thing is, when I seen Debra in the attic that night she was with another guy besides Rex. We never figured out who this guy was, but I'm pretty sure she left with him after she double-crossed Rex and took all the money they had. A few days later we found out that Rex was murdered and the guy who did it then started coming after us down in Florida."

Joe looked shocked. "What do you mean, why would he come after you guys, who was he?"

"That's the thing we found out that this guy's name was supposedly Bill Atwood and that he had been wanted by police for years. We don't know how he found us but we knew what he wanted."

"What did he want?"

"He was after the document, dad. He tried attacking us twice while we were down there and we barely got away. Our boat guide, Walt, eventually saved us by shooting the guy," James said, and then paused to let his father absorb it all... "After that we found out the guy's real name... It was your old friend Manny Jones," James said in one long breath.

He watched as his father processed the baffling information. Joe didn't say anything for several moments, he then looked up.

"That was my one greatest fear, and it happened when I couldn't protect you... I'm so sorry, James," Joe said, sounding defeated and hugging James.

"It's okay, it's not your fault, dad," James said, knowing he was going to have to continue explaining everything now.

It ended up taking James the next half an hour to thoroughly go over everything with his father. Joe was naturally upset by the rest of the news, but again expressed how proud he was of James. Joe admitted to James that he always thought Manny might one day come back, but he never thought that he would ever go this far to satisfy his obsession. James could tell his father was somewhat depressed about the fact that his friend had done these things to his son and him. He knew his dad would want to talk with Pop and Miss Nichols more about the situation. The whole thing seemed quite simple now that James had all the pieces. He was relieved to have finally told his father the rest of the story, even though it caused him a lot of heart ache. As much of a relief as it all was to know, James didn't look forward to explaining everything again to Pop, Neil, and Miss Nichols. He took comfort in knowing that for now all he had to do was rest and spend some quality time with his dad.

After the long discussion they both got cleaned up and then sat down and began watching a movie on the big screen television in the living room. Everything seemed finally back to normal again for James; it was almost like his father had never been gone at all. After the movie, they went out for pizza and then both picked up some new clothes. At around five, James called Neil and they decided to go to The Rack steak house downtown in the city for dinner. The plan was to meet there at eight o'clock and to dress nice. After James informed his father of the arrangements, they figured since they still had three hours they would go ahead and watch a football game. Joe sat in one of the large armchairs in the hotel living room and James laid down on the couch next to it.

"I'm kind of tired," James said, as he yawned and stretched out.

"It sounds like you didn't get much sleep last night," his father said, as he sat with the remote and his feet kicked up in front of the TV.

"No, actually I haven't got much in the past week."

"Well, why don't you take a nap, I'll wake you up in a couple hours or so," Joe said. "I think I've had enough rest to last me for the rest of the year," he joked, and James laughed.

"Yeah, no kidding, well, wake me up at seven okay, dad? Remember I told Neil we'd be there at eight," James said, as he closed his eyes and relaxed.

He easily fell asleep knowing his father was okay and near by again.

Some time later when James slowly awoke, he sat up and noticed his father was gone. He got up and checked the clock on the table. It read 7:03, he had been asleep for over two hours. *Why didn't he wake me up,* James thought, as he began looking around the huge hotel room for his father.

"Dad," he yelled, opening the door to the bedroom, "Dad, are you in here… Dad, come on it's after seven we need to get ready to go!"

But, there was no answer. He checked the large bathroom and peeked in the small kitchen, but still no sign of him…After he was positive his father was not in the hotel room, James put on his shoes, grabbed his room key, and walked out to the long carpeted hallway. Everything was quiet as he walked down towards the lobby where they had checked in. Once he got there, he looked around but still didn't see him. He then decided to go ask the young woman at the front desk if she had seen his father anywhere. *He probably went out for something and just didn't want to wake me*, James told himself. *Heck, he might even be in the pool.*

"Excuse me," James said, his eyes still adjusting to the bright chandelier lights.

"Yes, how may I help you?"

"Um, I'm in room," he said, checking his key card, "room one-eighteen, and I was wondering if you had seen or talked to my dad. He's not in the room and it's not like him to leave and not tell me where he was going."

The young woman checked the computer and shuffled some papers around.

"It's Mr. Greene, correct?" she asked.

"Yes, that's right," James said.

"Um, no I'm sorry it doesn't look like he's left any messages at the desk for anyone, and I haven't seen him since you two checked in here earlier."

James shook his head. "Okay, well if you do see him will you tell him I'm looking for him please?"

"No problem and you are?"

"I'm his son, James Greene."

"Okay, I will give him the message," she politely said.

Frustrated, James walked out front of the building and looked up and down the busy street. He didn't see anyone even slightly resembling his dad. After a few minutes of watching different people walk by he went back in and through the lobby. He turned the opposite way down the hall and saw a sign for some new restaurant inside the hotel. After following a few arrows he found out that the place was not yet opened for business. *Where is he?* James asked himself, as he hurried back down the hallway. He tried to ignore it but the truth was he was beginning to worry him a little now.

Finally, after another five minutes of wandering around the huge lobby areas aimlessly, he decided to head back to the room and hoped he had somehow missed him coming back. When he turned the last corner and looked down the hallway, he saw what he thought was his father reentering their room.

"Hey dad, wait, hey I've been looking for you," James shouted, as the door quickly slammed. *What's he doing?* James thought to himself as he began to jog down the hallway towards their hotel room. Once he got in front of the door he checked the room number again and then quickly inserted his key card. The tiny light turned green and he turned the handle and pushed open the door.

"No, James don't!" his father yelled, as he stepped into the room.

"What the—" James said, as the door was slammed shut behind him. What James saw next was something he couldn't believe… Astonishingly, there was Debra standing beside the couch with a gun pointed at his father. James turned around and saw the same red-headed man from the attic standing there looking nervous.

"Hello, James," Debra said, with a crazed look in her eyes. "Go sit down in that chair right there, now!" she shouted, as she aimed the pistol at James.

"What's going on, Dad, are you okay?"

"Oh, calm down, James, you're always acting like such a little baby," she said, as James sat down in the chair across from his dad. James took another look at the red-headed man, now standing in the middle of the room still looking unsure of the situation before him.

"Tie him up too," Debra commanded. The red-headed man hesitated and then walked over and tied James' hands around the chair. The knots were not even tight and James could have sworn the man apologized to him as he completed the job.

"You better not hurt him, it's going to be alright, James, don't worry," Joe said, and then Debra laughed.

"Yes, it's going to be just fine as long as you give me what I want," she snarled, as she walked around in front of James, like a tiger stalking its prey. "I know you have that document of your father's, James. You've been a thorn in my side long enough you little brat," she said, as she looked at James with her piercing, greedy eyes.

James was still too shocked to speak, instead he just stared at the red-headed man; for some reason he now seemed oddly familiar to James. He knew he hadn't felt like this the first time he had seen the man in the attic, but this time there was something different. Something about the man's hair and sharp blue eyes that reminded James of someone, but he wasn't sure who.

"I'm speaking to you!" Debra yelled, her voice getting aggressive. "Now, where is it James! And don't you dare lie to me, because if you do I'll make sure you and your father never see each other again."

"I don't have it, it's at Neil's house in Pop's safe," James said, as his stomach churned with nervousness.

"You expect me to believe that you'd leave something of your father's behind," Debra hissed.

"He's telling you the truth, Debra," Joe blurted out. "He told me the same thing."

"I don't think I was talking to you, Joe, see that's always been your problem you never know when to shut up do you? You're so easy to get information out of, but now James here, well, that's a different story. He likes to hide things don't you?" She said, grabbing James face and squeezing it tight in her hands. James couldn't believe what was happening. He didn't care about the document anymore, it had given him everything he wanted but the problem was that he honestly didn't have it, but he knew Debra would never believe him.

"Leave him alone, Debra, he's telling you the truth—he doesn't have it," Joe said.

Debra let go of James, turned around walked over and hit James' father in the face with her gun. James jumped up and as he quickly approached Debra she suddenly reached out and stuck him in the chest with something. Immediately, he felt a tight very hot sensation on his chest, his arms and legs went stiff and he couldn't move. The next thing he knew he was being helped back up and into the chair by the red-headed man.

"I thought you said nobody was going to get hurt?" the strange man quietly said to Debra, as James slowly regained consciousness.

"Don't ever question my methods, I told you to tie him tight didn't I? I'm going to do whatever it takes to get that document and the money... You're not the only one who wants it remember. Anyway, now they know I mean business, and he won't try that again," Debra said, as she showed James the stun-gun she had just used on him.

"You okay, James?" Joe mumbled through his bloody mouth.

"I think so," James slowly said.

"Now James, you understand how serious I am, so you better think about it and tell me right where that document is?" She said, as James ignored her and looked over at the strange red-headed man again, this time with newfound interest. Suddenly, a vision flashed into James' mind, he saw somebody, they were fuzzy at first and then they became clear. It was a man, it was an older man, he had blue eyes and light hair, and he was-

"Are you listening to me young man," Debra yelled directly in James' ear, causing him to come back from his deep thoughts.

"Yes, I heard you, and I told you already it's at Neil's house, I swear," James said loudly.

"Neil's house huh, do you really expect me to believe that?" Debra barked. "I don't have time for these games."

"Is that all you have ever cared about is money? I can't believe you're doing this—I thought you cared about us…"

Debra turned around and approached Joe with a sinister look in her eyes. She pushed him back and James noticed they had tied his hands to the couch leg.

"Tell me something, Joe," Debra said, "how could I ever care about a man like you? You're so gullible, and like all the others you fell for it. Ha, a mysterious disease, you never caught on did you?"

"What are you talking about?" Joe asked, looking confused as James listened closely now.

"You never had a disease, you idiot…" Debra said as she turned back around and smiled menacingly at James. "I poisoned you. And it would have been much easier if you would have just told me where that document was and then died. I would have never had to hire that manic friend of yours to hunt down sweet James here," she walked by James and pushed him back in his chair. "I would have simply taken the money and left you and your pathetic life alone… I've been doing this for a long time now, Joe, but I've never met someone as easily deceived as you—And it would have been over a long time ago if you hadn't of stopped by to visit that doctor friend of yours and gotten yourself admitted in the hospital… You know, I spent a lot of time and money finding and buying just the right kind of poison… A little bit here in your oatmeal, and a little there in your morning coffee… I didn't know the process took so long and that was my mistake, I should have done like I always did and just hire a killer from the beginning. But no, it was too late and now look what has happened? So, why don't you tell James to give me the document and it can all be over right now… I'm going to kill you anyway," Debra said, but no one said a word back to her. "Fine, you can have it your way."

James couldn't believe what he had just heard. Debra had poisoned his father, and who knows how many other men. For the first time since he had known Debra, he was actually afraid of her. He watched the gun in her hand closely as Debra began tearing through the hotel room searching for the document. James looked back over at the strange man and noticed that he seemed to be just as nervous as he and his father were. Debra was now turning things over and tearing through James and his father's luggage like a raving lunatic. After she tossed everything out of the fridge, she stomped into the bedroom; it was then James looked back over at the strange man and suddenly realized who he reminded him of. The next idea appeared so fast and so brilliantly in his mind that he wanted to kick himself for not thinking it before now. The strange man was a spitting image of Hunter Wipley. Sure he was a lot younger, but his eyes were the same bright blue, his short red hair had the same coarse texture, it was as if James was staring at Wipley from forty years ago. He had been so shocked by everything and it had all happened so quickly that he figured his mind had some how missed it. He took a deep breath as another realization hit him… He remembered Wipley telling him and Pop how his son had felt betrayed and left the night Wipley had given him the document. Wipley said that his son vowed to take revenge on his father for never being in his life. Wipley said that he had left his son's mother before he was born. James knew Wipley had said his son's name, but he couldn't remember what it was. He knew he could use this information as a way to connect with this strange man. There was no telling what Debra might do after she realized the document was indeed not there, she had proven herself to be quite dangerous and even deadly. James had no other choice and little time, like always he had to try.

"Do you know Hunter Wipley?" James softly asked the strange man as he stood in between him and his father.

The strange man looked at James as if he had splashed cold water on his face.

"What did you say?" he asked as he looked down at James.

"You're Hunter Wipley's son aren't you?"

"What do you know about it?" the strange man sternly asked as James struggled to think of his name.

Finally it came to him. "Your name's Ray isn't it?" James asked, "Ray Wipley?"

"You know this man," Joe asked from across the room as Debra yelled and threw something in the bedroom.

"He's Wipley's son," James said, as he looked up at the man. "I met your father a few days ago on the island."

"You really think I'm going to believe that crazy story my father wrote," Ray said with an angry look on his face.

"Yes, because I know that's why you're really here. You want the document back so you can go and find him," James said, surprising even himself with his insight. "I would do the same thing to find my dad."

The man shook his head. "Or maybe I tracked down the document after all these years because I decided to destroy it. But after I found out there was money involved I figured I'd get some of that first and then destroy it."

"He's on the island waiting for you," James said, as he heard Debra break something else and knew he was running out of time. "He told us all about you, and he was heart broken the night you left. He said all he ever wanted was to know you and that if he could take back what he did he would."

"You shut your mouth; you don't know anything about my father. He doesn't deserve to get to know me… And after I get back his document I'm going to burn it so no one can ever find that old selfish man," Ray angrily said as Debra reentered the room, looking even more deranged.

"What's going on out here, I told you not to talk to them," Debra yelled at Ray, as she rushed over to Joe and held the stun-gun to his side.

"Look here, James, unless you want me to hurt your father real bad you're going to tell me where you hid that damn document," she screamed.

"It's not here, it's at Neil's house," James exclaimed, and then Debra shocked Joe in the ribs with the stun-gun and he jerked and convulsed and then fell back unconscious.

"Stop it, leave him alone," James pleaded, as she shocked him again. "Stop you're killing him…"

James watched in horror as his father slumped over and fell off the couch, he could tell by his chest that he wasn't breathing. This was it, everything he had worked so hard to fix was about to be ruined again because of one person's greed and there was nothing he could do about it.

"I warned you," Debra said, as James looked over at Ray for help. He could tell that he had surprised the man by knowing who he was and he hoped he would be intrigued enough by James' knowledge and understanding of the situation that he might change his mind about committing this vicious act.

## HEALING WATER

"Please, stop her, she's going to kill him," James pleaded.

The next several seconds that passed were the longest of his life. James watched as his father laid there motionless. Without warning, he suddenly woke back up gasping for air.

"That hurts doesn't it, Joe, well that's just the beginning if your precious little James over there doesn't tell me what I want to know."

"Look if you don't believe me call Neil's house, you can listen as I talk to him," James said, trying desperately to convince Debra that he was telling her the truth.

"Okay," Joe suddenly said. "Okay, it's in my car—the keys are, are in my pants pocket, it's in the truck you can have it," he stammered.

"What are you talking about, dad, no it's not, it's at—"

"Shut up, James," Debra yelled. "See, now that wasn't so hard, was it?"

She reached into Joe's pocket and pulled out his car keys. "Watch them closely while I go get the document, if either one of them moves shoot the other one," she commanded Ray.

As soon as she left the room, James realized his father had just bought him precious time alone with Wipley's son again. His father was in no condition to talk, but he had an understanding of what James was trying to do.

"Listen Ray, can't you see Debra doesn't care about you? She's never cared about anyone she's just using you like she did my dad. She knew you wanted the same thing she did so she promised to help you get it. It's a con you heard what she said."

"What do you know you're just a kid…? You don't understand what it's like to not have a father, he left us, and when he came back he told me about some paradise island in the ocean somewhere he wanted me to go, he sounded crazy. I mean how would you feel to finally meet your father after twenty-five years and learn he's really nuts like all the kids in school told you he was. I'll tell you how, for the first five years after that you'd let it eat you up inside—then you'd start telling yourself that you need to go find him but you can't because you sold the directions to the island he lives on… And then, then you, you hate him, you hate him even more because he's made you crazy just like him. So, while you're stuck here he's out there in paradise where he can't be found."

"Stop," James said, "Just stop… Your father's not crazy. He's a great man. Now quit blaming him and go tell him how you feel, I'll give you back the document if you let us go…"

Ray looked deeply at James. There was something in the way James had been trying to protect his father that must have clicked in Ray's head. He slowly walked over to James and kneeled down. "But he said the document's in the car."

"It's not in the car, it's hidden at my friend Neil's house just like we've been saying all along. Don't you see that once Debra gets a hold of that document she's not going to have a use for you anymore..."

"I hated him for so long," Ray confessed, as he looked over at Joe and then back to James.

"He doesn't hate you," James seriously said. "He told me that if you found him and if you wanted that he would leave the island and come back to the main land with you. He said you're the only family he's got left and he's sorry, but he thought you meant what you said that night you left him. Ray, he waited for you to come back for two days."

"He did?" Raymond asked, his eyes looking kind and relaxed.

"Yeah, he did... Now come on hurry before Debra gets back and we'll help you find him again."

Ray nodded his head. "I haven't done much good with my life and I've always blamed my father for everything bad that has happened, but I'm going to change all that right now," he said. "I believe you for some reason and I do want to find him, I have for a long time now. I don't know what I was thinking here, I've never even held a gun before... I have just been so angry for so long."

James thought he had misheard Raymond, but then Joe sat up.

"We knew you weren't like her," Joe said, as he winked at James.

"You're not a bad person Ray and we can tell," James honestly expressed.

"Thank you, and it's nice to meet you James," Ray said, as he untied James and helped him up.

"You too Ray," James said, as they shook hands.

"Okay, James, you untie your dad, I'll wait for Debra behind the door; she's going to put up a fight and remember she's still got a gun and she will use it."

James tried to quickly untie his father but his knots were tight.

"You okay, dad?" he asked, as he and his father worked together to get the ropes off his wrists and ankles.

"Yes, I'm fine, that was amazing you know, I had no idea how much you have grown up lately. You sounded smarter than most adult's right then."

"Thanks dad, come on we need to hurry," James said.

"You call for help, and we'll contain her," Joe said, as James made his way over to the phone. He dialed the police and was explaining the situation when the door to the room was activated. Debra tried to open the door, but it caught on the chain Ray had latched.

"Hey, open this door Ray, what are you doing you idiot? I said open this door," she yelled as she kicked at the door several times. James was still on the phone and watching the scene across the room as his father and Ray stood on both sides of the door and waited. Without warning a loud bang rang out and the chain exploded into pieces. Debra had shot the door open and was now entering the room with the gun extended in front of her.

"Grab her," Joe exclaimed.

Debra went to aim for Joe only to be grabbed from behind by Ray.

"I'm not going to let you do this," he shouted, as he tried to wrestle the gun away from behind. Suddenly there was another loud gun shot and James threw the phone down and instinctively ducked.

"Get off of me," Debra screamed, as she managed to pull the trigger yet again.

Another gun shot rang out and ricocheted off the wall. James crawled over behind the bar and heard Debra fighting off Ray.

"Let go of me you little piece of nothing," she screamed, as James jumped up and turned the corner just in time to stop Debra from escaping. He pulled at her from behind as Joe finally managed to get the pistol away from her. Everything seemed like it was in slow motion from this point on as Debra turned toward James now, trying to grab her second gun. Luckily, Ray caught her arm and stopped her. Joe ducked down and wrestled her by the legs to the ground. *He saved my life*; James thought, as Ray now had her arm bunched up and was struggling to get the pistol. She was trying desperately to continue the fight, but they finally subdued her. James heard and saw the second gun go sliding across the kitchen floor, afterwards, he and Debra knew it was all over. Joe and Ray held her on the ground and it didn't take long until she completely gave up.

"Your all gonna pay, this isn't over believe me," she hissed.

"Go grab that rope James," Joe said, as she remained on the ground struggling. She had amazing strength for a woman her size and she continued to cuss and threaten them, even up until the police arrived and took her away in handcuffs. James knew now that it was finally all over. The moment was very bitter-sweet for all.

A few minutes later, the police questioned everyone and Ray told them the complete truth of how he was involved; this stunned James and his father. They were both prepared to wipe the slate clean for Ray since he turned the situation around and helped them out. They both figured without Ray's sudden change of heart who knows what might have happened to them. Seeing how crazy Debra had become, James knew she was capable of anything if it helped her get what she wanted. They both felt in some weird way that they owed Ray something. But seeing that he wanted to prove furthermore that he was truly sorry for what he did, Ray continued to claim his guilt in the matter. It wasn't until James and his father both told the detectives the rest of the story that it was left up to Joe weather or not to press charges. After a brief discussion between James and his dad they declined this action and instead stayed true to their word to help Ray find his father. James called the restaurant where Pop, Neil, and Miss Nichols were waiting and explained the situation to a stunned Pop.

"No," James said into the phone, as he stood in the hotel bedroom, "we're not going to press charges because the guy saved our lives… I know but can you believe he's Wipley's son? Okay, yeah that's fine we'll just meet you back there in half an hour then. Yes, we want him to have the document. Okay, thanks." James said, and then hung up the phone. He walked back into the living room area where his father and Ray sat along with a few police officers.

"Pop said they're going to leave the restaurant right now and meet us back at their house," James reported.

The detective in charge looked over and flipped his notepad closed. "I think it would be in everyone's best interest if we escorted, Mr. Wipley here, just to be sure everything stays worked out between everyone.

"That's fine you can have a car follow us over then," Joe said, as he stood up and shook hands with the detective.

"Maybe I should ride with the police?" Ray said.

No one said anything as Joe looked at James. "You can ride with us," James said.

As James and Joe walked around the hotel room and collected their things so they could leave, James noticed Debra's black purse on the chair in the kitchen.

"Hey dad, look at this," he said, as he picked up the bag and showed it to his father.

"Is that Debra's?"

"I guess," James said, as he looked down inside and saw the plastic baggie with the page from the document inside it. "Look, here it is," he exclaimed, as he pulled the baggie out. "It's the page we were missing from the document, I thought Rex had it."

"Well, it looks like the last piece of the puzzle has been found after all, huh?" Joe said, with a smile.

"Yep, that's right," James said, as he and his father left the hotel room and met Ray in the hall. "Here you go," James said. "We were missing this page from the document, but I found it in Debra's purse."

"Look at that," Ray said, as he held up the page. "I haven't seen this is a long time, thank you, James. I'm sure my father will be happy to have his collection back after all these years."

As James and his father left the parking lot with Ray Wipley in the back seat it seemed a little strange to James at first. Less than an hour ago, Ray had been the enemy and now they were all friends? But, after talking more with him and hearing him apologize several times during the ride James felt confident that they had made the right decision. Ray also confessed he had never known Debra's plan. He said he was only working with Debra to get the document back and that was it. He said he never really like her but she had promised to give the pages to him once she got what she wanted from them. James realized that Ray was far from being a dangerous person; he just had years and years of built up resentment, which would make anyone a little angry.

After breaking the ice with Ray, the rest of the drive over to Neil's was spent with them talking non-stop about his father Hunter. James told him how he helped save his father's life and how the water had healed Pop's hip. Ray seemed more than relieved to know that his father was truly not crazy; and James was amazed to find Ray to be just as nice as his father had been. He swore to James and Joe that he was going to find his father and that he would be sure to tell him what a great thing they did for him.

"Just returning the favor," James said.

When they finally arrived at Neil's, the police stayed out in the driveway as James, Joe, and Ray were met at the front door by Pop. After all walking in, James was pleasantly surprised to see Miss Nichols still with them. Neil's mother Judy also walked into the room from the kitchen and gave James a big hug.

"It's so good to see you, James," Judy said, and then noticed James' father behind him. "Oh my, is that really you, Joe, come here… We're all so happy to hear that you're okay. It's just a miracle, it really is."

"I want to thank you and Tim for taking James in like you did. It really means a lot to me." Joe said.

"He's like family to us you know that, and it was our pleasure, we're just happy that Neil has such a kind and smart friend like James."

After everyone was introduced to Ray, they all gathered in Pop's study. Everyone sat around the large desk in a semicircle as James and Joe explained everything to the shocked audience. No one could believe what Debra had done and how much had happened because of the document. Of course, there were plenty of questions afterwards that lead to an hour long conversation. It was then that Pop stood up, went over, and removed the document from the safe. He passed it slowly to James along with a letter he had written to Wipley. James took the document and gave his father the introduction, which contained the pass code and had caused its own share of the problems. He then took one last look at the leather-bound pages and then handed them over to Ray.

"The coordinates are here," James said, as he pointed to the last page. "It may take you some time to find them and it won't be easy, but if you really want to see your father again you will."

"That's funny," Ray said. "That's the exact same thing my father said when he gave this to me… I don't know what to say… Thanks, you guys really—you don't how much this all means to me," Ray sincerely said.

Pop stood up and stuck out his hand. "Every man deserves a second chance; now make sure you make the best of yours. Find your father and tell him everything, you'd be surprised at how much we old men understand things."

As more questions and conversation went on about everything that had happened, James just felt glad it was all over with. He was ready to start living a normal life with his father again; one that didn't include any guns, violence, or fear, the three things he despised most now in the world.

It was nine in the evening when Ray declined an invitation to dinner and instead called a taxi and said his goodbyes to everyone. He told James that he would be preparing tonight to go down to Florida tomorrow and begin the search for his father. He promised to stay in touch somehow and let James know when he had found the island. James watched as the taxi pulled up out front of Neil's house and drove off with Ray Wipley, the document, and the police behind it. It was another bittersweet moment, but James knew deep down that Ray would be reunited with his father the same way he had been with his. He realized that he and his father must have been the overwhelming inspiration that caused the drastic and sudden change in Ray. A change that he wished every person could make in their own lives.

Neil's dad, Tim, came home from work just in time to go to dinner with everyone. He was overjoyed to see Joe out of the hospital and healthy again. As Joe drove to the Italian restaurant Bunnucci's, James and Neil got their first real chance to talk privately since getting back from Florida. Miss Nichols decided to ride along as well and sat in the front seat beside Joe while James and Neil were in back. The night was unusually warm and James had his window rolled down a little which allowed in a nice breeze. He secretly watched Miss Nichol's hair blowing lightly in the air as she chatted openly with his father. Neil, noticing that James wasn't paying attention, hit him on the shoulder.

"Hey, I'm talking to you."

"Ow, I know I'm listening, now what?" James said.

"I asked you what you thought was going to happen to Debra?" Neil said.

This was the last thing James wanted to discuss. "I don't know, and I seriously don't care... I told you I'm kind of tired of talking about it. Have you really thought about everything that has happened over the last couple weeks, I'm lucky I didn't go crazy."

"What do you mean man, it was an adventure... I mean come on how many people do you know who have explored the ocean and found an unknown island with healing water? And then got attacked by two crazed-maniacs and came out on top of it all and lived to tell about it."

"I don't know, but I think everything that happened was mostly due to luck, not skill. I can't explain how or why, but I'm just glad it's all over," James said, as his mind flashed scenes from the island and he remembered Hunter Wipley's friendly face.

"Man, once everybody knows what happened we're gonna get all the babes next year in school."

"Shut up," James laughed. "Is that all you think about?"

"Yeah, why what's wrong with that? I've seen you sneak a few peeks as well," Neil said as he pointed at Miss Nichols.

James smiled and Neil laughed. The rest of the ride they talked about which girls they each liked the most at school.

Once they arrived at the restaurant, everyone met inside and was then seated at a large round table in back. A few minutes later, after receiving their drinks, Pop announced that he would be coming out of retirement and working with Miss Nichols and the CIA again. As far as James knew, no one ever explained to Judy or Tim how Pop had suddenly become healed, but it seemed as if they thought it best not to ask too many questions. Over dinner, James and his father discussed plans to rebuild their house in the same spot down the street from Neil's. Of course, Neil had plenty of ideas on how it should look.

"You gotta build a huge deck out back, with a hot tub and grill for all the parties we're going to throw this summer," Neil said. "Oh yeah, and a full basement with a game room and theater for all the chicks."

"Looks like you better install an alarm system too if you want to keep Neil out," Tim jokingly said.

Halfway through dinner, James sat back in his chair and watched as his father chatted with Miss Nichols and Pop. Meanwhile Judy, Tim, and Neil all talked about going on a vacation of their own to Florida. It was a very satisfying moment for James. He hated to admit it to himself, but Neil was right, it did feel as if he had won some huge battle over the bad things in this world. He felt proud of himself, and finally his nerves and heart were getting to take a break for once. He thought about the canteen he had stored away in Pop's safe at Neil's. It was still half full with the healing water, and he had no idea what, if anything he should do with it. He knew they would be discussing that question some other time, but James didn't know where he stood on the issue of whether or not to make the island and its healing water public. It could help so many people and it could save lives like it had done for his father, but then again one of the last great places and mysteries would become commercial and eventually lose all meaning. It was a tough decision and one that he was not about to ponder any more tonight. He had done enough thinking over the past month to last him for the rest of the year. He had accomplished many things a young man his age only dreams of doing. Proving that miracles really did still exist was something he knew he would never top. Yet, as he sat there and watched his new family talk and laugh, he felt he didn't need to.

After dinner, everyone walked out to the parking lot together. The night was still warm and the trees in the parking lot were covered with beautiful white lights.

"Where are you two going to stay until you build your new house?" Miss Nichols asked, as they all stood beside the cars.

"I think we might go looking for an apartment tomorrow somewhere close," Joe said, as he stood with his arm around James.

"When are you planning on starting the new house, Joe?" Pop asked.

"Hopefully by the end of the week."

"Make sure you call me when you do because I'd like to lead a hand. I decided I'm going to start back at work in the fall," Pop said.

"Thanks again, Pop," James said with a smile.

"Make sure you call me now," he said.

"Yeah, I want to help too," Neil said, as he slapped James five.

"Maybe we can just make a neighborhood thing out of it and all pitch in and help," Neil's dad suggested as he shook hands with Joe and James.

"We'd like that," Joe said.

"We'll call you from the hotel," James announced, as he, Miss Nichols and his dad got into the car.

The ride back was fairly a quiet one. Once there, Miss Nichols got out and James got in front beside his father.

"Goodbye, James," Miss Nichols said as she stood at the car door.

"Thanks, and I really can't thank you enough for everything you did to help us."

"I'm just glad everything worked out the way it did… I hope I see you both soon," Miss Nichols said. James and his father waved as they backed out of the driveway.

"We need to get you some real rest," Joe said, noticing how tired James had become again.

"I think we both need a few days off," James said.

"You're not kidding. I'm hitting the sack as soon as we get checked into a different room."

"Hey dad, can we get another suite I like the big screen TV?" James grinned.

"Yeah sure, anything for the next great detective in the family," Joe said.

After they got back to the hotel and switched rooms, they both went straight to sleep. James actually had good dreams for once and didn't wake up until ten the next morning. The next couple days were filled with James and his father swimming in the hotel pool, and relaxing. They only left the building to go get lunch and dinner. With this great change of events, it didn't take long before James felt like his old self again. He was happy and carefree, but most of all he was with his father again.

# Chapter Twenty-One
# Creating Their New World

A week had gone by and everything almost seemed completely back to normal now. James and his father found a nice apartment only about a half-mile from their old house and Neil's. They had already bought all new furniture and even recovered several valuable items from their old fire damaged home. It was Sunday and tomorrow morning they were planning to start construction on the new place. After several days of clean up by bulldozers and dump trucks Joe had hired, they had still yet to even see the place. So, that day at around noon, James and his father stopped by the lot to see what it looked like and if there was anything they could do before starting work tomorrow.

As they pulled up, James saw the huge dark spot on the ground where their old house used to be. It was now a large patch of fresh dirt with pipes coming up from the ground. James and his father both got out of the car and walked around in the front yard, evaluating the condition of things. The landscaping still seemed to be in decent shape, along with the tall bushes in front, only a few of which had been smashed by all the fire trucks. The concrete walkway leading out to the short driveway looked a little dirty but defiantly reusable.

"It doesn't look too bad now that it's all cleaned up and cleared away, does it?" Joe asked, as he walked around with his hands in his pockets.

James heard his father's remark, but was distracted by something down the street. He saw two people walking towards him waving their arms and yelling.

"Hey, dad, come here quick," James said. "Look at this..."

Joe walked over and put his hand up to his face to block out the sun, he immediately began laughing as soon as he saw what James was looking at. It was Pop and Neil, both wearing hardhats and carrying hammers.

"Let's build a house," Neil shouted, as he and Pop continued towards them. A minute later, after all saying hello and having a couple laughs together, they all got into Joe's car and left for the lumber yard. Right after they took off, something suddenly popped into James' mind.

"Has anyone here ever built a house before?" James asked, as he looked around at everyone in the car.

"No, but we'll figure it out," his dad said with a grin.

"Yeah, how hard can it be?" Neil said from the back seat.

"I did some research on it and printed off some helpful tips," Pop announced.

James knew now that it was going to take another miracle to build this house, and probably some of the healing water too.

# Chapter Twenty-Two
# Four Months Later…

It was a windy October day as James and Neil sat out front on the wrap-around porch of the new house they both helped build. It was a two story Victorian style home; just like the one James' real mother had always wanted. It had ended up taking several different contractors to help finish the project along with Joe, Pop, James, Neil, and Tim. But, now that it was done, the place looked great and was the talk of the town. Like the past brought back to life, the house stood for a new beginning to everyone.

The wind was blowing several newly planted trees around in the front yard, as the boys sat quietly and waited for something. Eventually, a small, white mail truck slowly pulled up along side the new mail box James helped his father install only a few weeks ago.

"There it is," James said, as he popped up and hurried out to check the mail. Hoping this would be the day that he got word from Ray Wipley.

"Man, what do you think he's just going to send a post card, yeah I bet it'll say something like: Greetings from nowhere," Neil joked, as he reluctantly followed James across the yard. There James pulled open the mailbox and grabbed all the envelopes inside. He quickly filed through them like a robot, "bill, bill, advertisement, bill." And then, there on the bottom was a small dirty envelope addressed to one: James Greene.

"Hey, look at this," James said, as he immediately ripped open the envelope and took out the small card inside. He turned it over and read it out loud. "Attention, James Greene, call 219-555-2734 immediately after receiving this card." James looked up with bright eyes. "Well, this has to be it. Let's go Neil it's Ray Wipley."

"Oh man, come on James we got the Halloween dance tonight, I gotta get ready; and you don't even know who you're going as yet," he complained as he followed James inside and over to the phone.

## HEALING WATER

James snatched up the receiver and typed the numbers into an old antique phone his father had recently bought. He waited as it rang once, and then again, and then again. While James was on the phone, Neil began putting on his mummy costume for the Halloween dance.

"Nobody's there, James, now come on its—"

"Shhh," James said, as a voicemail box picked up. "You've reached the voicemail box of, 'James, if you're calling it means you got my card before they did. Listen, I found my father, but something terrible has happened. We need your help—" Suddenly, James heard what sounded like yelling in the back ground and then some kind of small explosions. "I have to go, take the card and go to 115 North Manor Street in Bogstown, your father will know it, asked for—"

But James couldn't hear the rest of what Ray was saying, it was like the line was full of static or something. 'Need you—cal—immed… Help da." And that was it.

"So, who was it?" Neil asked, as he wrapped more mummy tape around his neck. James stood with a look of shock on his face. "It was Ray, he and his father are in trouble. They need our help," James said, as he rushed off to tell his dad the news.

"James, wait a minute, what about the Halloween dance?" Neil called out, as he chased after James with longs trails of mummy fabric flying around behind him.

"Dad, hey dad, where are you?" James shouted, running down the hall and up the stairs.

"I'm in here, what's wrong?" Joe said, as he met James in the doorway to his room.

"I got the letter from Ray, come on you have to hear this, he and his dad are in trouble," James quickly explained, as he led his father back to the phone and called the number again. After playing the message for his father, he looked very alarmed; it was obvious that something had to be done.

"What do you think we should do?" James asked.

"I think you need to call Pop, this sounds serious," Joe said, as he looked curiosity at Neil who was now halfway dressed like a mummy with gaze wrapped around his neck and body.

"Halloween dance tonight," Neil halfheartedly explained. Before Neil could protest any further, James had already dialed the phone and was talking to Pop.

"Hey Pop, it's James, listen, Wipley's in trouble he needs our help… Yes, okay I will, thanks, bye." James hung up the phone.

"What'd he say?" Neil asked.

"He's on his way down here, he thinks we should leave now," James said, as he grabbed his coat and his father's keys.

"I agree, and I know this Bogstown very well," Joe said, putting on his jacket. "It's where I purchased the document."

James couldn't believe it, he didn't know what was going on but he knew it was serious. Less then five minutes later Pop was parked in the driveway.

"Come on, I'll drive," he called out from his new sports jeep.

"You coming?" James asked Neil, as he and his father climbed in the vehicle with Pop.

"Yeah, I guess I have to now," he said, climbing in back beside James. "Man, I really wanted to go to that dance though. Nikki's gonna be so mad."

"I'm sure she'll get over it," James said. "Just tell her you had to go save some people again."

The jeep sped off out of the driveway with three men and one mummy in it. Pop made a sharp left turn on Main Street and headed directly for the highway. Little did James or anyone else know that in less then four hours another adventure would begin. This one even more profound than the first, this one would definitely change things, perhaps even the world…